PENGUIN CLASSICS

AGNES GREY

ANNE BRONTË was born in 1820, the youngest of the Brontë family. She was educated mainly at home and, as a child, was especially close to Emily. Together they invented the imaginary world of Gondal, the setting for many of their dramatic poems. Like her sisters, Emily and Charlotte, she tried to make a living as a governess and held two posts, the first with the Inghams at Blake Hall and later with the Robinsons at Thorp Green Hall, near York. Her experiences with the over-indulged young children and the worldly older children of these two households are vividly portrayed in *Agnes Grey*, which was first published in 1847. Her second novel *The Tenant of Wildfell Hall* appeared in 1848. She died at Scarborough in 1849.

ANGELINE GOREAU is the author of *Reconstructing Aphra: A Social Biography of Aphra Behn* and *The Whole Duty of a Woman: Female Writers in Seventeenth-Century England*. She has contributed articles on history and literature to a number of books and journals and is Hodder Fellow of the Humanities Council of Princeton University. She has also received awards from the National Endowment for the Humanities, the National Endowment for the Arts and the Belgian Ministry of Culture.

ANNE BRONTË

AGNES GREY

EDITED WITH AN INTRODUCTION AND NOTES
BY ANGELINE GOREAU

PENGUIN BOOKS

PENGUIN BOOKS

Published by the Penguin Group
Penguin Books Ltd, 27 Wrights Lane, London W8 5TZ, England
Penguin Books USA Inc., 375 Hudson Street, New York, New York 10014, USA
Penguin Books Australia Ltd, Ringwood, Victoria, Australia
Penguin Books Canada Ltd, 10 Alcorn Avenue, Toronto, Ontario, Canada M4V 3B2
Penguin Books (NZ) Ltd, 182–190 Wairau Road, Auckland 10, New Zealand

Penguin Books Ltd, Registered Offices: Harmondsworth, Middlesex, England

First published 1847
Published in Penguin Classics 1988
10

Introduction and notes copyright © Angeline Goreau, 1988
All rights reserved

Printed in England by Clays Ltd, St Ives plc
Set in 9/11 Sabon

CONTENTS

6   CONTENTS

INTRODUCTION

AGNES GREY IS THE FIRST NOVEL of the youngest Brontë. Anne wrote it at the same time that her sisters worked on their own first attempts at the novel-form – Charlotte's *The Professor*, Emily's *Wuthering Heights*. According to Mrs Gaskell, who had it from Charlotte, the three sisters would put away their needle-work at nine in the evening and give themselves over to 'study'. Pacing up and down the parsonage sitting room, they talked through the stories each was writing, delineating plot, describing character. Once or twice a week, each read aloud from the work she had finished and heard what the others had to say.

Long after her sisters were dead, Charlotte remembered that the 'readings were of great and stirring interest to all'.[1] The sisterly collaboration that Charlotte looked back upon so fondly was not without an element of discord, however. In a preface to the posthumous edition of her sisters' work, Charlotte complained that Emily was not 'amenable' to the 'influence of other intellects'. Anne, though 'milder and more subdued', was equally capable of 'taciturnity'.[2]

By the summer of 1846, *Agnes Grey*, *Wuthering Heights* and *The Professor* were ready to be sent out into the world, their authors rather ambiguously disguised under the pseudonyms Acton, Ellis and Currer Bell. Charlotte obtained a list of publishers and 'perseveringly obtruded' the manuscripts upon various editors. When the trio failed to meet with a sympathetic reading at half a dozen houses, Charlotte adopted the practice of neatly crossing out the name of the latest source of rejection – with what motive one can only imagine – and sending on what must have been an increasingly dog-eared specimen to the next address, bearing its history of failure on the wrapper.

Finally, a Mr Newby, of Messrs Thomas Cautley Newby, 72 Mortimer Street, Cavendish Square, sent a letter offering to publish the novels of Acton and Ellis Bell, but declining Currer Bell's *The Professor*. He requested, however, that the authors of *Agnes Grey* and *Wuthering Heights* contribute £50 toward the expenses of publication, to be returned once the sales had reimbursed the publisher for his outlays. The niggardly terms were not what Emily and Anne had hoped for, but as the authors of first novels rejected by a number of publishers, they were hardly in a position to argue for better.

Separated from its companions, *The Professor* had few chances of ever seeing the light of publication, since the prevailing fashion among publishers and circulating libraries was the triple-decker novel. By that standard, Charlotte's narrative was too short to be published on its own. She nevertheless continued unflaggingly to submit her manuscript for inspection and, what is more, started another novel. The first had met with several more gruff returns when a letter came from W. S. Williams, the reader at Messrs Smith, Elder & Co., extending the first word of encouragement the author had had.

Smith, Elder & Co. did not volunteer to publish *The Professor*, but their reader evidently saw some spark of talent in Currer Bell, because he sent an invitation to submit more work. In a matter of weeks, *Jane Eyre* arrived on his desk. Williams enthusiastically accepted the manuscript and Smith, Elder & Co. brought it out within two months. *Jane Eyre* was at once declared 'the best novel of the season'.[3] Thackeray, having read the first few pages, was unable to put the tale down until he had come to the end and wrote to George Smith to ask who the author of this remarkable book might be.

While the laudatory reviews of *Jane Eyre* rained down on their elder sister, Anne and Emily were still waiting to hear that their novels had been published. They had finished correcting proofs even before *Jane Eyre* had been sent to Smith, Elder & Co., but had had no further news from Mr Newby. On 10 November, Charlotte wrote to Mr Williams to ask whether Newby was a man whose word might be relied upon, or whether he 'often acts as he has done to my relations'.⁴

In the meantime, the dilatory Newby awakened to the fact that he was in possession of a manuscript whose authors might well be connected with the author of the season's literary sensation, *Jane Eyre*. He sped into publication and by mid-December Emily and Anne had their first copies. *Wuthering Heights* occupied two volumes of a claret-coloured set, and *Agnes Grey* the third. The girls were horrified to find that the multitude of printers' errors they had corrected in proof had returned in the finished copies. 'The orthography and punctuation of the books,' Charlotte remarked to her publisher, 'are mortifying to a degree.'⁵

The critical reception afforded Acton and Ellis Bell was no less humiliating. Neither novel could escape the effects of Currer Bell's success. Several reviewers expressed disappointment that the new publication was not as 'pleasing' as the first 'Bell' novel. One even made a point of noting that the 'extraordinary popularity of *Jane Eyre* will give this book a reputation which it would not, perhaps, have otherwise acquired for itself'. Few readers who admired the earlier work, he warned 'will find in this a worthy successor'.⁶

Agnes Grey and *Wuthering Heights* were generally reviewed together, but Emily's novel engrossed the larger share of critical attention – in the form of astonishment, perplexity, outrage, even disgust. A number of critics acknowledged the 'extraordinary power' of *Wuthering Heights*, but most thought it a power misspent. The critic from *New Monthly Magazine* could not resist remarking that 'it should have been called *Withering Heights*, for any thing from which the mind and body would more instinctively shrink, than the mansion and its tenants, cannot be easily imagined.' *Graham's Magazine* characterized the novel as a 'compound of vulgar depravity and unnatural horrors', while the reviewer from *Douglas Jerrold's Weekly* recorded that 'in *Wuthering Heights* the reader is shocked, disgusted, almost sickened by details of cruelty, inhumanity, and the most diabolical hate and vengeance . . .'⁶

Since the transgressions of *Wuthering Heights* required such a

large expense of wrath on the part of critics, they had little
energy left over to address *Agnes Grey*. For the most part, reviewers were satisfied to observe that it was 'less ambitious and
less repulsive' than its sister volume. When critics did accord
Anne's novel serious attention, they usually compared it un-
favourably to *Jane Eyre*: '*Agnes Grey* is the tale of a governess
who undergoes much that is the real bond of a governess's
endurance,' the *Athenaeum* opined, but 'the new victim's trials
are of a more ignoble quality than those which awaited *Jane
Eyre*.'[7]

Only one critic came close to understanding Anne Brontë's
intention in writing *Agnes Grey* when he remarked on the relentless accuracy of her portrayal of the 'torments' that make up a
governess's life. Acton Bell, the critic speculated, 'must have
bribed some governess very largely ... to reveal to him the
secrets of her prison-house, or, he must have devoted extraordinary powers of observation and discovery to the elucidation of
the subject.' The critic concluded that '*Agnes Grey* is a tale well
worth the writing and the reading,' but having paid Anne that
compliment, he felt compelled to add immediately: 'The heroine
is a sort of younger sister to *Jane Eyre*; but inferior to her in
every way.'[8]

All through the unhappy publication of *Agnes Grey*, Anne
Brontë continued to work at her second novel, *The Tenant of
Wildfell Hall*. Charlotte had assumed that after their shoddy
treatment at the hands of Mr Newby, her sisters would be grateful for the chance to transfer their allegiance to her own publisher. But Anne and Emily resisted. On 5 February 1848, Charlotte
huffily reported to W. S Williams that Newby was 'getting into
marvulously good tune with his authors.'[9]

As agreed, Anne Brontë sent Mr Newby the completed manuscript of *The Tenant of Wildfell Hall*, and he published it in
early summer, 1848, just two years after her first novel had
begun its frustrating tour of editors. The new novel represented
a startling departure from the style and subject matter of *Agnes
Grey*. Its heroine, against the advice of her family, marries
Arthur Huntingdon, a young man whose character might have

given pause to a young woman less befuddled by romantic illusion. The young man fulfills his dark promise and subjects the heroine to an array of humiliations she could have scarcely imagined in her former (unmarried) life.

A good Victorian wife, Helen Huntingdon endures all stoically for a time, but finally rebels and slams the bedroom door in her husband's face. Arthur Huntingdon has thus far shown little regard for conventional morality, but in this case he knows his duty – he locks up his wife. She nevertheless escapes with her son and, under another name, supports both of them by painting landscapes. In the end, Anne Brontë liberates Helen and punishes Arthur Huntingdon by killing him off at a suitably early age.

It is hardly surprising that contemporary critics found *The Tenant of Wildfell Hall* shocking. Sharpe's London Magazine deemed the book 'unfit for perusal':

... so revolting are many of the scenes, so coarse and disgusting the language put into the mouths of some of the characters, that the reviewer to whom we entrusted it returned it to us, saying it was unfit to be noticed in the pages of *Sharpe*; and we are so far of the same opinion, that our object in the present paper is to warn our readers, and more especially our lady-readers, against being induced to peruse it, either by the powerful interest of the story, or the talent with which it is written.[10]

The reviewer went on to speculate on the sex of the author. No one but a man, he thought, could write with such 'bold coarseness', such 'reckless freedom of language'; no one but a man could 'make so daring an exhibition as this book presents to us'. On the other hand, no man would have written a work in which all women 'are so far superior in every quality, moral and intellectual, to all the men'. Could it be that *The Tenant of Wildfell Hall* was written by 'an authoress assisted by her husband'?

There were few reviewers who disputed the general verdict that Acton Bell's new novel was wilfully 'coarse' but, with this caveat, a surprising number of critics also echoed the *Athenaeum*'s 'honest recommendation of *Wildfell Hall* as the most interesting novel which we have read for a month past'. The *Literary World* condemned Acton Bell's 'vulgarity' but praised his 'vigor of thought, freshness and naturalness of expression, and remarkable reality of description'. The *North American Review* deplored the 'tendency of the author to degrade passion into appetite', but nevertheless concluded that 'All the characters are drawn with great power and precision of outline, and the scenes are as vivid as life itself.'[11]

Despite the divided reaction of reviewers, *The Tenant of Wildfell Hall* proved an immediate success with the reading public. The books were snapped up with such eagerness that within a month of publication Newby was bringing out a second edition. Anne Brontë, stunned by the degree to which her work had been misunderstood by critics, asked to add a preface. She thanked the critics for their praise and acknowledged that the success of *The Tenant of Wildfell Hall* was 'greater than I anticipated', but nevertheless admitted that 'it has been censured with an asperity which I was as little prepared to expect, and which my judgement, as well as my feelings, assures me is more bitter than just.'[12]

While she did not deem it the province of the author to vindicate her own work, Anne continued, she felt it necessary in this case to correct some of the critics' 'misapprehensions' and clear herself of the charge of prurient motive. Her object in writing *The Tenant of Wildfell Hall* was not simply to amuse the reader, nor to indulge 'a morbid love of the coarse' (as the *Spectator* had charged). 'I wished to tell the truth, for truth always conveys its own moral . . . but as the priceless treasure too frequently hides at the bottom of a well, it needs some courage to dive for it.' She did not, Anne Brontë modestly told her readers, consider herself 'competent to reform the errors and abuses of society' alone, but would 'fain contribute my humble quota towards so good an aim.'

Finally, Acton Bell wished to resolve the question of his identity once and for all. Responsibility for *The Tenant of Wildfell Hall* lay with him alone; its fault sought not to be laid at the feet either of Currer or Ellis Bell. To the 'discovery' by one or two critics that the author was in fact a woman, Acton Bell answered: 'I take the imputation in good part, as a compliment to the just delineation of my female characters; and though I am bound to attribute much of the severity of my censors to this suspicion, I make no effort to refute it . . .'

Anne Brontë ended her preface with one of the most forceful protests against the critical double-standard that had yet been made by a woman writer of her time:

I am satisfied that if a book is a good one, it is so whatever the sex of the author may be. All novels are or should be written for both men and women to read, and I am at a loss to conceive how a man should permit himself to write anything that would be really disgraceful to a woman, or why a woman should be censured for writing anything that would be proper and becoming for a man.

II

Less than a year after the publication of *The Tenant of Wildfell Hall* Anne Brontë was dead – at the age of twenty-nine. Anne's death followed that of her beloved Emily by only a few months: Emily died in December, Anne in May. Of the three writing sisters, only Charlotte was left to address posterity.

Most of what we know about Anne Brontë comes from Charlotte – from the 'memoir' of her sisters, from her letters or from what she told Mrs Gaskell. Aside from Anne's two novels and her poems, the only extant first-hand testimony to a life that from an early age was busily occupied with writing is five letters and two diary papers. A famously perplexing remark Charlotte made in a letter led many scholars to believe that she had destroyed her sisters' papers after they died, but this has never been definitively proven.

What is certain is that, from the first, Anne's posthumous reputation was very much under Charlotte's governorship. In 1850, W. S. Williams wrote to Charlotte to propose that Smith, Elder & Co. publish a definitive edition of Anne and Emily's work – including any unpublished compositions that might be among their literary remains. There was indeed a good deal of unpublished work – mainly poetry – but Charlotte declined to supply Mr Williams with any 'additional compositions', on the

grounds that she believed her sisters would have objected. She
agreed to a new edition of *Agnes Grey* and *Wuthering Heights*,
but opposed in no uncertain terms a reprint of *The Tenant of
Wildfell Hall*. ' "Wildfell Hall" it hardly appears to me desireable
to preserve,' she wrote to W. S. Williams. 'The choice of subject
in that work is a mistake: it was too little consonant with the
character, tastes, and ideas, of the gentle, retiring, inexperienced
writer.'[13]

In her 'Biographical Notice' prefacing the posthumous edition
of *Agnes Grey* and *Wuthering Heights*, Charlotte made public
her conviction that Anne's final work was an 'entire mistake',
once again explaining that 'nothing less congrous with the
writer's nature could be conceived'.[14] The nature that Charlotte
went on to describe was indeed incongruous with the boldly
daring character contemporary critics had observed in the author
of *The Tenant of Wildfell Hall*. According to Charlotte, 'a
constitutional reserve and taciturnity placed and kept Anne in
the shade, covered her mind, and especially her feelings, with
a sort of nun-like veil, which was rarely lifted.' Anne was
'well-endowed with quiet virtues', wrote Charlotte; even when
attacked by critics, she 'bore it, as it was her custom to bear
whatever was unpleasant, with mild, steady patience'. This last
information must have come as something of a surprise to
readers familiar with Anne Brontë's spirited defence of her
motives in writing *The Tenant of Wildfell Hall*.

Mrs Gaskell echoed Charlotte's view of Anne, describing her
as 'docile, pensive Anne', who from childhood was 'always
patient and tractable'. Subsequent biographers and critics also
followed Charlotte's lead in writing about Anne, and eventually
'gentle Anne' was incorporated into the standard equipment of
Brontë legend as the dull partner of an otherwise passionate
clan. Charlotte's reading of her sister has since been challenged
by critics who have taken up Anne's defence, but the full
complexity of feeling that lay behind Charlotte's attitude and its
determining effect on Anne's life and work has not perhaps been
sufficiently explored.

To a certain degree, Anne's image was fixed for her eldest

sister from birth. When Anne was still a baby, the children's nurse used to tell, Charlotte rushed into her father's study to announce that there was an angel standing beside Anne's cradle. When Patrick Brontë entered the room, he could discover no trace of the angel, but Charlotte nevertheless held to her story. Charlotte hardly ever referred to Anne in later years without mentioning her 'goodness', but the angel by her cradle may have also had another association for Charlotte – the death of her mother. Mrs Brontë's sixth child in seven years, Anne was born asthmatic. It may have been that her mother never really recovered her strength after Anne's birth; just two weeks after the baby's first birthday, the family already knew Mrs Brontë was dying. She lay in that condition for eight long months, suffering unspeakably. When Aunt Branwell took charge of the household after Mrs Brontë's death, she took the sickly baby into her own room and Anne slept there for the next twenty years.

The overprotectiveness that Anne's difficulty in breathing inspired in the rest of the family was no doubt considerably increased by the deaths of Maria and Elizabeth in 1825, when Anne was only five. Charlotte, now the eldest, did her best to adopt Maria's motherly attitude toward the younger siblings, but she was by nature less suited to the role. What came most naturally to Charlotte was taking command. With the imperious Branwell for ally, Charlotte orchestrated the imaginative lives of the Brontë children. The 'Plays' which would later develop into the obsessive spinning of tales so central to the Brontë's literary evolution, were Charlotte's inspiration – according to her. In the 'History of the Year 1829', twelve-year-old Charlotte gave an account of the origin of the 'Young Men's Plays':

Papa bought Branwell some wooden soldiers at Leeds . . . I snatched one up and exclaimed: 'This is the Duke of Wellington! This shall be the Duke!' When I had said this Emily likewise took one up and said it should be hers; when Anne came down, she said one should be hers. Mine was the prettiest of the whole, and the tallest, and the most perfect in every part. Emily's was a grave-looking fellow, and we called him 'Gravey'. Anne's was a queer little thing, much like herself, and we called him 'Waiting-boy'. Branwell chose his, and called him Buonaparte.[15]

Of Charlotte's importance there could be no doubt: her soldier was necessarily the 'prettiest', the 'tallest', the 'most perfect in every part'. Branwell was allowed to name his own soldier, while 'we' named Emily's and Anne's.

That Anne chafed under the condescension that went along with being the baby of the family is made clear by a story Mr Brontë told Mrs Gaskell. When Charlotte was 'about ten' and Anne 'about four', he attempted to learn more about his children's characters by placing each behind a mask in order to allow them to speak more freely. 'I told them all to stand and speak boldly from under the mask,' he recalled. 'I began with the youngest (Anne, afterwards Acton Bell) and asked what a child like her most wanted; she answered, "Age and experience." '[16]

When Anne was eleven, Charlotte was sent away to Miss Wooler's school at Roe Head. Without her, Branwell was unable to keep his younger sisters effectively under his command. Anne and Emily formed the habit of escaping by themselves to the moors. They declared their independence by inventing a dramatic cycle of their own. From this time on, Charlotte and Branwell continued to elaborate the Angrian tales (often through correspondence), while Anne and Emily shared their private world of Gondal. When Charlotte's school-friend Ellen Nussey visited the parsonage in 1833, she noted that Emily and Anne were 'like twins – inseparable companions, and in the very closest sympathy, which never had any interruption.'[17]

It was probably about this time that Anne and Emily began writing a common 'diary paper' – a tiny square of paper folded into four parts – that was to be sealed and opened four years later. On 24 November 1834, they recorded the ordinary comings-and-goings of the household thus: 'Anne and I have been peeling Apples for Charlotte to make an apple pudding . . . Taby said just now Come Anne pilloputate (i.e., peel a potato) Aunt has come into the kitchen just now and said where are your feet Anne Anne answered On the floor Aunt . . .'[18]

Such a saucy reply suggests a very different Anne from the 'always good' girl Charlotte portrayed. The diary paper shows the two youngest Brontës commonly allied in a faintly rebellious attitude toward their elders (Charlotte, Taby, Aunt) who wish to enlist them for chores or correct their behaviour: 'Anne and I have not tidied ourselves, done our bed work or done our lessons and we want to go out to play.' The diary casually – almost unconsciously – opposes the world of the elder Brontës to the private domain of Emily and Anne in an interesting sequence: 'Papa opened the parlour door and gave Branwell a letter saying here Branwell read this and show it to your Aunt and Charlotte – The Gondals are discovering the interior of Gaaldine.' Papa, Aunt, Charlotte and Branwell may share their letter among themselves, but Emily and Anne have Gondal.

Less than a year after writing the diary paper, Emily and Anne were separated. Charlotte's former teacher, Miss Wooler, had written to offer her a post as governess at her old school, Roe Head. The salary Miss Wooler named was small indeed, but she included free tuition for one of Miss Brontë's sisters. As the elder of the two, Emily was the natural choice. She and Charlotte left for Roe Head in July 1835. Writing to a friend to announce their departure, Mr Brontë remarked: 'my dear little Anne I intend to keep at home for another year under her Aunt's tuition and my own.'[19]

Charlotte explained the circumstances surrounding her decision to take up Miss Wooler's offer in a letter she wrote not long after to the poet Southey: 'My father is a clergyman of limited . . . income, and I am the eldest of his children. He expended quite as much in my education as he could afford in justice to the rest. I thought it therefore my duty, when I left school, to become a governess.'[20] To her friend Ellen Nussey Charlotte confided a further consideration – Branwell was to be sent to London, at great expense to his father and aunt, to train for a career as artist. 'Papa [will] have enough to do with his limited income,' Charlotte wrote, 'should Branwell be placed at the Royal Academy.'[21]

Emily's decision to accompany Charlotte to Roe Head was almost certainly influenced by painful consciousness of the 'burden' she represented to her father as a dependent young

woman with few prospects of marriage. However much she felt
it her duty to fit herself for a career as teacher, though, Emily
was unable to adjust simultaneously to the loss of moors, home
and freedom. The school routine that Charlotte had earlier flour-
ished under as a pupil Emily found unbearable. After only three
months, she fled. Interpreting her sudden departure years later,
Charlotte wrote: 'Liberty was the breath of Emily's nostrils;
without it, she perished . . . Her nature proved here too strong
for her fortitude. Every morning when she woke the vision of
home and the moors rushed on her, and darkened and saddened
the day that lay before her. Nobody knew what ailed her but
me . . .'[22] In arranging for Emily's education at Roe Head, Charlotte had clearly underestimated the exigencies of her sister's
nature. The contradiction between Charlotte's certainty that she
alone knew Emily's heart and her failure to foresee that Emily
could not survive school-life would inform their relations for
years to come.

   Anne and Emily were reunited for only a matter of days. The
precious free tuition at Roe Head was now offered to the youngest Miss Brontë and she accepted. Her motivation was very
probably dual: she wished to lighten the burden of failure for
Emily by taking her place at school, but she was also very much
determined to equip herself to make a living. In the three years
she and Emily had been under Charlotte's tuition at home, Anne
had studied at secondhand most of the subjects Miss Wooler
taught, but she would need formal training if she were to offer
her services as a governess. An alteration in circumstances
at home also provided Anne with a third pressing motive: Branwell had returned home penniless and with no prospect of employment. He had indeed gone up to London to enrol at the
Royal Academy as planned, but squandered the ample funds his
father and aunt had supplied on 'little squibs of rum' without
ever even presenting the letters of introduction he carried to the
Secretary of the Academy.

   Anne was no less unhappy at school than Emily had been, but
she was resolved to persist and lasted a little more than a year
before collapsing. The circumstances she had to endure placed

her in an emotional bind of increasing complexity: Anne thought of her separation from home and Emily as a sacrifice she was making for the future happiness of all, but at the same time she was well aware of the sacrifice Charlotte was making on her behalf. That she had not asked for such a sacrifice did not alter matters. Furthermore, as weeks passed, the cost to Charlotte – both emotional and material – was more and more evident. Charlotte had hoped to be able to save something out of her small salary but according to her friend Mary Taylor, 'she owned that, after clothing herself and Anne, there was nothing left . . . She confessed it was not brilliant, but what could she do?'[23]

The private journal Charlotte kept during her tenure at Roe Head records her passionate resentment: she saw herself 'encompassed by bulls (query calves of Bashan) . . . A C[ook] on one side of me, E L[ister] on the other and Miss W[ooler] in the background, stupidity the atmosphere, school-books the employment, asses the society.' Never good at hiding her feelings, Charlotte further resented having to do so: '. . . am I to spend all the best part of my life,' she wrote in her journal, 'in this wretched bondage forcibly suppressing my rage at the idleness the apathy the hyperbolical and most asinine stupidity of those flatheaded oafs and on compulsion assuming an air of kindness patience and assiduity?'[24]

Anne's presence is never mentioned as a mitigating factor in her sister's bleak situation. Charlotte confided her innermost thoughts to her journal and to her friend Ellen Nussey in a rain of letters, but apparently held Anne at a distance. The full measure of that distance is indicated by a mention Charlotte made of a letter from Branwell: 'I lived on its contents for days . . . it came . . . bringing with it agreeable thoughts such as I had for many months been a stranger to.'[25]

Charlotte hated her employment, her students and eventually her formerly beloved Miss Wooler. Did her resentment also spill over onto her sister Anne? Given Charlotte's character, she would have almost certainly repressed such a feeling, but may well have unconsciously expressed it, as she would habitually do later on.

The bind that Charlotte's palpable anger and frustration put
Anne in must have added immeasurably to the emotional hardship school represented for her. Like Emily, Anne felt severely
the loss of her freedom and the moors they were accustomed to
roam. The poems she wrote during this period centre on the
themes of bereavement and imprisonment. 'A Voice from the
Dungeon', composed in October 1837, begins:

> I'm buried now; I've done with life;
> I've done with hate, revenge and strife;
> I've done with joy, and hope and love
> And all the bustling world above.
>
> Long have I dwelt forgotten here
> In pining woe and dull despair;
> This place of solitude and gloom
> Must be my dungeon and tomb.
>
> No hope, no pleasure can I find;
> I am grown weary of my mind . . .[26]

'The Captive's Dream' and 'The North Wind' also speak in the
voice of a prisoner 'pining in a dungeon'. The protagonist of the
latter poem hears the north wind say:

> I have passed over thy own mountains dear,
> Thy northern mountains – and they still are free,
> Still lonely, wild, majestic, bleak and drear,
> And stern and lovely, as they used to be
>
> When thou, a young enthusiast,
> As wild and free as they,
> O'er rocks and glens and snowy heights
> Didst often love to stray.

The poem ends with the plea:

> Confined and hopeless as I am,
> O speak of liberty,
> O tell me of my mountain home,
> And I will welcome thee.[27]

The loss of home was inseparably tied to the loss of Emily's companionship for Anne. The diary paper they wrote together on 26 June 1837, while Anne and Charlotte were briefly at the parsonage during school holidays, testifies to the perfectly easy accord between the two: 'Anne and I writing in the drawing-room – Anne a poem beginning "Fair was the evening and brightly the sun" – I August Almeda's life . . .'[28] The diary ends with Aunt Branwell interrupting Anne and Emily, prompting the following exchange:

Anne: 'Well, do you intend to write in the evening.'
Emily: 'Well, what think you.'
    (We agreed to go out[side] to make sure if we got into the humour.
    We may stay in –)

The separate alliances within the family still hold: while Anne and Emily are writing together, Charlotte is sewing in Aunt's room while Branwell reads a new novel to her.

The poem Anne was working on in the drawing-room deals with grief over parting. 'Can I be happy when I know/ Tomorrow we must part?' Anne's Gondalian heroine asks. '*Must* we be torn away?' her partner replies. '*Shall* I be left to mourn alone? Must hearts that have grown together,' he pleads, 'be rent away and kept apart for ever?'[29]

Anne's brief reunion with Emily may have made it even more difficult for her to return to isolation and loneliness at school. Excluded from Charlotte's confidence, she could hope for little sisterly sympathy from that quarter, nor could she offer any herself under the circumstances. Powerless to act, Anne could only hide her feelings. The penalty she paid was a physical collapse not unlike Emily's. Charlotte was so self-absorbed and Anne so adept at disguise that no notice was taken of the younger sister's deteriorating condition until it had reached an advanced stage. Suddenly awakened, Charlotte transferred her own guilt to Miss Wooler and in a rage accused her of neglecting Anne. This 'eclaircissement', as Charlotte called it, was the means of making a break she had no doubt intensely wished for: 'I told Miss Wooler one or two plain truths, which set her a-crying,'

Charlotte wrote to Ellen Nussey, 'and the next day, she wrote to papa, telling him that I had reproached her bitterly . . . Papa sent for us the day after he received the letter.'[30]

Characteristically, Charlotte was unable to admit the possibility that she might have contributed to Anne's decline, or even to recognize her own blindness in the matter. On the contrary, she claimed special insight into the true nature of her sister's condition: 'I looked upon her case in a different light to what I could wish or expect any uninterested person to view it in,' she told her friend Ellen. As she had been in Emily's case, Charlotte was firmly convinced – and never lost that conviction – that 'no one knew what ailed her but me'.

The complicated pattern of feeling that evolved between the two sisters during their stay at Roe Head would increasingly mark their relationship. They remained bound by strong family affection and loyalty, but Anne had developed a strategy of hiding her feelings from Charlotte who was, in any case, slow to recognize them and unable to accommodate any change in the fixed image she held of her youngest sister.

Anne, on recovering her health after returning home from Roe Head, was determined to prove that she was *not* the helpless child Charlotte thought her and to shoulder her fair share of the burden of making a living. To this end she applied for a post as governess. She was engaged by the Ingham family at Blake Hall and left home on 8 April 1839. Charlotte reported her departure to Ellen Nussey with affectionate condescension: 'Poor child! she left us last Monday . . . We have had one letter from her since she went. She expresses herself very well satisfied, and says that Mrs Ingham is extremely kind . . . You would be astonished what a sensible, clever letter she writes; it is only the talking part that I fear.'[31]

Anne was evidently covering up her real circumstances again: as we know from the autobiographical account in *Agnes Grey* of her arrival at her first post, Anne's reception was anything but 'kind'. The truth necessarily emerged, however, when Anne returned home once again after only two terms, unjustly dismissed by Mrs Ingham for incompetence.

By the time Anne left to take up her second post, at Thorp Green Hall in the spring of 1841, Charlotte was dimly aware that her sister might be concealing things from her. She wrote to Emily from her own post as governess in the White family: 'I had a letter from Anne yesterday; she says she is well. I hope she speaks absolute truth.'[32] At the beginning of summer, Charlotte wrote to Ellen Nussey, mentioning that she hoped her employers wouldn't put off her holiday, or 'I shall miss the chance of seeing Anne this vacation . . . I *should like* to see her to judge for myself of the state of her health. I cannot trust any other person's report no one seems minute enough in their observations.'[33] This presumably included Emily, who was then at home with Anne.

Emily was far more privy to Anne's confidence than Charlotte realized. In a diary paper written on 30 July, destined for Anne's eyes alone, Emily sent 'from afar an exhortation of courage, boys, courage, to exiled and harrassed [sic] Anne, wishing she was here.'[34] In the corresponding diary paper that Anne wrote at the same moment from Thorp Green, she confessed: 'I dislike my situation and wish to change it.'[35] She had some hope of doing so at that point: Aunt Branwell had offered to put up the capital that would allow her three nieces to set up a school of their own. Emily's diary paper eagerly projects a happy outcome to this plan: 'We, i.e. Charlotte, Anne, and I – shall be all merrily seated in our sitting-room in some pleasant and flourishing seminary . . . Our debts will be paid off and we shall have cash in hand to a considerable amount. Papa, Aunt Branwell will either have been, or be coming – to visit us . . . Anne and I will perchance slip out into the garden for a few minutes to piruse [sic] our papers.'

Miss Wooler suggested that the Brontë girls take over her school and Charlotte had begun negotiating the terms when a letter came from Mary Taylor in Brussels, urging Charlotte to join her there. A stint at school on the Continent, Mary argued, would enhance the accomplishments Charlotte could advertise for the proposed school. Charlotte dropped the negotiations with Miss Wooler and wrote to Aunt Branwell to persuade her to use her capital to send herself and Emily to Brussels. In view of Emily's unhappy experience at Roe Head and her indelible attachment to home, it seems unlikely that she welcomed Charlotte's idea. She also evidently objected to Anne's exclusion, because on 7 November Charlotte wrote to reassure her: 'Anne seems omitted in the present plan, but if all goes right I trust she will derive her full share of benefit from it in the end. I exhort all to hope. I believe in my heart this is acting for the best; my only fear is lest others should doubt and be dismayed.'[36] Charlotte was by this time aware of Anne's deep unhappiness at Thorp Green, but nevertheless chose to pursue her determined course of action: 'I burn to go somewhere else,' she confided to Ellen Nussey.[37] She persuaded Aunt Branwell to accept her plan by assuring her that 'Anne might take her turn at some future period, if our school answered.'[38]

If Anne doubted that 'this is acting for the best', she hid her dismay from Charlotte. She was also masking her feelings on another subject. Just before the departure for Brussels, Charlotte observed to Ellen Nussey that her father's handsome curate, William Weightman, 'sits opposite to Anne at church sighing softly and looking out of the corners of his eyes to win her attention – and Anne is so quiet, her look so downcast – they are a picture – He would be the better of a comfortable wife like you to settle him, you would settle him I believe – nobody else would.'[39]

As Anne's poetry amply documents, she was hardly indifferent to Willy Weightman. He was very probably the love of her life. Charlotte had earlier carried on a mild flirtation with him herself and then had promoted a romance between the curate and Ellen Nussey, which had come to nothing. Her remarks to Ellen on the subject of Anne and Willy Weightman are open to two interpretations. It may be that Anne had once again succeeded in hiding her real feelings from Charlotte; it also seems possible, however, that Charlotte had partly divined them, but was scornful about her 'gentle' sister's capacity to take on the 'fickle' Mr Weightman and was still pushing her friend Ellen as an appropriate wife for him. Whether or not Charlotte had any inkling of Anne's passionate attachment was soon a moot point. Willy Weightman died of cholera that autumn while Anne was at Thorp Green and Charlotte and Emily at the Pensionnat Heger in Brussels. From her lonely exile, Anne wrote:

> I will not mourn thee. lovely one,
> Though thou art torn away

> . . . if thy life as transient proved,
> It hath been full as bright,
> For thou wert hopeful and beloved;
> Thy spirit knew no blight.

> If few and short the joys of life
> That thou on earth couldst know,
> Little thou knew'st of sin and strife
> Nor much of pain and woe.[40]

She is determined to remember that 'thy brightest hopes were fixed above', but still,

> . . . I cannot check my sighs,
> Thou wert so young and fair,
> More bright than summer morning skies,
> But stern death would not spare . . .

> That angel smile that late so much
> Could my fond heart rejoice;
> And he had silenced by his touch
> The music of thy voice.

> I'll weep no more thine early doom
> But O! I still must mourn
> The pleasures buried in thy tomb,
> For they will not return.

As it turned out, Anne quite rightly felt that with Willy Weightman's death, her only chance for love had vanished.

It may have been of some comfort to Anne that in November, Emily returned home. Charlotte had originally asked for six months at school on the Continent, but even before she and

Emily left home had resolved to spend a year abroad. After they had been gone nine months, Aunt Branwell's death recalled them. Emily was no doubt glad of the opportunity to return home, but Charlotte was eager to regain Brussels and her beloved professor, Monsieur Heger. She left in January of 1843 and did not return for another year. Anne, in the meantime, had returned to Thorp Green, accompanied by Branwell. Her brother's own attempts at finding himself employment having ended the previous summer with a humiliating dismissal by the Railway Company from his post as clerk at Luddenfoot Station, Anne had taken it upon herself to persuade her own employers, the Robinsons, to hire Branwell as tutor to their son.

The school that Anne and Emily had looked forward to with such hope had been delayed for more than two years by Charlotte's desire to go abroad. When she finally came home in January, 1844, it was clear that the project as originally conceived was out of the question. Aunt Branwell's death and Mr Brontë's increasing blindness made it imperative that someone remain at home to look after him. It was not until mid-summer that the possibility of setting up their school at the parsonage occurred to the girls. Oddly enough, when Charlotte wrote to Monsieur Heger to outline her plan and ask his advice, she did not mention Anne at all. Of Emily she said: '[she] does not care much for teaching but she would look after the housekeeping and, although something of a recluse, she is too good-hearted not to do all she could for the well-being of the children.'[41]

Anne and Emily, probably unaware of the terms in which Charlotte had described their project to Monsieur Heger, certainly regarded themselves as equal parties to the plan and eagerly supported the efforts to find students for their parsonage school. After a year's trying, however, they recruited no pupils and the hoped-for liberation from governess-ship came to an end when Branwell returned home in disgrace after Mr Robinson learnt of his tutor's affair with Mrs Robinson. Branwell's subsequent collapse and descent into the hell of opium addiction definitively excluded any possibility of a school or pupils at the parsonage.

Anne had evidently kept secret from Charlotte the bad news about Branwell's activities at Thorp Green. Charlotte, for her part, had failed to observe any change in Branwell's behaviour until recognition of what was going on was forced upon her. When Anne apprised her of the truth behind Branwell's collapse, Charlotte reacted with shock and disapproval: 'My hopes ebb low indeed about Branwell,' she wrote to Ellen Nussey. 'I sometimes fear he will never be fit for much. His bad habits seem more deeply rooted than I thought ... One ought, indeed to hope to the very last; I try to do so, but occasionally, hope, in his case, seems a fallacy ...'[42] Anne, who had much more to complain of, resisted condemning Branwell or letting him feel her disapproval. In her diary paper of 31 July, she simply noted: 'Branwell had left Ludden Foot, and been a tutor at Thorp Green, and had much tribulation and ill health ... We hope he will be better and do better in the future.'[43] In her own corresponding diary paper, Emily echoed Anne's generous sentiments toward Branwell almost exactly. 'We are all in decent health,' she wrote, 'with the exception of Branwell who I hope will be better and do better, hereafter.' While Emily and Anne continued to extend to Branwell their sympathy, Charlotte was hardening her rejection of him: 'I wish I could say one word in his favour,' she told Ellen Nussey in November, 'but I cannot, therefore I will hold my tongue.'[44]

Anne refused to denounce Branwell, but the disaster at Thorp Green that she was forced to witness took an enormous toll emotionally. In her diary paper, she recorded opening the paper she had written in 1841, thinking, 'How many things have happened since ... I was then at Thorp Green, and now I am only just escaped from it. I was wishing to leave it then, and if I had known that I had four years longer to stay how wretched I should have been; but during my stay I have had some very unpleasant and undreamt-of experiences of human nature.'[45]

Anne's relation to Branwell at Thorp Green repeated in certain respects her unhappy experience with Charlotte at Roe Head. Branwell's presence, which ought to have mitigated her loneliness, in the end only served to reinforce Anne's isolation. And, though in this case she had taken Charlotte's former role of self-sacrifice for the benefit of a sibling, Anne no doubt experienced once again a sense of powerlessness no less great than it had been at Roe Head. Her physical collapse was not repeated, but she acknowledged in her diary paper that 'I . . . [could not] well be flatter or older in mind than I am now.'

The single pleasure in Anne's life was reunion with Emily. They were still writing the Gondal saga and had taken their first long journey together, to York. They had wanted to go to Scarborough, but Charlotte asked them to give up the idea because she wanted to take a trip to see Ellen Nussey. Emily reported in her diary that the trip was a great success, nevertheless – 'though the weather was broken we enjoyed ourselves very much . . .'[46] Emily was clearly making a large effort to cheer up Anne – against rather overwhelming odds. Of the entire household, only Emily was 'undesponding': Mr Brontë was sinking further into blindness, Branwell was stunning his sorrows with drink, and Charlotte had for the last year been suffering unspeakable anguish over her unrequited feelings for Monsieur Heger.

It was at this juncture that Charlotte discovered Emily's poems. According to the famous account in Charlotte's 'Biographical Notice of Ellis and Acton Bell', she 'accidentally lighted' on a manuscript in Emily's handwriting and read it – though, by her own admission, 'unlicensed' to do so. Emily was outraged by this intrusion into the 'recesses of [her] mind and feelings', as Charlotte put it, so much so that 'it took hours to reconcile her to the discovery I had made, and days to persuade her that such poems merited publication. I knew, however, that a mind like hers could not be without some latent spark of honourable ambition, and refused to be discouraged in my attempts to fan that spark to flame.'[47] Anne attempted to distract Charlotte's attention by 'quietly' producing some poems of her own, but Charlotte was not to be diverted from her campaign. As she later told W. S. Williams, 'by dint of entreaty and reason I at last wrung out a reluctant consent to have the "rhymes" as they were contemptuously termed, published.'[48]

Charlotte's discovery of Emily's poems radically revised and complicated the relationship among the three sisters. From the beginning, Charlotte's writing life had been shared with Branwell. Even when she was away at Roe Head as a teacher, they continued to spin out the Angrian saga by letter. Their partnership gradually dwindled, however, and had already come to an end some time before the revelation of Branwell's moral perfidy caused Charlotte to reject him. She had, moreover, under Southey's discouragement and M. Heger's advice, definitively renounced their common dream of pursuing a career of letters. Writing to M. Heger in the summer of 1844, Charlotte complained of 'désoeuvrement' and consequent 'léthargie des facultés', remarking that, 'I would not know this lethargy if I could write. Formerly I passed whole days and weeks and months in writing . . .'[49]

Charlotte was apparently unaware that Anne and Emily's writing partnership had continued unabated. Her account in the 'Biographical Notice' of the way matters stood in the autumn of 1845 states that 'formerly we used to show each other what we wrote, but of late years this habit of communication and consultation had been discontinued; hence it ensued, that we were mutually ignorant of the progress we might respectively have made.'[50]

The corresponding diary papers that Emily and Anne wrote the summer before Charlotte's discovery tell a different story: both casually refer to the literary exchange that was a matter of habit with them. Emily records that 'the Gondals still flourish bright as ever', and notes both her own and Anne's contributions to the Chronicles, happily adding: 'We intend sticking firm by the rascals as long as they delight us which I am glad to say they do at present.' Anne notes that Emily is writing the Emperor Julius's life and remarks that 'she has read some of it, and I want her very much to hear the rest'. Anne also mentions that Emily is writing some poetry. Evidently Emily had not yet shown it to her, since she remarked: 'I wonder what it is about.' Anne's attitude could not be more different from Charlotte's; she tacitly assumes that when Emily is ready to show her work she will do so of her own accord. It may well have been this willingness to allow each other autonomy within twinship that accounted for Anne and Emily's perfect ease with each other.

At the very moment Charlotte had 'lost' Branwell, she 'discovered' her sisters – with the characteristic energy and zeal that she gave to all her projects. She wrote enthusiastically to her former teacher: 'You my dear Miss Wooler know full well as I do the value of sisters' affection to each other; there is nothing like it in the world, I believe, when they are nearly equal in age and similar in education, tastes, and sentiments.'[51]

Whatever ideal of sisterhood Charlotte held in her mind, in practice she inserted herself into Anne and Emily's partnership not as an equal, but as leader. Emily and Anne resented her uninvited eruption into their private world, but the multiple losses that Charlotte had recently undergone may have acted as powerful emotional blackmail. Nevertheless, there is a good deal of evidence of resistance on their part. In the same letter to Miss Wooler in which Charlotte extols the 'value of sisters' affection', she also complains that Anne and Emily refuse to be persuaded 'to regard the affair [of investment in railway shares] precisely from my point of view.' Emily, Charlotte told Miss Wooler, is 'not quite so tractable or open as I could wish [but] I must remember perfection is not the lot of humanity and as long as we can regard those we love, and to whom we are closely allied, with profound and never-shaken esteem, it is a small thing that they should vex us occasionally by, what appear to us, unreasonable and headstrong notions.'

Emily had acceded to Charlotte's burning desire to publish, but apparently could not control her feelings of resentment. About the same time Aylott and Jones published *Poems, by Currer, Ellis and Acton Bell*, Anne wrote a poem describing the painful sense of loss and domestic discord that dominated the parsonage. Under the title 'Monday Night May 11 1846' she questioned:

> Why should such gloomy silence reign;
> And why is all the house so drear,

When neither danger, sickness, pain,
Nor death, nor want have entered here?

We are as many as we were
That other night, when all were gay,
And full of hope, and free from care;
Yet, is there something gone away.[52]

Charlotte's violation not only damaged her own relations with
Emily and Anne, but interfered with the intimacy between the
two younger sisters as well: 'Each feels the bliss of all destroyed,'
Anne wrote, 'And mourns the change – but each apart.' From
the beginning, when she brought out her own poems to distract
Charlotte from her 'persuasion' of Emily, Anne had taken upon
herself the role of mediator. Since Charlotte was not generally
inclined to take her seriously, it is hardly surprising that her
efforts were unsuccessful. Anne steps back from assigning any
blame to Charlotte, however, and merely laments the absence of
'Mirth', 'Love' and '*Peace*' (the last underlined in the manuscript), commenting:

We rudely drove thee from our hearth,
And vainly sigh for thy return.

After Anne died, Charlotte included this poem in the 1830 edition
of her sister's work, under her own title: 'Domestic Peace'.

The account Charlotte gave Mrs Gaskell of the sisters' working habits while writing their first novels describes a thrilling
commonality of purpose, each sister reading aloud to the others.
But the 'Editor's Preface' Charlotte wrote for the posthumous
edition of *Wuthering Heights* offers a darker version of the same
exchange. 'If the auditor of her work when read in manuscript,'
she wrote, 'shuddered under the grinding influence of natures so
relentless and implacable, of spirits so lost and fallen; if it was
complained that the mere hearing of certain vivid and fearful
scenes banished sleep by night, and disturbed mental peace by
day, Ellis Bell would wonder what was meant, and suspect the
complaintant of affectation.'[53] Behind Charlotte's strong reaction to hearing *Wuthering Heights* read aloud was the feeling

that what Emily had written was morally reprehensible: 'Whether it is right or advisable to create beings like Heathcliff I do not know: I scarcely think it is,' she remarked.

Charlotte's attempts to impose her point of view were clearly unsuccessful; she repeatedly complained that Emily was not 'amenable' to her 'influence'. She pointed out, for example, that the qualities of constancy and tenderness 'do not shine so well incarnate in a man as they would do in a woman . . . [but] Ellis Bell could never be brought to comprehend this notion.'[54] Anne received the same sort of 'advice' from Charlotte while she was writing *The Tenant of Wildfell Hall*. In the 'Biographical Notice', Charlotte says she 'reasoned' with her. But like Emily, Anne chose to ignore her sister's admonition and pursue her own course.

The summer after *Wuthering Heights* and *Agnes Grey* were published – the summer before Emily died – Charlotte repeated her violation of Emily's privacy. When she and Anne rushed to London to counter Mr Newby's deceptive advertising of *The Tenant of Wildfell Hall*, Charlotte revealed Ellis Bell's true identity to her publishers. Afterward, she wrote to W. S. Williams to caution him not to mention her sisters in any letters to her. She had 'betrayed' Emily 'inadvertently', Charlotte told Mr Williams, adding that 'I regret it bitterly now, for I find it is against every feeling and intention of Ellis Bell.'[55] This latest indiscretion may well have contributed to a hardening of attitude on Emily's part. At the end of November, Charlotte protested to Ellen Nussey that '[Emily] will not give an explanation of her feelings . . .' Five days later, Charlotte wrote again: 'she is too intractable. I *do* wish I knew her feelings more clearly.'[56]

Charlotte's perplexing ambivalence is nowhere more apparent than in a letter she wrote to W. S. Williams while Emily was dying and Anne very ill. 'To-day, as Emily appeared a little easier,' Charlotte recounted, 'I thought the "Review" would amuse her, so I read it aloud to her and Anne. As I sat between them at our quiet but now somewhat melancholy fireside, I studied the two ferocious authors. Ellis, the "man of uncommon talents, but dogged, brutal and morose," sat leaning back in his easy-chair drawing her impeded breath as best he could . . . it is not his wont to laugh, but he smiled half-amused and half in scorn as he listened. Acton . . . smiled too, dropping . . . a single word of calm amazement to hear his character so darkly portrayed.'[57]

The review in question began by insulting the 'whole firm of Bell & Co.', but thereafter principally concentrated its attack on Acton Bell:

Acton, when left together to his own imaginations, seems to take a morose satisfaction in developing a full and complete science of human brutality. In *Wuthering Heights* he has succeeded in reaching the summit of this laudable ambition . . . he details all the ingenuities of animal malignity, and exhausts the whole rhetoric of stupid blasphemy, in order that there may be no mistake as to the kind of person he intends to hold up to the popular gaze.

The reviewer concludes with the observation that 'Nightmares and dreams, through which devils dance and wolves howl, make bad novels.'[58]

The idea that Charlotte could read aloud to her dying sisters a personal attack of such violence, even under the self-delusion that they might find it amusing, seems nearly incredible. That Charlotte knew that Anne at least had most definitely *not* been amused by what the critics had to say about her work is evidenced by an earlier letter she wrote to W. S. Williams: 'You will have seen some of the notices of "Wildfell Hall". I wish my sister felt the unfavourable ones less keenly. She does not *say* much, for she is reserved even with her nearest of kin, but I cannot avoid seeing that her spirits are depressed sometimes.'[59] Charlotte went on to explain to Mr Williams that it had come as a great surprise to Anne, as well as to Emily and herself, that the critics questioned her intentions in writing. After blaming the critics for objecting to Anne's choice of subject, Charlotte told Mr Williams that she herself considered the subject 'unfortunately chosen – it was one the author was not qualified to handle at once vigorously and truthfully'. Acton Bell would do much better to stick to 'quiet description and simple pathos', her sister opined.

Charlotte responded to Anne's last request with similarly per-

plexing behaviour. Two months before Anne died, Ellen Nussey
invited her to come for a visit at Brookroyd, her family's estate.
Charlotte answered for her failing sister, saying that Anne had
proposed that Ellen accompany her to Scarborough instead, since
Charlotte could not do so because she had to stay home with Mr
Brontë. In the same letter, Charlotte asked Ellen to refuse Anne's
proposal, on the grounds that Ellen must not assume responsibility for a patient who might die on her hands. On
5 April 1849, Anne replied to Ellen herself, regretting that
'visitors' prevented her from going to Scarborough in the month
of May, but adding that she hoped Charlotte 'will by some
means make it possible to accompany me after all'. She did not
wish to delay the trip any further, Anne explained, because she
had been assured by doctors that a change of air would 'hardly
ever fail of success in consumptive cases, if the remedy be taken
in time; but the reason there are so many disappointments is that
it is generally deferred till it is too late . . . Under these circumstances, I think there is no time to be lost.'[60]

Motivated by the old conviction that she alone knew best what
her sister needed, Charlotte continued to procrastinate for nearly
another month. She wrote to Ellen Nussey: '[Anne] seems herself
but half-conscious of the necessity for such a delay. She wonders,
I believe, why I don't talk more about the journey: it grieves me
to think she may even be hurt by my seeming tardiness.'[61] Charlotte told Ellen she was waiting for some improvement in Anne's
condition, but by the time they finally set out for Scarborough at
the end of May, Anne was already dying and lasted only a few
days after arriving at her passionately desired destination.

Charlotte described her sister's death in a letter to W. S.
Williams: 'She died very calmly and gently . . . Anne had had
enough of life such as it was – in her twenty-eighth year she laid
it down as a burden.'[62] Yet Anne herself had said the month
before, in her letter to Ellen, that 'I wish it would please God to
spare me not only for Papa's and Charlotte's sakes, but because
I long to do some good in the world before I leave it. I have
many schemes in my head for future practice . . .'[63]

*

When read against the background of the extremely complex, ambivalent relationship that evolved between Charlotte and her sisters, the portrait Charlotte fixed for posterity in the 'Biographical Notice of Ellis and Acton Bell' emerges more as a manifestation of the strategy Anne developed for dealing with her domineering sister than a definitive record of her character. When Charlotte writes that 'a constitutional reserve and taciturnity . . . covered [Anne's] mind, and especially her feelings, with a sort of nun-like veil, which was rarely lifted,'[64] we cannot help remembering that Anne had long been in the habit of hiding her feelings from Charlotte and resisting her schemes by evasion. At the same time, it is useful to consider that Charlotte's all-important role in Anne's life may have had a good deal to do with shaping her character.

The masking of feeling that began with Charlotte may have eventually become a standard response for Anne. In a telling passage, the heroine of *Agnes Grey* describes the disguise she habitually adopted: 'I was accustomed, now, to keeping silence when things distasteful to my own ear were uttered, and, now, too, I was used to wearing a placid smiling countenance when my heart was bitter within me. Only those who have felt the like can imagine my feelings, as I sat with an assumption of smiling indifference . . .' A few pages later, she sums up: 'I was a close and resolute dissembler . . .'

The influence of 'family' is of paramount importance in *Agnes Grey*. It is their insistence on condescending to Agnes as the helpless 'baby' of the family that supplies an important motivation for going out as a governess. Interestingly enough, Agnes Grey, like her creator, had six siblings, but Anne Brontë chose to kill them all off by the time the story begins – all except one dear sister. One can't help thinking that Anne's chosen survivor would have been Emily.

In one instance, though, the inspiration for Agnes's sister Mary must surely have been Charlotte. Attempting to dissuade her younger sister from taking her first post as governess, Mary says: 'Only think what you would do in a house full of strangers, without me or Mama to speak and act for you . . .' Agnes replies:

'You think, because I always do as you bid me, I have no judgment of my own: but only try me . . .'

III

In the 'Biographical Notice of Ellis and Acton Bell', Charlotte
Brontë recorded that after the publication of *Poems, by Currer,
Ellis and Acton Bell* in 1846, 'we each set to work on a prose
tale: Ellis Bell produced *Wuthering Heights*, Acton Bell *Agnes
Grey*, and Currer Bell also wrote a narrative in one volume [*The
Professor*].' But the diary paper that Anne Brontë wrote almost a
whole year earlier mentions that she was already beginning the
third volume of *Passages in the Life of an Individual* – the novel
that in its final form was published under the title *Agnes Grey*.

Since bringing her Angrian chronicles to a close in 1839, Charlotte had attempted several narratives with a realistic setting,
but her plots and characters were still strongly influenced by the
romantic excesses of her juvenilia. Anne's *Passages in the Life of
an Individual*, begun while she was at Thorp Green and Charlotte in Brussels, was very probably the first fully realized work
by any of the Brontës that had its origin in observed reality,
rather than the more extravagant 'clime' of Gondal or Angria.

Agnes Grey is based on Anne Brontë's experiences as a governess in the two posts she held successively between 1839 and
1845. Anne's first post was with the Ingham family at Blake
Hall, Mirfield. Miss Wooler's school was not far away, and it
may well have been Anne's former teacher who obtained the
post for her. In the novel, Agnes Grey obtains her first post
through the offices of her Aunt Grey, who 'asserted [Mrs Bloom-
field] to be a very nice woman'. The Inghams had five children:
Joshua, who was six; Mary, aged five; Martha, aged three; Emily,
aged two; and Harriette, still a baby. Anne was engaged to
educate the two eldest children; the others were still confined to
the nursery. Like Agnes Grey, she was peremptorily dismissed
from her post after only two terms.

Anne Brontë's second 'situation' was with the family of the
Rev. Edmund Robinson, who was ordained as a minister but

lived as a gentleman on the income of an estate he had inherited at his father's death, when he was only three months old. His wife, Lydia Robinson, was the daughter of a clergyman, the Rev. Gisborne, a Canon of Durham. Her father also had an independent income, and the family was socially prominent. The Edmund Robinsons had three daughters and one son: Lydia, the eldest, was fifteen and a half when Anne was engaged as governess, and her sisters Elizabeth and Mary were fourteen and eleven. The son, Edmund, was nine years old. He was under Anne's tutorship for two years before Branwell was hired to take him over. Thorp Green Hall, which had been in the Robinson family for nearly fifty years, stood in the midst of fields and hedgerows, two miles from the village of Little Ouseburn and twelve miles from York. From the beginning, Anne disliked her situation and wished to leave, but she remained for four years – first, out of a sense of duty to those at home and later on out of a desire to secure steady employment for Branwell. She was rewarded by a humiliating and painful forced witness of Branwell's love-affair with the mistress of the house.

Agnes Grey follows the particulars of Anne Brontë's actual experience fairly closely. Like her creator, Agnes Grey is the youngest child of a clergyman of the north of England, whose narrow income motivates his daughter to seek employment as a governess. Agnes Grey, like Anne Brontë, was nineteen when she took up her first post. Her deliberately solitary departure from home is very much like the leave-taking Charlotte described in a letter to Ellen Nussey on the occasion of Anne's going to Blake Hall for the first time. Countless other details of landscape, character and event in the novel have their counterparts in the author's own life.

Anne Brontë herself insisted on the autobiographical 'truth' of her novel. The first line of Agnes Grey establishes the novel as a 'true history'. Later on in the introductory paragraph, the speaker confides: 'Shielded by my own obscurity, and by the lapse of years and a few fictitious names, I do not fear to venture, and will candidly lay before the public what I would not disclose to the most intimate friend.' The novel closes with the statement that 'my diary, from which I have compiled these pages, goes but little further'.

The author's assertion that her novel is a true history was of course a convention that originated with the novel-form itself more than a century before, but Anne Brontë's emphasis on the truth of her narrative is especially important because believability was essential to her purpose in writing. As she declared of her second novel in the preface to the second edition, what Anne Brontë aimed at was reform. Through the coolly objective narration of Agnes Grey's experience, she meant to provide her contemporaries with as thorough an exposition as she possibly could of the plight of the governess. In an aside to the reader, the narrator of Agnes Grey declares: '. . . my design in writing the last few pages, was not to amuse, but to benefit those whom it might concern.' Naturally Anne Brontë was distressed when, as she related in the preface to *The Tenant of Wildfell Hall*, 'the story of *Agnes Grey* was accused of extravagant over-colouring in those very parts that were carefully copied from life, with a most scrupulous avoidance of all exaggeration . . .'

The plight of the governess was inseparable from the larger dilemma of marriage for a woman of Anne Brontë's generation. Since the beginning of the nineteenth century, and perhaps even before, there had been a steadily increasing surplus of women in England. According to the census of 1851, this excess amounted to 365,000 – an understated figure at that, because the 100,000 men resident abroad in the military were counted as part of the population in England.

The unequal distribution of the sexes meant that there were large numbers of women who could never hope to marry. Between 1800 and 1840, the periodical literature of the day – which the young Brontës eagerly devoured whenever the opportunity presented itself – was full of articles debating 'what to do with our old maids?' It seems to have been tacitly assumed in the Brontë household that there was little likelihood of the girls ever finding husbands. Agnes Grey's mother refers to a happy married future for her daughters, and her husband mournfully replies: '*They* married – poor penniless things! Who will take them, I wonder!'

Outside of marriage, the prospects for supporting oneself were achingly few. In the same letter that Charlotte Brontë announced to Ellen Nussey Anne's departure for her first post as governess, she gave an ironic catalogue of the possibilities for earning a living that she herself could look forward to: 'I am as yet "wanting a situation" . . . I've lately discovered that I've quite a talent for cleaning – sweeping up hearths dusting rooms – making beds &c. so if everything else fails – I can turn my hand to that . . . I won't be a cook – I hate cooking – I won't be a nursery-maid – nor a lady's maid far less a lady's companion – or a mantua-maker – or a straw-bonnet maker or a taker-in of plain-work – I will be nothing but a house-maid.'[65]

When Agnes Grey and her sister Mary ask how they might contribute to the dwindling family finances, the only sort of work their mother can suggest is painting water-colours – an occupation that ladies commonly resorted to to fill leisure hours. Margaret Ibbotson, the heroine of Harriet Martineau's novel *Deerbrook* (1839), asks the same question of her governess friend, Maria, and is told that a woman of the 'uneducated classes' can earn a subsistence by washing or cooking, milking cows or going into service, but for an educated woman 'there is in all England no chance of subsistence but by teaching . . . or by being a superior Miss Nares – the feminine gender of the tailor and the hatter.' Margaret, who has hitherto been protected from any such exigency, incredulously asks: 'The tutor, the tailor, and the hatter. Is this all?' 'All,' Maria replies, 'except that there are departments of art and literature from which it is impossible to shut women out. These are not, however, to be regarded as resources for bread.'[66] Charlotte Brontë's school-friend Mary Taylor found that she had to emigrate to New Zealand in order to establish any sort of career outside this meagre sphere of alternatives. 'Mary has made up her mind that she can not and will not be a governess, a teacher, a milliner, a bonnet-maker nor housemaid,' Charlotte wrote to Emily in 1844. 'She sees no means of obtaining employment she would like in England, so she is leaving it.'[67]

In the eyes of Anne Brontë's contemporaries, the idea of seeking any sort of employment at all outside the home irreparably compromised a woman's gentility. 'Society has thought fit to assert that the woman who works . . . loses her social position,' comments Elizabeth Missing Sewell in her *Principles of Education*. Ladies of decent family would 'shrink from it as from an insult.'[68] The author of an article on 'The Market for Educated Female Labor' pointed out in a contemporary journal that 'If a lady has to work for her livelihood, it is universally considered to be misfortune, an exception to the ordinary rule.' The theory of 'civilized life', the author continued, holds that women of the upper and middle classes are supported either by their fathers or husbands: 'All our laws are framed strictly in accordance with this hypothesis; and all our social customs adhere to it more strictly still. We make no room in our social framework for any other idea.'[69]

Mary Taylor referred scornfully to the influence of this social prohibition against work in a letter she wrote to Ellen Nussey in 1849, urging her to come to New Zealand:

I hear from Charlotte Brontë that you are staying in Sussex. What in the world are you doing there? Getting your living in any way? Not at all, you are only wishing to do so; wishing for something to turn up that would enable you to work for yourself instead of for other people, and that no one should know that you were working . . . Try and persuade some of your twenty brothers to fit you out for New Zealand. You could get your living here at any of the trades I have mentioned, which you would only die of in England. As to 'society' position in the world, you must have found it is all my eye seeking society without the means to enjoy it.[70]

Mary and her sister Ellen had made a success of the shop they set up together, but even in New Zealand, it had not been as easy as she claimed. When the shop was first set up, Mary had written to Charlotte Brontë: 'Our keeping shop astonishes everybody here; I believe they think we do it for fun. Some think we shall make nothing of it, or that we shall get tired; and all laugh at us.'[71]

Mary and Ellen Taylor, as they themselves readily acknowledged, were exceptional. As a rule, single women who had to earn their keep overwhelmingly preferred to be employed as a governess because it involved the least injury to social standing. As a contemporary writer pointed out in 1844, distressed gentle-women 'found, if they would not sink in the scale, they must work with their heads, and not with their hands'.[72] At best, he admitted, governesses could only enjoy 'equivocal gentility', however. The very fact of their employment left them pitifully 'hanging between two ranks' – not good enough to associate with their employers, but too good to be friendly with the ser-vants.

The unhappy lot of governesses had worsened considerably in the years just before Anne Brontë took up her first post. The bank failures of the 1830s and consequent economic hardship had swollen the ranks of gently bred women who were driven to seek employment. The strong competition further depressed sal-aries that were already marginal. 'The policy of the world is to take advantage of want,' an observer remarked of the gover-nesses' situation. With such a large supply of desperate young women available, employers found 'no difficulty in driving a bar-gain'.[73]

The largest remuneration a governess could hope to earn was £100 a year. That salary was offered only in the most extraordin-ary circumstances. Salaries of £30 to £40 a year were more common. Agnes Grey's first employer was 'a retired tradesman, who had realized a very comfortable fortune; but could not be prevailed upon to give a greater salary than twenty-five pounds to the instructress of his children'. She stipulates that her second employer must pay her £50 a year, but out of that sum she had to buy 'decent clothes becoming my station', pay for them to be washed, and finance four annual journeys home. At her last post as governess, Charlotte Brontë accepted a salary of £20, out of which her employer deducted £4 to cover the expense of washing. Salaries of as little as £12 a year were not unheard of.

The author of an article published in *Fraser's* magazine on 'The Modern Governess System' calculated that the minimum expenses a governess needed to cover amounted to £27 a year – £16 for dress; £6 for laundry; £3 for postage and stationery; and

£2 for casualties. This sum did not include travel, and made no allowance for illness. Even if a governess earned the maximum salary she could expect, that income still put her hopelessly out of the sphere of middle-class comfort. In Harriet Martineau's *Deerbrook*, a household of three adults and one servant find themselves sinking inexorably into poverty on an income of more than £150 a year. Mrs Belloc, in her *Essays on Women's Work* (1865), referred to second-rate professional men and merchants living on the edge of gentility on £300 to £400 a year. The Brontë girls assumed without question that their father's income of £200 a year was insufficient to support all of them living at home together as adults.

The plight of the governess was just beginning to be recognized as a 'cause' worthy of public attention in the early 1840s. In 1841, a Governesses' Benevolent Institution was founded to 'delicately' provide destitute members of that class assistance in old age or illness. Some attempt to establish professional standards for governesses was made in 1848, when Queen's College for Women was established. Graduates of that institution could, in theory at least, command better salaries with a certificate of proficiency in hand.

Novels portraying the 'wrongs' of governesses eventually became a standard feature of Victorian fiction, but when Anne Brontë began writing *Agnes Grey* the subject was still new. The Countess of Blessington had taken it up in a fashionable novel called *The Governess* (1839), but her treatment was highly romantic. The governess in question was a startlingly beautiful, rich young lady who had been orphaned when her father committed suicide after financial ruin. Her trials are so various and extreme as to defy probability, and the narrative concludes with the restoration of her fortune, followed by a brilliant marriage. The governess in Harriet Martineau's *Deerbrook*, published the same year, is more realistically portrayed, but she is a minor character and the main focus of the novel lies elsewhere.

It would not have been difficult, then, for Anne Brontë to persuade herself that in writing *Agnes Grey* she was filling the urgent need for a true account of the governess's condition. If she had any doubts during the composition of her first novel, the article on governesses in *Fraser's* (which Aunt Branwell subscribed to) would have reassured her: '*Punch* has admirably pleaded in the cause of salaries and qualifications. The statistics touching lunatic asylums give a frightful proportion of governesses in the list of the insane. But has the whole life in home schoolrooms even been investigated? We ask this with a real wish to be informed, with a hope of directing eyes to this unknown page of human life.'[74] An article written by a governess which appeared a few years later in the same magazine noted that her friends had urged her to write about 'the social position of governesses' because the public needed to hear the story from 'one *within* not *without* the "pale".'[75]

Anne Brontë's Agnes Grey differs from the stock Victorian governess heroine in one essential respect: she actively chooses her employment rather than being constrained to do so by a father's bankruptcy or husband's death – though certainly the financial condition of her family plays an important part in her desire to help. The fact that Agnes Grey looks forward to her first post as governess with eagerness and enthusiasm is crucial to the structure of the book; through the successive lessons in the 'art of instruction', we witness the dismantling of the heroine's illusions. The repetition of Agnes Grey's unhappy experience in two different families serves to underline the point that Agnes's difficulties are not the result of any one set of circumstances but are inherent in the condition of her employment. The advice Mrs Grey gives Agnes after her first failure as governess is an important transition in the novel: 'This time,' she says, 'you shall try your fortune in a somewhat higher family – in that of some genuine thorough-bred gentleman; for such are far more likely to treat you with proper respect and consideration than those purse-proud tradespeople and arrogant upstarts.'

In portraying the Bloomfields as 'tradespeople' Anne Brontë significantly departed from her autobiographical model. The Inghams of Blake Hall in fact belonged to the squirearchy; Mr Ingham more or less fit the mould of a typical Yorkshire country gentleman. Anne's alteration of her actual experience was part of a careful structuring of the novel that allowed her to illustrate the hypocrisy of Victorian notions of gentility. Agnes Grey's second employer, Mrs Murray, is much more a 'lady' than Mrs Bloomfield, but her behaviour toward the governess is no more 'genteel' than that arrogant upstart's.

Agnes Grey's loss of caste as a result of her employment comes as a great surprise to her. Clearly she had expected to be treated as a friend of the family and is shocked when her first employer behaves toward her as she would an upper-servant. Rosalie Murray, Agnes Grey's eldest pupil, is initially haughty, insolent and overbearing. But even when later 'she became as deeply attached to me as it was possible for *her* to be . . . she seldom lost sight, for above half an hour at a time, of the fact of my being a hireling and a poor curate's daughter.' The Murrays' friends treat her with the same condescension. When Mr Weston questions why Agnes has never 'exchanged a word' with the Misses Green, she explains: 'Very likely they are not so [reserved] to people of their own class; but they consider themselves as moving in quite a different sphere from me!'

Agnes Grey finds herself inescapably enmeshed in a painful contradiction: because she has been 'genteely bred', she has been hired to teach her charges to be 'ladies', and yet her status as a hireling irrevocably bars her from that class. Agnes Grey's conflict over whether to walk *with* or *behind* her pupils on the way home from church epitomizes the whole of her impossible position. Since the Murrays' friends pretend not to notice her, she finds it disagreeable to walk with them, 'as if listening to what they said, or wishing to be thought one of them . . .' On the other hand, 'it was disagreeable, too, to walk behind, and thus appear to acknowledge my own inferiority; for, in truth, I considered myself pretty nearly as good as the best of them, and wished them to know that I did so, and not to imagine that I looked upon myself as a mere domestic, who knew her own place too well to walk beside such fine ladies and gentlemen as they were . . . [Thus] I gave myself no little trouble in my endeavours (if I did keep up with them) to appear perfectly unconscious or regardless of their presence, as if I were wholly

absorbed in my own reflections, or the contemplation of surrounding objects . . .'

The way in which consideration of class and money distorts
every kind of human relationship is underscored over and over
in *Agnes Grey*. At the very beginning of the novel, Agnes Grey's
mother is cut off from her family because she chooses to marry a
poor curate. After his death, her father offers to restore his
daughter to her proper place in society, but at the cost of formally
renouncing her marriage. Even the happy marriage between
Agnes Grey's parents, which represents a rejection of materialism, is derailed from its natural course by Mr Grey's guilty
obsession with the loss of his small savings through foolish specu-
lation. Prosperity corrupts just as surely as loss in the novel,
however. The spectacle of Mr and Mrs Bloomfield quarrelling
over dinner is chilling. The Murrays' marriage is clearly as little
based on love as the Bloomfields'. Worst of all is Mrs Murray's
betrayal of her daughter Rosalie when she hurries the girl into a
socially advantageous marriage that is to bring utmost misery.

In her famous attack on *Jane Eyre*, Lady Eastlake accused
Charlotte Brontë of subverting the 'natural' order, 'murmuring
against the comforts of the rich and against the privation of the
poor, which . . . is a murmuring against God's appointment'.[76]
In its own way, *Agnes Grey* was equally subversive. Through
her 'simple' exposition of the case of the governess, Anne Brontë
also gave her contemporaries an indictment of the ruthless
materialism at the heart of Victorian life.

IV

As an exposition of the conflicts that informed the lives of the
'droves of spirit-broken governesses' who haunted the Victorian
era, *Agnes Grey* is an entire success. As a work of art, it is less
successful. In framing the narrative of her first novel, Anne
Brontë mistakenly assumed that in order to create a realistic
work of fiction, she had to eschew drama, excitement and suspense. Charlotte Brontë took a similar stance when she undertook *The Professor*, rejecting the 'poetical and imaginative',

as she later explained in a preface to her still unpublished first novel. On the part of both sides, this attitude grew out of a desire to make a definitive break from the overwrought dramatic sagas of their childhood. In Anne's case, however, there may have been a further motivation. She may have felt that in order to avoid the charge that her motive in writing *Agnes Grey* was personal revenge, her narrator must at all costs maintain a coolly objective distance.

It seems quite possible, however, that there is yet another explanation for Agnes Grey's apparent detachment. The natural response to the relentless catalogue of insults that the heroine narrates would be anger. On the rare occasions that Agnes Grey allows herself to acknowledge any resentment, she immediately follows that admission with the assurance that she means to suppress it. 'I judged it my wisest plan to subdue every resentful impulse,' she says early on in the book. Later, when the check on her feelings momentarily slips, Agnes Grey tells herself: '. . . next time I am determined to take things coolly.' It may well be that the emotional flatness that dampens the narrative of Anne Brontë's first novel has its source in the supreme effort she was making to control her anger at the humiliation she was subjected to.

In writing her second novel, Anne Brontë allowed herself far more emotional freedom. As a result, *The Tenant of Wildfell Hall* is a much more interesting and engaging novel. It also represents an enormous leap in Anne Brontë's control over her craft. The handling of plot and character are far more assured and the author's insight into the workings of a marriage in dissolution is astonishing. Unfortunately, Anne chose to frame her compelling narrative within another, less compelling, story. *The Tenant of Wildfell Hall*'s flawed construction distracts from the novel's otherwise impressive achievement. Ironically, *Agnes Grey*'s greatest strength is its structure. George Moore called it 'the most perfect prose narrative in English literature'.

In considering whether Anne in fact deserves her place as 'literary Cinderella' of the parsonage – the least talented, mildest Brontë – it is useful to compare her development with Charlotte's.

They both wrote their first novels at about the same time, but *Agnes Grey* was published, while *The Professor* appeared only posthumously as a footnote to Charlotte's successful career. In many respects, *Agnes Grey* is the superior novel. Both sisters began writing their second novels almost immediately after completion of the first; both demonstrated a stunning advance as artists. *The Tenant of Wildfell Hall*, though, is flawed where *Jane Eyre* is fully achieved. Anne Brontë's early death ended her career after her second novel, but if it had not, she might well have evolved into a writer as great as her sister Charlotte. Emily's mysterious genius, of course, was beyond duplication.

It is a mistake to judge Anne Brontë by the same standards that apply either to Emily's or Charlotte's work, however. She was, above all, a novelist whose purpose was reform. She would surely have felt that she had fulfilled her aim in writing *Agnes Grey* if she could have read the comment Lady Amberly recorded in her diary more than a score of years after the book was published: 'read *Agnes Grey* ... and should like to give it to every family with a governess and shall read it through again when I have a governess to remind me to be human.' [77]

For modern readers, *Agnes Grey* serves as an important historical document. There is perhaps no other novel of the period which gives such an intimately revealing account of the quotidian horrors of the only 'respectable' employment open to a gentlewoman in the mid-nineteenth century – that of governess.

NOTE ON THE TEXT

AGNES GREY WAS FIRST PUBLISHED in December 1847 by T. C. Newby of 72 Mortimer Street, Cavendish Square, London. The novel was part of a three-volume, plum-coloured set: *Wuthering Heights* occupied the first two volumes and *Agnes Grey* the third. Newby had promised to publish 350 copies, but in the end only printed 250. As I have noted in the introduction, Charlotte Brontë reported to her publisher after her sisters received their copies of the books that 'The orthography and punctuation of the books are mortifying to a degree: almost all the errors that were corrected in the proof-sheets appear intact in what should have been the fair copies' (LL, II, p. 162).

The second edition of *Agnes Grey* was the 1850 publication by Smith, Elder and Co. (Charlotte's publishers) in a single volume with *Wuthering Heights* and a 'selection from the literary remains' of Ellis and Acton Bell. Charlotte Brontë edited the text of *Agnes Grey* extensively for this edition, changing punctuation, re-ordering paragraphs, correcting misprints and occasionally adding or altering words. She also made a large number of changes in *Wuthering Heights* and, in the poetry included in the selection of 'literary remains', she went so far as to alter titles and shorten texts. Most subsequent editions have their source in this edition, but there is no evidence that Charlotte's revisions have any connection to the authors themselves.

There is no extant manuscript of *Agnes Grey*, but the Parrish Collection of the Princeton University Library possesses a copy of the first edition that is catalogued as Anne Brontë's own copy, with emendations to the text pencilled in the margins in her own hand. The possibility has been raised that these emendations may have been made by Charlotte instead, when she was preparing the posthumous edition of her sisters' work, but this seems highly unlikely, since few of the changes in the Parrish Collection copy correspond to those in the 1850 edition. Careful comparison of the Parrish Collection copy with other examples of Anne Brontë's handwriting – letters, poems and the signature she habitually recorded in books she acquired – has convinced me that the marginal emendations are indeed in the author's own hand.

After weighing all the evidence, I have concluded that the Parrish Collection copy of the 1847 Newby edition with Anne Brontë's emendations must be the ultimate authority for a new edition of *Agnes Grey*. My study of these emendations has been considerably aided by my discovery in the Amy Lowell Collection of the Houghton Library at Harvard University of what appears to be Anne Brontë's own copy of *The Tenant of Wildfell Hall*, signed and dated by the author herself, with marginal emendations pencilled in the author's handwriting. The nature of the changes Anne Brontë made in her second novel is remarkably consistent with those she made in the Parrish Collection copy of *Agnes Grey*.

It is not clear whether Anne Brontë corrected her own copy of *Agnes Grey* because she hoped for a second edition, or whether she pencilled in the corrections for her own satisfaction – a perfectly understandable response to the 'mortifying' errors sprinkled throughout the text. Newby, who printed the book himself, dropped, inverted, substituted and transposed letters, mistook one word for another, and introduced incorrect punctuation. Anne Brontë corrected most of the obvious printer's errors, but left some misspellings unaltered. As one cannot be sure in these cases whether the errors went unnoticed by the author, or whether they in fact represent her original intention, I have corrected them in the text and recorded the original spelling in the notes.

In addition to correcting obvious misprints, Anne Brontë also occasionally altered words ('different' to 'distinct'; 'expected' to 'expressed'; 'my' to 'any') and added words or even in a few cases whole phrases. The nature of these changes suggests that the author was correcting the printer's misreadings or omissions rather than making changes in the text as an afterthought.

Editors of *Wuthering Heights* and *The Tenant of Wildfell Hall* have pointed out Newby's inconsistent use of the comma – sometimes unduly heavy (even by nineteenth-century standards), sometimes unduly light. In her marginal emendations, Anne Brontë often re-inserts commas that have been incorrectly left out, but on occasion adds one where it does not belong and fails to remove others that are incorrect. The inconsistent use of the comma most probably, therefore, reflects an uncertain command of punctuation on Anne Brontë's part, no doubt abetted by Newby's own carelessness and ignorance. Charlotte, whose formal training was far more extensive than Anne's, was grateful to her publisher for repunctuating *Jane Eyre* and assumed as a matter of course that he would do so in the novels that followed. Clearly, Newby took it upon himself to do the same, but his incompetence produced a very different result.

I have attempted, in the present edition, to re-establish a text that is as close as possible to what Anne Brontë originally intended. To this end I have restored a number of now-obsolete spellings ('visiters' for 'visitors', 'shew' for 'show', 'canvass' for 'canvas'). A number of these were already archaic when Ann Brontë was writing. Any departures from her emended copy of the 1847 Newby edition are recorded in the notes, except in the case of punctuation. Since Anne Brontë's use of punctuation is inconsistent at best and Newby's incompetence in this matter further complicates the issue of author's intention, I have thought it best to correct punctuation and remove commas where they prove awkward or irritating for a modern reader. The double quotes used in the Newby edition have been changed to single quotes to conform with Penguin style.

ANGELINE GOREAU

BIOGRAPHICAL NOTICE
OF
ELLIS AND ACTON BELL

BY CHARLOTTE BRONTË

IT HAS BEEN THOUGHT THAT all the works published under the names of Currer, Ellis, and Acton Bell, were, in reality, the production of one person. This mistake I endeavoured to rectify by a few words of disclaimer prefixed to the third edition of *Jane Eyre*. These, too, it appears, failed to gain general credence, and now, on the occasion of a reprint of *Wuthering Heights* and *Agnes Grey*, I am advised distinctly to state how the case really stands.

Indeed, I feel myself that it is time the obscurity attending those two names – Ellis and Acton – was done away. The little mystery, which formerly yielded some harmless pleasure, has lost its interest; circumstances are changed. It becomes, then, my duty to explain briefly the origin and authorship of the books written by Currer, Ellis, and Acton Bell.

About five years ago, my two sisters and myself, after a somewhat prolonged period of separation, found ourselves reunited, and at home. Resident in a remote district where education had made little progress, and where, consequently, there was no inducement to seek social intercourse beyond our own domestic circle, we were wholly dependent on ourselves and each other, on books and study, for the enjoyments and occupations of life. The highest stimulus, as well as the liveliest pleasure we had known from childhood upwards, lay in attempts at literary composition; formerly we used to show each other what we wrote, but of late years this habit of communication and consultation had been discontinued; hence it ensured that we were mutually ignorant of the progress we might respectively have made.

One day, in the autumn of 1845, I accidentally lighted on a MS. volume of verse in my sister Emily's handwriting. Of course, I was not surprised, knowing that she could and did write verse: I looked it over, and something more than surprise seized me – a deep conviction that these were not common effusions, nor at all like the poetry women generally write. I thought them condensed and terse, vigorous and genuine. To my ear, they had also a peculiar music – wild, melancholy, and elevating.

My sister Emily was not a person of demonstrative character, nor one, on the recesses of whose mind and feelings, even those nearest and dearest to her could, with impunity, intrude un-licensed; it took hours to reconcile her to the discovery I had made, and days to persuade her that such poems merited publica-tion. I knew, however, that a mind like hers could not be without some latent spark of honourable ambition, and refused to be discouraged in my attempts to fan that spark to flame.

Meantime, my younger sister quietly produced some of her own compositions, intimating that since Emily's had given me pleasure, I might like to look at hers. I could not but be a partial judge, yet I thought that these verses too had a sweet sincere pathos of their own.

We had very early cherished the dream of one day becoming authors. This dream, never relinquished even when distance divi-ded and absorbing tasks occupied us, now suddenly acquired strength and consistency: it took the character of a resolve. We agreed to arrange a small selection of our poems, and, if possible, get them printed. Averse to personal publicity, we veiled our own names under those of Currer, Ellis, and Acton Bell; the ambiguous choice being dictated by a sort of conscientious scru-ple at assuming Christian names positively masculine, while we did not like to declare ourselves women, because – without at that time suspecting that our mode of writing and thinking was not what is called 'feminine' – we had a vague impression that authoresses are liable to be looked on with prejudice; we had noticed how critics sometimes use for their chastisement the weapon of personality, and for their reward, a flattery, which is not true praise.

The bringing out of our little book was hard work. As was to be expected, neither we nor our poems were at all wanted; but for this we had been prepared at the outset; though inexperienced ourselves, we had read the experience of others. The great puzzle lay in the difficulty of getting answers of any kind from the publishers to whom we applied. Being greatly harassed by this obstacle, I ventured to apply to the Messrs. Chambers, of Edinburgh, for a word of advice; *they* may have forgotten the circumstance, but *I* have not, for from them I received a brief and business-like but civil and sensible reply, on which we acted, and at last made a way.

The book was printed: it is scarcely known, and all of it that merits to be known are the poems of Ellis Bell. The fixed conviction I held, and hold, of the worth of these poems has not indeed received the confirmation of much favourable criticism; but I must retain it notwithstanding.

Ill-success failed to crush us: the mere effort to succeed had given a wonderful zest to existence; it must be pursued. We each set to work on a prose tale: Ellis Bell produced *Wuthering Heights*, Acton Bell *Agnes Grey*, and Currer Bell also wrote a narrative in one volume. These MSS. were perseveringly obtruded upon various publishers for the space of a year and a half; usually, their fate was an ignominious and abrupt dismissal.

At last *Wuthering Heights* and *Agnes Grey* were accepted on terms somewhat impoverishing to the two authors; Currer Bell's book found acceptance nowhere, nor any acknowledgement of merit, so that something like the chill of despair began to invade his heart. As a forlorn hope, he tried one publishing house more – Messrs. Smith and Elder. Ere long, in a much shorter space than that on which experience had taught him to calculate – there came a letter, which he opened in the dreary expectation of finding two hard hopeless lines, intimating that Messrs. Smith and Elder 'were not disposed to publish the MS.,' and, instead, he took out of the envelope a letter of two pages. He read it trembling. It declined, indeed, to publish that tale, for business reasons, but it discussed its merits and demerits so courteously, so considerately, in a spirit so rational, with a discrimination so enlightened, that this very refusal cheered the author better than a vulgarly-expressed acceptance would have done. It was added that a work in three volumes would meet with careful attention.

I was then just completing *Jane Eyre*, at which I had been working while the one volume tale was plodding its weary round in London: in three weeks I sent it off; friendly and skilful hands took it in. This was in the commencement of September 1847; it came out before the close of October following, while *Wuthering Heights* and *Agnes Grey*, my sisters' works, which had already been in the press for months, still lingered under a different management.

They appeared at last. Critics failed to do them justice. The immature but very real powers revealed in *Wuthering Heights* were scarcely recognized; its import and nature were misunderstood; the identity of its author was misrepresented; it was said that this was an earlier and ruder attempt of the same pen which had produced *Jane Eyre*. Unjust and grievous error! We laughed at it at first, but I deeply lament it now. Hence, I fear, arose a prejudice against the book. That writer who could attempt to palm off an inferior and immature production under cover of one successful effort, must indeed be unduly eager after the secondary and sordid result of authorship, and pitiably indifferent to its true and honourable meed. If reviewers and the public truly believed this, no wonder that they looked darkly on the cheat.

Yet I must not be understood to make these things subject for reproach or complaint; I dare not do so; respect for my sister's memory forbids me. By her any such querulous manifestation would have been regarded as an unworthy and offensive weakness.

It is my duty, as well as my pleasure, to acknowledge one exception to the general rule of criticism. One writer,[1] endowed with the keen vision and fine sympathies of genius, has discerned the real nature of *Wuthering Heights*, and has, with equal accuracy, noted its beauties and touched on its faults. Too often do reviewers remind us of the mob of Astrologers, Chaldeans, and Soothsayers gathered before the 'writing on the wall', and unable to read the characters or make known the interpretation.[2] We have a right to rejoice when a true seer comes at last, some man in whom is an excellent spirit, to whom have been given light, wisdom, and understanding; who can accurately read the 'Mene, Mene, Tekel, Upharsin'[3] of an original mind (however unripe, however inefficiently cultured and partially expanded that mind may be); and who can say with confidence, 'This is the interpretation thereof.'

Yet even the writer to whom I allude shares the mistake about the authorship, and does me the injustice to suppose that there was equivoque in my former rejection of this honour (as an honour, I regard it). May I assure him that I would scorn in this and in every other case to deal in equivoque; I believe language to have been given us to make our meaning clear, and not to wrap it in dishonest doubt.

The Tenant of Wildfell Hall, by Acton Bell, had likewise an unfavourable reception. At this I cannot wonder. The choice of subject was an entire mistake. Nothing less congruous with the writer's nature could be conceived. The motives which dictated this choice were pure, but, I think, slightly morbid. She had, in the course of her life, been called on to contemplate, near at hand and for a long time, the terrible effects of talents misused and faculties abused; hers was naturally a sensitive, reserved, and dejected nature; what she saw sank very deeply into her mind; it did her harm. She brooded over it till she believed it to be a duty to reproduce every detail (of course with fictitious characters, incidents, and situations) as a warning to others. She hated her work, but would pursue it. When reasoned with on the subject, she regarded such reasonings as a temptation to self-indulgence. She must be honest; she must not varnish, soften, or conceal. This well-meant resolution brought on her misconstruction and some abuse, which she bore, as it was her custom to bear whatever was unpleasant, with mild, steady patience. She was a very sincere and practical Christian, but the tinge of religious melancholy communicated a sad shade to her brief, blameless life.

Neither Ellis nor Acton allowed herself for one moment to sink under want of encouragement; energy nerved the one, and endurance upheld the other. They were both prepared to try again; I would fain think that hope and the sense of power was yet strong within them. But a great change approached: affliction came in that shape which to anticipate is dread; to look back on, grief. In the very heat and burden of the day, the labourers failed over their work.

My sister Emily first declined. The details of her illness are deep-branded in my memory, but to dwell on them, either in thought or narrative, is not in my power. Never in all her life had she lingered over any task that lay before her, and she did not linger now. She sank rapidly. She made haste to leave us. Yet, while physically she perished, mentally, she grew stronger than we had yet known her. Day by day, when I saw with what a front she met suffering, I looked on her with an anguish of wonder and love. I have seen nothing like it; but, indeed, I have never seen her parallel in anything. Stronger than a man, simpler than a child, her nature stood alone. The awful point was, that, while full of ruth for others, on herself she had no pity; the spirit was inexorable to the flesh; from the trembling hand, the unnerved limbs, the faded eyes, the same service was exacted as they had rendered in health. To stand by and witness this, and not dare to remonstrate, was a pain no words can render.

Two cruel months of hope and fear passed painfully by, and the day came at last when the terrors and pains of death were to be undergone by this treasure, which had grown dearer and dearer to our hearts as it wasted before our eyes. Towards the decline of that day, we had nothing of Emily but her mortal remains as consumption left them. She died December 19, 1848.

We thought this enough; but we were utterly and presumptuously wrong. She was not buried ere Anne fell ill. She had not been committed to the grave a fortnight, before we received distinct intimation that it was necessary to prepare our minds to see the younger sister go after the elder. Accordingly, she followed in the same path with slower step, and with a patience that equalled the other's fortitude. I have said that she was religious, and it was by leaning on these Christian doctrines in which she firmly believed, that she found support through her most painful journey. I witnessed their efficacy in her latest hour and greatest trial, and must bear my testimony to the calm triumph with which they brought her through. She died May 28, 1849.

What more shall I say about them? I cannot and need not say much more. In externals, they were two unobtrusive women; a perfectly secluded life gave them retiring manners and habits. In Emily's nature the extremes of vigour and simplicity seemed to meet. Under an unsophisticated culture, inartificial tastes, and an unpretending outside, lay a secret power and fire that might have informed the brain and kindled the veins of a hero; but she had no worldly wisdom; her powers were unadapted to the practical business of life; she would fail to defend her most manifest rights, to consult her most legitimate advantage. An interpreter ought always to have stood between her and the world. Her will was not very flexible, and it generally opposed her interest. Her temper was magnanimous, but warm and sudden; her spirit altogether unbending.

Anne's character was milder and more subdued; she wanted the power, the fire, the originality of her sister, but was well-endowed with quiet virtues of her own. Long-suffering, self-denying, reflective, and intelligent, a constitutional reserve and taciturnity placed and kept her in the shade, and covered her mind, and especially her feelings, with a sort of nun-like veil, which was rarely lifted. Neither Emily nor Anne was learned; they had no thought of filling their pitchers at the well-spring of other minds; they always wrote from the impulse of nature, the dictates of intuition, and from such stores of observation as their limited experience had enabled them to amass. I may sum up all by saying, that for strangers they were nothing, for superficial observers less than nothing; but for those who had known them all their lives in the intimacy of close relationship, they were genuinely good and truly great.

This notice has been written, because I felt it a sacred duty to wipe the dust off their gravestones, and leave their dear names free from soil.

CURRER BELL
September 19, 1850

AGNES GREY

I

THE PARSONAGE

ALL TRUE HISTORIES CONTAIN instruction; though, in some,
the treasure may be hard to find, and when found, so trivial in
quantity that the dry, shrivelled kernel scarcely compensates for
the trouble of cracking the nut. Whether this be the case with my
history or not, I am hardly competent to judge; I sometimes
think it might prove useful to some, and entertaining to others,
but the world may judge for itself: shielded by my own obscurity,
and by the lapse of years, and a few fictitious names, I do not
fear to venture, and will candidly lay before the public what I
would not disclose to the most intimate friend.

My father was a clergyman of the north of England, who was
deservedly respected by all who knew him and, in his younger
days, lived pretty comfortably on the joint income of a small
incumbency, and a snug little property of his own. My mother,
who married him against the wishes of her friends, was a squire's
daughter, and a woman of spirit. In vain it was represented to
her that, if she became the poor parson's wife, she must relinquish her carriage and her lady's-maid, and all the luxuries and
elegancies of affluence, which to her were little less than the
necessaries of life. A carriage and a lady's-maid were great con-
veniences; but, thank Heaven, she had feet to carry her, and
hands to minister to her own necessities. An elegant house and
spacious grounds were not to be despised, but she would rather
live in a cottage with Richard Grey than in a palace with any
other man in the world.

Finding arguments of no avail, her father, at length, told the
lovers they might marry if they pleased, but, in so doing, his
daughter would forfeit every fraction of her fortune. He expected this would cool the ardour of both; but he was mistaken.

My father knew too well my mother's superior worth, not to be sensible that she was a valuable fortune in herself; and if she would but consent to embellish his humble hearth, he should be happy to take her on any terms; while she, on her part, would rather labour with her own hands than be divided from the man she loved, whose happiness it would be her joy to make, and who was already one with her in heart and soul. So her fortune went to swell the purse of a wiser sister, who had married a rich nabob, and she, to the wonder and compassionate regret of all who knew her, went to bury herself in the homely village parsonage among the hills of —. And yet, in spite of all this, and in spite of my mother's high spirit, and my father's whims, I believe you might search all England through, and fail to find a happier couple.

Of six children, my sister Mary and myself were the only two that survived the perils of infancy and early childhood. I, being the younger by five or six years, was always regarded as the *child*, and the pet of the family – father, mother, and sister, all combined to spoil me – not by foolish indulgence to render me fractious and ungovernable, but by ceaseless kindness to make me too helpless and dependent, too unfit for buffeting with the cares and turmoils of life.

Mary and I were brought up in the strictest seclusion. My mother, being at once highly accomplished, well informed, and fond of employment, took the whole charge of our education on herself, with the exception of Latin – which my father undertook to teach us – so that we never even went to school; and, as there was no society in the neighbourhood, our only intercourse with the world consisted in a stately tea-party, now and then, with the principal farmers and tradespeople of the vicinity, just to avoid being stigmatized as too proud to consort with our neighbours, and an annual visit to our paternal grandfather's, where himself, our kind grandmamma, a maiden aunt, and two or three elderly ladies and gentlemen were the only persons we ever saw. Sometimes our mother would amuse us with stories and anecdotes of her younger days, which, while they entertained us amazingly, frequently awoke – in *me*, at least – a vague and secret wish to see a little more of the world.

I thought she must have been very happy; but she never seemed to regret past times. My father, however, whose temper was neither tranquil nor cheerful by nature, often unduly vexed himself with thinking of the sacrifices his dear wife had made for him, and troubled his head with revolving endless schemes for the augmentation of his little fortune, for her sake, and ours. In vain my mother assured him she was quite satisfied, and if he would but lay by a little for the children, we should all have plenty, both for time present, and to come: but saving was not my father's forte: he would not run in debt (at least, my mother took good care he should not), but while he had money, he must spend it; he liked to see his house comfortable, and his wife and daughters well clothed, and well attended; and besides, he was charitably disposed, and liked to give to the poor, according to his means, or, as some might think, beyond them.

At length, however, a kind friend suggested to him a means of doubling his private property at one stroke; and further increasing it, hereafter, to an untold amount. This friend was a merchant, a man of enterprising spirit, and undoubted talent, who was somewhat straitened in his mercantile pursuits for want of capital, but generously proposed to give my father a fair share of his profits, if he would only intrust him with what he could spare, and he thought he might safely promise that whatever sum the latter chose to put into his hands, it should bring him in cent per cent. The small patrimony was speedily sold, and the whole of its price was deposited in the hands of the friendly merchant, who as promptly proceeded to ship his cargo, and prepare for his voyage.

My father was delighted, so were we all, with our brightening prospects: for the present, it is true, we were reduced to the narrow income of the curacy; but my father seemed to think there was no necessity for scrupulously restricting our expenditure to that; so, with a standing bill at Mr Jackson's, another at Smith's, and a third at Hobson's, we got along even more comfortably than before: though my mother affirmed we had better keep within bounds, for our prospects of wealth were but precarious after all; and if my father would only trust everything to her management, he should never feel himself stinted; but he, for once, was incorrigible.

What happy hours Mary and I have passed,[1] while sitting at our work by the fire, or wandering on the heath-clad hills, or idling under the weeping birch (the only considerable tree in the garden), talking of future happiness to ourselves and our parents, of what we would do, and see, and possess; with no firmer foundation for our goodly superstructure than the riches that were expected to flow in upon us from the success of the worthy merchant's speculations. Our father was nearly as bad as ourselves; only, that he affected not to be so much in earnest, expressing his bright hopes and sanguine expectations in jests and playful sallies that always struck me as being exceedingly witty and pleasant. Our mother laughed with delight to see him so hopeful and happy; but still she feared he was setting his heart too much upon the matter; and once, I heard her whisper as she left the room,

'God grant he be not disappointed! I know not how he would bear it.'

Disappointed he was; and bitterly too. It came like a thunder-clap on us all that the vessel, which contained our fortune, had been wrecked,[2] and gone to the bottom with all its stores, together with several of the crew, and the unfortunate merchant himself. I was grieved for him; I was grieved for the overthrow of all our air-built castles; but, with the elasticity of youth, I soon recovered the shock.

Though riches had charms, poverty had no terrors for an inexperienced girl like me. Indeed, to say the truth, there was something exhilarating in the idea of being driven to straits, and thrown upon our own resources. I only wished papa, mamma,[3] and Mary were all of the same mind as myself; and then, instead of lamenting past calamities, we might all cheerfully set to work to remedy them; and the greater the difficulties, the harder our present privations, the greater should be our cheerfulness to endure the latter, and our vigour to contend against the former.

Mary did not lament, but she brooded continually over the misfortune, and sank into a state of dejection from which no effort of mine could rouse her. I could not possibly bring her to regard the matter on its bright side as I did; and indeed I was so fearful of being charged with childish frivolity, or stupid insensibility, that I carefully kept most of my bright ideas and cheering notions to myself, well knowing they could not be appreciated.

My mother thought only of consoling my father, and paying our debts and retrenching our expenditure by every available means; but my father was completely overwhelmed by the calamity – health, strength, and spirits sank beneath the blow; and he never wholly recovered them. In vain my mother strove to cheer him by appealing to his piety, to his courage, to his affection for herself and us. That very affection was his greatest torment: it was for our sakes he had so ardently longed to increase his fortune – it was our interest that had lent such brightness to his hopes, and that imparted such bitterness to his present distress. He now tormented himself with remorse at having neglected my mother's advice, which would, at least, have saved him from the additional burden of debt – he vainly reproached himself for having brought her from the dignity, the ease, the luxury of her former station to toil with him through the cares and toils of poverty. It was gall and wormwood to his soul to see that splendid, highly accomplished woman, once so courted and admired, transformed into an active managing housewife, with hands and head continually occupied with household labours and household economy. The very willingness with which she performed these duties, the cheerfulness with which she bore her reverses, and the kindness which withheld her from imputing the smallest blame to him, were all perverted by this ingenious self-tormentor into further aggravations of his sufferings. And thus the mind preyed upon the body, and disordered the system of the nerves, and they in turn increased the troubles of the mind, till by action, and reaction, his health was seriously impaired; and not one of us could convince him that the aspect of our affairs was not half so gloomy, so utterly hopeless as his morbid imagination represented it to be.

The useful pony phaeton was sold, together with the stout

well-fed pony – the old favourite that we had fully determined should end its days in peace, and never pass from our hands; the little coach-house and stable were let, the servant boy and the more efficient (being the more expensive) of the two maid-servants were dismissed. Our clothers were mended, turned, and darned to the utmost verge of decency; our food, always plain, was now simplified to an unprecedented degree – except my father's favorite dishes: our coals and candles were painfully economized – the pair of candles reduced to one, and that most sparingly used: the coals carefully husbanded in the half-empty grate, especially when my father was out on his parish duties, or confined to bed through illness -- then we sat with our feet on the fender, scraping the perishing embers together from time to time, and occasionally adding a slight scattering of the dust and fragments of coal, just to keep them alive. As for our carpets, they in time were worn threadbare, and patched and darned even to a greater extent than our garments. To save the expense of a gardener, Mary and I undertook to keep the garden in order; and all the cooking and household work that could not easily be managed by one servant girl was done by my mother and sister, with a little occasional help from me – only a little, because though a woman in my own estimation, I was still a child in theirs; and my mother, like most active, managing women, was not gifted with very active daughters: for this reason – that being so clever and diligent herself, she was never tempted to trust her affairs to a deputy, but on the contrary, was willing to act and think for others as well as for number one; and whatever was the business in hand, she was apt to think that no one could do it so well as herself; so that whenever I offered to assist her, I received such an answer as – 'No, love, you cannot indeed – there's nothing here you can do. Go and help your sister, or get her to take a walk with you – tell her she must not sit so much, and stay so constantly in the house as she does – she may well look thin and dejected.'

'Mary, mamma says I'm to help you; or get you to take a walk with me; she says you may well look thin and dejected, if you sit so constantly in the house.'

'Help me you cannot, Agnes; and I cannot go out with *you* – I have far too much to do.'

'Then let me help you.'

'You cannot indeed my dear child. Go and practise your music, or play with the kitten.'

There was always plenty of sewing on hand; but I had not been taught to cut out a single garment; and except plain hemming and seaming, there was little I could do, even in that line; for they both asserted that it was far easier to do the work themselves than to prepare it for me; and, besides, they liked better to see me prosecuting my studies, or amusing myself – it was time enough for me to sit bending over my work, like a grave matron, when my favourite little pussy was become a steady old cat. Under such circumstances, although I was not many degrees more useful than the kitten, my idleness was not entirely without excuse.

Through all our troubles, I never but once heard my mother complain of our want of money. As summer was coming on, she observed to Mary and me,

'What a desirable thing it would be for your papa to spend a few weeks at a watering-place. I am convinced the sea air, and the change of scene, would be of incalculable service to him. But then you see there's no money,' she added with a sigh.

We both wished exceedingly that the thing might be done, and lamented greatly that it could not.

'Well, well!' said she, 'it's no use complaining. Possibly something might be done to further the project after all. Mary, you are a beautiful drawer. What do you say to doing a few more pictures, in your best style, and getting them framed, with the water-colour drawings you have already done, and trying to dispose of them to some liberal picture-dealer, who has the sense to discern their merits?'

'Mamma, I should be delighted if you think they *could* be sold; and for anything worth while.'

'It's worth while trying, however, my dear, do you procure the drawings and I'll endeavour to find a purchaser.'

'I wish *I* could do something,' said I.

'You, Agnes! well, who knows? You draw pretty well[4] too: if you choose some simple piece for your subject, I dare say you will be able to produce something we shall all be proud to exhibit.'

'But I have another scheme in my head, mamma, and have had long . . . only I did not like to mention it.'

'Indeed! pray tell us what it is.'

'I should like to be a governess.'

My mother uttered an exclamation of surprise, and laughed. My sister dropped her work in astonishment, exclaiming, '*You* a governess, Agnes! What *can* you be dreaming of?'

'Well! I don't see anything so *very* extraordinary in it. I do not pretend to be able to instruct great girls; but surely I could teach little ones . . . and I should like it *so* much . . . I am so fond of children. Do let me mamma!'

'But, my love, you have not learned to take care of *yourself* yet; and young children require more judgment and experience to manage than elder ones.'

'But mamma, I am above eighteen, and quite able to take care of myself, and others too. You do not know half the wisdom and prudence I possess, because I have never been tried.'

'Only think,' said Mary, 'what would you do in a house full of strangers, without me or mamma to speak and act for you . . . with a parcel of children, besides yourself, to attend to; and no one to look to for advice? You would not even know what clothes to put on.'

'You think, because I always do as you bid me, I have no judgment of my own: but only try me – that is all I ask – and you shall see what I can do.'

At that moment my father entered, and the subject of our discussion was explained to him.

'What, my little Agnes, a governess!' cried he, and in spite of his dejection, he laughed at the idea.

'Yes, papa, don't *you* say anything against it; I should like it *so* much; and I'm sure I could manage delightfully.'

'But, my darling, we could not spare you.' And a tear glistened in his eye as he added – 'No, no! afflicted as we are, surely we are not brought to that pass yet.'

'Oh, no!' said my mother. 'There is no necessity, whatever, for such a step; it is merely a whim of her own. So you must hold your tongue, you naughty girl, for though you are so ready to leave *us*, you know very well we cannot part with *you*.'

I was silenced for that day, and for many succeeding ones; but still, I did not wholly relinquish my darling scheme. Mary got her drawing materials and steadily set to work. I got mine too; but while I drew, I thought of other things.

How delightful it would be to be a governess! To go out into the world; to enter upon a new life; to act for myself; to exercise my unused faculties; to try my unknown powers; to earn my own maintenance, and something to comfort and help my father, mother, and sister, besides exonerating them from the provision of my food and clothing; to show papa what his little Agnes could do; to convince mamma and Mary that I was not quite the helpless, thoughtless being they supposed. And then, how charming to be intrusted with the care and education of children! Whatever others said, I felt I was fully competent to the task: the clear remembrance of my own thoughts and feelings in early childhood would be a surer guide than the instructions of the most mature adviser. I had but to turn from my little pupils to myself at their age, and I should know, at once, how to win their confidence and affections; how to waken the contrition of the erring; how to embolden the timid, and console the afflicted; how to make Virtue practicable, Instruction desirable, and Religion lovely and comprehensible.

> '– Delightful task!
> To teach the young idea how to shoot!' [5]

To train the tender plants, and watch their buds unfolding day by day!

Influenced by so many inducements, I determined still to persevere; though the fear of displeasing my mother, or distressing my father's feelings prevented me from resuming the subject for several days. At length, again, I mentioned it to my mother in private, and, with some difficulty, got her to promise to assist me with her endeavours. My father's reluctant consent was next

obtained, and then, though Mary still sighed her disapproval,
my dear, kind mother began to look for a situation for me. She
wrote to my father's relations, and consulted the newspaper
advertisements – her own relations she had long dropped all
communication with – a formal interchange of occasional letters
was all she had ever had since her marriage, and she would not,
at any time, have applied to them in a case of this nature. But so
long, and so entire had been my parent's seclusion from the
world, that many weeks elapsed before a suitable situation could
be procured. At last, to my great joy, it was decreed that I
should take charge of the young family of a certain Mrs Bloomfield, whom my kind, prim Aunt Grey had known in her youth,
and asserted to be a very nice woman. Her husband was a
retired tradesman, who had realized a very comfortable fortune,
but could not be prevailed upon to give a greater salary than
twenty-five pounds to the instructress of his children. I, however,
was glad to accept this rather than refuse the situation – which
my parents were inclined to think the better plan.

But some weeks more were yet to be devoted to preparation.
How long, how tedious those weeks appeared to me! Yet they
were happy ones in the main – full of bright hopes and ardent
expectations. With what peculiar pleasure I assisted at the
making of my new clothes and, subsequently, the packing of my
trunks! But there was a feeling of bitterness mingling with the
latter occupation too – and when it was done, when all was
ready for my departure on the morrow, and the last night at
home approached, a sudden anguish seemed to swell my heart.
My dear friends looked so sad, and spoke so very kindly, that I
could scarcely keep my eyes from overflowing; but I still affected
to be gay. I had taken my last ramble with Mary on the moors,
my last walk in the garden and round the house; I had fed, with
her, our pet pigeons for the last time – the pretty creatures that
we had tamed to peck their food from our hands. I had given a
farewell stroke to all their silky backs as they crowded in my
lap. I had tenderly kissed my own peculiar favourites, the pair of
snow-white fantails; I had played my last tune on the old familiar
piano, and sung my last song to papa; not the last, I hoped, but

the last for, what appeared, to me, a very long time; and perhaps when I did these things again, it would be with different feelings – circumstances might be changed, and this house might never be my settled home again.

My dear little friend, the kitten, would certainly be changed; she was already growing a fine cat; and when I returned, even for a hasty visit at Christmas, would, most likely, have forgotten both her playmate and her merry pranks. I had romped with her for the last time; and when I stroked her soft bright fur, while she lay purring herself to sleep in my lap, it was with a feeling of sadness I could not easily disguise. Then, at bed-time, when I retired with Mary to our own quiet little chamber, where already my drawers were cleared out, and my share of the bookcase was empty, and where, hereafter, she would have to sleep alone, in dreary solitude, as she expressed it, my heart sank[6] more than ever: I felt as if I had been selfish and wrong to persist in leaving her; and when I knelt once more beside our little bed, I prayed for a blessing on her and on my parents more fervently than ever I had done before. To conceal my emotion, I buried my face in my hands, and they were presently bathed in tears. I perceived, on rising, that she had been crying too; but neither of us spoke; and in silence we betook ourselves to our repose, creeping more closely together, from the consciousness that we were to part so soon.

But the morning brought a renewal of hope and spirits. I was to depart early, that the conveyance which took me (a gig, hired from Mr Smith, the draper, grocer, and tea-dealer of the village) might return the same day. I rose, washed, dressed, swallowed a hasty breakfast, received the fond embraces of my father, mother, and sister, kissed the cat, to the great scandal of Sally, the maid, shook hands with her, mounted the gig, drew my veil over my face, and then, but not till then, burst into a flood of tears.

The gig rolled on – I looked back – my dear mother and sister were still standing at the door, looking after me, and waving their adieux: I returned their salute, and prayed God to bless them from my heart: we descended the hill, and I could see them no more.

'It's a coldish mornin' for you, Miss Agnes,' observed Smith; 'and a darksome un too; but we's, happen, get to yon' spot afore there come much rain to signify.'

'Yes, I hope so,' replied I, as calmly as I could.

'It's comed a good sup last night too.'

'Yes.'

'But this cold wind ull, happen, keep it off.'

'Perhaps it will.'

Here ended our colloquy; we crossed the valley, and began to ascend the opposite hill. As we were toiling up, I looked back again: there was the village spire, and the old grey parsonage beyond it, basking in a slanting beam of sunshine – it was but a sickly ray, but the village and surrounding hills were all in sombre shade, and I hailed the wandering beam as a propitious omen to my home. With clasped hands, I fervently implored a blessing on its inhabitants, and hastily turned away, for I saw the sunshine was departing; and I carefully avoided another glance, lest I should see it in gloomy shadow, like the rest of the landscape.

II

FIRST LESSONS IN THE ART
OF INSTRUCTION

AS WE DROVE ALONG, MY spirits revived again, and I turned, with pleasure, to the contemplation of the new life upon which I was entering; but though it was not far past the middle of September, the heavy clouds and strong north-easterly wind combined to render the day extremely cold and dreary, and the journey seemed a very long one, for, as Smith observed, the roads were 'very heavy'; and, certainly, his horse was very heavy too; it crawled up the hills, and crept down them, and only condescended to shake its sides in a trot where the road was at a dead level or a very gentle slope, which was rarely the case in those rugged regions: so that it was nearly one o'clock before we reached the place of our destination. Yet, after all, when we entered the lofty iron gateway, when we drove softly up the smooth, well-rolled carriage road, with the green lawn on each side, studded with young trees, and approached the new but stately mansion of Wellwood, rising above its mushroom poplar groves, my heart failed me, and I wished it were a mile or two farther off: for the first time in my life, I must stand alone – there was no retreating now – I must enter that house, and introduce myself among its strange inhabitants – but how was it to be done? True, I was near nineteen, but, thanks to my retired life, and the protecting care of my mother and sister, I well knew that many a girl of fifteen, or under, was gifted with a more womanly address, and greater ease and self-possession, than I was. Yet, if Mrs Bloomfield were a kind, motherly woman, I might do very well after all; and the children, of course, I should soon be at ease with them – and Mr Bloomfield, I hoped, I should have but little to do with.

'Be calm, be calm, whatever happens,' I said within myself, and truly I kept this resolution so well, and was so fully occupied in steadying my nerves, and stilling the rebellious flutter of my heart, that when I was admitted into the hall, and ushered into the presence of Mrs Bloomfield, I almost forgot to answer her polite salutation; and it afterwards struck me that the little I did say, was spoken in the tone of one half-dead or half-asleep. The lady too was somewhat chilly in her manner, as I discovered when I had time to reflect. She was a tall, spare, stately woman, with thick black hair, cold grey eyes, and extremely sallow complexion.

With due politeness, however, she showed me my bed-room, and left me there to take off my things, desiring me afterwards to come down and take a little refreshment. I was somewhat dismayed at my appearance on looking in the glass ... the cold wind had swelled and reddened my hands, uncurled and entangled my hair, and dyed my face of a pale purple; add to this my collar was horribly crumpled, my frock splashed with mud, my feet clad in stout new boots, and as the trunks were not brought up, there was no remedy, so having smoothed my hair as well as I could, and repeatedly twitched my obdurate collar, I proceeded to clomp down the two flights of stairs, philosophising as I went, and with some difficulty, found my way into the room where Mrs Bloomfield awaited me.

She led me into the dining-room, where the family luncheon had been laid out. Some beefsteaks and half-cold potatoes were set before me; and while I dined upon these, she sat opposite, watching me (as I thought) and endeavouring to sustain something like a conversation – consisting chiefly of a succession of common-place remarks, expressed with frigid formality: but this might be more my fault than hers, for I really *could* not converse. In fact, my attention was almost wholly absorbed in my dinner, not from ravenous appetite, but from distress at the toughness of the beefsteaks, and the numbness of my hands, almost palsied by their five hours' exposure to the bitter wind. I would gladly have eaten the potatoes and let the meat alone, but having got a large piece of the latter on my plate, I could not be so impolite as to leave it; so, after many awkward and unsuccessful attempts to cut it with the knife, or tear it with the fork, or pull it asunder between them, sensible that the awful lady was a spectator to the whole transaction, I at last desperately grasped the knife and fork in my fists, like a child of two years old, and fell to work with all the little strength I possessed. But this needed some apology – with a feeble attempt at a laugh, I said, 'My hands are so benumbed with the cold that I can scarcely handle my knife and fork.'

'I dare say you would find it cold,' replied she with a cool, immutable gravity that did not serve to re-assure me.

When the ceremony was concluded, she led me into the sitting-room again, where she rung, and sent for the children.

'You will find them not very far advanced in their attainments,' said she, 'for I have had so little time to attend to their education myself, and we have thought them too young for a governess till now; but I think they are clever children, and very apt to learn, especially the little boy; he is, I think, the flower of the flock – a generous, noble-spirited boy, one to be led, but not driven, and remarkable for always speaking the truth. He seems to scorn deception' (this was good news). 'His sister Mary Ann will require watching,' continued she, 'but she is a very good girl upon the whole: though I wish her to be kept out of the nursery as much as possible, as she is now almost six years old, and might acquire bad habits from the nurses.[1] I have ordered her crib to be placed in your room, and if you will be so kind as to overlook her washing and dressing, and take charge of her clothes, she need have nothing further to do with the nursery-maid.'

I replied I was quite willing to do so; and at that moment, my young pupils entered the apartment with their two younger sisters. Master Tom Bloomfield was a well-grown boy of seven, with a somewhat wiry frame, flaxen hair, blue eyes, small turned-up nose, and fair complexion. Mary Ann was a tall girl too, somewhat dark like her mother, but with a round, full face, and a high colour in her cheeks. The second sister was Fanny, a very pretty little girl; Mrs Bloomfield assured me she was a remarkably gentle child, and required encouragement: she had not learnt anything yet; but, in a few days, she would be four years old, and then she might take her first lesson in the alphabet, and be promoted to the school-room. The remaining one was Harriet, a little, broad, fat, merry, playful thing of scarcely two, that I coveted more than all the rest – but with her I had nothing to do.

I talked to my little pupils as well as I could, and tried to render myself agreeable; but with little success, I fear, for their mother's presence kept me under an unpleasant restraint. They, however, were remarkably free from shyness. They seemed bold, lively children, and I hoped I should soon be on friendly terms with them – the little boy, especially, of whom I had heard such a favourable character from his mamma. In Mary Ann there was a certain affected simper, and a craving for notice, that I was sorry to observe. But her brother claimed all my attention to himself: he stood bolt upright between me and the fire, with his hands behind his back, talking away like an orator, occasionally interrupting his discourse with a sharp reproof to his sisters when they made too much noise.

'O Tom, what a darling you are!' exclaimed his mother. 'Come and kiss dear mamma – and then won't you show Miss Grey your school-room, and your nice new books?'

'I won't kiss *you*, mamma; but I *will* show Miss Grey my school-room, and my new books.'

'And *my* school-room, and *my* new books, Tom,' said Mary Ann. 'They're mine too.'

'They're *mine*,' replied he decisively. 'Come along, Miss Grey – I'll escort you.'

When the room and books had been shown, with some bickering between the brother and sister that I did my utmost to appease or mitigate, Mary Ann brought me her doll, and began to be very loquacious on the subject of its fine clothes, its bed, its chest of drawers, and other appurtenances; but Tom told her to hold her clamour, that Miss Grey might see his rocking-horse, which, with a most important bustle, he dragged forth from its corner into the middle of the room, loudly calling on me to attend to it. Then, ordering his sister to hold the reins, he mounted, and made me stand for ten minutes, watching how manfully he used his whip and spurs. Meantime, however, I admired Mary Ann's pretty doll, and all its possessions; and then told Master Tom he was a capital rider, but I hoped he would not use his whip and spurs so much when he rode a real pony.

'Oh yes, I will!' said he, laying on with redoubled ardour. 'I'll cut into him like smoke! Eeh! my word! but he shall sweat for it.'

This was very shocking, but I hoped in time to be able to work a reformation.

'Now you must put on your bonnet and shawl,' said the little hero, 'and I'll show you my garden.'

'And *mine*,' said Mary Ann.

Tom lifted his fist with a menacing gesture, she uttered a loud, shrill scream, ran to the other side of me, and made a face at him.

'Surely, Tom, you would not strike your sister! I hope I shall *never* see you do that.'

'You will sometimes; I am obliged to do it now and then to keep her in order.'

'But it's not your business to keep her in order, you know – that is for –'

'Well, now go and put on your bonnet.'

'I don't know – it is so very cloudy and cold, it seems likely to rain; – and you know I have had a long drive.'

'No matter – you *must* come; I shall allow of no excuses,' replied the consequential little gentleman. And as it was the first day of our acquaintance, I thought I might as well indulge him. It was too cold for Mary Ann to venture out, so she stayed with her mamma, to the great relief of her brother, who liked to have me all to himself.

The garden was a large one, and tastefully laid out; besides several splendid dahlias, there were some other fine flowers still in bloom; but my companion would not give me time to examine them: I must go with him, across the wet grass, to a remote, sequestered corner, the most important place in the grounds – because it contained *his* garden. There were two round beds,

stocked with a variety of plants. In one, there was a pretty little
rose tree. I paused to admire its lovely blossoms.

'Oh, never mind that!' said he contemptuously. 'That's only
Mary Ann's garden; look, THIS is mine.'

After I had observed every flower, and listened to a disquisi-
tion on every plant, I was permitted to depart; but first, with
great pomp, he plucked a polyanthus and presented it to me, as
one conferring a prodigious favour. I observed, on the grass
about his garden certain apparatus of sticks and cord, and asked
what they were.

'Traps for birds.'

'Why do you catch them?'

'Papa says they do harm.'

'And what do you do with them, when you catch them?'

'Different things. Sometimes I give them to the cat; sometimes
I cut them in pieces with my penknife; but the next, I mean to
roast alive.'

'And why do you mean to do such a horrible thing?'

'For two reasons; first, to see how long it will live – and then,
to see what it will taste like.'

'But don't you know it is extremely wicked to do such things?
Remember, the birds can feel as well as you; and think, how
would you like it yourself?'

'Oh, that's nothing! I'm not a bird, and I can't feel what I do
to them.'

'But you will have to feel it sometime, Tom – you have heard
where wicked people go to when they die; and if you don't leave
off torturing innocent birds, remember, you will have to go
there, and suffer just what you have made them suffer.'

'Oh, pooh! I shan't. Papa knows how I treat them, and he
never blames me for it; he says it's just what *he* used to do when
he was a boy. Last summer he gave me a nest full of young
sparrows, and he saw me pulling off their legs and wings, and
heads, and never said anything, except that they were nasty
things, and I must not let them soil my trousers; and Uncle
Robson was there too, and he laughed, and said I was a fine
boy.'

'But what would your mamma say?'

'Oh she doesn't care – she says it's a pity to kill the pretty singing birds, but the naughty sparrows, and mice and rats I may do what I like with. So now, Miss Grey, you see it is *not* wicked.'

'I still think it is, Tom; and perhaps your papa and mamma would think so too, if they thought much about it. However,' I internally added, 'they may say what they please, but I am determined you shall do nothing of the kind, as long as I have power to prevent it.'

He next took me across the lawn to see his mole-traps, and then into the stack-yard to see his weasel-traps, one of which, to his great joy, contained a dead weasel; and then into the stable to see, not the fine carriage horses, but a little rough colt, which he informed me had been bred on purpose for him, and he was to ride it as soon as it was properly trained.

I tried to amuse the little fellow, and listened to all his chatter as complacently as I could; for I thought if he had any affections at all, I would endeavour to win them; and then, in time, I might be able to show him the error of his ways; but I looked in vain for that generous, noble spirit his mother talked of; though I could see he was not without a certain degree of quickness and penetration, when he chose to exert it.

When we re-entered the house it was nearly tea-time. Master Tom told me that, as papa was from home, he and I and Mary Ann were to have tea with mamma for a treat; for, on such occasions, she always dined at luncheon time with them, instead of at six o'clock. Soon after tea, Mary Ann went to bed, but Tom favoured us with his company and conversation till eight. After he was gone, Mrs Bloomfield further enlightened me on the subject of her children's dispositions and acquirements, and on what they were to learn, and how they were to be managed, and cautioned me to mention their defects to no one but herself. My mother had warned me before to mention them as little as possible to *her*, for people did not like to be told of their children's faults, and so I concluded I was to keep silence on them altogether. About half-past nine, Mrs Bloomfield invited me to

partake a frugal supper[2] of cold meat and bread. I was glad
when that was over, and she took her bed-room candle-stick and
retired to rest, for though I wished to be pleased with her, her
company was extremely irksome to me, and I could not help
feeling that she was cold, grave, and forbidding – the very opposite of the kind, warm-hearted matron my hopes had depicted
her to be.

III
A FEW MORE LESSONS

I ROSE, NEXT MORNING, with a feeling of hopeful exhilaration, in spite of the disappointments already experienced; but I found the dressing of Mary Ann was no light matter, as her abundant hair was to be smeared with pomade, plaited in three long tails, and tied with bows of ribbon, a task my unaccustomed fingers found great difficulty in performing. She told me her nurse could do it in half the time, and, by keeping up a constant fidget of impatience, contrived to render me still longer. When all was done, we went into the school-room, where I met my other pupil, and chatted with the two till it was time to go down to breakfast. That meal being concluded, and a few civil words having been exchanged with Mrs Bloomfield, we repaired to the school-room again, and commenced the business of the day. I found my pupils very backward indeed; but Tom, though averse to every species of mental exertion, was not without abilities. Mary Ann could scarcely read a word, and was so careless and inattentive that I could hardly get on with her at all. However, by dint of great labour and patience, I managed to get something done in the course of the morning, and then accompanied my young charge out into the garden and adjacent grounds, for a little recreation before dinner. There we got along tolerably together, except that I found they had no notion of going with *me*: I must go with *them* wherever they chose to lead me. I must run, walk, or stand exactly as it suited their fancy. This, I thought, was reversing the order of things; and I found it doubly disagreeable,[1] as on this as well as subsequent occasions, they seemed to prefer the dirtiest places, and the most dismal occupations. But there was no remedy; either I must follow them, or keep entirely apart from them, and thus appear neglectful of my charge. To-day, they manifested a particular attachment to a well at the bottom of the lawn, where they persisted in dabbling with sticks and pebbles for above half an hour. I was in constant fear that their mother would see them from the window, and blame me for allowing them thus to draggle their clothes, and wet their feet and hands, instead of taking exercise; but no arguments, commands, or intreaties could draw them away. If *she* did not see them, some one else did – a gentleman on horse-back had entered the gate, and was proceeding up the road; at the distance of a few paces from us, he paused, and calling to the children in a waspish penetrating tone, bade them 'keep out of that water'. 'Miss Grey,' said he, '(I suppose it *is* Miss Grey) I am surprised you should allow them to dirty their clothes in that manner – Don't you see how Miss Bloomfield has soiled her frock? – and that Master Bloomfield's socks are quite wet? – and both of them without gloves! Dear! Dear! Let me *request* that in future you will keep them *decent*, at least!' So saying, he turned away, and continued his ride up to the house. This was Mr Bloomfield. I was surprised that he should nominate his children Master and Miss Bloomfield, and still more so, that he should speak so uncivilly to me – their governess, and a perfect stranger to himself. Presently the bell rang to summon us in. I dined with the children at one, while he and his lady took their luncheon at the same table. His conduct there did not greatly raise him in my estimation. He was a man of ordinary stature – rather below than above, and rather thin than stout, apparently between thirty and forty years of age: he had large mouth, pale, dingy complexion, milky blue eyes, and hair the colour of a hempen cord. There was a roast leg of mutton before him: he helped Mrs Bloomfield, the children, and me, desiring me to cut up the children's meat; then, after twisting about the mutton in various directions, and eyeing it from different points, he pronounced it not fit to be eaten, and called for the cold beef.

'What is the matter with the mutton, my dear?' asked his mate.

'It is quite overdone. Don't you taste, Mrs Bloomfield, that all the goodness is roasted out of it? And can't you see that all that nice, red gravy is completely dried away?'

'Well, I think the *beef* will suit you.'

The beef was set before him, and he began to carve, but with the most rueful expressions of discontent.

'What is the matter with the *beef*, Mr Bloomfield? I'm sure I thought it was very nice.'

'And so it *was* very nice. A nicer joint could not be; but it is *quite* spoiled,' replied he, dolefully.

'How so?'

'How so! Why, don't you see how it is cut? Dear – dear! it is quite shocking!'

'They must have cut it wrong in the kitchen, then, for I'm sure I carved it quite properly here yesterday.'

'No *doubt* they cut it wrong in the kitchen – the savages! Dear – dear! Did ever any one see such a fine piece of beef so completely ruined? But remember that, in future, when a decent dish leaves this table, they shall not *touch* it in the kitchen. Remember *that*, Mrs Bloomfield!'

Notwithstanding the ruinous state of the beef, the gentleman managed to cut himself some delicate slices, part of which he ate in silence. When he next spoke it was, in a less querulous tone, to ask what there was for dinner.

'Turkey and grouse,' was the concise reply.

'And what besides?'

'Fish.'

'What kind of fish?'

'I don't know.'

'*You don't know?*' cried he, looking solemnly up from his plate, and suspending his knife and fork in astonishment.

'No. I told the cook to get some fish – I did not particularise what.'

'Well, that beats everything! A lady professes to keep house, and doesn't even know what fish is for dinner! professes to order fish, and doesn't specify what!'

'Perhaps, Mr Bloomfield, you will order dinner yourself in future.'

Nothing more was said; and I was very glad to get out of the room with my pupils; for I never felt so ashamed and uncomfortable in my life for anything that was not my own fault.

In the afternoon we applied to lessons again; then went out again; then had tea in the school-room; then I dressed Mary Ann for dessert; and when she and her brother were gone down to the dining-room, I took the opportunity of beginning a letter to my dear friends at home; but the children came up before I had half completed it.

At seven, I had to put Mary Ann to bed; then I played with Tom till eight, when he too went, and I finished my letter, and unpacked my clothes, which I had hitherto found no opportunity for doing, and, finally, went to bed myself.

But this is a very favourable specimen of a day's proceedings.

My task of instruction and surveillance, instead of becoming easier as my charges[2] and I got better accustomed to each other, became more arduous as their characters unfolded. The name of governess, I soon found, was a mere mockery as applied to me; my pupils had no more notion of obedience than a wild, un-broken colt. The habitual fear of their father's peevish temper, and the dread of the punishments he was wont to inflict when irritated, kept them generally within bounds in his immediate presence. The girls, too, had some fear of their mother's anger; and the boy might occasionally be bribed to do as she bid him by the hope of reward; but I had no rewards to offer, and as for punishments, I was given to understand, the parents reserved that privilege to themselves; and yet they expected me to keep my pupils in order. Other children might be guided by the fear of anger, and the desire of approbation; but neither the one nor the other had any effect upon these.

Master Tom, not content with refusing to be ruled, must needs set up as a ruler, and manifested a determination to keep, not only his sisters, but his governess in order, by violent manual and pedal applications; and, as he was a tall, strong boy of his years, this occasioned no trifling inconvenience. A few sound boxes on the ear,[3] on such occasions, might have settled the matter easily enough: but as, in that case, he might make up some story to his mother, which she would be sure to believe, as she had such unshaken faith in his veracity – though I had already discovered it to be by no means unimpeachable, I determined to refrain from striking him even in self-defence; and, in his most violent moods, my only resource was to throw him on his back, and hold his hands and feet till the frenzy was somewhat abated.

To the difficulty of preventing him from doing what he ought not, was added that of forcing him to do what he ought. Often he would positively refuse to learn, or to repeat his lessons, or even to look at his book. Here again, a good birch rod might have been serviceable; but, as my powers were so limited, I must make the best use of what I had. As there were no settled hours for study and play, I resolved to give my pupils a certain task, which, with moderate attention, they could perform in a short time; and till this was done, however weary I was, or however perverse they might be, nothing short of parental interference should induce me to suffer them to leave the school-room; even if I should sit with my chair against the door to keep them in. Patience, Firmness, and Perseverance were my only weapons; and these I resolved to use to the utmost.

I determined always strictly to fulfil the threats and promises I made; and, to that end, I must be cautious to threaten and promise nothing that I could not perform. Then, I would carefully refrain from all useless irritability and indulgence of my own ill-temper: when they behaved tolerably, I would be as kind and obliging as it was in my power to be, in order to make the widest possible distinction between good and bad conduct; I would reason with them too in the simplest and most effective manner. When I reproved them, or refused to gratify their wishes, after a glaring fault, it should be more in sorrow than in anger: their little hymns and prayers I would make plain and clear to their understanding; when they said their prayers at night, and asked pardon for their offences, I would remind them of the sins of the past day, solemnly, but in perfect kindness, to avoid raising a spirit of opposition; penitential hymns should be said by the naughty, cheerful ones by the comparatively good; and every kind of instruction, I would convey to them, as much as possible, by entertaining discourse – apparently with no other object than their present amusement in view.

By these means I hoped, in time, both to benefit the children, and to gain the approbation of their parents; and, also, to convince my friends at home that I was not so wanting in skill and prudence as they supposed. I knew the difficulties I had to contend with were great; but I knew (at least I believed), unremitting patience and perseverance could overcome them; and night and morning I implored Divine assistance to this end. But either the children were so incorrigible, the parents so unreasonable, or myself so mistaken in my views, or so unable to carry them out, that my best intentions and most strenuous efforts seemed productive of no better result than sport to the children, dissatisfaction to their parents, and torment to myself.

The task of instruction was as arduous for the body as the mind. I had to run after my pupils to catch them, to carry, or drag them to the table, and often forcibly to hold them there, till the lesson was done. Tom, I frequently put into a corner, seating myself before him in a chair, with the book which contained the little task that must be said, or read, before he was released, in my hand. He was not strong enough to push both me and the chair away, so he would stand twisting his body and face into the most grotesque and singular contortions – laughable, no doubt, to an unconcerned spectator, but not to me – and uttering loud yells and doleful outcries, intended to represent weeping, but wholly without the accompaniment of tears. I knew this was done solely for the purpose of annoying me; and, therefore, however I might inwardly tremble with impatience and irritation, I manfully strove to suppress all visible signs of molestation, and affected to sit, with calm indifference, waiting till it should please him to cease this pastime, and prepare for a run in the garden, by casting his eye on the book, and reading or repeating the few words he was required to say.

Sometimes he would determine to do his writing badly; and I had to hold his hand to prevent him from purposely blotting or disfiguring the paper. Frequently, I threatened that, if he did not do better, he should have another line: then, he would stubbornly refuse to write this line; and I, to save my word, had finally to resort to the expedient of holding his fingers upon the pen, and forcibly drawing his hand up and down till, in spite of his resistance, the line was in some sort completed.

Yet Tom was by no means the most unmanageable of my pupils: sometimes, to my great joy, he would have the sense to see that his wisest policy was to finish his tasks, and go out and amuse himself till I and his sisters came to join him, which, frequently was not at all, for Mary Ann seldom followed his example in this particular. She apparently preferred rolling on the floor to any other amusement. Down she would drop like a leaden weight; and when I, with great difficulty, had succeeded in rooting her thence, I had still to hold her up with one arm, while, with the other, I held the book from which she was to read or spell her lesson. As the dead weight of the big girl of six became too heavy for one arm to bear, I transferred it to the other; or, if both were weary of the burden, I carried her into a corner, and told her she might come out when she could find the use of her feet, and stand up; but she generally preferred lying there like a log till dinner or tea time, when, as I could not deprive her of her meals, she must be liberated, and would come crawling out with a grin of triumph on her round, red face.

Often she would stubbornly refuse to pronounce some particular word in her lesson; and now I regret the lost labour I have had in striving to conquer her obstinacy. If I had passed it over as a matter of no consequence, it would have been better for both parties, than vainly striving to overcome it, as I did; but I thought it my absolute duty to crush this vicious tendency in the bud; and so it was, if I could have done it: and, had my powers been less limited, I might have enforced obedience; but as it was, it was but a trial of strength between her and me, in which she generally came off victorious; and every victory served to encourage and strengthen her for a future contest.

In vain I argued, coaxed, entreated, threatened, scolded; in vain I kept her in from play, or, if obliged to take her out, refused to play with her, or to speak kindly, or have anything to do with her; in vain I tried to set before her the advantages of doing as she was bid, and being loved and kindly treated in consequence, and the disadvantages of persisting in her absurd perversity. Sometimes, when she asked me to do something for her, I would answer –

'Yes, I will, Mary Ann, if you will only say that word. Come! you'd better say it at once, and have no more trouble about it.'

'No.'

'Then, of course, I can do nothing for you!'

With me, at her age, or under, neglect and disgrace were the most dreadful punishments; but on her they made no impression.

Sometimes, exasperated to the utmost pitch, I would shake her violently by the shoulders, or pull her long hair, or put her in the corner, – for which she punished me with loud, shrill, piercing screams, that went through my head like a knife. She knew I hated this, and when she had shrieked her utmost, would look into my face with an air of vindictive satisfaction, exclaiming –

'*Now* then! *that's* for you.'

And then shriek again and again, till I was forced to stop my ears. Often these dreadful cries would bring Mrs Bloomfield up to inquire what was the matter?

'Mary Ann is a naughty girl, ma'am.'

'But what are these shocking screams?'

'She is screaming in a passion.'

'I never heard such a dreadful noise! You might be killing her. Why is she not out with her brother?'

'I cannot get her to finish her lessons.'

'But Mary Ann must be a *good* girl, and finish her lessons.' This was blandly spoken to the child. 'And I hope I shall *never* hear such terrible cries again!'

And fixing her cold, stony eyes on me with a look that could not be mistaken, she would shut the door, and walk away.

Sometimes I would try to take the little obstinate creature by surprise, and casually ask her the word whilst she was thinking of something else: frequently she would begin to say it, and then suddenly check herself, with a provoking look that seemed to say, 'Ah! I'm too sharp for you; you shan't trick it out of me either.'

On another occasion, I pretended to forget the whole affair; and talked and played with her as usual, till night, when I put her to bed, then bending over her, while she lay all smiles and good-humour, just before departing, I said, as cheerfully and kindly as before –

'Now, Mary Ann, just tell me that word before I kiss you good-night: you are a good girl now, and, of course, you will say it.'

'No. I won't.'

'Then I can't kiss you!'

'Well, I don't care.'

In vain I expressed my sorrow; in vain I lingered for some symptom of contrition; she really 'didn't care,' and I left her alone, and in darkness, wonderimg most of all at this last proof of insensate stubbornness. In *my* childhood I could not imagine more afflictive punishment than for my mother to refuse to kiss me at night: the very idea was terrible; more than the idea I never felt, for, happily, I never committed a crime that was deemed worthy of such a penalty; but once, I remember, for some transgression of my sister's our mother thought proper to inflict it upon her; what *she* felt, I cannot tell; but my sympathetic tears and suffering for her sake, I shall not soon forget.

Another troublesome trait in Mary Ann, was her incorrigible propensity to keep running into the nursery to play with her little sisters and the nurse. This was natural enough, but, as it was against her mother's express desire, I, of course, forbade her to do so, and did my utmost to keep her with me, but that only increased her relish for the nursery; and the more I strove to keep her out of it, the oftener she went, and the longer she stayed – to the great dissatisfaction of Mrs Bloomfield, who, I well knew, would impute all the blame of the matter to me.

Another of my trials was the dressing in the morning: at one time she would not be washed; at another she would not be dressed, unless she might wear some particular frock that, I knew, her mother would not like her to have; at another she would scream and run away if I attempted to touch her hair. So that, frequently, when after much trouble and toil, I had, at length, succeeded in bringing her down, the breakfast was nearly half over; and black looks from 'mamma', and testy observations from 'papa', spoken at me, if not to me, were sure to be my meed;[4] for few things irritated the latter so much as want of punctuality at meal-times.

Then, among the minor annoyances, was my inability to satisfy Mrs Bloomfield with her daughter's dress; and the child's hair 'was never fit to be seen'. Sometimes, as a powerful reproach to me, she would perform the office of tire-woman[5] herself, and then complain bitterly of the trouble it gave her.

When little Fanny came into the school-room, I hoped *she* would be mild and inoffensive, at least; but a few days, if not a few hours, sufficed to destroy the illusion: I found her a mischievous, intractable little creature, given up to falsehood and deception, young as she was, and alarmingly fond of exercising her two favourite weapons of offence and defence: that of spitting in the faces of those who incurred her displeasure, and bellowing like a bull when her unreasonable desires were not gratified. As she, generally, was pretty quiet in her parents' presence, and they were impressed with the notion of her being a remarkably gentle child, her falsehoods were readily believed, and her loud uproars led them to suspect harsh and injudicious treatment on my part; and when, at length, her bad disposition became manifest, even to their prejudiced eyes, I felt that the whole was attributed to me.

'What a naughty girl Fanny is getting,' Mrs Bloomfield would say to her spouse. 'Don't you observe, my dear, how she is altered since she entered the school-room? She will soon be as bad as the other two; and, I am sorry to say, they have quite deteriorated of late.'

'You may say that,' was the answer. 'I've been thinking that same myself. I thought when we got them a governess they'd improve; but instead of that, they get worse and worse: I don't know how it is with their learning; but their habits, I know, make no sort of improvement; they get rougher, and dirtier, and more unseemly every day.'

I knew this was all pointed at me; and these, and all similar innuendoes affected me far more deeply than any open accusations would have done; for against the latter I should have been roused to speak in my own defence: now, I judged it my wisest plan to subdue every resentful impulse, suppress every sensitive shrinking, and go on perseveringly doing my best; for, irksome as my situation was, I earnestly wished to retain it. I thought, if I could struggle on with unremitting firmness and integrity, the children would, in time, become more humanized: every month would contribute to make them some little wiser, and, consequently, more manageable; for a child of nine or ten as frantic and ungovernable as these at six and seven would be a maniac.

I flattered myself I was benefiting my parents and sister by my continuance here; for, small as the salary was, I still was earning something, and with strict economy I could easily manage to have something to spare for them, if they would favour me by taking it. Then, it was by my own will that I had got the place: I had brought all this tribulation on myself, and I was determined to bear it; nay, more than that, I did not even regret the step I had taken, and I longed to show my friends that, even now, I was competent to undertake the charge, and able to acquit myself honourably to the end; and if ever I felt it degrading to submit so quietly, or intolerable to toil so constantly, I would turn towards my home, and say within myself –

'They may crush, but they shall not subdue me;
'Tis of thee that I think, not of them.'[6]

About Christmas I was allowed a visit home, but only of a fortnight's duration. 'For,' said Mrs Bloomfield, 'I thought, as you had seen your friends so lately, you would not care for a longer stay.'

I left her to think so still; but she little knew how long, how wearisome those fourteen weeks of absence had been to me, how intensely I had longed for my holidays, how greatly I was disappointed at their curtailment. Yet she was not to blame in this; I had never told her my feelings, and she could not be expected to divine them; I had not been with her a full term, and she was justified in not allowing me a full vacation.

IV
THE GRANDMAMMA

I SPARE MY READERS THE account of my delight on coming home, my happiness while there – enjoying a brief space of rest and liberty in that dear, familiar place, among the loving and the loved, and my sorrow on being obliged to bid them, once more, a long adieu.

I returned, however, with unabated vigour to my work – a more arduous task than anyone can imagine, who has not felt something like the misery of being charged with the care and direction of a set of mischievous, turbulent rebels, whom his utmost exertions cannot bind to their duty, while, at the same time, he is responsible for their conduct to a higher power, who exacts from him what cannot be achieved without the aid of the superior's more potent authority, which, either from indolence, or the fear of becoming unpopular with the said rebellious gang, the latter refuses to give. I can conceive few situations more harassing than that wherein, however you may long for success, however you may labour to fulfil your duty, your efforts are baffled and set at naught by those beneath you, and unjustly censured and misjudged by those above.

I have not enumerated half the vexatious propensities of my pupils, or half the troubles resulting from my heavy responsibilities, for fear of trespassing too much upon the reader's patience, as, perhaps, I have already done; but my design, in writing the last few pages, was not to amuse, but to benefit those whom it might concern: he that has no interest in such matters will doubtless have skipped them over with a cursory glance, and, perhaps, a malediction against the prolixity of the writer; but if a parent has, therefrom, gathered any useful hint, or an unfortunate governess received thereby the slightest benefit, I am well rewarded for my pains.

To avoid trouble and confusion, I have taken my pupils one by one, and discussed their various qualities; but this can give no adequate idea of being worried by the whole three together, when, as was often the case, all were determined to 'be naughty, and to tease Miss Grey, and put her in a passion'.

Sometimes, on such occasions, the thought has suddenly occurred to me – 'if *they* could see me now!' meaning, of course, my friends at home, and the idea of how they would pity me has made me pity myself – so greatly that I have had the utmost difficulty to restrain my tears; but I have restrained them, till my little tormentors were gone to dessert, or cleared off to bed (my only prospects of deliverance), and then, in all the bliss of solitude, I have given myself up to the luxury of an unrestricted burst of weeping. But this was a weakness I did not often indulge: my employments were too numerous, my leisure moments were too precious to admit of much time being given to fruitless lamentations.

I particularly remember one wild, snowy afternoon, soon after my return in January – the children had all come up from dinner, loudly declaring that they meant 'to be naughty'; and they had well kept their resolution, though I had talked myself hoarse, and wearied every muscle in my throat, in the vain attempt to reason them out of it. I had got Tom pinned up in a corner, whence, I told him, he should not escape till he had done his appointed task. Meantime, Fanny had possessed herself of my work bag,[1] and was rifling its contents – and spitting into it besides. I told her to let it alone, but to no purpose, of course.

'Burn it, Fanny!' cried Tom; and *this* command she hastened to obey. I sprang to snatch it from the fire, and Tom darted to the door.

'Mary Ann, throw her desk out of the window!' cried he, and my precious desk, containing my letters and papers, my small amount of cash, and all my valuables, was about to be precipitated from the three-story window. I flew to rescue it. Meanwhile Tom had left the room, and was rushing down the stairs, followed by Fanny. Having secured my desk, I ran to catch them, and Mary Ann came scampering after. All three escaped me, and ran out of the house into the garden, where they plunged about in the snow, shouting and screaming in exultant glee.

What must I do? If I followed them, I should probably be unable to capture one, and only drive them farther away; if I did not, how was I to get them in? and what would their parents think of me, if they saw or heard the children rioting, hatless, bonnetless, gloveless, and bootless, in the deep, soft snow?

While I stood in this perplexity, just without the door, trying, by grim looks and angry words, to awe them into subjection, I heard a voice behind me, in harshly piercing tones, exclaiming, –

'Miss Grey! Is it possible! What, in the d – l's name, can you be thinking about?'

'I can't get them in, sir,' said I, turning round, and beholding Mr Bloomfield, with his hair on end and his pale blue eyes bolting from their sockets.

'But I INSIST upon their being got in!' cried he, approaching nearer, and looking perfectly ferocious.

'Then, sir, you must call them yourself, if you please, for they won't listen to me,' I replied, stepping back.

'Come in with you, you filthy brats, or I'll horsewhip you every one!' roared he; and the children instantly obeyed. 'There, you see! they come at the first word!'

'Yes, when *you* speak.'

'And it's very strange, that when you've the care of 'em, you've no better control over 'em than that! – Now there they are – gone up-stairs with their nasty, snowy feet! Do go after 'em and see them made decent, for Heaven's sake!'

That gentleman's mother was then staying in the house; and as I ascended the stairs and passed the drawing-room door, I had the satisfaction of hearing the old lady declaiming aloud to her daughter-in-law to this effect (for I could only distinguish the most emphatic words) –

'Gracious Heavens! – never in all my life – ! – get their death as sure as – ! Do you think, my dear, she's a *proper person?* Take my word for it –'

I heard no more; but that sufficed.

The senior Mrs Bloomfield had been very attentive and civil to me; and, till now, I had thought her a nice, kind-hearted, chatty old body. She would often come to me and talk in a confidential strain, nodding, and shaking her head, and gesticulating with hands and eyes, as a certain class of old ladies are wont to do, though I never knew one that carried the peculiarity to so great an extent: she would even sympathise with me for the trouble I had with the children, and express at times, by half sentences, interspersed with nods and knowing winks, her sense of the injudicious conduct of their mamma in so restricting my power, and neglecting to support me with her authority. Such a mode of testifying disapprobation was not much to my taste; and I generally refused to take it in, or understand anything more than was openly spoken; at least, I never went farther than an implied acknowledgement that, if matters were otherwise ordered, my task would be a less difficult one, and I should be better able to guide and instruct my charge; but now I must be doubly cautious. Hitherto, though I saw the old lady had her defects (of which one was a proneness to proclaim her perfections), I had always been wishful to excuse them, and to give her credit for all the virtues she professed, and even imagine others yet untold. Kindness, which had been the food of my life through so many years, had lately been so entirely denied me, that I welcomed with grateful joy the slightest semblance of it. No wonder then that my heart warmed to the old lady, and always gladdened at her approach, and regretted her departure.

But now, the few words, luckily, or unluckily, heard in passing had wholly revolutionized my ideas respecting her; now I looked upon her as hypocritical and insincere, a flatterer, and a spy upon my words and deeds. Doubtless it would have been my interest still to meet her with the same cheerful smile and tone of respectful cordiality as before; but I could not, if I would; my manner altered with my feelings, and became so cold and shy that she could not fail to notice it. She soon did notice it, and *her* manner altered too: the familiar nod was changed to a stiff bow, the gracious smile gave place to a glare of Gorgon ferocity,[2] her vivacious loquacity was entirely transferred from me to 'the darling boy and girls' whom she flattered and indulged more absurdly than ever their mother had done.

I confess, I was somewhat troubled at this change: I feared the consequences of her displeasure, and even made some efforts to recover the ground I had lost – and with better apparent success than I could have anticipated. At one time, I, merely in common civility, asked after her cough – immediately her long visage relaxed into a smile, and she favoured me with a particular history of that and her other infirmities, followed by an account of her pious resignation, delivered in the usual emphatic, declamatory style, which no writing can pourtray.

'But there's one remedy for all, my dear, and that's resignation' (a toss of the head) 'resignation to the will of Heaven!' (an uplifting of the hands and eyes). 'It has always supported me through all my trials, and always will do' (a succession of nods). 'But then, it isn't everybody that can say that' (a shake of the head) 'but I'm one of the pious ones, Miss Grey!' (a very significant nod and toss). 'And, thank Heaven, I always was' (another nod) 'and I glory in it!' (an emphatic clasping of the hands and shaking of the head), and with several texts of Scripture, misquoted, or misapplied, and religious exclamations so redolent of the ludicrous in the style of delivery and manner of bringing in, if not in the expressions themselves, that I decline repeating them, she withdrew, tossing her large head in high good humour – with herself at least – and left me hoping that, after all, she was rather weak than wicked.

At her next visit to Wellwood House, I went so far as to say I was glad to see her looking so well. The effect of this was magical: the words, intended as a mark of civility, were received as a flattering compliment; her countenance brightened up, and from that moment she became as gracious and benign as heart could wish[3] – in outward semblance at least; and from what I now saw of her, and what I heard from the children, I knew that in order to gain her cordial friendship, I had but to utter a word of flattery at each convenient opportunity; but this was against my principles; and for lack of this, the capricious old dame soon deprived me of her favour again, and I believe did me much secret injury.

She could not greatly influence her daughter-in-law against me, because between that lady and herself there was a mutual dislike – chiefly shewn by her in secret detractions and calumniations, by the other, in an excess of frigid formality in her demeanour; and no fawning flattery of the older could thaw away the wall of ice which the younger interposed between them. But with her son, the old lady had better success: he would listen to all she had to say, provided she could soothe his fretful temper, and refrain from irritating him by her own asperities; and I have reason to believe that she considerably strengthened his prejudice against me. She would tell him that I shamefully neglected the children, and even his wife did not attend to them as she ought; and that he must look after them himself, or they would all go to ruin.

Thus urged, he would frequently give himself the trouble of watching them from the windows during their play; at times, he would follow them through the grounds, and too often came suddenly upon them while they were dabbling in the forbidden well, talking to the coachman in the stables, or revelling in the filth of the farm-yard – and I, meanwhile, stupidly standing by, having previously exhausted my energy in vain attempts to get them away; often too he would unexpectedly pop his head into the school-room while the young people were at meals, and find them spilling their milk over the table and themselves, plunging their fingers into their own, or each other's mugs, or quarrelling over their victuals like a set of tiger's cubs. If I were quiet at the moment, I was conniving at their disorderly conduct, if (as was frequently the case), I happened to be exalting my voice to enforce order, I was using undue violence, and setting the girls a bad example by such ungentleness of tone and language.

I remember one afternoon in spring, when, owing to the rain, they could not go out; but, by some amazing good fortune, they had all finished their lessons, and yet abstained from running down to tease their parents – a trick that annoyed me greatly, but which, on rainy days, I seldom could prevent their doing; because, below, they found novelty and amusement – especially when visiters were in the house; and their mother, though she

bid me keep them in the school-room, would never chide them
for leaving it, or trouble herself to send them back; but to-day
they appeared satisfied with their present abode, and what is
more wonderful still, seemed disposed to play together without
depending on me for amusement, and without quarrelling with
each other. Their occupation was a somewhat puzzling one:
they were all squatted together on the floor by the window, over
a heap of broken toys, and a quantity of birds' eggs, or rather
egg-shells, for the contents had luckily been abstracted; these
shells they had broken up and were pounding into small fragments, to what end, I could not imagine; but so long as they
were quiet, and not in positive mischief, I did not care; and, with
a feeling of unusual repose, I sat by the fire, putting the finishing
stitches to a frock for Mary Ann's doll, intending, when that
was done, to begin a letter to my mother. But suddenly the door
opened, and the dingy head of Mr Bloomfield looked in.

'All very quiet here! What are you doing?' said he.

'No harm *to-day*, at least,' thought I.

But he was of a different opinion. Advancing to the window,
and seeing the children's occupation, he testily exclaimed –

'What in the world are you about?'

'We're grinding egg-shells, papa!' cried Tom.

'How *dare* you make such a mess, you little d – ls? Don't you
see what confounded work you're making of the carpet?' (The
carpet was a plain, brown drugget.[4]) 'Miss Grey, did you know
what they were doing?'

'Yes, sir.'

'*You knew it?*'

'Yes.'

'You *knew* it! and you actually sat there and permitted them
to go on, without a word of reproof!'

'I didn't think they were doing any harm.'

'Any harm! Why, look there? Just look at that carpet, and see
– was there ever anything like it in a Christian house before? No
wonder your room is not fit for a pigsty – no wonder your
pupils are worse than a litter of pigs! – no wonder – Oh! I
declare, it puts me quite past my patience!' and he departed,

shutting the door after him with a bang that made the children laugh.

'It puts *me* quite past my patience too!' muttered I, getting up; and, seizing the poker, I dashed it repeatedly into the cinders, and stirred them up with unwonted energy; thus easing my irritation, under pretence of mending the fire.

After this, Mr Bloomfield was continually looking in to see if the school-room was in order; and, as the children were continually littering the floor with fragments of toys, sticks, stones, stubble, leaves, and other rubbish, which I could not prevent their bringing, or oblige them to gather up, and which the servants refused to 'clean after them', I had to spend a considerable portion of my valuable leisure moments on my knees upon the floor, in painfully[5] reducing things to order. Once, I told them that they should not taste their supper till they had picked up everything from the carpet; Fanny might have hers when she had taken up a certain quantity, Mary Ann when she had gathered twice as much,[6] and Tom was to clear away the rest.

Wonderful to state, the girls did their part; but Tom was in such a fury that he flew upon the table, scattered the bread and milk about the floor, struck his sisters, kicked the coals out of the coal-pan, attempted to overthrow the table and chairs, and seemed inclined to make a Douglas-larder[7] of the whole contents of the room; but I seized upon him, and, sending Mary Ann to call her mamma, held him, in spite of kicks, blows, yells, and execrations, till Mrs Bloomfield made her appearance.

'What is the matter with my boy?' said she.

And when the matter was explained to her, all she did was to send for the nursery-maid to put the room in order, and bring Master Bloomfield his supper.

'There now,' cried Tom, triumphantly, looking up from his viands with his mouth almost too full for speech. 'There now, Miss Grey! you see I have got my supper in spite of you: and I haven't picked up a single thing!'

The only person in the house who had any real sympathy for me was the nurse; for she had suffered like afflictions, though in a smaller degree, as she had not the task of teaching, nor was she so responsible for the conduct of her charge.

'Oh, Miss Grey!' she would say, 'you have some trouble with them childer!'

'I have indeed, Betty; and I dare say you know what it is.'

'Ay, I do so! But I don't vex myself o'er 'em as you do. And then, you see, I hit 'em a slap sometimes; and them little uns – I gives 'em a good whipping[8] now and then – there's nothing else ull do for 'em, as what they say. Howsever, I've lost my place for it.'

'Have you, Betty? I heard you were going to leave.'

'Eh, bless you, yes! Misses gave me warning a three-wik sin'. She told be afore Christmas how it mud be, if I hit 'em again; but I couldn't hold my hand off 'em at nothing – I know not how *you* do, for Miss Mary Ann's worse by the half nor her sisters!'

V

THE UNCLE

BESIDES THE OLD LADY, THERE was another relative of the family, whose visits were a great annoyance to me – this was 'Uncle Robson,' Mrs Bloomfield's brother, a tall, self-sufficient fellow, with dark hair and sallow complexion like his sister, a nose that seemed to disdain the earth, and little grey eyes, frequently half closed, with a mixture of real stupidity and affected contempt of all surrounding objects. He was a thick-set, strongly-built man, but he had found some means of compressing his waist into a remarkably small compass, and that, together with the unnatural stiffness of his form, showed that the lofty-minded, manly Mr Robson, the scorner of the female sex, was not above the foppery of stays.

He seldom deigned to notice me; and when he did, it was with a certain supercilious insolence of tone and manner that convinced me that he was no gentleman, though it was intended to have a contrary effect. But it was not for that I disliked his coming, so much as for the harm he did the children – encouraging all their evil propensities, and undoing, in a few minutes, the little good it had taken me months of labour to achieve.

Fanny and little Harriet he seldom condescended to notice; but Mary Ann was something of a favourite. He was continually encouraging her tendency to affectation (which I had done my utmost to crush) talking about her pretty face, and filling her head with all manner of conceited notions concerning her personal appearance (which I had instructed her to regard as dust in the balance compared with the cultivation of her mind and manners); and I never saw a child so susceptible of flattery as she was. Whatever was wrong, in either her or her brother, he would encourage by laughing at, if not by actually praising; and people little know the injury they do to children by laughing at their faults, and making a pleasant jest of what their true friends have endeavoured to teach them to hold in great abhorrence.

Though not a positive drunkard, Mr Robson habitually swallowed great quantities of wine, and took with relish an occasional glass of brandy and water. He taught his nephew to imitate him in this to the utmost of his ability, and to believe that the more wine and spirits he could take, and the better he liked them, the more he manifested his bold and manly spirit, and rose superior to his sisters. Mr Bloomfield had not much to say against it, for *his* favourite beverage was gin and water, of which he took a considerable portion every day, by dint of constant sipping – and to that, I chiefly attributed his dingy complexion and waspish temper.

Mr Robson likewise encouraged Tom's propensity to persecute the lower creation, both by precept and example. As he frequently came to course or shoot over his brother-in-law's grounds, he would bring his favourite dogs with him, and he treated them so brutally that, poor as I was, I would have given a sovereign any day to see one of them bite him, provided the animal could have done it with impunity. Sometimes, when in a very complacent mood, he would go a bird-nesting with the children, a thing that irritated and annoyed me exceedingly, as, by frequent and persevering attempts, I flattered myself I had partly shown them the evil of this pastime, and hoped, in time, to bring them to some general sense of justice and humanity; but ten minutes' bird-nesting with Uncle Robson, or even a laugh from him at some relation of their former barbarities, was sufficient, at once, to destroy the effect of my whole elaborate course of reasoning and persuasion. Happily, however, during that spring, they never, but once, got anything but empty nests, or eggs – being too impatient to leave them till the birds were hatched; that once, Tom, who had been with his uncle into the neighbouring plantation, came running in high glee into the garden with a brood of little callow nestlings in his hands.

Mary Ann and Fanny, whom I was just bringing out, ran to admire his spoils, and to beg each a bird for themselves.

'No, not one!' cried Tom. 'They're all mine. Uncle Robson gave them to me – one, two, three, four, five – you shan't touch one of them! no, not one, for your lives!' continued he, exultantly, laying the nest on the ground and standing over it with his legs wide apart, his hands thrust into his breeches-pockets, his body bent forward, and his face twisted into all manner of contortions in the ecstacy of his delight.

'But you shall see me fettle 'em off.[1] My word, but I *will* wallop 'em! See if I don't now. By gum! but there's rare sport for me in that nest.'

'But, Tom,' said I, 'I shall not allow you to torture those birds. They must either be killed at once, or carried back to the place you took them from, that the old birds may continue to feed them.'

'But you don't know where that is, madam. It's only me and Uncle Robson that knows that.'

'But if you don't tell me, I shall kill them myself – much as I hate it.'

'You daren't. You daren't touch them for your life! because you know papa and mamma, and Uncle Robson, would be angry. Ha, hah! I've caught you there, miss!'

'I shall do what I think right in a case of this sort, without consulting any one. If your papa and mamma don't happen to approve of it, I shall be sorry to offend them, but your Uncle Robson's opinions, of course, are nothing to me.'

So saying – urged by a sense of duty – at the risk of both making myself sick, and incurring the wrath of my employers – I got a large flat stone that had been reared up for a mouse-trap by the gardener, then, having once more vainly endeavoured to persuade the little tyrant to let the birds be carried back, I asked what he intended to do with them. With fiendish glee he commenced a list of torments, and while he was busied in the relation, I dropped the stone upon his intended victims and crushed them flat beneath it.

Loud were the outcries, terrible the execrations consequent upon this daring outrage; Uncle Robson had been coming up the walk with his gun, and was, just then, pausing to kick his dog.

Tom flew towards him, vowing he would make him kick me instead of Juno. Mr Robson leant upon his gun, and laughed excessively at the violence of his nephew's passion, and the bitter maledictions and opprobrious epithets he heaped upon me.

'Well, you *are* a good 'un!' exclaimed he, at length, taking up his weapon and proceeding towards the house. 'Damme, but the lad has some spunk in him too. Curse me, if ever I saw a nobler little scoundrel than that. He's beyond petticoat government already: – by G –, he defies mother, granny, governess, and all! Ha, ha, ha. Never mind, Tom, I'll get you another brood to-morrow.'

'If you do, Mr Robson, I shall kill them too,' said I.

'Humph!' replied he, and having honoured me with a broad stare, which, contrary to his expectations, I sustained without flinching, he turned away with an air of supreme contempt, and stalked into the house.

Tom next went to tell his mamma. It was not her way to say much on any subject; but, when she next saw me, her aspect and demeanour were doubly dark and chill.

After some casual remark about the weather, she observed –

'I am sorry, Miss Grey, you should think it necessary to inter-fere with Master Bloomfield's amusements; he was *very* much distressed about your destroying the birds.'

'When Master Bloomfield's amusements consist in injuring sentient creatures,' I answered, 'I think it is my duty to interfere.'

'You seem to have forgotten,' said she, calmly, 'that the crea-tures were all created for our convenience.'

I thought that doctrine admitted some doubt, but merely replied –

'If they were, we have no right to torment them for our amuse-ment.'

'I think,' said she, 'a child's amusement is scarcely to be weighed against the welfare of a soulless brute.'

'But, for the child's own sake, it ought not to be encouraged to have such amusements,' answered I, as meekly as I could, to make up for such unusual pertinacity.

'Blessed are the merciful, for they shall obtain mercy.'[2]

'Oh, of course! but that refers to our conduct towards each other.'

'The merciful man shows mercy to his beast,' I ventured to add.

'I think *you* have not shown much mercy,' replied she, with a short, bitter laugh; 'killing the poor birds by wholesale, in that shocking manner, and putting the dear boy to such misery, for a mere whim.'

I judged it prudent to say no more.

This was the nearest approach to a quarrel I ever had with Mrs Bloomfield, as well as the greatest number of words I ever exchanged with her at one time, since the day of my first arrival.

But Mr Robson and old Mrs Bloomfield were not the only guests whose coming to Wellwood House annoyed me; every visiter disturbed me, more or less, not so much because they neglected me (though I did feel their conduct strange and disagreeable in that respect), as because I found it impossible to keep my pupils away from them, as I was repeatedly desired to do: Tom must talk to them, and Mary Ann must be noticed by them. Neither the one nor the other knew what it was to feel any degree of shame-facedness, or even common modesty. They would indecently and clamorously interrupt the conversation of their elders, teaze them with the most impertinent questions, roughly collar the gentlemen, climb their knees uninvited, hang about their shoulders or rifle their pockets, pull the ladies' gowns, disorder their hair, tumble their collars, and importunately beg for their trinkets.

Mrs Bloomfield had the sense to be shocked and annoyed at all this, but she had not sense to prevent it. She expected me to prevent it; – and how could I – when the guests, with their fine clothes and new faces, continually flattered and indulged them out of complaisance to their parents – how could I, with my homely garments, every-day face, and honest words draw them away? I strained every nerve to do so; – by striving to amuse them, I endeavoured to attract them to my side; by the exertion of such authority as I possessed, and by such severity as I dared to use, I tried to deter them from tormenting the guests; and by reproaching their unmannerly conduct, to make them ashamed to repeat it. But they knew no shame – they scorned authority which had no terrors to back it, and as for kindness and affection, either they had no hearts, or such as they had were so strongly guarded, and so well concealed, that I, with all my efforts, had not yet discovered how to reach them.

But soon my trials in this quarter came to a close – sooner than I either expected or desired; for one sweet evening towards the close of May, as I was rejoicing in the near approach of the holidays, and congratulating myself upon having made some progress with my pupils (as far as their learning went at least, for I *had* instilled *something* into their heads, and I had at length brought them to be a little – a very little – more rational about getting their lessons done in time to leave some space for recreation, instead of tormenting themselves and me all day long to no purpose), Mrs Bloomfield sent for me, and calmly told me that after Midsummer my services would be no longer required. She assured me that my character and general conduct were unexceptionable; but the children had made so little improvement since my arrival, that Mr Bloomfield and she felt it their duty to seek some other mode of instruction. Though superior to most children of their years in abilities, they were decidedly behind them in attainments, their manners were uncultivated, and their tempers unruly. And this she attributed to a want of sufficient firmness, and diligent, persevering care on my part.

Unshaken firmness, devoted diligence, unwearied perseverance, unceasing care, were the very qualifications on which I had secretly prided myself, and by which I had hoped in time to overcome all difficulties, and obtain success at last. I wished to say something in my own justification, but in attempting to speak, I felt my voice falter, and rather than testify any emotion, or suffer the tears to overflow that were already gathering in my eyes, I chose to keep silence, and bear all, like a self-convicted culprit.

Thus was I dismissed, and thus I sought my home. Alas! what would they think of me? unable, after all my boasting, to keep my place even for a single year, as governess to three small

children, whose mother was asserted, by my own aunt, to be a
'very nice woman'. Having been thus weighed in the balance and
found wanting, I need not hope they would be willing to try me
again. And this was an unwelcome thought, for vexed, harassed,
disappointed as I had been, and greatly as I had learnt to love
and value my home, I was not yet weary of adventure, nor
willing to relax my efforts. I knew all parents were not like Mr
and Mrs Bloomfield, and I was certain all children were not like
theirs. The next family must be different, and any change must
be for the better. I had been seasoned by adversity, and tutored
by experience, and I longed to redeem my lost honour in the eyes
of those whose opinion was more than that of all the world
to me.

VI
THE PARSONAGE AGAIN

FOR A FEW MONTHS I REMAINED peaceably at home, in the quiet enjoyment of liberty and rest, and genuine friendship, from all of which I had fasted so long, and in the earnest prosecution of my studies, to recover what I had lost during my stay at Wellwood House, and to lay in new stores for future use.

My father's health was still very infirm, but not materially worse than when I last saw him, and I was glad I had it in my power to cheer him by my return, and to amuse him with singing his favorite songs.

No one triumphed over my failure, or said I had better have taken his or her advice, and quietly stayed at home. All were glad to have me back again, and lavished more kindness than ever upon me, to make up for the sufferings I had undergone; but not one would touch a shilling of what I had so cheerfully earned, and so carefully saved, in the hope of sharing it with them. By dint of pinching here, and scraping there, our debts already were nearly paid. Mary had had good success with her drawings, but our father had insisted upon *her* likewise keeping all the produce of her industry to herself. All we could spare from the supply of our humble wardrobe and our little casual expenses, he directed us to put into the savings' bank, saying, we knew not how soon we might be dependent[1] on that alone for support, for he felt he had not long to be with us, and what would become of our mother and us when he was gone, God only knew.

Dear papa! if he had troubled himself less about the afflictions that threatened us in case of his death, I am convinced that dreaded event would have not taken place so soon. My mother would never suffer him to ponder the subject if she could help it.

'Oh Richard!' exclaimed she, on one occasion, 'if you would but dismiss such gloomy subjects from your mind, you would live as long as any of us – at least you would live to see the girls married, and yourself a happy grandfather, with a canty old dame[2] for your companion.'

My mother laughed, and so did my father, but his laugh soon perished in a dreary sigh.

'*Them* married – poor penniless things!' said he, 'who will take them, I wonder?'

'Why, nobody shall, that isn't thankful for them – Wasn't I penniless when you took me? and you *pretended*, at least, to be vastly pleased with your acquisition. – But it's no matter whether they get married or not: we can devise a thousand honest ways of making a livelihood; and I wonder, Richard, you can think of bothering your head about our *poverty* in case of your death, as if *that* would be anything compared with the calamity of losing you – an affliction that, you well know, would swallow up all others, and which you ought to do your utmost to preserve us from; and there is nothing like a cheerful mind for keeping the body in health.'

'I know, Alice, it is wrong to keep repining as I do, but I cannot help it; you must bear with me.'

'I *won't* bear with you, if I can alter you!' replied my mother: but the harshness of her words was undone by the earnest affection of her tone and pleasant smile that made my father smile again, less sadly, and less transiently than was his wont.

'Mamma,' said I, as soon as I could find an opportunity of speaking with her alone, 'my money is but little, and cannot last long; if I could increase it, it would lessen papa's anxiety on one subject at least. I cannot draw like Mary, and so the best thing I could do would be to look out for another situation.'

'And so you would actually try again, Agnes?'

'Decidedly, I would.'

'Why, my dear, I should have thought you had had enough of it.'

'I know,' said I, 'everybody is not like Mr and Mrs Bloomfield –'

'Some are worse,' interrupted my mother.

'But not many, I think,' replied I, 'and I'm sure all children are not like theirs; for I and Mary were not; we always did as you bid us, didn't we?'

'Generally: but then, I did not spoil you; and you were not perfect angels after all: Mary had a fund of quiet obstinacy, and you were somewhat faulty in regard to temper; but you were very good children on the whole.'

'I know I was sulky sometimes, and I should have been glad to see these children sulky sometimes too; for then I could have understood them; but they never were; for they *could* not be offended, nor hurt, nor ashamed: they could not be unhappy in any way, except when they were in a passion.'

'Well, if they *could* not, it was not their fault; you cannot expect stone to be as pliable as clay.'

'No, but still it is very unpleasant to live with such un-impressible, incomprehensible creatures. You cannot love them, and if you could, your love would be utterly thrown away; they could neither return it, nor value, nor understand it. – But, however, even if I should stumble on such a family again, which is quite unlikely, I have all this experience to begin with, and I should manage better another time; and the end and aim of this preamble is, let me try again.'

'Well, my girl, you are not easily discouraged, I see – I am glad of that. – But, let me tell you, you are a good deal paler and thinner than when you first left home, and we cannot have you undermining your health to hoard up money, either for your-self or others.'

'Mary tells me I am changed too; and I don't much wonder at it, for I was in a constant state of agitation and anxiety all day long; but next time I am determined to take things coolly.'

After some further discussion, my mother promised once more to assist me, provided I would wait and be patient; and I left her to broach the matter to my father, when, and how, she deemed it most advisable, never doubting her ability to obtain his consent.

Meantime, I searched, with great interest, the advertising columns of the newspapers, and wrote answers to every 'Wanted a Governess,' that appeared at all eligible; but all my letters, as well as the replies, when I got any, were dutifully shewn to my mother; and she, to my chagrin, made me reject the situations one after another – These were low people, these were too exacting in their demands, and these too niggardly in their remunerations.

'Your talents are not such as every poor clergyman's daughter possesses, Agnes,' she would say, 'and you must not throw them away.' Remember, you promised to be patient – there is no need of hurry – you have plenty of time before you, and may have many chances yet.'

At length, she advised me to put an advertisement, myself, in the paper, stating my qualifications, etc.

'Music, singing, drawing, French, Latin, and German,' said she, 'are no mean assemblage; many will be glad to have so much in one instructor; and this time, you shall try your fortune in a somewhat higher family – in that of some genuine, thorough-bred gentleman, for such are far more likely to treat you with proper respect and consideration, than those purse-proud trades-people and arrogant upstarts. I have known several among the higher ranks, who treated their governesses quite as one of the family; though some, I allow, are as insolent and exacting as anyone else can be: for there are bad and good in all classes.'

The advertisement was quickly written and despatched. Of the two parties who answered it, but one would consent to give me fifty pounds, the sum my mother bade me name as the salary I should require; and here, I hesitated about engaging myself, as I feared the children would be too old, and their parents would require some one more showy, or more experienced, if not more accomplished than I; but my mother dissuaded me from declining it on that account: I should do vastly well, she said, if I would only throw aside my diffidence, and acquire a little more confidence in myself. I was just to give a plain, true statement of my acquirements and qualifications, and name what stipulations I chose to make, and then await the result.

The only stipulation I ventured to propose, was that I might be allowed two months' holiday during the year to visit my friends, at Midsummer and Christmas. The unknown lady, in her reply, made no objection to this, and stated that, as to my acquirements, she had no doubt I should be able to give satisfaction; but in the engagement of governesses, she considered those things as but subordinate points, as, being situated in the neighbourhood of O–, she could get masters to supply any deficiencies in that respect, but, in her opinion, next to unimpeachable morality, a mild and cheerful temper, and obliging disposition were the most essential requisites.

My mother did not relish this at all, and now made many objections to my accepting the situation, in which my sister warmly supported her; but, unwilling to be baulked again, I overruled them all; and, having first obtained the consent of my father, who had, a short time previously, been apprised of these transactions, I wrote a most obliging epistle to my unknown correspondent, and, finally, the bargain was concluded.

It was decreed that, on the last day of January, I was to enter upon my new office as governess in the family of Mr Murray, of Horton Lodge, near O–, about seventy miles from our village – a formidable distance to me, as I had never been above twenty miles from home in all the course of my twenty years' sojourn on earth, and as, moreover, every individual in that family and in the neighbourhood was utterly unknown to myself and all my acquaintances. But this rendered it only the more piquant to me: I had now, in some measure, got rid of the *mauvaise honte* that had formerly oppressed me so much; there was a pleasing excitement in the idea of entering these unknown regions, and making my way alone among its strange inhabitants; I now flattered myself I was going to see something of the world; Mr Murray's residence was near a large town, and not in a manufacturing district, where the people had nothing to do but to make money; his rank, from what I could gather, appeared to be higher than that of Mr Bloomfield, and doubtless he was one of those genuine thorough-bred gentry my mother spoke of, who would treat his governess with due consideration as a respectable, well-educated lady, the instructor and guide of his children, and not a mere upper servant; then, my pupils, being older, would be more rational, more teachable, and less troublesome than the last, they would be less confined to the school-room, and not require that constant labour and incessant watching; and finally – bright visions mingled with my hopes, with which the care of children and the mere duties of a governess had little or nothing to do; so that the reader will see I had no claim to be regarded as a martyr to filial piety, going forth to sacrifice peace and liberty for the sole purpose of laying up stores for the comfort and support of my parents; though, certainly, the comfort of my father, and the future support of my mother, had a large share in my calculations, and fifty pounds appeared to be no ordinary sum. I must have decent clothes becoming my station, I must, it seemed, put out my washing, and also pay for my four annual journeys between Horton Lodge and home; but with strict attention to economy, surely twenty pounds, or little more, would cover those expenses, and then there would be thirty for the bank, or little less; what a valuable addition to our stock! Oh! I *must* struggle to keep this situation, whatever it might be! both for my own honour among my friends, and for the solid services I might render them by my continuance there.

VII

HORTON LODGE

THE THIRTY-FIRST OF JANUARY WAS A wild, tempestuous day; there was a strong north wind, with a continual storm of snow drifting on the ground and whirling through the air. My friends would have had me delay my departure, but fearful of prejudicing my employers against me by such want of punctuality at the commencement of my undertaking, I persisted in keeping the appointment.

I will not inflict upon my readers an account of my leaving home on that dark winter morning, the fond farewells, the long, long journey to O–, the solitary waitings in inns for coaches or trains – for there were some railways then – and, finally, the meeting at O– with Mr Murray's servant, who had been sent with the phaeton to drive me from thence to Horton Lodge.

I will just state that the heavy snow had thrown such impediments in the way of both horses and steam-engines, that it was dark some hours before I reached my journey's end, and that a most bewildering storm came on at last, which made the few miles' space between O– and Horton Lodge a long and formidable passage. I sat resigned, with the cold, sharp snow drifting through my veil and filling my lap, seeing nothing, and wondering how the unfortunate horse and driver could make their way even as well as they did, and indeed it was but a toilsome, creeping style of progression, to say the best of it.

At length we paused; and, at the call of the driver, someone unlatched and rolled back upon their creaking hinges what appeared to be the park gates. Then we proceeded along a smoother road, whence, occasionally, I perceived some huge, hoary mass gleaming through the darkness, which I took to be a portion of a snow-clad tree.

After a considerable time, we paused again, before the stately portico of a large house with long windows descending to the ground.

I rose with some difficulty from under the superincumbent snowdrift, and alighted from the carriage, expecting a kind and hospitable reception would indemnify me for the toils and hardships of the day. A gentlemanly person in black opened the door, and admitted me into a spacious hall lighted by an amber-coloured lamp suspended from the ceiling; he led me through this, along a passage, and, opening the door of a back room, told me that was the school-room. I entered, and found two young ladies and two young gentlemen, my future pupils, I supposed. After a formal greeting, the elder girl, who was trifling over a piece of canvas and a basket of German wools,[1] asked if I should like to go upstairs.

I replied in the affirmative, of course.

'Matilda, take a candle, and show her her room,' said she.

Miss Matilda, a strapping hoyden[2] of about fourteen, with a short frock and trousers, shrugged her shoulders and made a slight grimace,[3] but took a candle and proceeded before me, up the back stairs, a long, steep, double flight, and through a long, narrow passage, to a small, but tolerably comfortable room. She then asked me if I would take some tea or coffee. I was about to answer no, but remembering that I had taken nothing since seven o'clock that morning, and feeling faint in consequence, I said I would take a cup of tea. Saying she would tell 'Brown,' the young lady departed; and by the time I had divested myself of my heavy, wet cloak, shawl, bonnet, etc., a mincing damsel came to say, the young ladies desired to know whether I would take my tea up there or in the school-room. Under the plea of fatigue, I chose to take it there. She withdrew; and after a while returned again with a small tea-tray, and placed it on the chest of drawers which served as a dressing-table. Having civilly thanked her, I asked at what time I should be expected to rise in the morning.

'The young ladies and gentlemen breakfast at half-past eight, ma'am,' said she; 'they rise early; but, as they seldom do any lessons before breakfast, I should think it would do if you rise soon after seven.'

I desired her to be so kind as to call me at seven; and, promising to do so, she withdrew. Then, having broken my long fast on a cup of tea and a little thin bread and butter, I sat down beside the small, smouldering fire, and amused myself with a hearty fit of crying; after which I said my prayers, and then, feeling considerably relieved, began to prepare for bed; but finding that none of my luggage was brought up, I instituted a search for the bell; and failing to discover any signs of such a convenience in any corner of the room, I took my candle and ventured through the long passage, and down the steep stairs, on a voyage of discovery. Meeting a well-dressed female on the way, I told her what I wanted, but not without considerable hesitation, as I was not quite sure whether it was one of the upper servants, or Mrs Murray herself. It happened, however, to be the lady's maid.

With the air of one conferring an unusual favour, she vouchsafed to undertake the sending up of my things; and when I had re-entered my room, and waited and wondered a long time greatly fearing that she had forgotten or neglected to perform her promise, and doubting whether to keep waiting, or go to bed, or go down again, my hopes, at length, were revived by the sound of voices and laughter, accompanied by a tramp of feet along the passage, and presently the luggage was brought in by a rough-looking maid and a man, neither of them very respectful in their demeanour to me.

Having shut the door upon their retiring footsteps and unpacked a few of my things, I, at length, betook myself to rest, gladly enough, for I was weary in body and mind.

It was with a strange feeling of desolation, mingled with a strong sense of the novelty of my situation, and a joyless kind of curiosity concerning what was yet unknown, that I awoke the next morning feeling like one whirled away by enchantment, and suddenly dropped from the clouds into a remote and unknown land, widely and completely isolated from all he had ever seen or known before; or like a thistle-seed borne on the wind to some strange nook of uncongenial soil, where it must lie long enough before it can take root and germinate, extracting nourishment from what appears so alien to its nature, if indeed it ever can; but this gives no proper idea of my feelings at all; and no one that has not lived such a retired, stationary life as mine, can possibly imagine what they were – hardly even if he has known what it is to awake some morning and find himself at Port Nelson, in New Zealand, with a world of waters between himself and all that knew him.

I shall not soon forget the peculiar feeling with which I raised my blind and looked out upon the unknown world – a wide, white wilderness was all that met my gaze, a waste of –

> Deserts tossed in snow,
> And heavy-laden groves.

I descended to the school-room with no remarkable eagerness to join my pupils, though not without some feeling of curiosity respecting what a further acquaintance would reveal. One thing, among others of more obvious importance, I determined with myself; I must begin with calling them Miss and Master. It seemed to me a chilling and unnatural piece of punctilio between the children of a family and their instructor and daily companion, especially where the former were in their early childhood, as at Wellwood House; but even there my calling the little Bloomfields by their simple names had been regarded as an offensive liberty, as their parents had taken care to show me, by carefully designating them *Master* and *Miss* Bloomfield, etc., in speaking to me. I had been very slow to take the hint, because the whole affair struck me as so very absurd; but now I determined to be wiser, and began at once with as much form and ceremony as any member of the family would be likely to require; and indeed, the children being so much older, there would be less difficulty; though the little words Miss and Master seemed to have a surprising effect in repressing all familiar, open-hearted kindness, and extinguishing every gleam of cordiality that might arise between us.

As I cannot, like Dogberry,[4] find it in my heart to bestow *all* my tediousness upon the reader, I will not go on to bore him with a minute detail of all the discoveries and proceedings of this and the following day. No doubt he will be amply satisfied with a slight sketch of the different members of the family, and a general view of the first year or two of my sojourn among them.

To begin with the head, Mr Murray was, by all accounts, a blustering, roystering,[5] country squire, a devoted fox-hunter, a skilful horse-jockey and farrier, an active, practical farmer, and a hearty *bon-vivant* – by all accounts, I say, for, except on Sundays, when he went to church, I never saw him from month to month, unless, in crossing the hall or walking in the grounds, the figure of a tall, stout gentleman with scarlet cheeks and crimson nose, happened to come across me; on which occasions, if he passed near enough to speak, an unceremonious nod, accompanied by a 'Morning, Miss Grey,' or some such brief salutation, was usually vouchsafed. Frequently, indeed, his loud laugh reached me from afar, and oftener still I heard him swearing and blaspheming against the footmen, groom, coachman, or some other hapless dependent.

Mrs Murray was a handsome, dashing lady of forty, who certainly required neither rouge nor padding to add to her charms, and whose chief enjoyments were, or seemed to be, in giving or frequenting parties, and in dressing at the very top of the fashion.

I did not see her till eleven o'clock on the morning after my arrival, when she honoured me with a visit, just as my mother might step into the kitchen to see a new servant girl – yet not so, either, for my mother would have seen her immediately after her arrival, and not waited till the next day; and, moreover, she would have addressed her in a more kind and friendly manner, and given her some words of comfort as well as a plain exposition of her duties; but Mrs Murray did neither the one nor the other. She just stepped into the school-room on her return from ordering dinner in the housekeeper's room, bid me good morning, stood for two minutes by the fire, said a few words about the weather, and the 'rather rough' journey I must have had yesterday, petted her youngest child – a boy of ten, who had just been wiping his mouth and hands on her gown, after indulging in some savoury morsel from the housekeeper's stores – told me what a sweet, good boy he was, and then sailed out, with a self-complacent smile upon her face, thinking, no doubt, that she had done quite enough for the present, and had been delightfully condescending into the bargain. Her children evidently held the same opinion, and I alone thought otherwise.

After this she looked in upon me once or twice, during the absence of my pupils, to enlighten me concerning my duties towards them. For the girls, she seemed anxious only to render them as superficially attractive and showily accomplished as they could possibly be made, without present trouble [or] discomfort to themselves;[6] and I was to act accordingly – to study and strive to amuse and oblige, instruct, refine, and polish, with the least possible exertion on their part, and no exercise of authority on mine. With regard to the two boys, it was much the same, only instead of accomplishments, I was to get the greatest possible quantity of Latin grammar and Valpy's Delectus[7] into their heads, in order to fit them for school – the greatest possible quantity, at least, *without* trouble to themselves. John might be a 'little high-spirited,' and Charles might be a little 'nervous and tedious –'

'But at all events, Miss Grey,' said she, 'I hope *you* will keep your temper, and be mild and patient throughout; especially with the dear little Charles, he is so extremely nervous and susceptible, and so utterly unaccustomed to anything but the tenderest treatment. You will excuse my naming these things to you; for the fact is, I have hitherto found all the governesses, even the very best of them, faulty in this particular. They wanted that meek and quiet spirit[8] which St Matthew, or some of them, says is better than the putting on of apparel – you will know the passage to which I allude, for you are a clergyman's daughter; but I have no doubt you will give satisfaction in this respect as well as the rest. And remember, on all occasions, when any of the young people do anything very improper, if persuasion and gentle remonstrance will not do, let one of the others come and tell me; for *I* can speak to them more plainly than it would be proper for you to do. And make them as happy as you can, Miss Grey, and I dare say you will do very well.'

I observed that while Mrs Murray was so extremely solicitous for the comfort and happiness of her children, and continually talking about it, she never once mentioned mine, though they were at home surrounded by friends, and I an alien among strangers; and I did not yet know enough of the world, not to be considerably surprised at this anomaly.

Miss Murray,[9] otherwise Rosalie, was about sixteen when I came, and decidedly a very pretty girl; and in two years longer, as time more completely developed her form, and added grace to her carriage and deportment, she was positively beautiful; and that in no common degree. She was tall and slender, but not thin, perfectly formed, exquisitely fair, but not without a brilliant, healthy bloom; her hair, which she wore in a profusion of long ringlets, was of a very light brown, strongly inclining to yellow, her eyes were pale blue, but so clear and bright that few would wish them darker, the rest of her features were small, but not quite regular, and not remarkably otherwise, but altogether you could not hesitate to pronounce her a very lovely girl. I wish I could say as much for her mind and disposition as I can for her form and face.

Yet think not I have any dreadful disclosures to make: she was lively, light-hearted, and could be very agreeable, with those who did not cross her will. Towards me, when I first came she was cold and haughty, then insolent and overbearing; but on a further acquaintance, she gradually laid aside her airs, and in time, became as deeply attached to me as it was possible for *her* to be to one of my character and position; for she seldom lost sight, for above half an hour at a time, of the fact of my being a hireling, and a poor curate's daughter; and yet, upon the whole, I believed she respected me more than she herself was aware of, because I was the only person in the house who steadily professed good principles, habitually spoke the truth, and generally endeavoured to make inclination bow to duty; and this I say, not of course in commendation of myself, but to show the unfortunate state of the family to which my services were, for the present, devoted. There was no member of it in whom I regretted this sad want of principle so much as Miss Murray herself; not only because she had taken a fancy to me, but because there was so much of what was pleasing and pre-possessing in herself, that, in spite of her failings, I really liked her – when she did not rouse my indignation, or ruffle my temper by *too* great a display of her faults, which, however, I would fain persuade myself, were rather the effect of her education than her disposition: she had never been properly taught the distinction between right and wrong; she had, like her brothers and sisters, been suffered from infancy to tyrannize over nurses, governesses, and servants; she had not been taught to moderate her desires, to control her temper or bridle her will, or to sacrific her own pleasure for the good of others; her temper being naturally good, she was never violent or morose, but from constant indulgence and habitual scorn of reason, she was often testy and capricious; her mind had never been cultivated: her intellect at best was somewhat shallow; she possessed considerable vivacity, some quickness of perception, and some talent for music and the acquisition of languages, but till fifteen she had troubled herself to acquire nothing; – then the love of display had roused her faculties, and induced her to apply herself, but only to the more showy accomplishments; and when I came, it was the same – everything was neglected but French, German, music, singing, dancing, fancy-work,[10] and a little drawing – such drawing as might produce the greatest show with the smallest labour, and the principal parts of which were generally done by me. For music and singing, besides my occasional instruction, she had the attendance of the best master the country afforded; and in them, as well as in dancing, she certainly attained great proficiency. To music, indeed, she devoted too much of her time, as, governess though I was, I frequently told her: but her mother thought that if *she* liked it, she *could* not give too much time to the acquisition of so attractive an accomplishment.

Of fancy-work I knew nothing but what I gathered from my pupil and my own observation; but no sooner was I initiated, than she made me useful in twenty different ways: all the tedious parts of her work were shifted on to my shoulders; such as stretching the frames, stitching in the canvas, sorting the wools and silks, putting in the grounds, counting the stitches, rectifying mistakes, and finishing the pieces she was tired of.

At sixteen, Miss Murray was something of a romp, yet not more so than is natural and allowable for a girl of that age; but at seventeen, that propensity, like all other things, began to give way to the ruling passion, and soon was swallowed up in the all-absorbing ambition to attract and dazzle the other sex. But enough of her: now let us turn to her sister.

Miss Matilda Murray was a veritable hoyden, of whom little need be said. She was about two years and a half younger than her sister; her features were larger, her complexion much darker. She might possibly make a handsome woman, but she was far too big-boned and awkward ever to be called a pretty girl, and, at present, she cared little about it. Rosalie knew all her charms, and thought them even greater than they were, and valued them more highly than she ought to have done, had they been three times as great; Matilda thought she was well enough, but cared little about the matter; still less did she care about the cultivation of her mind and the acquisition of ornamental accomplishments. The manner in which she learnt her lessons and practised her music was calculated to drive any governess to despair. Short and easy as her tasks were, if done at all, they were slurred over, at any time, and in any way, but generally in the way least beneficial to herself, and least satisfactory to me; and the short half-hour of practising was horribly strummed through; she, meantime, unsparingly abusing me, either for interrupting her with corrections, or for not rectifying her mistakes before they were made, or something equally unreasonable.

Once or twice, I ventured to remonstrate with her seriously for such irrational conduct; but, on each of these occasions, I received such reprehensive expostulations from her mother, as convinced me that, if I wished to keep the situation, I must even let Miss Matilda go on in her own way.

When her lessons were over, however, her ill-humour was generally over too; while riding her spirited pony, or romping with the dogs or her brothers and sister, but especially with her dear brother John, she was as happy as a lark.

As an animal, Matilda was all right, full of life, vigour, and activity; as an intelligent being, she was barbarously ignorant, indocile, careless, and irrational, and consequently very distressing to one who had the task of cultivating her understanding, reforming her manners, and aiding her to acquire those ornamental attainments which, unlike her sister, she despised as much as the rest: her mother was partly aware of her deficiencies, and gave me many a lecture as to how I should try to form her tastes, and endeavour to rouse and cherish her dormant vanity, and, by insinuating, skilful flattery, to win her attention to the desired objects – which I would not do – and how I should prepare and smooth the path of learning till she could glide along it without the least exertion to herself, which I could not, for nothing can be taught to any purpose without some little exertion on the part of the learner.

As a moral agent, she was reckless, headstrong, violent, and unamenable to reason. One proof of the deplorable state of her mind was that, from her father's example, she had learnt to swear like a trooper.

Her mother was greatly shocked at the 'unlady-like trick,' and wondered 'how she had picked it up.'

'But you can soon break her of it, Miss Grey,' said she; 'it is only a habit; and if you will just gently remind her every time she does so, I am sure she will soon lay it aside.'

I not only 'gently reminded' her, I tried to impress upon her how wrong it was, and how distressing to the ears of decent people; but all in vain, I was only answered by a careless laugh, and –

'Oh, Miss Grey, how shocked you are! I'm so glad!'

Or –

'Well! I can't help it; papa shouldn't have taught me: I learnt it all from him; and may be a bit from the coachman.'

Her brother John, *alias* Master Murray, was about eleven when I came, a fine, stout, healthy boy, frank and good-natured in the main, and might have been a decent lad, had he been properly educated, but now he was as rough as a young bear, boisterous, unruly, unprincipled, untaught, unteachable – at least for a governess under his mother's eye; his masters at school might be able to manage him better – for to school he was sent, greatly to my relief, in the course of a year; in a state, it is true, of scandalous ignorance as to Latin, as well as the more useful, though more neglected things; and this, doubtless would all be laid to the account of his education having been entrusted to an ignorant female teacher, who had presumed to take in hand what she was wholly incompetent to perform. I was not delivered from his brother till full twelve months after, when he also was despatched in the same state of disgraceful ignorance as the former.

Master Charles was his mother's peculiar darling. He was a little more than a year younger than John, but much smaller, paler, and less active and robust; a pettish, cowardly, capricious, selfish little fellow, only active in doing mischief, and only clever in inventing falsehoods, not simply to hide his faults, but, in mere malicious wantonness, to bring odium upon others; in fact, Master Charles was a very great nuisance to me: it was a trial of patience to live with him peaceably; to watch over him was worse; and to teach him, or pretend to teach him, was inconceivable.

At ten years old, he could not read, correctly, the easiest line in the simplest book; and as, according to his mother's principle, he was to be told every word, before he had time to hesitate or examine its orthography, and never even to be informed, as a stimulant to exertion, that other boys were more forward than he, it is not surprising that he made but little progress during the two years I had charge of his education.

His minute portions of Latin grammar, etc., were to be repeated over to him, till he chose to say he knew them; and then, he was to be helped to say them: if he made mistakes in his little easy sums in arithmetic, they were to be shewn him at once, and the sum done for him, instead of his being left to exercise his faculties in finding them out himself; so that, of course, he took no pains to avoid mistakes, but frequently set down his figures at random without any calculation at all.

Yet I did not invariably confine myself to these rules; it was against my conscience to do so; but I seldom could venture[11] to deviate from them in the slightest degree, without incurring the wrath of my little pupil, and subsequently of his mamma, to whom he would relate my transgressions, maliciously exaggerated, or adorned with embellishments of his own; and often, in consequence, was I on the point of losing or resigning my situation; but for their sakes at home, I smothered my pride and suppressed my indignation, and managed to struggle on till my little tormentor was despatched to school, his father declaring that home education was 'no go' for him, it was plain; his mother spoiled him outrageously, and his governess could make no hand of him at all.

A few more observations about Horton Lodge and its ongoings, and I have done with dry description for the present.

The house was a very respectable one, superior to Mr Bloomfield's both in age, size, and magnificence: the garden was not so tastefully laid out; but instead of smooth-shaven lawn, the young trees guarded by palings, the grove of upstart poplars and the plantation of firs, there was a wide park, stocked with deer, and beautified by fine old trees. The surrounding country itself was pleasant, as far as fertile fields, flourishing trees, quiet green lanes, and smiling hedges, with wild flowers scattered along their banks, could make it; but it was depressingly flat to one born and nurtured among the rugged hills of –.

We were situated nearly two miles from the village church, and, consequently, the family carriage was put in requisition every Sunday morning, and sometimes oftener.

Mr and Mrs Murray generally thought it sufficient to show themselves at church once in the course of the day; but frequently the children preferred going a second time to wandering about the grounds all the day with nothing to do.

If some of my pupils chose to walk and take me with them, it was well for me; otherwise, my position in the carriage was to be crushed into the corner farthest from the open window, and with my back to the horses, a position which invariably made me sick; and, if I were not actually obliged to leave the church in the middle of the service, my devotions were disturbed with a feeling of languor and sickliness, and the tormenting fear of its becoming worse; and a depressing head-ache was generally my companion throughout the day, which would otherwise have been one of welcome rest, and holy, calm enjoyment.

'It's very odd, Miss Grey, that the carriage should always make you sick; it never makes *me*,' remarked Miss Matilda.

'Nor me either,' said her sister, 'but I dare say it would, if I sat where she does – such a nasty, horrid place, Miss Grey; I wonder how you can bear it!'

I am obliged to bear it, since no choice is left me – I might have answered; but in tenderness for their feelings, I only replied –

'Oh! it is but a short way, and if I am not sick in church, I don't mind it.'

If I were called upon to give a description of the usual divisions and arrangements of the day, I should find it a very difficult matter. I had all my meals in the school-room with my pupils, at such times as suited their fancy: sometimes they would ring for dinner before it was half-cooked; sometimes they would keep it waiting on the table for above an hour, and then be out of humour because the potatoes were cold, and the gravy covered with cakes of solid fat; sometimes they would have tea at four; frequently, they would storm at the servants because it was not in precisely at five, and when these orders were obeyed, by way of encouragement to punctuality, they would keep it on the table till seven or eight.

The hours of study were managed in much the same way: my judgment or convenience was never once consulted. Sometimes Matilda and John would determine 'to get all the plaguy business over before breakfast,' and send the maid to call me up at half-past five, without any scruple or apology; sometimes, I was told to be ready precisely at six, and, having dressed in a hurry, came down to an empty room and after waiting a long time in suspense, discovered that they had changed their minds, and were still in bed; or, perhaps, if it were a fine summer morning, Brown would come to tell me that the young ladies and gentlemen had taken a holiday, and were gone out; and then, I was kept waiting for breakfast, till I was almost ready to faint;

they having fortified themselves with something before they went.

Often they would do their lessons in the open air, which I had nothing to say against, except that I frequently caught cold by sitting on the damp grass, or from exposure to the evening dew, or some such insidious draught, which seemed to have no injurious effect on them. It was quite right that they should be hardy; yet, surely, they might have been taught some consideration for others who were less so. But I must not blame them for what was, perhaps, my own fault; for I never made any particular objections to sitting where they pleased, foolishly choosing to risk the consequences, rather than trouble them for my convenience.

Their indecorous manner of doing their lessons was quite as remarkable as the caprice displayed in their choice of time and place. While receiving my instructions, or repeating what they had learnt, they would lounge upon the sofa, lie on the rug, stretch, yawn, talk to each other, or look out of the window; whereas, I could not so much as stir the fire, or pick up the handkerchief I had dropped, without being rebuked for inattention by one of my pupils, or told that 'mamma would not like me to be so careless.'

The servants, seeing in what little estimation the governess was held by both parents and children, regulated their behaviour by the same standard.

I have frequently stood up for *them*, at the risk of some injury to myself, against the tyranny and injustice of their young masters and mistresses; and I always endeavoured to give them as little trouble as possible; but they entirely neglected my comfort, despised my requests, and slighted my directions. All servants, I am convinced, would not have done so; but the domestics in general, being ignorant and little accustomed to reason and reflection, are too easily corrupted by the carelessness and bad example of those above them; and these, I think, were not of the best order to begin with.

I sometimes felt myself degraded by the life I led, and ashamed of submitting to so many indignities; and sometimes, I thought myself a precious fool for caring so much about them, and feared I must be sadly wanting in Christian humility, or that charity which suffereth long and is kind, seeketh not her own, is not easily provoked, beareth all things, endureth all things.[12]

But, with time and patience, matters began to be slightly ameliorated, slowly, it is true, and almost imperceptibly; but I got rid of my male pupils (that was no trifling advantage), and the girls, as I intimated before concerning one of them, became a little less insolent, and began to show some symptoms of esteem.

Miss Grey was a queer creature; she never flattered, and did not praise them half enough, but whenever she did speak favourably of them, or anything belonging to them, they could be quite sure her approbation was sincere.

She was very obliging, quiet, and peaceable in the main, but there were some things that put her out of temper; they did not much care for that, to be sure, but still, it was better to keep her in tune, as when she was in a good humour, she would talk to them, and be very agreeable and amusing sometimes, in her way, which was quite different from mamma's, but still very well for a change. She had her own opinions on every subject, and kept steadily to them – very tiresome opinions they often were, as she was always thinking of what was right and what was wrong, and had a strange reverence for matters connected with religion, and an unaccountable liking to good people.

VIII

THE 'COMING OUT'

AT EIGHTEEN, MISS MURRAY was to emerge from the quiet obscurity of the school-room into the full blaze of the fashionable world – as much of it, at least, as could be had out of London, for her papa could not be persuaded to leave his rural pleasures and pursuiits, even for a few weeks' residence in town.

She was to make her debut[1] on the third of January, at a magnificent ball, which her mamma proposed to give to all nobility and choice gentry of O– and its neighbourhood for twenty miles round. Of course, she looked forward to it with the wildest impatience, and the most extravagant anticipations of delight.

'Miss Grey,' said she, one evening, a month before the all-important day – as I was perusing a long and extremely interesting letter of my sister's which I had just glanced at in the morning to see that it contained no very bad news, and kept till now, unable before to find a quiet moment for reading it. 'Miss Grey, do put away that dull, stupid letter, and listen to me! I'm sure my talk must be far more amusing than that.'

She seated herself on the low stool at my feet; and I, suppressing a sigh of vexation, began to fold up the epistle.

'You should tell the good people at home not to bore you with such long letters,' said she; 'and above all, do bid them to write on proper note-paper, and not on those great vulgar sheets! You should see the charming little lady-like notes mamma writes to her friends.'

'The good people at home,' replied I, 'know very well that the longer their letters are, the better I like them. I should be very sorry to receive a charming little lady-like note from any of them; and I thought you were too much of a lady yourself, Miss

Murray, to talk about the "vulgarity" of writing on a large sheet of paper.'

'Well, I only said it to tease you. But now I want to talk about the ball; and to tell you that you positively must put off your holidays till it is over.'

'Why so? – I shall not be present at the ball.'

'No, but you will see the rooms decked out before it begins, and hear the music, and, above all, see me in my splendid new dress! I shall be so charming, you'll be ready to worship me – you really must stay.'

'I should like to see you very much; but I shall have many opportunities of seeing you equally charming, on the occasion of some of the numberless balls and parties that are to be, and I cannot disappoint my friends by postponing my return so long.'

'Oh, never mind your friends! Tell them we won't let you go.'

'But to say the truth, it would be a disappointment to myself: I long to see them as much as they to see me – perhaps more.'

'Well, but it is such a short time.'

'Nearly a fortnight by my computation; and, besides, I cannot bear the thoughts of a Christmas spent from home; and, moreover, my sister is going to be married.'

'Is she – when?'

'Not till next month; but I want to be there to assist her in making preparations, and to make the best of her company while we have her.'

'Why didn't you tell me before?'

'I've only got the news in this letter, which you stigmatize as dull and stupid, and won't let me read.'

'Who is she to be married to?'

'To Mr Richardson, the vicar of a neighbouring parish.'

'Is he rich?'

'No, – only comfortable.'

'Is he handsome?'

'No, – only decent.'

'Young?'

'No, – only middling.'

'O mercy! what a wretch! What sort of a house is it?'

'A quiet little vicarage, with an ivy-clad porch, an old-fashioned garden, and –'

'O stop! – you'll make me sick. How *can* she bear it?'

'I expect she'll not only be able to bear it, but to be very happy. You did not ask me if Mr Richardson were a good, wise, or amiable man; I could have answered yes to all these questions – at least so Mary thinks, and I hope she will not find herself mistaken.'

'But – miserable creature! how can she think of spending her life there, cooped up with that nasty old man; and *no* hope of change?'

'He is not old; he is only six or seven-and-thirty; and she herself is twenty-eight, and as sober as if she were fifty.'

'Oh! that's better then – they're well matched; but do they call him the "worthy vicar"?'

'I don't know; but if they do, I believe he merits the epithet.'

'Mercy, how shocking! and will she wear a white apron, and make pies and puddings?'

'I don't know about the white apron, but I dare say, she will make pies and puddings, now and then; but that will be no great hardship, as she has done it before.'

'And will she go about in a plain shawl, and a large straw bonnet, carrying tracts and bone soup to her husband's poor parishioners?'

'I'm not clear about that, but I dare say she will do her best to make them comfortable in body and mind, in accordance with our mother's example.'

IX

THE BALL

'NOW MISS GREY,' EXCLAIMED Miss Murray, immediately I entered the school-room, after having taken off my out-door garments, upon returning from my four weeks' recreation, 'Now shut the door, and sit down, and I'll tell you all about the ball.'

'No, – d– it, no!' shouted Miss Matilda. 'Hold your tongue, can't ye! and let me tell her about my new mare – *such* a splendour, Miss Grey! a fine blood mare –'

'Do be quiet, Matilda; and let me tell my news first.'

'No, no, Rosalie! you'll be such a d– long time over it – she *shall* hear me first – I'll be hanged if she doesn't!'

'I'm sorry to hear, Miss Matilda, that you've not got rid of that shocking habit yet.'

'Well I can't help it; but I'll never say a wicked word again, if you'll only listen to me, and tell Rosalie to hold her confounded tongue.'

Rosalie remonstrated, and I thought I should have been torn in pieces between them; but, Miss Matilda having the loudest voice, her sister at length gave in, and suffered her to tell her story first: so I was doomed to hear a long account of her splendid mare, its breeding and pedigree, its paces, its action, its spirit, etc., and of her own amazing skill and courage in riding it, concluding with an assertion that she could clear a five-barred gate 'like winking', that papa said she might hunt next time the hounds met, and mamma had ordered a bright scarlet hunting-habit for her.

'Oh, Matilda! what stories you are telling!' exclaimed her sister.

'Well,' answered she, no whit abashed, 'I know I *could* clear a five-barred gate, if I tried, and papa *will* say I may hunt, and mamma *will* order the habit when I ask it.'

'Well, now get along,' replied Miss Murray; 'and do, dear Matilda, try to be a little more lady-like. Miss Grey, I wish you *would* tell her not to use such shocking words; she *will* call her horse a mare;[1] it is so *inconceivably* shocking! and then she uses such dreadful expressions in describing it: she *must* have learnt it from the grooms. It nearly puts me into fits when she begins.'

'I learnt it from papa, you ass! and his jolly friends,' said the young lady, vigorously cracking a hunting-whip, which she habitually carried in her hand. 'I'm as good a judge of horse flesh as the best of 'em.'

'Well now get along, you shocking girl: I really shall take a fit if you go on in such a way. And now, Miss Grey, attend to me; I'm going to tell you about the ball. You must be dying to hear about it, I know. Oh, *such* a ball! You never saw or heard, or read, or dreamt of anything like it in all your life! The decorations, the entertainment, the supper, the music, were indescribable! and then the guests! There were two noblemen, three baronets, and five titled ladies! – and other ladies and gentlemen innumerable. The ladies, of course, were of no consequence to me, except to put me in a good humour with myself, by showing how ugly and awkward most of them were; and the best, mamma told me, – the most transcendent beauties among them, were nothing to me. As for *me*, Miss Grey – I'm so *sorry* you didn't see me! I was *charming* – wasn't I, Matilda?'

'Middling.'

'No, but I really *was* – at least so mamma said . . . and Brown and Williamson. Brown said she was sure no gentleman could set eyes on me without falling in love that minute; and so I may be allowed to be a little vain. I know you think me a shocking, conceited, frivolous girl, but then, you know, I don't attribute it *all* to my personal attractions: I give some praise to the hairdresser, and some to my exquisitely lovely dress – you must see it to-morrow – white gauze over pink satin . . . and so *sweetly* made! and a necklace and bracelet of beautiful, large pearls!'

'I have no doubt you looked very charming; but should that delight you so *very* much?'

'Oh, no! – not that alone: but then, I was so much admired; and I made so *many* conquests in that one night – you'd be astonished to hear –'

'But what good will they do you?'

'What good? Think of any woman asking that!'

'Well, I should think one conquest would be enough, and too much, unless the subjugation were mutual.'

'Oh, but you know I never agree with you on those points. Now wait a bit, and I'll tell you my principal admirers – those who made themselves very conspicuous on that night and after, for I've been to two parties since. Unfortunately the two noblemen, Lord G– and Lord F–, were married, or I might have condescended to be particularly gracious to *them*; as it was, I did not, though Lord F–, who hates his wife, was evidently much struck with me. He asked me to dance with him twice – he is a charming dancer, by-the-bye, and so am I ... you can't think how well I did ... I was astonished at myself. My lord was very complimentary too – rather too much so in fact, and I thought proper to be a little haughty and repellent; but I had the pleasure of seeing his nasty, cross wife ready to perish with spite and vexation –'

'Oh Miss Murray! you don't mean to say that such a thing could really give you pleasure! However such cross or –'

'Well I know it's very wrong; – but never mind! I mean to be good sometime – only don't preach now, there's a good creature – I haven't told you half yet ... Let me see ... Oh! I was going to tell you how many unmistakable admirers I had: – Sir Thomas Ashby was one, – Sir Hugh Meltham and Sir Broadley Wilson are old codgers, only fit companions for papa and mamma. Sir Thomas is young, rich, and gay, but an ugly beast nevertheless: however, mamma says I should not mind that after a few months' acquaintance. Then, there was Harry Meltham, Sir Hugh's younger son, rather good-looking, and a pleasant fellow to flirt with; but *being* a younger son, that is all he is good for: then there was young Mr Green, rich enough, but of no family, and a great stupid fellow, a mere country booby; and then, our good Rector, Mr Hatfield, an *humble* admirer, he ought to consider himself; but I fear he has forgotten to number humility among his stock of Christian virtues.'

'Was Mr Hatfield at the ball?'

'Yes, to be sure. Did you think he was too good to go?'

'I thought he might consider it unclerical.'

'By *no* means. He did not profane his cloth by dancing; but it was with difficulty he could refrain, poor man: he looked as if he were dying to ask my hand just for *one* set; and – Oh! by-the-bye – he's got a new curate . . . that seedy old fellow Mr Bligh has got his long-wished-for living at last, and gone.'

'And what is the new one like?'

'Oh – *such* a beast! Weston his name is. I can give you his description in three words . . . an insensate, ugly, stupid block-head. That's four, but no matter . . . enough of *him* now.'

Then she returned to the ball, and gave me a further account of her deportment there, and at the several parties she had since attended, and further particulars respecting Sir Thomas Ashby, and Messrs Meltham, Green and Hatfield, and the ineffaceable impression she had wrought upon each of them.

'Well, which of the four do you like best?' said I, suppressing my third or fourth yawn.

'I detest them all,' replied she, shaking her bright ringlets in vivacious scorn.

'That means, I suppose, I like them all – but which most?'

'No, I really do detest them all; but Harry Meltham is the handsomest and most amusing, and Mr Hatfield the cleverest, Sir Thomas the wickedest, and Mr Green the most stupid. But the one I'm to have, I suppose, if I'm doomed to have any of them, is Sir Thomas Ashby.'

'Surely not, if he is so wicked, and if you dislike him?'

'Oh, I don't mind his being wicked; he's all the better for that; and as for disliking him – I shouldn't greatly object to being Lady Ashby of Ashby Park, if I must marry; but if I could be always young, I would be always single. I should like to enjoy myself thoroughly, and coquet with all the world, till I am on the verge of being called an old maid; and then, to escape the infamy of that, after having made ten thousand conquests, to break all their hearts save one, by marrying some high-born, rich, indulgent husband, whom, on the other hand, fifty ladies were dying to have.'

'Well, as long as you entertain those views, keep single by all means, and never marry at all, not even to escape the infamy of old-maidenhood.'

X
THE CHURCH

'WELL, MISS GREY, WHAT do you think of the new curate?' asked Miss Murray, on our return from church the Sunday after the re-commencement of my duties.

'I can scarcely tell,' was my reply: 'I have not even heard him preach.'

'Well, but you saw him, didn't you?'

'Yes; but I cannot pretend to judge a man's character by a single, cursory glance at his face.'

'But *isn't* he ugly?'

'He did not strike me as being particularly so; I don't dislike that cast of countenance: but the only thing I particularly noticed about him was his style of reading, which appeared, to me, good – infinitely better, at least, than Mr Hatfield's. He read the lessons as if he were bent on giving full effect to every passage: it seems as if the most careless person could not have helped attending, nor the most ignorant have failed to understand; and the prayers, he read as if he were not reading at all, but praying earnestly and sincerely from his own heart.'

'Oh, yes! that's all he is good for: he can plod through the service well enough; but he has not a single idea beyond it.'

'How do you know?'

'Oh! I know perfectly well; I'm an excellent judge in such matters. Did you see how he went out of church? stumping along, as if there were nobody there but himself – never looking to the right hand or the left, and evidently thinking of nothing but just getting out of the church, and perhaps, home to his dinner – his great stupid head could contain no other idea.'

'I suppose you would have had him cast a glance into the squire's pew,' said I, laughing at the vehemence of her hostility.

'Indeed! I should have been highly indignant if he had dared to do such a thing!' replied she, haughtily tossing her head; then, after a moment's reflection, she added – 'Well, well! I suppose he's good enough for his place; but I'm glad I'm not dependent on *him* for amusement – that's all. Did you see how Mr Hatfield hurried out to get a bow from me, and be in time to put us into the carriage?'

'Yes,' answered I, internally adding, 'and I thought it some-what derogatory to his dignity as a clergyman to come flying from the pulpit in such eager haste to shake hands with the squire, and hand his wife and daughters into their carriage; and, moreover, I owe him a grudge for nearly shutting me out of it;' for, in fact, though I was standing before his face, close beside the carriage steps, waiting to get in, he would persist in putting them up and closing the door, till one of the family stopped him by calling out that the governess was not in yet: then, without a word of apology, he departed, wishing them good morning, and leaving the footman to finish the business. *Nota bene*[1] – Mr Hatfield never spoke to me, neither did Sir Hugh or Lady Mel-tham, nor Mr Harry or Miss Meltham, nor Mr Green or his sisters, nor any other lady or gentleman who frequented that church, nor, in fact, any one that visited at Horton Lodge.

Miss Murray ordered the carriage again, in the afternoon, for herself and her sister: she said it was too cold for them to enjoy themselves in the garden; and besides, she believed Harry Mel-tham would be at church.

'For,' said she, smiling slyly at her own fair image in the glass, 'he has been a most exemplary attendant at church these last few Sundays. You would think he was quite a good Christian. And you may go with us, Miss Grey, I want you to see him; he is so greatly improved since he returned from abroad – you can't think! And besides, then you will have an opportunity of seeing the beautiful Mr Weston again, and of hearing him preach.'

I did hear him preach, and was decidedly pleased with the evangelical truth of his doctrine, as well as the earnest simplicity of his manner, and the clearness and force of his style.

It was truly refreshing to hear such a sermon, after being so

long accustomed to the dry, prosy discourses of the former
curate, and the still less edifying harangues of the rector, who
would come sailing up the aisle, or rather sweeping along like a
whirlwind, with his rich silk gown flying behind him and rustling
against the pew doors, mount the pulpit like a conqueror ascend-
ing his triumphal car; then, sinking on the velvet cushion in an
attitude of studied grace, remain in silent prostration[2] for a
certain time, then mutter over a Collect, and gabble through the
Lord's Prayer, rise, draw off one bright lavender glove to give
the congregation the benefit of his sparkling rings, lightly pass
his fingers through his well-curled hair, flourish a cambric handkerchief, recite a very short passage, or, perhaps, a mere phrase
of Scripture, as a head-piece to his discourse, and, finally, deliver
a composition which, as a composition, might be considered
good, though far too studied and too artificial to be pleasing to
me; the propositions were well laid down, the arguments logically conducted; and yet, it was sometimes hard to listen quietly
throughout, without some slight demonstrations of disapproval
or impatience.

His favourite subjects were Church discipline,[3] rites and
ceremonies, apostolical succession, the duty of reverence and
obedience to the clergy, the atrocious criminality of Dissent, the
absolute necessity of observing all the forms of godliness, the
reprehensible presumption of individuals who attempted to think
for themselves in matters connected with religion, or to be guided
by their own interpretations of Scripture, and occasionally (to
please his wealthy parishioners) the necessity of deferential
obedience from the poor to the rich – supporting his maxims and
exhortations throughout with quotations from the Fathers, with
whom he appeared to be far better acquainted than with the
Apostles and Evangelists, and whose importance he seemed to
consider at least equal to theirs.

But now and then he gave us a sermon of a different order –
what some would call a very good one, but sunless and severe,
representing the Deity as a terrible task-master, rather than a
benevolent father. Yet, as I listened, I felt inclined to think the
man was sincere in all he said; he must have changed his views,

and become decidedly religious, gloomy and austere, yet still devout: but such illusions were usually dissipated, on coming out of church, by hearing his voice in a jocund colloquy with some of the Melthams or Greens, or, perhaps, the Murrays themselves, probably laughing at his own sermon, and hoping that he had given the rascally people something to think about; perchance, exulting in the thought[4] that old Betty Holmes would now lay aside the sinful indulgence of her pipe, which had been her daily solace for upwards of thirty years, that George Higgins would be frightened out of his Sabbath evening walks, and Thomas Jackson would be sorely troubled in his conscience, and shaken in his sure and certain hope of a joyful resurrection at the last day.

Thus, I could not but conclude that Mr Hatfield was one of those who bind heavy burdens, and grievous to be borne, and lay them upon men's shoulders, while they themselves will not move them with one of their fingers,[5] and that make the word of God of none effect by their traditions, teaching for doctrines the commandments of men.[6] I was well pleased to observe that the new curate resembled him, as far as I could see, in none of these particulars.

'Well, Miss Grey! what do you think of him now?' said Miss Murray, as we took our places in the carriage after service.

'No harm still,' replied I.

'No harm!' repeated she, in amazement. 'What do you mean?'

'I mean, I think no worse of him than I did before.'

'No worse! I should think not indeed – quite the contrary! Is he not greatly improved?'

'Oh, yes! very much indeed,' replied I; for I had now discovered that it was Harry Meltham she meant, not Mr Weston. That gentleman had eagerly come forward to speak to the young ladies, a thing he would hardly have ventured to do had their mother been present; he had likewise politely handed them into the carriage – he had not attempted to shut me out like Mr Hatfield; neither, of course, had he offered me his assistance (I should not have accepted it, if he had), but as long as the door had remained open he had stood smirking and chatting with

them, and then lifted his hat and departed to his own abode; –
but I had scarcely noticed him all the time. My companions,
however, had been more observant; and, as we rolled along,
they discussed between them not only his looks, words, and
actions, but every feature of his face, and every article of his
apparel.

'You shan't have him all to yourself, Rosalie,' said Miss
Matilda, at the close of the discussion; 'I like him: I know he'd
make a nice, jolly companion for me.'

'Well, you're quite welcome to him, Matilda,' replied her
sister, in a tone of affected indifference.

'And I'm sure,' continued the other, 'he admires me quite as
much as he does you – doesn't he, Miss Grey?'

'I don't know; I'm not acquainted with his sentiments.'

'Well, but he *does* though!'

'My *dear* Matilda! nobody will ever admire you till you get
rid of your rough, awkward manners.'

'Oh stuff! Harry Meltham likes such manners; and so do
papa's friends.'

'Well, you *may* captivate old men, and younger sons; but
nobody else, I'm sure, will ever take a fancy to you.'

'I don't care: I'm not always grubbing after money, like you
and mamma. If my husband is able to keep a few good horses
and dogs, I shall be quite satisfied; and all the rest may go to the
devil!'

'Well, if you use such shocking expressions, I'm sure no real
gentleman will ever venture to come near you – really, Miss
Grey, you should not let her do so!'

'I can't possibly prevent it, Miss Murray.'

'And you're quite mistaken, Matilda, in supposing that Harry
Meltham admires you: I assure you he does nothing of the kind.'

Matilda was beginning an angry reply; but, happily, our journey was now at an end; and the contention was cut short by the
footman's opening the carriage door, and letting down the steps
for our descent.

XI

THE COTTAGERS

As I had now only one regular pupil – though she contrived to give me as much trouble as three or four ordinary ones, and though her sister still took lessons in German and drawing – I had considerably more time at my own disposal than I had ever been blessed with before, since I had taken upon me the governess's yoke; which time I devoted partly to correspondence with my friends, partly to reading, study, and the practice of music, singing, etc., partly to wandering in the grounds or adjacent fields, with my pupils, if they wanted me, alone if they did not.

Often, when they had no more agreeable occupation at hand, the Misses Murray would amuse themselves with visiting the poor cottagers on their father's estate,[1] to receive their flattering homage, or to hear the old stories, or gossiping news of the garrulous old women; or, perhaps, to enjoy the purer pleasure of making the poor people happy with their cheering presence and their occasional gifts, so easily bestowed, so thankfully received. Sometimes, I was called upon to accompany one or both of the sisters in these visits; and, sometimes, I was desired to go alone, to fulfil some promise which they had been more ready to make than to perform, to carry some small donation, or read to one who was sick, or seriously disposed: and thus I made a few acquaintances among the cottagers; and, occasionally, I went to see them on my own account.

I generally had more satisfaction in going alone than with either of the young ladies, for they, chiefly owing to their defective education, comported themselves towards their inferiors in a manner that was highly disagreeable for me to witness. They never in thought exchanged places with them;

and consequently had no consideration for their feelings, regarding them as an order of beings entirely distinct from themselves.

They would watch the poor creatures at their meals, making uncivil remarks about their food, and their manner of eating; they would laugh at their simple notions and provincial expressions, till some of them scarcely durst venture to speak; they would call the grave, elderly men and women old fools and silly old blockheads to their faces; and all this without meaning to offend.

I could see that the people were often hurt and annoyed by such conduct, though their fear of the 'grand ladies' prevented them from testifying any resentment; but *they* never perceived it. They thought that, as these cottagers were poor and untaught, they must be stupid and brutish; and as long as they, their superiors, condescended to talk to them, and to give them shillings and half-crowns, or articles of clothing, they had a right to amuse themselves, even at their expense; and the people must adore them as angels of light condescending to minister to their necessities, and enlighten their humble dwellings.

I made many and various attempts to deliver my pupils from these delusive notions without alarming their pride, which was easily offended, and not soon appeased, but with little apparent result; and I know not which was the more reprehensible of the two: Matilda was more rude and boisterous; but from Rosalie's womanly age and lady-like exterior better things were expected: yet she was as provokingly careless and inconsiderate as a giddy child of twelve.

One bright day in the last week of February, I was walking in the park, enjoying the threefold luxury of solitude, a book, and pleasant weather, for Miss Matilda had set out on her daily ride, and Miss Murray was gone in the carriage with her mamma to pay some morning calls. But it struck me that I ought to leave these selfish pleasures, and the park with its glorious canopy of bright blue sky, the west wind sounding through its yet leafless branches, the snow-wreaths still lingering in its hollows, but melting fast beneath the sun, and the graceful deer browsing on its moist herbage, already assuming the freshness and verdure of spring . . . and go to the cottage of one Nancy Brown, a widow, whose son was at work all day in the fields, and who was afflicted with an inflammation in the eyes which had, for some time, incapacitated her from reading, to her own grief, for she was a woman of a serious, thoughtful turn of mind.

I accordingly went, and found her alone, as usual, in her little, close, dark cottage, redolent of smoke and confined air, but as tidy and clean as she could make it. She was seated beside her little fire (consisting of a few red cinders and a bit of stick), busily knitting, with a small sackcloth cushion at her feet, placed for the accommodation of her gentle friend the cat, who was seated thereon with her long tail half encircling her velvet paws, and her half-closed eyes dreamingly gazing on the low, crooked fender.

'Well, Nancy, how are you to-day?'

'Why, middling, miss, i' myseln – my eyes is no better, but I'm a deal easier i' my mind nor I have been,' replied she, rising to welcome me with a contented smile, which I was glad to see, for Nancy had been somewhat afflicted with religious melancholy.[2]

I congratulated her upon the change. She agreed that it was a great blessing, and expressed herself 'right down thankful for it,' adding, 'If it please God to spare my sight, and make me so as I can read my Bible again, I think I shall be as happy as a queen.'

'I hope he will, Nancy,' replied I; 'and, meantime, I'll come and read to you now and then when I have a little time to spare.'

With expressions of grateful pleasure, the poor woman moved to get me a chair; but, as I saved her the trouble, she busied herself with stirring the fire, and adding a few more sticks to the decaying embers; and then, taking her well-used Bible from the shelf, dusted it carefully, and gave it to me. On my asking if there was any particular part she would like me to read, she answered –

'Well, Miss Grey, if it's all the same to you, I'd like to hear that chapter in the First Epistle of St John, that says, "God is love, and he that dwelleth in love dwelleth in God, and God in him."'

With a little searching, I found these words in the fourth chapter. When I came to the seventh verse[3] she interrupted me, and, with needless apologies for such a liberty, desired me to read it very slowly, that she might take it all in, and dwell on every word; hoping I would excuse her, as she was but a 'simple body.'

'The wisest person,' I replied, 'might think over each of these verses for an hour, and be all the better for it; and I would rather read them slowly than not.'

Accordingly, I finished the chapter as slowly as need be, and at the same time as impressively as I could. My auditor listened most attentively all the while, and sincerely thanked me when I had done. I sat still about half a minute to give her time to reflect upon it; when, somewhat to my surprise, she broke the pause by asking me how I liked Mr Weston.

'I don't know,' I replied, a little startled by the suddenness of the question; 'I think he preaches very well.'

'Ay, he does so; and talks well too!'

'Does he?'

'He does. Maybe, you haven't seen him – not to talk to much, yet?'

'No, I never see any one to talk to – except the young ladies of the Hall.'

'Ah; they're nice, kind young ladies; but they can't talk as he does!'

'Then he comes to see you, Nancy?'

'He does, miss; and I'se thankful for it. He comes to see all us poor bodies a deal ofter nor Maister Bligh, or th' Rector ever did; an' it's well he does, for he's always welcome, and we can't say as much for th' Rector – there is 'at says they're fair feared on him. When he comes into a house, they say he's sure to find summut wrong, and begin a calling 'em as soon as he crosses th' doorstuns: but may-be, he thinks it his duty like to tell 'em what's wrong; and very oft he comes o' purpose to reprove folk for not coming to church, or not kneeling an' standing when other folks does, or going to th' Methody chapel, or summut o' that sort; but I can't say 'at he ever fund much fault wi' me. He came to see me once or twice, afore Maister Weston come, when I was so ill troubled in my mind; and as I had only very poor health besides, I made bold to send for him – and he came right enough. I was sore distressed, Miss Grey – thank God it's owered now – but when I took my Bible, I could get no comfort of it at all. That very chapter 'at you've just been reading troubled me as much as aught –⁴ "He that loveth not, knoweth not God."⁵ It seemed fearsome to me; for I felt that I loved neither God nor man as I should do, and could not, if I tried ever so. And th' chapter afore, where it says, "He that is born of God cannot commit sin." And another place where it says, "Love is the fulfilling of the Law." And many – many others, miss; I should fair weary you out, if I was to tell them all. But all seemed to condemn me, and to show me 'at I was not in the right way; and as I knew not how to get into it, I sent our Bill to beg Maister Hatfield to be as kind as look in on me some day; and when he came, I told him all my troubles.'

'And what did he say, Nancy?'

'Why miss, he like seemed to scorn me. I might be mista'en – but he like gave a sort of a whistle, and I saw a bit of a smile on his face; and he said "Oh it's all stuff! You've been among the Methodists,⁶ my good woman." But I told him I'd never been near the Methodies. And then he said, –

'"Well," says he, "you must come to church, where you'll hear the Scriptures properly explained, instead of sitting poring over your Bible at home."'

'But I told him, I always used coming to church when I had my health; but this very cold winter weather I hardly durst venture so far – and me so bad i' th' rheumatiz an' all.

'But he says, "It'll do your rheumatiz good to hobble to church: there's nothing like exercise for the rheumatiz. You can walk about the house well enough; why can't you walk to church? The fact is," says he, "you're getting too fond of your ease. It's always easy to find excuses for shirking one's duty."'

'But then, you know, Miss Grey, it wasn't so. However, I told him I'd try. "But please, sir," says I, "if I do go to church, what the better shall I be? I want to have my sins blotted out, and to feel that they are remembered no more against me, and that the love of God is shed abroad in my heart; and if I can get no good by reading my Bible an' saying my prayers at home, what good shall I get by going to church?"'

'"The church," says he, "is the place appointed by God for his worship. It's your duty to go there as often as you can. If you want comfort, you must seek it in the path of duty" – an' a deal more he said, but I cannot remember all his fine words. However, it all come to this, that I was to come to church as oft as ever I could, and bring my prayer-book with me, an' read up all the sponsers after the clerk, an' stand, an' kneel, an' sit, an' do – all as I should, an' take the Lord's Supper at every opportunity, an' hearken his sermons, an' Maister Bligh's, an' it 'ud be all right: if I went on doing my duty I should get a blessing at last.

'"But if you get no comfort that way," says he, "it's all up."'

'"Then, sir," says I, "should you think I'm a reprobate?"'

'"Why," says he – he says, "if you do your best to get to Heaven and can't manage it, you must be one of those that seek to enter in at the strait gate[7] and shall not be able."'

'An' then he asked me if I'd seen any of the ladies o' th' Hall about that mornin'; so I told him where I had seen the young misses go on th' Moss Lane; – an' he kicked my poor cat[8] right across th' floor, an' went after 'em as gay as a lark; but I was very sad. That last word o' his fair sunk into my heart, an' lay there like a lump o' lead, till I was weary to bear it.

'Howsever, I follered his advice: I thought he meant it all for th' best, though he *had* a queer way with him – but you know, miss, he's rich an' young, and such like cannot right understand the thoughts of a poor old woman such as me. But howsever, I did my best to do all as he bade me – but may-be I'm plaguing you, miss, wi' my chatter.'

'Oh no, Nancy! Go on, and tell me all.'

'Well, my rheumatiz got better – I know not whether wi' going to church or not, but one frosty Sunday I got this cold i' my eyes. Th' inflammation didn't come on all at once like, but bit by bit – but I wasn't going to tell you about my eyes, I was talking about my trouble o' mind; – and to tell the truth, Miss Grey, I don't think it was any-ways eased by coming to church – naught to speak on at least: I like got my health better; but that didn't mend my soul. I hearkened and hearkened the ministers, and read an' read at my prayer-book; but it was all like sounding brass and a tinkling cymbal:[9] the sermons I couldn't understand, an' th' Prayer-book only served to show me how wicked I was, that I could read such good words, an' never be no better for it, and oftens feel it a sore labour an' a heavy task beside, instead of a blessing and a privilege as all good Christians does. It seemed like as all were barren an' dark to me. And then, them dreadful words, "Many shall seek to enter in, and shall not be able." They like as they fair dried up my sperrit.'

'But one Sunday, when Maister Hatfield gave out about the sacrament, I noticed where he said, "If there be any of you that cannot quiet his own conscience, but requireth further comfort or counsel, let him come to me, or some other discreet and learned minister of God's word, and open his grief!" So next Sunday morning, afore service, I just looked into th' vestry, an' began a talking to th' Rector again . . . I hardly could fashion to take such a liberty, but I thought when my soul was at stake, I shouldn't stick at a trifle. But he said he hadn't time to attend to me then.'

'"And indeed," says he, "I've nothing to say to you but what I've said before . . . take the sacrament, of course, and go on doing your duty; if that won't serve you, nothing will. So don't bother me any more."

'So then, I went away. But I heard Maister Weston . . . Maister Weston was there, miss – this was his first Sunday at Horton, you know, an' he was i' th' vestry in his surplice, helping th' Rector on with his gown.'

'Yes, Nancy.'

'And I heard him ask Maister Hatfield who I was; an' he said "Oh! She's a canting[10] old fool."'

'And I was very ill grieved, Miss Grey; but I went to my seat, and I tried to do my duty as aforetime: but I like got no peace. An' I even took the sacrament; but I felt as though I were eating and drinking to my own damnation all th' time. So I went home, sorely troubled.

'But next day, afore I'd gotten fettled up – for indeed miss, I'd no heart to sweeping an' fettling, an' washing pots; so I sat me down i' th' muck – but who should come in but Maister Weston! I started siding[11] stuff then, an' sweeping an' doing; and I expected he'd begin a calling me for my idle ways as Maister Hatfield would a' done; but I was mista'en: he only bid me good mornin' like, in a quiet, dacent way. So I dusted him a chair, an' fettled up th' fire-place a bit; but I hadn't forgotten th' Rector's words, so says I, –

' "I wonder, sir, you should give yourself that trouble, to come so far to see a 'canting old fool', such as me."

'He like seemed taken aback at that; but he would fain persuade me 'at th' Rector was only in jest; and when that wouldn't do, he says, –

' "Well, Nancy you shouldn't think so much about it: Mr Hatfield was a little out of humour just then; you know we're none of us perfect – even Moses spoke unadvisedly with his lips.[12] But now sit down a minute, if you can spare the time, and tell me all your doubts and fears; and I'll try to remove them."

'So I sat me down anent him.[13] He was quite a stranger, you know, Miss Grey, and even *younger* nor Maister Hatfield, I believe; an' I had thought him not so pleasant looking as him, and rather a bit crossish, at first, to look at; but he spake so civil like – and when th' cat, poor thing, jumped on to his knee, he only stroked her, and gave a bit of a smile: so I thought that was a good sign; for once, when she did so to th' Rector, he knocked her off, like as it might be in scorn or anger, poor thing. But you can't expect a cat to know manners like a Christian, you know, Miss Grey.'

'No; of course not, Nancy. But what did Mr Weston say then?'

'He said naught; but he listened to me as steady an' patient as could be, an' never a bit o' scorn about him; so I went on, an' told him all, just as I've telled you – *an' more too.*

' "Well," says he, "Mr Hatfield was quite right in telling you to persevere in doing your duty; but in advising you to go to church and attend to the service, and so on, he didn't mean that was the whole of a Christian's duty, he only thought you might there learn what more was to be done, and be led to take delight in those exercises, instead of finding them a task and a burden. And if you had asked him to explain those words that trouble you so much, I think he would have told you that if many shall seek to enter in at the strait gate and shall not be able, it is their own sins that hinder them; just as a man with a large sack on his back might wish to pass through a narrow doorway, and find it impossible to do so unless he would leave his sack behind him. But you, Nancy, I dare say, have no sins that you might not gladly throw aside, if you knew how?"

'"Indeed, sir, you speak truth," says I.

'"Well," says he, "you know the first and great commandment – and the second, which is like unto it – on which two commandments hang all the law and prophets? You say you cannot love God; but it strikes me, that if you rightly consider who and what He is, you cannot help it. He is your father, your best friend; every blessing, everything good, pleasant, or useful, comes from Him; and everything evil, everything you have reason to hate, to shun, or to fear, comes from Satan, *His* enemy as well as ours; and for *this* cause was God manifest in the flesh,[14] that he might destroy the works of the devil: in one word, God is LOVE; and the more of love we have within us, the nearer we are to Him, and the more of His spirit we possess."

'"Well, sir," I said, "if I can always think on these things, I think I might well love God; but how can I love my neighbours – when they vex me, and be so contrairy and sinful as some on 'em is?"

'"It may seem a hard matter," says he, "to love our neighbours, who have so much of what is evil about them, and whose faults so often awaken the evil that lingers within ourselves, but remember that *He* made them, and *He* loves them; and whosoever loves Him that begat, loveth him that is begotten also.[15] And if God so loveth us, that He gave His only begotten son to die for us, we ought also to love one another. But if you cannot

feel positive affection for those who do not care for you, you can
at least try to do to them as you would they should do unto you;
you can endeavour to pity their failings and excuse their offences,
and to do all the good you can to those about you. And if you
accustom yourself to this, Nancy, the very effort itself will make
you love them in some degree – to say nothing of the goodwill
your kindness would beget in them, though they might have
little else that is good about them. If we love God and wish to
serve Him, let us try to be like Him, to do His work, to labour
for His glory, which is the good of man, to hasten the coming of
His kingdom, which is the peace and happiness of all the world
– however powerless we may seem to be, in doing all the good we
can through life, the humblest of us may do much towards it;
and let us dwell in love,[16] that He may dwell in us, and we in
Him. The more happiness we bestow, the more we shall receive,
even here, and the greater will be our reward in Heaven when
we rest from our labours."

'I believe, miss, them is his very words, for I've thought them
ower many a time. An' then he took that Bible, an' read bits here
and there, an' explained 'em as clear as the day: and it seemed
like as a new light broke in on my soul; an' I felt fair aglow
about my heart, an' only wished poor Bill an' all the world could
a' been there an' heard it all, and rejoiced wi' me.

'After he was gone, Hannah Rogers, one o' th' neighbours,
came in and wanted me to help her to wash. I told her I
couldn't just then, for I hadn't set on th' potaties for th' dinner,
nor washed up th' breakfast stuff yet. So then she began a calling
me for my nasty, idle ways. I was a little bit vexed at first, but I
never said nothing wrong to her: I only told her, like all in a
quiet way, 'at I'd had th' new parson to see me; but I'd get done
as quick as ever I could, and then come an' help her. So then she
softened down; and my heart like as it warmed towards her, an'
in a bit, we was very good friends.

'An' so it is, Miss Grey, "a soft answer turneth away wrath;
but grievous words stir up anger."[17] It isn't only in them you
speak to, but in yourself.'

'Very true, Nancy, if we could always remember it.'

'Ay, if we could!'

'And did Mr Weston ever come to see you again?'

'Yes, many a time; and since my eyes has been so bad, he's sat an' read to me by the half-hour together; but you know, miss, he has other folks to see, and other things to do – God bless him! An' that next Sunday he preached *such* a sermon! His text was, "Come unto me, all ye that labour and are heavy laden, and I will give you rest," [18] and them two blessed verses that follows. [19] You wasn't there miss, you was with your friends then – but it made me *so* happy! and I *am* happy now, thank God! an' I take a pleasure, now, in doing little bits o' jobs for my neighbours – such as a poor old body 'at's half blind can do . . . and they take it kindly of me, just as he said. You see, miss, I'm knitting a pair o' stockings now: – they're for Thomas Jackson: he's a queerish old body, an' we've had many a bout at threaping, [20] one anent t' other; an' at times we've differed sorely. So I thought I couldn't do better nor knit him a pair o' warm stockings; an' I've felt to like him a deal better, poor old man, sin' I began. It's turned out just as Maister Weston said.'

'Well I'm very glad to see you so happy, Nancy, and so wise: but I must go now; I shall be wanted at the Hall,' said I; and bidding her good bye, I departed, promising to come again when I had time, and feeling nearly as happy as herself.

At another time, I went to read to a poor labourer who was in the last stage of a consumption. The young ladies had been to see him, and somehow, a promise of reading to him had been extracted from them; but it was too much trouble, so they begged *me* to do it instead. I went, willingly enough, and there too I was gratified with the praises of Mr Weston, both from the sick man and his wife. The former told me that he derived great comfort and benefit from the visits of the new parson, who frequently came to see him, and was 'another guess sort of man' [21] to Mr Hatfield, who before the other's arrival at Horton had now and then paid him a visit, on which occasions, he would always insist upon having the cottage door kept open to admit the fresh air for his own convenience, without considering how it might injure the sufferer, and having opened his Prayer-book and hastily read over a part of the service for the sick, would hurry away again, if he did not stay to administer some harsh rebuke to the afflicted wife, or to make some thoughtless, not to say heartless, observation, rather calculated to increase than diminish the troubles of the suffering pair.

'Whereas,' said the man, 'Maister Weston 'ull pray with me quite in a different fashion, an' talk to me as kind as owt'; an' oft read to me, too, an' beside me just like a brother.'

'Just for all the world!' exclaimed his wife, 'an' about three wik sin', when he seed how poor Jem shivered wi' cold, an' what pitiful fires we kept, he axed if wer stock o' coals was nearly done. I told him it was, an' we was ill set to get more – but you know, mum, I didn' think o' him helping us – but howsever, he sent us a sack o' coals next day; an' we've had good fires ever sin': an' a great blessing it is, this winter time. But that's his way, Miss Grey – when he comes into a poor body's house a seein' sick folk, he like notices what they most stand i' need on, an' if he thinks they can't readily get it therseln, he never says nowt about it, but just gets it for 'em: – an' it isn't everybody 'at 'ud do that,' at has as little as he has; for you know mum, he's now't at all to live on but what he gets fr' th' Rector; an' that's little enough, they say.'

I remembered then, with a species of exultation, that he had frequently been styled a vulgar brute by the amiable Miss Murray, because he sported a silver watch, and clothes not quite so bright and fresh as Mr Hatfield's.

In returning to the lodge, I felt very happy, and thanked God that I had now something to think about, something to dwell on as a relief from the weary monotony, the lonely drudgery of my present life – for I *was* lonely – never, from month to month, from year to year, except during my brief intervals of rest at home, did I see one creature to whom I could open my heart, or freely speak my thoughts with any hope of sympathy, or even comprehension; never one, unless it were poor Nancy Brown, with whom I could enjoy a single moment of real social inter-course, or whose conversation was calculated to render me better, wiser, or happier than before; or who, as far as I could

see, could be greatly benefited by mine. My only companions
had been unamiable children, and ignorant, wrong-headed girls,
from whose fatiguing folly, unbroken solitude was often a relief
most earnestly desired and dearly prized. But to be restricted to
such associates was a serious evil, both in its immediate effects
and the consequences that were likely to ensue.

Never a new idea or a stirring thought came to me from
without; and such as rose within me were, for the most part,
miserably crushed at once, or doomed to sicken and fade away,
because they could not see the light.

Habitual associations are known to exercise a great influence
over each other's minds and manners. Those whose actions are
for ever before our eyes, whose words are ever in our ears, will
naturally lead us, albeit against our will – slowly – gradually –
imperceptibly, perhaps, to act and speak as they do. I will not
presume to say how far this irresistible power of assimilation
extends; but if one civilized man were doomed to pass a dozen
years amid a race of intractable savages, unless he had power to
improve them, I greatly question whether, at the close of that
period, he would not have become, at least, a barbarian himself.
And I, as I could not make my young companions better, feared
exceedingly that they would make me worse – would gradually
bring my feelings, habits, capacities, to the level of their own,
without, however, imparting to me their light-heartedness and
cheerful vivacity. Already, I seemed to feel my intellect deteriorating, my heart petrifying, my soul contracting, and I trembled lest
my very moral perceptions should become deadened, my distinc-
tions of right and wrong confounded, and all my better faculties
be sunk, at last, beneath the baleful influence of such a mode of
life. The gross vapours of earth were gathering round me, and
closing in upon my inward heaven; and thus it was that Mr
Weston rose at length upon me, appearing like the morning star
in my horizon, to save me from the fear of utter darkness; and I
rejoiced that I had now a subject for contemplation that was
above me, not beneath. I was glad to see that all the world was
not made up of Bloomfields, Murrays, Hatfields, Ashbys,
etc.; and that human excellence was not a mere dream of the

imagination. When we hear a little good and no harm of a person, it is easy and pleasant to imagine more – in short, it is needless to analyze all my thoughts, but Sunday was now become a day of peculiar delight to me (I was now almost broken in to the back corner in the carriage), for I liked to hear him – and I liked to see him, too, though I knew he was not handsome, or even what is called agreeable, in outward aspect; but, certainly, he was not ugly.

In stature, he was a little – a very little – above the middle size; perfectly symmetrical in figure, deep-chested, and strongly-built; the outline of his face would be pronounced too square for beauty, but to me it announced decision of character; his dark brown hair was not carefully curled, like Mr Hatfield's, but simply brushed aside over a broad, white forehead; the eyebrows, I suppose, were too projecting, but from under those dark brows there gleamed an eye of singular power, brown in colour, not large, and somewhat deep set, but strikingly brilliant, and full of expression; there was character, too, in the mouth, something that bespoke a man of firm purpose and an habitual thinker, and when he smiled – but I will not speak of that yet, for, at the time I mention, I had never seen him smile; and indeed, his general appearance did not impress me with the idea of a man given to such a relaxation, nor of such an individual as the cottagers described him. I had early formed my opinion of him, and, in spite of Miss Murray's objurgations, was fully convinced that he was a man of strong sense, firm faith, and ardent piety, but thoughtful and stern: and when I found that, to his other good qualities, was added that of true benevolence and gentle, considerate kindness, the discovery, perhaps, delighted me the more, as I had not been prepared to expect it.

XII

THE SHOWER

THE NEXT VISIT I PAID[1] TO Nancy Brown was in the second week in March, for, though I had many spare minutes during the day, I seldom could look upon an hour as entirely my own, since, where everything was left to the caprices of Miss Matilda and her sister, there could be no order or regularity, and whatever occupation I chose, when not actually busied about them or their concerns, I had, as it were, to keep my loins girded, my shoes on my feet, and my staff in my hand; for not to be immediately forthcoming when called for, was regarded as a grave and inexcusable offence, not only by my pupils and their mother, but by the very servant, who came in breathless haste to call me, exclaiming –

'You're to go to the school-room *directly*, mum – the young ladies is WAITING!!'

Climax of horror! actually waiting for their governess!!!

But this time, I was pretty sure of an hour or two to myself, for Matilda was preparing for a long ride, and Rosalie was dressing for a dinner party at Lady Ashby's: so I took the opportunity of repairing to the widow's cottage, where I found her in some anxiety about her cat, which had been absent all day. I comforted her with as many anecdotes of that animal's roving propensities as I could recollect.

'I'm feared o' th' gamekeepers,' said she, 'that's all 'at I think on. If th' young gentlemen had been at home, I should a' thought they'd been setting their dogs at her, an' worried her, poor thing, as they did *many* a poor body's cat; but I haven't that to be feared on now.'

Nancy's eyes were better, but still far from well: she had been trying to make a Sunday shirt for her son, but told me she could only bear to do a little bit at it now and then, so that it progressed but slowly, though the poor lad wanted it sadly. So I proposed to help her a little, after I had read to her, for I had plenty of time that evening, and need not return till dusk. She thankfully accepted the offer.

'An' you'll be a bit o' company for me too, miss,' said she, 'I like as I feel lonesome without my cat.'

But when I had finished reading, and done the half of a seam, with Nancy's capacious brass thimble fitted on to my finger by means of a roll of paper, I was disturbed by the entrance of Mr Weston with the identical cat in his arms. I now saw that he could smile, and very pleasantly too.

'I've done you a piece of good service, Nancy,' he began; then seeing me, he acknowledged my presence by a slight bow. I should have been invisible to Hatfield, or any other gentleman of those parts. 'I've delivered your cat,' he continued, 'from the hands, or rather the gun, of Mr Murray's gamekeeper.'

'God bless you, sir!' cried the grateful old woman, ready to weep for joy as she received her favourite from his arms.

'Take care of it,' said he, 'and don't let it go near the rabbit warren, for the gamekeeper swears he'll shoot it if he sees it there again. He would have done so to-day, if I had not been in time to stop him. I believe it is raining, Miss Grey,' added he, more quietly, observing that I had put aside my work, and was preparing to depart. 'Don't let me disturb you – I shan't stay two minutes.'

'You'll *both* stay while this shower gets owered,' said Nancy as she stirred the fire, and placed another chair beside it: 'what! there's room for all.'

'I can see better here, thank you, Nancy,' replied I, taking my work to the window, where she had the goodness to suffer me to remain unmolested, while she got a brush to remove the cat's hairs from Mr Weston's coat, carefully wiped the rain from his hat, and gave the cat its supper, busily talking all the time; now thanking her clerical friend for what he had done; now wondering how the cat had found out the warren; and now lamenting the probable consequences of such a discovery. He listened with a quiet, good-natured smile, and at length took a seat in compliance with her pressing invitations, but repeated that he did not mean to stay.

'I have another place to go to,' said he, 'and I see' (glancing at the book on the table) 'some one else has been reading to you.'

'Yes sir, Miss Grey has been as kind as read me a chapter; an' now she's helping me with a shirt for our Bill – but I'm feared she'll be cold there. Won't you come to th' fire, miss?'

'No, thank you, Nancy, I'm quite warm. I must go as soon as this shower is over.'

'Aw, miss! You said you could stop till dusk!'[2] cried the provoking old woman, and Mr Weston seized his hat.

'Nay, sir,' exclaimed she, 'pray, don't go now, while it rains so fast.'

'But it strikes me I'm keeping your visitor away from the fire.'[3]

'No, you're not, Mr Weston,' replied I, hoping there was no harm in a falsehood of that description.

'No, sure!' cried Nancy, 'What! there's lot's o' room!'

'Miss Grey,' said he, half-jestingly, as if he felt it necessary to change the present subject, whether he had anything particular to say or not, 'I wish you would make my peace with the squire, when you see him. He was by when I rescued Nancy's cat, and did not quite approve of the deed. I told him I thought he might better spare all his rabbits than she her cat, for which audacious assertion, he treated me to some rather ungentlemanly language, and I fear I retorted a trifle too warmly.'

'Oh, lawful sir! I hope you didn't fall out wi' th' maister for sake o' my cat! he cannot bide answering again – can th' maister.'

'Oh! it's no matter, Nancy: I don't care about it, really: I said nothing *very* uncivil; and I suppose Mr Murray is accustomed to use rather strong language when he's heated.'

'Ay, sir: it's a pity!'

'And now, I really must go. I have to visit a place a mile beyond this; and you would not have me to return in the dark: besides, it has nearly done raining now – so good evening, Nancy. – Good evening, Miss Grey.'

'Good evening, Mr Weston . . . but don't depend upon me for making your peace with Mr Murray, for I never see him – to speak to.'

'Don't you? it can't be helped then,' replied he in dolorous resignation: then . . ., with a peculiar half-smile, he added, 'But never mind; I imagine the squire has more to apologize for than I,' and left the cottage.

I went on with my sewing as long as I could see; and then bid Nancy good evening, checking her too lively gratitude by the undeniable assurance that I had only done for her what she would have done for me, if she had been in my place, and I in hers, and hastened back to Horton Lodge, where, having entered the school-room, I found the tea-table all in confusion, the tray flooded with slops, and Miss Matilda in a most ferocious humour.

'Miss Grey, whatever have you been about? I've had tea half-an-hour ago, and had to make it myself, and drink it all alone! I wish you *would* come in sooner!'

'I've been to see Nancy Brown. I thought you would not be back from your ride.'

'How could I ride in the rain, I should like to know? That d–d pelting shower was vexatious enough – coming on when I was just in full swing: and then to come in and find nobody in to tea! – and you *know* I can't make the tea as I like it.'

'I didn't think of the shower,' replied I (and indeed, the thought of its driving her home had never entered my head).

'No, of course, you were under shelter yourself, and you never thought of other people.'

I bore her coarse reproaches with astonishing equanimity, even with cheerfulness; for I was sensible that I had done more good to Nancy Brown than harm to her; and perhaps some other thoughts assisted to keep up my spirits, and impart relish to a cup of cold, overdrawn tea, and a charm to the otherwise unsightly table, and – I had almost said – to Miss Matilda's unamiable face. But she soon betook herself to the stables, and left me to the quiet enjoyment of my solitary meal.

XIII

THE PRIMROSES

MISS MURRAY NOW ALWAYS went twice to church, for she so loved admiration that she could not bear to lose a single opportunity of obtaining it; and she was so sure of it, wherever she showed herself, that whether Harry Meltham and Mr Green were there or not, there was certain to be somebody present who would not be insensible to her charms, besides the Rector, whose official capacity generally obliged him to attend.

Usually, also, if the weather permitted, both she and her sister would walk home; Matilda, because she hated the confinement of the carriage; she, because she disliked the privacy of it, and enjoyed the company that generally enlivened the first mile of the journey in walking from the church to Mr Green's park-gates: near which commenced the private road to Horton Lodge, which lay in the opposite direction; while the highway conducted in a straight-forward course to the still more distant mansion of Sir Hugh Meltham. Thus, there was always a chance of being accompanied so far, either by Harry Meltham, with or without Miss Meltham, or Mr Green, with perhaps one or both of his sisters, and any gentleman visiters they might have.

Whether I walked with the young ladies or rode with their parents, depended entirely upon their own capricious will: if they chose to 'take' me, I went; if, for reasons best known to themselves, they chose to go alone, I took my seat in the carriage: I liked walking better, but a sense of reluctance to obtrude my presence on any one who did not desire it, always kept me passive on these and similar occasions; and I never inquired into the causes of their varying whims and indeed, this was the best policy – for to submit and oblige was the governess's part, to consult their own pleasure was that of the pupils. But when I did walk, this first half of the journey was generally a great nuisance to me. As none of the before-mentioned ladies and gentlemen ever noticed me, it was disagreeable to walk beside them, as if listening to what they said, or wishing to be thought one of them, while they talked over me or across, and if their eyes, in speaking, chanced to fall on me, it seemed as if they looked on vacancy – as if they either did not see me, or were very desirous to make it appear so.

It was disagreeable, too, to walk behind, and thus appear to acknowledge my own inferiority; for, in truth, I considered myself pretty nearly as good as the best of them, and wished them to know that I did so, and not to imagine that I looked upon myself as a mere domestic, who knew her own place too well to walk beside such fine ladies and gentlemen as they were ... though her young ladies might choose to have her with them, and even condescend to converse with her, when no better company were at hand.

Thus – I am almost ashamed to confess it – but indeed I gave myself no little trouble in my endeavours (if I did keep up with them) to appear perfectly unconscious or regardless of their presence, as if I were wholly absorbed in my own reflections, or the contemplation of surrounding objects; or, if I lingered behind, it was some bird or insect, some tree or flower, that attracted my attention, and having duly examined that, I would pursue my walk alone, at a leisurely pace, until my pupils had bid adieu to their companions, and turned off into the quiet, private road.

One such occasion I particularly well remember, it was a lovely afternoon about the close of March; Mr Green and his sisters had sent their carriage back empty, in order to enjoy the bright sunshine and balmy air in a sociable walk home along with their visiters, Captain Somebody and Lieutenant Somebody else (a couple of military fops), and the Misses Murray, who, of course, contrived to join them.

Such a party was highly agreeable to Rosalie; but not finding it equally suitable to my taste, I presently fell back, and began to botanize and entomologize along the green banks and budding hedges, till the company was considerably in advance of me, and misanthropy began to melt away beneath the soft, pure air and genial sunshine; but sad thoughts of early childhood, and yearnings for departed joys, or for a brighter future lot, arose instead.

As my eyes wandered over the steep banks covered with young grass and green-leaved plants, and surmounted by budding hedges, I longed intensely for some familiar flower that might recall the woody dales or green hill-sides of home – the brown moorlands, of course, were out of the question. Such a discovery would make my eyes gush out with water, no doubt; but that was one of my greatest enjoyments now.

At length, I descried, high up between the twisted roots of an oak, three lovely primroses, peeping so sweetly from their hiding place that the tears already started at the sight, but they grew so high above me, that I tried in vain to gather one or two, to dream over and to carry with me; I could not reach them unless I climbed the bank, which I was deterred from doing by hearing a footstep at that moment behind me, and was, therefore, about to turn away, when I was startled by the words, 'Allow me to gather them for you, Miss Grey,' spoken in the grave, low tones of a well-known voice.

Immediately the flowers were gathered, and in my hand. It was Mr Weston of course – who else would trouble himself to do so much for *me*?

I thanked him; whether warmly or coldly, I cannot tell: but certain I am, that I did not express half the gratitude I felt. It was foolish, perhaps, to feel any gratitude at all, but it seemed to me, at that moment, as if this were a remarkable instance of his good nature, an act of kindness which I could not repay, but never should forget: so utterly unaccustomed was I to receive such civilities, so little prepared to expect them – from any one within fifty miles of Horton Lodge.

Yet this did not prevent me from feeling a little uncomfortable in his presence; and I proceeded to follow my pupils at a much quicker pace than before; though perhaps, if Mr Weston had taken the hint, and let me pass without another word, I might have repented it an hour after: but he did not. A somewhat rapid walk for me was but an ordinary pace for him.

'Your young ladies have left you alone,' said he.

'Yes; they are occupied with more agreeable company.'

'Then don't trouble yourself to overtake them.'

I slackened my pace; but next moment regretted having done so; my companion did not speak: and I had nothing in the world to say, and feared he might be in the same predicament. At length, however, he broke the pause by asking, with a certain quiet abruptness peculiar to himself, if I liked flowers.

'Yes; very much,' I answered, 'wild flowers especially.'

'*I* like wild flowers,' said he, 'others I don't care about, because I have no particular associations connected with them – except one or two. What are your favourite flowers?'

'Primroses, blue-bells,[1] and heath-blossoms.'

'Not violets?'

'No; because, as you say, I have no particular associations connected with them; for there are no sweet violets among the hills and valleys round my home.'

'It must be a great consolation to you to have a home, Miss Grey,' observed my companion after a short pause, 'however remote, or however seldom visited, still it is something to look to.'

'It is so much that I think I could not live without it,' replied I, with an enthusiasm of which I immediately repented, for I thought it must have sounded essentially silly.

'Oh yes, you could!' said he, with a thoughtful smile. 'The ties that bind us to life are tougher than you imagine, or than any one can who has not felt how roughly they may be pulled without breaking. You might be miserable without a home, but even *you* could live, and not *so* miserably as you suppose. The human heart is like india-rubber, a little swells it, but great deal will not burst it. If "little more than nothing" will disturb it, "little less than all things will suffice" to break it. As in the outer members of our frame, there is a vital power inherent in itself, that streng-thens it against external violence. Every blow that shakes it will serve to harden it against a future stroke; as constant labour thickens the skin of the hand, and strengthens its muscles instead of wasting them away: so that a day of arduous toil that might

excoriate a lady's palm, would make no sensible impression on
that of a hardy ploughman.

'I speak from experience – partly my own. There was a time
when I thought as you do – at least, I was fully persuaded that
Home and its affections were the only things that made life
tolerable . . . that, if deprived of these, existence would become a
burden hard to be endured; but now, I have no home . . . unless
you would dignify my two hired rooms at Horton by such a
name; and not twelve months ago, I lost the last and dearest of
my early friends: and yet, not only I live, but I am not wholly
destitute of hope and comfort, even for this life; though I must
acknowledge that I can seldom enter even an humble cottage at
the close of day, and see its inhabitants peaceably gathered round
their cheerful hearth, without a feeling *almost* of envy at their
domestic enjoyment.'

'You don't know what happiness lies before you yet,' said I,
'you are now only in the commencement of your journey.'

'The best of happiness,' replied he, 'is mine already . . . the
power and the will to be useful.'

We now approached a stile communicating with a footpath
that conducted to a farm-house, where, I suppose, Mr Weston
purposed to make himself 'useful,' for he presently took leave of
me, crossed the stile, and traversed the path with his usual firm,
elastic tread, leaving me to ponder his words as I continued my
course alone.

I had heard before that he had lost his mother not many
months before he came. She then was the last and dearest of his
early friends; and he had *no home*. I pitied him from my heart; I
almost wept for sympathy. And this, I thought, accounted for
the shade of premature thoughtfulness that so frequently clouded
his brow, and obtained for him the reputation of a morose and
sullen disposition with the charitable Miss Murray and all her
kin.

'But,' thought I, 'he is not so miserable as I should be under
such a deprivation: he leads an active life; and a wide field for
useful exertion lies before him, he can *make* friends – and he can
make a home too, if he pleases, and doubtless he will please

some time; and God grant the partner of that home may be worthy of his choice, and make it a happy one ... such a home as he deserves to have! And how delightful it would be to –' But no matter what I thought.

I began this book with the intention of concealing nothing, that those who liked might have the benefit of perusing a fellow creature's heart: but we have *some* thoughts that all the angels in heaven are welcome to behold – but not our brother-men – not even the best and kindest amongst them.

By this time the Greens had taken themselves to their own abode, and the Murrays had turned down the private road, whither I hastened to follow them. I found the two girls lost in an animated discussion on the respective merits of the two young officers; but on seeing me Rosalie broke off in the middle of a sentence to exclaim, with malicious glee, –

'Oh, ho, Miss Grey! you're come at last, are you? No *wonder* you lingered so long behind! and no *wonder* you always stand up so vigorously for Mr Weston when I abuse him – Ah, ha! I see it all now!'

'Now, come, Miss Murray, don't be foolish,' said I, attempting a good-natured laugh, 'you know such nonsense can make no impression on me.'

But she still went on talking such intolerable stuff – her sister helping her with appropriate fictions coined for the occasion – that I thought it necessary to say something in my own justification.

'What humbug all this is!' I exclaimed. 'If Mr Weston's road happened to be the same as mine for a few yards, and if he chose to exchange a word or two in passing, what is there so remarkable in that? I assure you I never spoke to him before; except once.'

'Where? where? and when?' cried they eagerly.

'In Nancy's cottage.'

'Ah, ha! you've met him there, have you?' exclaimed Rosalie, with exultant laughter. 'Ah! now, Matilda, I've found out why she's so fond of going to Nancy Brown's! she goes there to flirt with Mr Weston!'

'Really, that is not worth contradicting! . . . I only saw him there once, I tell you . . . and how could I know he was coming?'

Irritated as I was at their foolish mirth and vexatious imputations, the uneasiness did not continue long: when they had had their laugh out, they returned again to the Captain and Lieutenant; and, while they disputed and commented upon them, my indignation rapidly cooled; the cause of it was quickly forgotten, and I turned my thoughts into a pleasanter channel.

Thus we proceeded up the park, and entered the hall; and as I ascended the stairs to my own chamber, I had but one thought within me, my heart was filled to overflowing with one single earnest wish. Having entered the room, and shut the door, I fell upon my knees and offered up a fervent, but not impetuous prayer: 'Thy will be done,' I strove to say throughout, but, 'Father, all things are possible with Thee,'[2] and may it be Thy will,' was sure to follow. That wish . . . that prayer – both men and women would have scorned me for . . . 'But, Father, *Thou* wilt *not* despise!'[3] I said – and felt that it was true. It seemed to me that another's welfare was at least as ardently implored as my own – nay, even that *that* was the principal object of my heart's desire. I might have been deceiving myself; but that idea gave me confidence to ask, and power to hope I did not ask in vain.

As for the primroses, I kept two of them in a glass in my room until they were completely withered, and the housemaid threw them out, and the petals of the other, I pressed between the leaves of my Bible – I have them still, and mean to keep them always.

XIV
THE RECTOR

THE FOLLOWING DAY WAS AS fine as the preceding one. Soon after breakfast, Miss Matilda, having galloped and blundered through a few unprofitable lessons, and vengibly[1] thumped the piano for an hour, in a terrible humour with both me and it, because her mamma would not give her a holiday, had betaken herself to her favorite places of resort, the yards, the stables, and the dog-kennels: and Miss Murray was gone forth to enjoy a quiet ramble with a new fashionable novel for her companion, leaving me in the school-room, hard at work upon a water-colour drawing I had promised to do for her, and which she insisted upon my finishing that day.

At my feet lay a little rough terrier. It was the property of Miss Matilda; but she hated the animal, and intended to sell it, alleging that it was quite spoiled. It was really an excellent dog of its kind; but she affirmed it was fit for nothing, and had not even the sense to know its own mistress.

The fact is, she had purchased it when but a small puppy, insisting, at first, that no one should touch it but herself; but, soon becoming tired of so helpless and troublesome a nursling, she had gladly yielded to my entreaties to be allowed to take charge of it; and I, by carefully nursing the little creature from infancy to adolescence, of course, had obtained its affections; a reward I should have greatly valued and looked upon as far outweighing all the trouble I had had with it, had not poor Snap's grateful feelings exposed him to many a harsh word and many a spiteful kick and pinch from his owner, and were he not now in danger of being 'put away,' in consequence, or transferred to some rough, stony-hearted master. But how could I help it? I could not make the dog hate me by cruel treatment; and she would not propitiate him by kindness.

However, while I thus sat, working away with my pencil, Mrs Murray came, half-sailing, half-bustling, into the room.

'Miss Grey,' she began, – 'Dear! how can you sit at your drawing such a day as this?' (she thought I was doing it for my own pleasure). 'I *wonder* you don't put on your bonnet and go out with the young ladies.'

'I think, ma'am, Miss Murray is reading; and Miss Matilda is amusing herself with her dogs.'

'If you would try to amuse Miss Matilda yourself a little more, I think she would not be *driven* to seek amusement in the companionship of dogs and horses, and grooms, so much as she is; and if you would be a little more cheerful and conversable with Miss Murray, she would not so often go wandering in the fields with a book in her hand. However, I don't want to vex you,' added she, seeing, I suppose, that my cheeks burned and my hand trembled with some unamiable emotion. 'Do, pray, try not to be so touchy! – there's no speaking to you else. And tell me if you know where Rosalie is gone: and why she likes to be so much alone?'

'She says she likes to be alone when she has a new book to read.'

'But why can't she read it in the park or the garden; – why should she go into the fields and lanes? and how is it that Mr Hatfield so often finds her out? She told me last week he'd walked his horse by her side all up Moss-lane;[2] and now I'm sure it was he I saw from my dressing-room window, walking so briskly past the park-gates, and on towards the field where she so frequently goes. I wish you would go and see if she is there; and just gently remind her that it is not proper for a young lady of her rank and prospects to be wandering about by herself in that manner, exposed to the attentions of any one that presumes to address her, like some poor neglected girl that has no park to walk in, and no friends to take care of her; and tell her that her papa would be extremely angry if he knew of her treating Mr Hatfield in that familiar manner that I fear she does; and – Oh! if you – if *any* governess had but half a mother's watchfulness – half a mother's anxious care, I should be saved this trouble; and you would see at once the necessity of keeping your eye upon her, and making your company agreeable to – Well, go – go; there's no time to be lost,' cried she, seeing that I had put away my drawing materials, and was waiting in the door-way for the conclusion of her address.

According to her prognostications, I found Miss Murray in her favorite field just without the park; and, unfortunately, not alone; for the tall, stately figure of Mr Hatfield was slowly sauntering by her side.

Here was a poser[3] for me. It was my duty to interrupt the *tête-a tête*[4]: but how was it to be done? Mr Hatfield could not be driven away by so insignificant a person as I; and to go and place myself on the other side of Miss Murray, and intrude my unwelcome presence upon her without noticing her companion, was a piece of rudeness I could not be guilty of: neither had I the courage to cry aloud from the top of the field that she was wanted elsewhere. So I took the intermediate course of walking slowly, but steadily towards them, resolving, if my approach failed to scare away the beau, to pass by and tell Miss Murray her mamma wanted her.

She certainly looked very charming as she strolled lingeringly along under the budding horse-chestnut trees that stretched their long arms over the park-palings, with her closed book in one hand, and in the other, a graceful sprig of myrtle which served her as a very pretty plaything ... her bright ringlets escaping profusely from her little bonnet, and gently stirred by the breeze, her fair cheek flushed with gratified vanity, her smiling blue eyes, now slyly glancing towards her admirer, now gazing downward at her myrtle sprig. But Snap, running before me, interrupted her in the midst of some half-pert, half-playful repartee, by catching hold of her dress and vehemently tugging thereat till Mr Hatfield, with his cane, administered a resounding thwack upon the animal's skull, and sent it yelping back to me, with a clamorous outcry that afforded the reverend gentleman great amusement; but seeing me so near, he thought, I suppose, he might as well be taking his departure; and as I stooped to caress the dog, with ostentatious pity to show my disapproval of his severity, I heard him say, –

'When shall I see you again, Miss Murray?'

'At church, I suppose,' replied she, 'unless your business chance to bring you here again, at the precise moment when I happen to be walking by.'

'I could always manage to have business here, if I knew precisely when and where to find you.'

'But if I would, I could not inform you, for I am so unmethodical,' I never can tell to-day what I shall do to-morrow.'

'Then give me that, meantime, to comfort me,' said he, half jestingly and half in earnest, extending his hand for the sprig of myrtle.

'No, indeed, I shan't.'

'Do, *pray* do! I shall be the most miserable of men if you don't. You cannot be so cruel as to deny me a favour so easily granted and yet so highly prized!' pleaded he, as ardently as if his life depended on it.

By this time, I stood within a very few yards of them, impatiently waiting his departure.

'There, then! take it and go,' said Rosalie.

He joyfully received the gift, murmured something that made her blush and toss aside her head, but with a little laugh that shewed her displeasure was entirely affected; and then with a courteous salutation withdrew.

'Did you ever see such a man, Miss Grey?' said she, turning to me, 'I'm so *glad* you came! I thought I never *should* get rid of him; – and I was so terribly afraid of papa seeing him.'

'Has he been with you long?'

'No, not long, but he's so extremely impertinent: and he's always hanging about, pretending his business or his clerical duties require his attendance in these parts, and really watching for poor me, and pouncing upon me wherever he sees me.'

'Well, your mamma thinks you ought not to go beyond the park or garden without some discreet, matronly person like me to accompany you, and keep off all intruders. She descried Mr Hatfield hurrying past the park-gates, and forthwith dispatched me with instructions to seek you up and to take care of you, and likewise to warn' –

'Oh, mamma's so tiresome! As if I couldn't take care of myself!
She bothered me before about Mr Hatfield; and I told her she
might trust me – I never should forget my rank and station for
the most delightful man that ever breathed – I wish he would go
down on his knees to-morrow, and implore me to be his wife,
that I might just shew her how mistaken she is in supposing that
I could ever – Oh! it provokes me so – To think that I could be
such as fool as to fall in *love*! It is quite beneath the dignity of a
woman to do such a thing. Love! I detest the word! as applied to
one of our sex, I think it a perfect insult! a preference I *might*
acknowledge; but never for one like poor Mr Hatfield, who has
not seven hundred a year to bless himself with. I like to talk to
him, because he's so clever and amusing – I wish Sir Thomas
Ashby were half as nice – besides, I must have *somebody* to flirt
with, and no one else has the sense to come here; and when we
go out, mamma won't let me flirt with anybody but Sir Thomas
– if he's there, and if he's *not* there, I'm bound hand and foot, for
fear somebody should go and make up some exaggerated story,
and put it into his head that I'm engaged, or likely to be engaged,
to somebody else; or, what is more probable, for fear his nasty
old mother should see, or hear of my ongoings, and conclude
that I'm not a fit wife for her excellent son; as if the said son
were not the greatest scamp in Christendom; and as if any
woman of common decency were not a world too good for him.'

'Is it really so, Miss Murray? and does you mamma know it,
and yet wish you to marry him?'

'To be sure she does! She knows more against him than I do, I
believe: she keeps it from me lest I should be discouraged; not
knowing how little I care about such things. For it's no great
matter really: he'll be all right when he's married, as mamma
says; and reformed rakes make the best husbands, *everybody*
knows. I only wish he were not so ugly – *that's* all I think about
– but then there's no choice here in the country, and papa *will not*
let us go to London –'

'But I should think Mr Hatfield would be far better.'

'And so he would, if he were lord of Ashby Park – there's not
a doubt of it; but the fact is, I *must* have Ashby Park, whoever
shares it with me.'

'But Mr Hatfield thinks you like him all this time; you don't consider how bitterly he will be disappointed when he finds himself mistaken.'

'No, indeed! It will be a proper punishment for his presumption – for ever *daring* to think I could like him. I should enjoy nothing so much as lifting the veil from his eyes.'

'The sooner you do it the better then.'

'No; I tell you, I like to amuse myself with him. Besides, he doesn't really think I like him. I take good care of that; you don't know how cleverly I manage. He may presume to think he can *induce* me to like him, for which I shall punish him as he deserves.'

'Well, mind you don't give too much reason for such presumption – that's all,' replied I.

But all my exhortations were in vain: they only made her somewhat more solicitous to disguise her wishes and her thoughts from me. She talked no more to me about the Rector; but I could see that her mind, if not her heart, was fixed upon him still, and that she was intent upon obtaining another interview; for though, in compliance with her mother's request, I was now constituted the companion of her rambles for a time, she still persisted in wandering in the fields and lanes that lay in the nearest proximity to the road; and, whether she talked to me, or read the book she carried in her hand, she kept continually pausing to look round her, or gaze up the road to see if anyone was coming; and if a horseman trotted by, I could tell by her unqualified abuse of the poor equestrian, whoever he might be, that she hated him *because* he was not Mr Hatfield.

'Surely,' thought I, 'she is not so indifferent to him as she believes herself to be, or would have others to believe her; and her mother's anxiety is not so wholly causeless as she affirms.'

Three days passed away, and he did not make his appearance. On the afternoon of the fourth, as we were walking beside the park-palings in the memorable field, each furnished with a book (for I always took care to provide myself with something to be doing when she did not require me to talk), she suddenly interrupted my studies by exclaiming, –

'Oh! Miss Grey, do be so kind as to go and see Mark Wood, and take his wife half-a-crown from me – I should have given or sent it a week ago, but quite forgot. There!' said she, throwing me her purse, and speaking very fast – 'Never mind getting it out now, but take the purse and give them what you like – I would go with you, but I want to finish this volume. I'll come and meet you when I've done it. Be quick, will you – and – Oh, wait; hadn't you better read to him a bit? Run to the house and get some sort of a good book – Anything will do.'

I did as I was desired; but, suspecting something from her hurried manner and the suddenness of the request, I just glanced back before I quitted the field, and there was Mr Hatfield about to enter at the gate below. By sending me to the house for a book, she had just prevented my meeting him on the road.

'Never mind!' thought I, 'there'll be no great harm done. Poor Mark will be glad of the half-crown and perhaps of the good book too; and if the Rector does steal Miss Rosalie's heart, it will only humble her pride a little; and if they do get married at last, it will only save her from a worse fate; and she will be quite a good enough partner for him, and him for her.'

Mark Wood was the consumptive labourer whom I mentioned before. He was now rapidly wearing away. Miss Murray, by her liberality, obtained literally the blessing of him that was ready to perish;[6] for though the half-crown could be of very little service to him, he was glad of it for the sake of his wife and children, so soon to be widowed and fatherless.

After I had sat a few minutes, and read a little for the comfort and edification of himself and his afflicted wife, I left them; but I had not proceeded fifty yards before I encountered Mr Weston, apparently on his way to the same abode.

He greeted me in his usual quiet, unaffected way, stopped to inquire about the condition of the sick man and his family, and with a sort of unconscious, brotherly disregard to ceremony, took from my hand the book out of which I had been reading, turned over the pages, made a few brief but very sensible remarks, and restored it; then, told me about some poor sufferer he had just been visiting, talked a little about Nancy Brown, made a few observations upon my little rough friend the terrier, that was frisking at his feet, and finally upon the beauty of the weather, and departed.

I have omitted to give a detail of his words, from a notion that they would not interest the reader as they did me, and not because I have forgotten them. No; I remember them well; for I thought them over and over again in the course of that day and many succeeding ones, I know not how often, and recalled every intonation of his deep, clear voice, every flash of his quick, brown eye, and every gleam of his pleasant, but too transient smile. Such a confession will look very absurd, I fear – but no matter – I have written it; and they that read it will not know the writer.

While I was walking along, happy within, and pleased with all around, Miss Murray came hastening to meet me; her buoyant step, flushed cheek, and radiant smiles shewing that she, too, was happy, in her own way. Running up to me, she put her arm in mine, and without waiting to recover breath, began, –

'Now, Miss Grey, think yourself highly honoured, for I'm come to tell you my news before I've breathed a word of it to anyone else.'

'Well, what is it?'

'Oh, *such* news! In the first place, you must know that Mr Hatfield came upon me just after you were gone. I was in *such* a way for fear papa or mamma should see him! – but you know I couldn't call you back again; and so I – Oh, dear! I can't tell you all about it now, for there's Matilda, I see, in the park, and I must go and open my budget to her.[7] But, however, Hatfield was most uncommonly audacious, unspeakably complimentary, and unprecedentedly[8] tender – tried to be so at least – he didn't succeed very well in *that*, because it's not his vein. I'll tell you all he said another time!'

'But what did *you* say? – I'm more interested in that.'

'I'll tell you that, too, at some future period. I happened to be in a very good humour just then; but, though I was complaisant and gracious enough, I took care not to compromise myself in any possible way. But, however, the conceited wretch chose to interpret my amiability of temper his own way, and at length presumed upon my indulgence so far that – what do you think? – he actually – made me an offer!'

'And you –'

'I proudly drew myself up, and with the greatest coolness expressed my astonishment at such an occurrence, and hoped he had seen nothing in my conduct to justify his expectations. You should have *seen* how his countenance fell! He went perfectly white in the face. I assured him that I esteemed him and all that, but could not possibly accede to his proposals; and if I did, papa and mamma could never be brought to give their consent.'

'"But if they could," said he, "would yours be wanting?"'

'"Certainly, Mr Hatfield," I replied, with a cool decision which quelled all hope at once. Oh, if you had seen how dreadfully mortified he was – how crushed to the earth by his disappointment! really, I almost pitied him myself!

'One more desperate attempt, however, he made. After a silence of considerable duration, during which he struggled to be calm, and I to be grave – for I felt a strong propensity to laugh – which would have ruined all – he said, with the ghost of a smile; –

'"But tell me plainly, Miss Murray; if I had the wealth of Sir Hugh Meltham, or the prospects of his eldest son, would you still refuse me? answer me truly, upon your honour."

'"Certainly," said I. "That would make no difference whatever."

'It was a great lie, but he looked so confident in his own attractions still, that I determined not to leave him one stone upon another.' He looked me full in the face; but I kept my countenance so well that he could not imagine I was saying anything more than the actual truth.

'"Then it's all over, I suppose," he said, looking as if he could have died on the spot with vexation and the intensity of his despair. But he was angry as well as disappointed. There was he, suffering so unspeakably, and there was I, the pitiless cause of it all, so utterly impenetrable to all the artillery of his looks and words, so calmly cold and proud, he could not but feel some resentment; and with singular bitterness he began, –

'"I certainly did not expect this, Miss Murray. I might say something about your past conduct, and the hopes you have led me to foster; but I forbear, on condition –"

'"No conditions, Mr Hatfield!" said I, now truly indignant at his insolence.

'"Then let me beg it as a favour," he replied, lowering his voice at once, and taking an humbler tone; "let me entreat that you will not mention this affair to anyone whatever. If you will keep silence about it, there need be no unpleasantness on either side – nothing, I mean, beyond what is quite unavoidable, for my own feelings, I will endeavour to keep to myself, if I cannot annihilate them;[10] I will try to forgive if I cannot forget the cause of my sufferings. I will not suppose, Miss Murray, that you know how deeply you have injured me. I would not have you aware of it; but if, in addition to the injury you have already done me – pardon me, but whether innocently or not, you *have* done it – and if you add to it by giving publicity to this unfortunate affair, or naming it *at all*, you will find that I too can speak; and though you scorned my love, you will hardly scorn my – "

'He stopped, but he bit his bloodless lip and looked so terribly fierce that I was quite frightened. However, my pride upheld me still, and I answered disdainfully, –

'"I do not know what motive you suppose I could have for naming it to anyone, Mr Hatfield; but if I were disposed to do so, you would not deter me by threats; and it is scarcely the part of a gentleman to attempt it."

'"Pardon me, Miss Murray," said he, "I have loved you so intensely – I do still adore you so deeply that I would not willingly offend you; but though I never have loved, and never *can* love any woman as I have loved you, it is equally certain that I never was so ill-treated by any. On the contrary, I have always found your sex the kindest – and most tender and obliging of God's creation, till now." (Think of the conceited fellow saying that!) "And the novelty and the harshness of the lesson you have taught me to-day, and the bitterness of being disappointed in the only quarter on which the happiness of my life depended, must

excuse any appearance of asperity. If my presence is disagreeable
to you, Miss Murray," he said (for I was looking about me to
show how little I cared for him, so he thought I was tired of him,
I suppose), – "If my presence is disagreeable to you, Miss
Murray, you have only to promise me the favour I named, and I
will relieve you at once. There are many ladies – some even in
this parish – that would be delighted to accept what you have so
scornfully trampled under your feet. They would be naturally
inclined to hate one whose surpassing loveliness has so completely estranged my heart from them and blinded me to their
attractions; and a single hint of the truth, from me to one of
these, would be sufficient to raise such a talk against you as
would seriously injure your prospects, and diminish your chance
of success with any other gentleman you or your mamma might
design to entangle."

'"What do you mean, sir?" said I, ready to stamp with passion.

'"I mean that this affair from beginning to end appears to me
like a case of arrant – flirtation, to say the least of it – such a case
as you would find it rather inconvenient to have blazoned through
the world – especially with the additions and exaggerations of
your female rivals, who would be too glad to publish the matter,
if I only gave them a handle to it. But I promise you, on the faith
of a gentleman, that no word or syllable that could tend to your
prejudice shall ever escape my lips, provided you will – "

'"Well, well, I won't mention it," said I. "You may rely upon
my silence, if that can afford you any consolation."

'"You promise it?"

'"Yes," I answered, for I wanted to get rid of him now.

'"Farewell, then!" said he, in a most doleful heart-sick tone;
and with a look where pride vainly struggled against despair, he
turned and went away, longing, no doubt, to get home, that he
might shut himself up in his study and cry – if he doesn't burst
into tears before he gets there.'

'But you have broken your promise already!' said I, truly
horrified at her perfidy.

'Oh! it's only to you – I know you won't repeat it.'

'Certainly, I shall not; but you say you are going to tell your sister; and she will tell your brothers when they come home, and Brown immediately, if you do not tell her yourself, and Brown will blazon it, or be the means of blazoning it, throughout the country.'

'No, indeed she won't – We shall not tell her at all, unless it be under the promise of the strictest secrecy.'

'But how can you expect her to keep her promises better than her more enlightened mistress?'

'Well, well, she shan't hear it then,' said Miss Murray, somewhat snappishly.

'But you will tell your mamma, of course,' pursued I; 'and she will tell your papa.'

'Of course, I shall tell mamma: that is the very thing that pleases me so much. I shall now be able to convince her how mistaken she was in her fears about me.'

'Oh, *that's* it, is it? I was wondering what it was that delighted you so much.'

'Yes; and another thing is, that I've humbled Mr Hatfield so charmingly; and another – why, you must allow me some share of female vanity; I don't pretend to be without that most essential attribute of our sex – and if you had seen poor Hatfield's intense eagerness in making his ardent declaration, and his flattering proposal, and his agony of mind that no effort of pride could conceal, on being refused, you would have allowed I had some cause to be gratified.'

'The greater his agony, I should think the less your cause for gratification.'

'Oh, nonsense!' cried the young lady, shaking herself with vexation. 'You either can't understand me, or you won't. If I had not confidence in your magnanimity, I should think you envied me. But you will perhaps comprehend *this* cause of pleasure – which is as great as any – namely, that I am delighted with myself for my prudence, my self-command, my *heartlessness*, if you please; I was not a bit taken by surprise, not a bit confused, or awkward, or foolish; I just acted and spoke as I ought to have done, and was completely my own mistress

throughout. And here was a man, decidedly good-looking – Jane
and Susan Green call him bewitchingly handsome – I suppose
they're two of the ladies he pretends would be so glad to have
him – but, however, he was certainly a very clever, witty, agreeable companion – not what *you* call clever, but just enough to
make him entertaining; and a man one needn't be ashamed of
anywhere, and would not soon grow tired of; and, – to confess
the truth, I rather liked him – better even, of late than Harry
Meltham – and he evidently idolized me; and yet, though he came
upon me all alone and unprepared, I had the wisdom, and the
pride, and the strength to refuse him – and so scornfully and
coolly as I did: I have good reason to be proud of that!'

'And are you equally proud of having told him that his having
the wealth of Sir Hugh Meltham would make no difference to
you when that was not the case; and of having promised to tell
no one of his misadventure, apparently without the slightest
intention of keeping your promise?'

'Of course! what else could I do? You would not have had me
– but I see, Miss Grey, you're not in a good temper. – Here's
Matilda; I'll see what she and mamma have to say about it.'

She left me, offended at my want of sympathy, and thinking,
no doubt, that I envied her. I did not – at least, I firmly believe I
did not. I was sorry for her; I was amazed, disgusted at her
heartless vanity; I wondered why so much beauty should be
given to those who made so bad a use of it, and denied to some
who would make it a benefit to both themselves and others.

But God knows best, I concluded. There are, I suppose, some
men as vain, as selfish, and as heartless as she is, and, perhaps,
such women may be useful to punish them.

XV

THE WALK

'O DEAR! I WISH HATFIELD had not been so precipitate!' said Rosalie next day at four p.m., as, with a portentous yawn, she laid down her worsted-work and looked listlessly towards the window.

'There's no inducement to go out now; and nothing to look forward to. The days will be so long and dull when there are no parties to enliven them; and there are none this week, or next either, that I know of.'

'Pity you were so cross to him,' observed Matilda, to whom this lamentation was addressed. 'He'll never come again; and I suspect you liked him after all. I hoped you would have taken him for your beau, and left dear Harry to me.'

'Humph! my beau must be an Adonis indeed, Matilda, the admired of all beholders, if I am to be contented with him alone. I'm sorry to lose Hatfield, I confess; but the first decent man, or number of men, that come to supply his place, will be more than welcome. It's Sunday to-morrow – I do wonder how he'll look, and whether he'll be able to go through the service. Most likely he'll pretend he's got a cold and make Mr Weston do it all.'

'Not he!' exclaimed Matilda, somewhat contemptuously. 'Fool as he is, he's not so soft as that comes to.'

Her sister was slightly offended; but the event proved Matilda was right. The disappointed lover performed his pastoral duties as usual. Rosalie, indeed, affirmed he looked very pale and dejected: he might be a little paler, but the difference, if any, was scarcely perceptible. As for his dejection, I certainly did not hear his laugh ringing from the vestry as usual, nor his voice loud in hilarious discourse, though I did hear it uplifted in rating the sexton in a manner that made the congregation stare; and, in his transits to and from the pulpit and the communion-table there was more of solemn pomp, and less of that irreverent, self-confident, or rather self-delighted imperiousness with which he usually swept along – that air that seemed to say, 'You all reverence and adore me, I know; but if any one does not, I defy him to the teeth!'

But the most remarkable change was that he never once suffered his eyes to wander in the direction of Mr Murray's pew, and did not leave the church till we were gone.

Mr Hatfield had doubtless received a very severe blow; but his pride impelled him to use every effort to conceal the effects of it. He had been disappointed in his certain hope of obtaining not only a beautiful and, to him, highly attractive wife, but one whose rank and fortune might give brilliance to far inferior charms: he was likewise, no doubt, intensely mortified by his repulse, and deeply offended at the conduct of Miss Murray throughout.

It would have given him no little consolation to have known how disappointed she was to find him apparently so little moved, and to see that he was able to refrain from casting a single glance at her throughout both the services, though, she declared, it showed that he was thinking of her all the time, or his eyes would have fallen upon her, if it were only by chance; but if they had so chanced to fall, she would have affirmed it was because they could not resist the attraction. It might have pleased him too, in some degree, to have seen how dull and dissatisfied she was throughout that week (the greater part of it, at least), for lack of her usual source of excitement; and how often she regretted having 'used him up so soon,' like a child that, having devoured its plum-cake too hastily, sits sucking its fingers, and vainly lamenting its greediness.

At length, I was called upon, one fine morning, to accompany her in a walk to the village. Ostensibly she went to get some shades of Berlin wool at a tolerably respectable shop that was chiefly supported by the ladies of the vicinity: really – I trust there is no breach of charity in supposing that she went with the idea of meeting either with the Rector himself, or some other admirer by the way; for as we went along, she kept wondering 'what Hatfield would do or say if we met him,' etc., etc., as we passed Mr Green's park-gates, she 'wondered whether he was at home – great stupid blockhead;' as Lady Meltham's carriage passed us, she 'wondered what Mr Harry was doing this fine day;' and then began to abuse his elder brother for being 'such a fool as to get married and go and live in London.'

'Why,' said I, 'I thought you wanted to live in London yourself.'

'Yes, because it's so dull here; and then he makes it still duller by taking himself off; and if he were not married, I might have him instead of that odious Sir Thomas.'

Then, observing the prints of a horse's feet on the somewhat miry road, she 'wondered whether it was a gentleman's horse,' and finally concluded it was, for the impressions were too small to have been made by a 'great, clumsy cart-horse;' and then she 'wondered who the rider could be,' and whether we should meet him coming back, for she was sure he had only passed that morning; and lastly, when we entered the village and saw only a few of its humble inhabitants moving about, she 'wondered why the stupid people couldn't keep in their houses; she was sure she didn't want to see their ugly faces, and dirty, vulgar clothes – it wasn't for that she came to Horton!'

Amid all this, I confess, I wondered too, in secret, whether we should meet, or catch a glimpse of somebody else; and as we passed his lodgings, I even went so far as to wonder whether he was at the window.

On entering the shop, Miss Murray desired me to stand in the doorway while she transacted her business, and tell her if any one passed. But alas! there was no one visible besides the villagers, except Jane and Susan Green coming down the single street, apparently returning from a walk.

'Stupid things!' muttered she, as she came out after having concluded her bargain. 'Why couldn't they have their dolt of a brother with them? even *he* would be better than nothing!'

She greeted them, however, with a cheerful smile, and protestations of pleasure at the happy meeting equal to their own. They placed themselves one on each side of her; and all three walked away chatting and laughing as young ladies do when they get together, if they be but on tolerably intimate terms. But I, feeling myself to be one too many, left them to their merriment and lagged behind, as usual on such occasions: I had no relish for walking beside Miss Green or Miss Susan like one deaf and dumb, who could neither speak nor be spoken to.

But this time, I was not long alone. It struck me, at first, as very odd, that just as I was thinking about Mr Weston he should come up and accost me; but afterwards, on due reflection, I thought there was nothing odd about it, unless it were the fact of his speaking to me, for, on such a morning and so near his own abode, it was natural enough that he should be about; and as for my thinking of him, I had been doing that, with little inter-mission, ever since we set out on our journey; so there was nothing remarkable in that.

'You are alone again, Miss Grey,' said he.

'Yes.'

'What kind of people are those ladies – the Misses Green?'

'I really don't know.'

'That's strange – when you live so near and see them so often!'

'Well, I suppose they are lively, good-tempered girls; but I imagine you must know them better than I do, yourself, for I never exchanged a word with either of them.'

'Indeed! They don't strike me as being particularly reserved.'

'Very likely they are not so to people of their own class; but they consider themselves as moving in quite a different sphere from me!'

He made no reply to this; but after a short pause, he said, –

'I suppose it's these things, Miss Grey, that make you think you could not live without a home?'

'Not exactly. The fact is I am too socially disposed to be able to live contentedly without a friend, and as the only friends I have, or am likely to have, are at home, if it – or rather, if they were gone – I will not say I could not live – but I would rather not live in such a desolate world.'

'But why do you say the only friends you are likely to have? Are you so unsociable that you cannot make friends?'

'No, but I never made one yet; and in my present position there is no possibility of doing so, or even of forming a common acquaintance. The fault may be partly in myself, but I hope not together.'

'The fault is partly in society, and partly, I should think, in your immediate neighbours, and partly, too, in yourself; for many ladies, in your position, would *make* themselves be noticed and accounted of. But your pupils should be companions for you in some degree; they cannot be many years younger than yourself.'

'Oh, yes, they are good company sometimes; but I cannot call them friends, nor would they think of bestowing such a name on me – they have other companions better suited to their tastes.'

'Perhaps you are too wise for them. How do you amuse yourself when alone – do you read much?'

'Reading is my favourite occupation, when I have leisure for it, and books to read.'

From speaking of books in general, he passed to different books in particular, and proceeded by rapid transitions from topic to topic, till several matters, both of taste and opinion, had been discussed considerably within the space of half-an-hour, but without the embellishment of many observations from himself; he being evidently less bent upon communicating his own thoughts and predilections, than on discovering mine. He had not the tact or the art to effect such a purpose by skilfully drawing out my sentiments or ideas through the real or apparent statement of his own, or leading the conversation by imperceptible gradations to such topics as he wished to advert to. But such gentle abruptness, and such single-minded straightforwardness could not possibly offend me.

'And why should he interest himself at all in my moral and intellectual capacities: what is it to him what I think or feel?' I asked myself.

And my heart throbbed in answer to the question.

But Jane and Susan Green soon reached their home. As they

stood parleying at the park-gates, attempting to persuade Miss Murray to come in, I wished Mr Weston would go, that she might not see him with me when she turned round; but unfortunately, his business, which was to pay one more visit to poor Mark Wood, led him to pursue the same path as we did, till nearly the close of our journey.

When, however, he saw that Rosalie had taken leave of her friends, and I was about to join her, he would have left me and passed on at a quicker pace; but, as he civilly lifted his hat in passing her, to my surprise, instead of returning the salute with a stiff, ungracious bow, she accosted him with one of her sweetest smiles, and, walking by his side, began to talk to him with all imaginable cheerfulness and affability; and so we proceeded all three together.

After a short pause in the conversation Mr Weston made some remark addressed particularly to me, as referring to something we had been talking of before; but, before I could answer, Miss Murray replied to the observation and enlarged upon it: he rejoined; and from thence to the close of the interview, she engrossed him entirely to herself.

It might be partly owing to my own stupidity, my want of tact and assurance; but I felt myself wronged; I trembled with apprehension; and I listened with envy to her easy, rapid flow of utterance, and saw with anxiety the bright smile with which she looked into his face from time to time, for she was walking a little in advance, for the purpose (as I judged) of being seen as well as heard.

If her conversation was light and trivial, it was amusing, and she was never at a loss for something to say, or for suitable words to express it in. There was nothing pert or flippant in her manner now, as when she walked with Mr Hatfield; there was only a gentle, playful kind of vivacity, which I thought must be peculiarly pleasing to a man of Mr Weston's disposition and temperament.

When he was gone she began to laugh, and muttered to herself, – 'I thought I could do it!'

'Do what?' I asked.

'Fix that man.'

'What in the world do you mean?'

'I mean that he will go home and dream of me. I have shot him through the heart!'

'How do you know?'

'By many infallible proofs: more especially the look he gave me when he went away. It was not an impudent look – I exonerate him from that – it was a look of reverential tender adoration. Ha, ha! he's not quite such a stupid blockhead as I thought him!'

I made no answer, for my heart was in my throat, or something like it, and I could not trust myself to speak. 'O, God, avert it!' I cried internally – 'for his sake, not for mine!'

Miss Murray made several trivial observations as we passed up the park, to which (in spite of my reluctance to let one glimpse of my feelings appear) I could only answer by monosyllables.

Whether she intended to torment me, or merely to amuse herself, I could not tell – and did not much care; but I thought of the poor man and his one lamb,[1] and the rich man with his thousand flocks; and I dreaded I knew not what for Mr Weston, independently of my own blighted hopes.

Right glad was I to get into the house, and find myself alone once more in my own room. My first impulse was to sink into the chair beside the bed, and, laying my head on the pillow, to seek relief in a passionate burst of tears: there was an imperative craving for such an indulgence; but alas! I must restrain and swallow back my feelings still: there was the bell – the odious bell for the school-room dinner; and I must go down with a calm face, and smile, and laugh, and talk nonsense – yes, and eat, too, if possible, as if all were right, and I were just returned from a pleasant walk.

XVI

THE SUBSTITUTION

NEXT SUNDAY WAS ONE OF the gloomiest of April days, a day of thick dark clouds, and heavy showers. None of the Murrays were disposed to attend church in the afternoon, excepting Rosalie: she was bent upon going as usual; so she ordered the carriage, and I went with her, nothing loth, of course, for at church I might look without fear of scorn or censure upon a form and face more pleasing to me than the most beautiful of God's creations; I might listen without disturbance to a voice more charming than the sweetest music to my ears; I might seem to hold communion with that soul in which I felt so deeply interested, and imbibe its purest thoughts and holiest aspirations, with no alloy to such felicity, except the secret reproaches of my conscience, which would too often whisper that I was deceiving my own self, and mocking God with the service of a heart more bent upon the creature than the Creator.

Sometimes, such thoughts would give me trouble enough; but sometimes I could quiet them with thinking –

'It is not the man, it is his goodness that I love.'

'Whatsoever things are pure, whatsoever things are lovely, whatsoever things are honest and of good report, think on these things.'[1]

We do well to worship God in his works; and I know none of them in which so many of his attributes – so much of his own spirit shines, as [in] this his faithful servant, whom to know and not to appreciate, were obtuse insensibility in me, who have so little else to occupy my heart.

Almost immediately after the conclusion of the service, Miss Murray left the church. We had to stand in the porch; for it was raining, and the carriage was not yet come. I wondered at her coming forth so hastily, for neither young Meltham nor Squire Green were there; but I soon found it was to secure an interview with Mr Weston as he came out, which he presently did, and having saluted us both, would have passed on, but she detained him; first with observations upon the disagreeable weather, and then with asking if he would be so kind as to come sometime tomorrow to see the granddaughter of the old woman who kept the porter's lodge, for the girl was ill of a fever, and wished to see him. He promised to do so.

'And at what time will you be most likely to come, Mr Weston? The old woman will like to know when to expect you – you know such people think more about having their cottages in order when decent people come to see them than we are apt to suppose.'

Here was a wonderful instance of consideration from the thoughtless Miss Murray.

Mr Weston named an hour in the morning at which he would endeavour to be there. By this time the carriage was ready, and the footman was waiting, with an open umbrella, to escort Miss Murray through the church-yard. I was about to follow; but Mr Weston had an umbrella too, and offered me the benefit of its shelter, for it was raining heavily.

'No, thank you, I don't mind the rain,' I said.

I always lacked common sense when taken by surprise.

'But you don't *like* it, I suppose? – an umbrella will do you no harm at any rate,' he replied, with a smile that showed he was not offended, as a man of worse temper or less penetration would have been at such a refusal of his aid.

I could not deny the truth of his assertion, and so went with him to the carriage; he even offered me his hand on getting in, an unnecessary piece of civility, but I accepted that too, for fear of giving offence. One glance he gave, one little smile at parting – it was but for a moment, but therein I read, or thought I read, a meaning that kindled in my heart a brighter flame of hope than had ever yet arisen.

'I would have sent the footman back for you, Miss Grey, if you'd waited a moment – you needn't have taken Mr Weston's

umbrella,' observed Rosalie, with a very unamiable cloud upon
her pretty face.

'I would have come without an umbrella, but Mr Weston
offered me the benefit of his, and I could not have refused it,
more than I did, without offending him,' replied I, smiling placid-
ly, for my inward happiness made that amusing, which would
have wounded me at another time.

The carriage was now in motion. Miss Murray bent forwards,
and looked out of the window as we were passing Mr Weston.
He was pacing homewards along the causeway, and did not turn
his head.

'Stupid ass!' cried she, throwing herself back again in the seat.
'You don't know *what* you've lost by not looking this way!'

'What has he lost?'

'A bow from me, that would have raised him to the seventh
heaven!'

I made no answer. I saw she was out of humour, and I derived
a secret gratification from the fact, not that she was vexed, but
that she thought she had reason to be so. It made me think my
hopes were not entirely the offspring of my wishes and imagination.

'I mean to take up Mr Weston instead of Mr Hatfield,' said
my companion after a short pause, resuming something of her
usual cheerfulness. 'The ball at Ashby Park takes place on Tuesday, you know; and mamma thinks it very likely that Sir Thomas
will propose to me then – such things are often done in the
privacy of the ball-room, when gentlemen are most easily en-
snared, and ladies most enchanting: – but if I am to be married
so soon, I must make the best of the present time: I am determined Hatfield shall not be the only man who shall lay his heart
at my feet, and implore me to accept the worthless gift in vain.'

'If you mean Mr Weston to be one of your victims,' said I,
with affected indifference, 'you will have to make such overtures
yourself that you will find it difficult to draw back when he asks
you to fulfil the expectations you have raised.'

'I don't suppose he will ask me to *marry* him – nor should I
desire it . . . that would be *rather* too much presumption! but I

intend him to feel my power – he has felt it already, indeed – but he shall *acknowledge* it too; and what visionary hopes he may have, he must keep to himself, and only amuse me with a result of them – for a time.'

'Oh! that some kind spirit would whisper those words in his ear!' I inwardly exclaimed. I was far too indignant to hazard a reply to her observation, aloud; and nothing more was said about Mr Weston that day, by me or in my hearing. But next morning, soon after breakfast, Miss Murray came into the school-room where her sister was employed with me at her studies ... or rather her lessons, for studies they were not ... and said, –

'Matilda, I want you to take a walk with me about eleven o'clock.'

'Oh, I can't, Rosalie! I have to give orders about my new bridle and saddle-cloth, and speak to the rat-catcher about his dogs ... Miss Grey must go with you.'

'No, I want *you*,' said Rosalie; and calling her sister to the window, she whispered an explanation in her ear, upon which the latter consented to go.

I remembered that eleven was the hour at which Mr Weston proposed to come to the porter's lodge; and remembering that, I beheld the whole contrivance.

Accordingly, at dinner, I was entertained with a long account of how Mr Weston had overtaken them as they were walking along the road; and how they had had a long walk and talk with him, and really found him quite an agreeable companion; and how he must have been, and evidently was, delighted with them and their amazing condescension, etc., etc.

XVII
CONFESSIONS

A s I A M I N T H E W A Y O F confessions, I may as well acknowledge that, about this time, I paid more attention to dress than ever I had done before . . . this is not saying much, for hitherto I had been a little neglectful in that particular . . . but now, also, it is no uncommon thing to spend as much as two minutes in the contemplation of my own image in the glass; though I never could derive any consolation from such a study: I could discover no beauty in those marked features,[1] that pale hollow cheek, and ordinary dark brown hair; there might be intellect in the forehead, there might be expression in the dark grey eyes, but what of that? . . . a low Grecian brow, and large black eyes devoid of sentiment would be esteemed far preferable.

It is foolish to wish for beauty. Sensible people never either desire it for themselves or care about it in others. If the mind be but well cultivated, and the heart well disposed, no one ever cares for the exterior.

So said the teachers of our childhood; and so say we to the children of the present day. All very judicious and proper no doubt; but are such assertions supported by actual experience?

We are naturally disposed to love what gives us pleasure, and what more pleasing than a beautiful face . . . when we know no harm of the possessor at least? A little girl loves her bird . . . Why? . . . Because it lives and feels, because it is helpless and harmless. A toad, likewise, lives and feels, and is equally helpless and harmless; but though she would not hurt a toad, she cannot love it like the bird, with its graceful form, soft feathers, and bright, speaking eyes. If a woman is fair and amiable, she is praised for both qualities, but especially the former, by the bulk of mankind: if, on the other hand, she is disagreeable in person and character, the plainness is commonly inveighed against as her greatest crime, because to common observers, it gives the greatest offence; while if she is plain and good, provided she is a a person of retiring manners and secluded life, no one ever knows of her goodness, except her immediate connections; others, on the contrary, are disposed to form unfavourable opinions of her mind and disposition, if it be but to excuse themselves for their instinctive dislike of one so unfavoured by nature; and *vice versa* with her whose angel form conceals a vicious heart, or sheds a false, deceitful charm over defects and foibles that would not be tolerated in another.

They that have beauty, let them be thankful for it, and make a good use of it, like any other talent: they that have it not, let them console themselves, and do the best they can without it – certainly, though liable to be over-estimated, it is a gift of God, and not to be despised. Many will feel this, who have felt that they could love, and whose hearts tell them that they are worthy to be loved again, while yet they are debarred, by the lack of this or some such seeming trifle, from giving and receiving that happiness they seem almost made to feel and to impart. As well might the humble glow-worm despise that power of giving light, without which, the roving fly might pass her and repass her a thousand times, and never light beside her; she might hear her winged darling buzzing over and around her; he vainly seeking her, she longing to be found, but with no power to make her presence known, no voice to call him, no wings to follow his flight . . . the fly must seek nother mate, the worm must live and die alone.

Such were some of my reflections about this period. I might go on prosing more and more, I might dive much deeper, and disclose other thoughts, propose questions the reader might be puzzled to answer, and deduce arguments that might startle his prejudices, or perhaps provoke his ridicule, because he could not comprehend them; but I forbear.

Now, therefore, let us return to Miss Murray. She accompanied her mamma to the ball on Tuesday; of course splendidly attired, and delighted with her prospects and her charms. As Ashby Park was nearly ten miles distant from Horton Lodge, they had to set out pretty early, and I intended to have spent the evening with Nancy Brown, whom I had not seen for a long time; but my kind pupil took care I should spend it neither there nor anywhere else beyond the limits of the school-room, by giving me a piece of music to copy, which kept me closely occupied till bed-time.

About eleven next morning, as soon as she had left her room, she came to tell me her news. Sir Thomas had indeed proposed to her at the ball, an event which reflected great credit on her mamma's sagacity, if not upon her skill in contrivance; I rather incline to the belief that she had first laid her plans, and then predicted their success.

The offer had been accepted of course, and the bridegroom-elect was coming that day to settle matters with Mr Murray.

Rosalie was pleased with the thoughts of becoming mistress of Ashby Park; she was elated with the prospect of the bridal ceremony and its attendant splendour and eclat,[2] the honeymoon spent abroad, and the subsequent gaieties she expected to enjoy in London and elsewhere; she appeared pretty well pleased too, for the time being, with Sir Thomas himself, because she had so lately seen him, danced with him, and been flattered by him; but, after all, she seemed to shrink from the idea of being so soon united: she wished the ceremony to be delayed some months, at least; and I wished it too. It seemed a horrible thing to hurry on the inauspicious match, and not to give the poor creature time to think and reason on the irrevocable step she was about to take. I made no pretension to 'a mother's watchful, anxious care,' but I was amazed and horrified at Mrs Murray's heartlessness, or want of thought for the real good of her child; and, by my unheeded warnings and exhortations, I vainly strove to remedy the evil. Miss Murray only laughed at what I said; and I soon found that her reluctance to an immediate union arose chiefly from a desire to do what execution she could among the young gentlemen of her acquaintance before she was incapacitated from further mischief of the kind. It was for this cause that, before she confided to me the secret of her engagement, she had extracted a promise that I would not mention a word on the subject to any one. And when I saw this, and when I beheld her plunge more recklessly than ever into the depths of heartless coquetry, I had no more pity for her.

'Come what will,' I thought, 'she deserves it. Sir Thomas cannot be too bad for her; and the sooner she is incapacitated from deceiving and injuring others the better.'

The wedding was fixed for the first of June. Between that and the critical ball was little more than six weeks; but, with Rosalie's accomplished skill and resolute exertion, much might be done, even within that period, especially as Sir Thomas spent most of the interim in London, whither he went up, it was said, to settle affairs with his lawyer, and make other preparations for the approaching nuptials.

He endeavoured to supply the want of his presence by a pretty constant fire of billets-doux;[3] but these did not attract the neighbours' attention, and open their eyes as personal visits would have done; and old Lady Ashby's haughty, sour spirit of reserve withheld her from spreading the news, while her indifferent health prevented her coming to visit her future daughter-in-law; so that, altogether, this affair was kept far closer than such things usually are.

Rosalie would sometimes shew her lover's epistles to me, to convince me what a kind, devoted husband he would make. She shewed me the letters of another individual, too, the unfortunate Mr Green, who had not the courage, or, as she expressed it, the 'spunk' to plead his cause in person, but whom one denial would not satisfy; he must write again and again.

He would not have done so if he could have seen the grimaces his fair idol made over his moving appeals to her feelings, and heard her scornful laughter, and the opprobrious epithets she heaped upon him for his perseverance.

'Why don't you tell him, at once, that you are engaged?' I asked.

'Oh, I don't want him to know that!' replied she. 'If he knew it, his sisters and everybody would know it, and then there would be an end of my – ahem – And besides, if I told him that, he would think my engagement was the only obstacle, and that I

would have him if I were free, which I could not bear that any
man should think, and he, of all others, the least. Besides, I don't
care for his letters,' she added contemptuously; 'he may write as
often as he pleases, and look as great a calf as he likes when I
meet him; it only amuses *me*.'

Meantime, young Meltham was pretty frequent in his visits to
the house or transits past it; and, judging by Matilda's execrations and reproaches, her sister paid more attention to him than
civility required – in other words, she carried on as animated a
flirtation as the presence of her parents would admit.

She made some attempts to bring Mr Hatfield once more to
her feet; but finding them unsuccessful, she repaid his haughty
indifference with still loftier scorn, and spoke of him with as
much disdain and detestation as she had formerly done of his
curate.

But, amid all this, she never for a moment lost sight of Mr
Weston. She embraced every opportunity of meeting him, tried
every art to fascinate him, and pursued him with as much perseverance as if she really loved him – and no other, and the happiness
of her life depended upon eliciting a return of affection. Such
conduct was completely beyond my comprehension. Had I seen
it depicted in a novel I should have thought it unnatural; had I
heard it described by others, I should have deemed it a mistake
or an exaggeration; but when I saw it with my own eyes, and
suffered from it too, I could only conclude that excessive vanity,
like drunkenness, hardens the heart, enslaves the faculties, and
perverts the feelings, and that dogs are not the only creatures
which, when gorged to the throat, will yet gloat over what they
cannot devour, and grudge the smallest morsel to a starving
brother.

She now became extremely beneficent to the poor cottagers.
Her acquaintance among them was more widely extended, her
visits to their humble dwellings were more frequent and ex-
cursive than they had ever been before. Hereby, she earned
among them the reputation of a condescending and very charitable young lady; and their encomiums were sure to be repeated
to Mr Weston, whom also she had, thus, a daily chance of

meeting in one or other of their abodes, or in her transits to and fro; and often, likewise, she could gather, through their gossip, to what places he was likely to go at such and such a time, whether to baptise a child, or to visit the aged, the sick, the sad, or the dying; and most skilfully she laid her plans accordingly.

In these excursions she would sometimes go with her sister, whom, by some means, she had persuaded or bribed to enter into her schemes, sometimes alone, never, now, with me; so that I was debarred the pleasure of seeing Mr Weston, or hearing his voice, even in conversation with another, which would certainly have been a very great pleasure, however hurtful or however fraught with pain.

I could not even see him at church, for Miss Murray, under some trivial pretext, chose to take possession of that corner in the family pew which had been mine ever since I came; and unless I had the presumption to station myself between Mr and Mrs Murray, I must sit with my back to the pulpit, which I accordingly did.

Now, also, I never walked home with my pupils: they said their mamma thought it did not look well to see three people out of the family walking, and only two going in the carriage; and, as they greatly preferred walking in fine weather, I should be honoured by going with the seniors.

'And besides,' said they, 'you can't walk as fast as we do; you know you're always lagging behind.'

I knew these were false excuses, but I made no objections, and never contradicted such assertions, well knowing the motives which dictated them.

And in the afternoons, during those six memorable weeks, I never went to church at all. If I had a cold, or any slight indisposition, they took advantage of that to make me stay at home; and often they would tell me they were not going again that day, themselves, and then pretend to change their minds, and set off without telling me, so managing their departure that I never discovered the change of purpose till too late.

Upon their return home, on one of these occasions, they entertained me with an animated account of a conversation they had had with Mr Weston as they came along.

'And he asked if you were ill, Miss Grey,' said Matilda: 'but we told him you were quite well, only you didn't want to come to church – so he'll think you're turned wicked.'

All chance meetings on weekdays were likewise carefully prevented; for, lest I should go to see poor Nancy Brown or any other person, Miss Murray took good care to provide sufficient employment for all my leisure hours. There was always some drawing to finish, some music to copy, or some work to do sufficient to incapacitate me from indulging in anything beyond a short walk about the grounds, however she or her sister might be occupied.

One morning, having sought and waylaid Mr Weston, they returned in high glee to give me an account of their interview.

'And he asked after you again,' said Matilda, in spite of her sister's silent but imperative intimation that she should hold her tongue. 'He wondered why you were never with us, and thought you must have delicate health, as you came out so seldom.'

'He didn't, Matilda – what nonsense you're talking!'

'Oh, Rosalie, what a lie! He did, you know; and you said – Don't, Rosalie – hang it! – I won't be pinched so! And, Miss Grey, Rosalie told him you were quite well, but you were always so buried in your books that you had had no pleasure in anything else.'

'What an idea he must have of me!' I thought.

'And,' I asked, 'does old Nancy ever inquire about me?'

'Yes, and we tell her you are so fond of reading and drawing that you can do nothing else.'

'That is not the case though; if you had told her I was so busy I *could* not come so see her, it would have been nearer the truth.'

'I don't think it would,' replied Miss Murray, suddenly kindling up; 'I'm sure you have plenty of time to yourself now, when you have so little teaching to do.'

It was no use beginning to dispute with such indulged, unreasoning creatures; so I held my peace. I was accustomed, now, to keeping silence when things distasteful to my ear were uttered; and now, too, I was used to wearing a placid smiling countenance when my heart was bitter within me. Only those who have felt the like can imagine my feelings, as I sat with an assumption of smiling indifference, listening to the accounts of those meetings and interviews with Mr Weston, which they seemed to find such pleasure in describing to me, and hearing things asserted of him which, from the character of the man, I knew to be exaggerations and perversions of the truth, if not entirely false – things derogatory to him, and flattering to them – especially to Miss Murray – which I burned to contradict, or, at least, to show my doubts about, but dared not, lest, in expressing my disbelief, I should display my interest too.

Other things I heard, which I felt or feared were indeed too true; but I must still conceal my anxiety respecting him, my indignation against them beneath a careless aspect; others again – mere hints of something said or done, which I longed to hear more of, but could not venture to inquire.

So passed the weary time. I could not even comfort myself with saying, 'She will soon be married; and then, there may be hope.'

Soon after her marriage the holidays would come; and when I returned from home, most likely, Mr Weston would be gone, for, I was told that he and the Rector could not agree (the Rector's fault of course), and he was about to remove to another place.

No – besides my hope in God, my only consolation was in thinking that, though he knew it not, I was more worthy of his love than Rosalie Murray, charming and engaging as she was; for I could appreciate his excellence, which she could not; I would devote my life to the promotion of his happiness; she would destroy his happiness for the momentary gratification of her own vanity.

'Oh, if he could but know the difference!' I would earnestly exclaim. 'But no! I would not have him see my heart – but, if he could but know her hollowness, her worthless, heartless frivolity – he would then be safe, and I should be – *almost* happy, though I might never see him more!'

I fear, by this time, the reader is well nigh disgusted with the

folly and weakness I have so freely laid before him. I never
disclosed it then, and would not have done so had my own sister
or my mother been with me in the house.

I was a close and resolute dissembler – in this one case at
least. My prayers, my tears, my wishes, fears, and lamentations,
were witnessed by myself and Heaven alone.

When we are harassed by sorrows or anxieties, or long oppressed by any powerful feelings which we must keep to ourselves, for which we can obtain and seek no sympathy from any
living creature, and which, yet, we cannot, or will not wholly
crush, we often, naturally, seek relief in poetry – and often find
it too – whether in the effusions of others, which seem to har-
monize with our existing case, or in our own attempts to give
utterance to those thoughts and feelings in strains less musical,
perchance, but more appropriate, and therefore more penetrating
and sympathetic, and, for the time, more soothing, or more
powerful to rouse and to unburden the oppressed and swollen
heart.

Before this time, at Wellwood House and here, when suffering
from home-sick melancholy, I had sought relief twice or thrice
at this secret source of consolation; and now I flew to it again,
with greater avidity than ever, because I seemed to need it more.
I still preserve those relics of past sufferings and experience, like
pillars of witness set up in travelling through the vale of life, to
mark particular occurrences.

The footsteps are obliterated now; the face of the country
may be changed, but the pillar is still there to remind me how all
things were when it was reared.

Lest the reader should be curious to see any of these effusions,
I will favour him with one short specimen: cold and languid as
the lines may seem, it was almost a passion of grief to which
they owed their being.

> "Oh, they have robbed me of the hope
>   My spirit held so dear;
> They will not let me hear that voice
>   My soul delights to hear.

"They will not let me see that face
    I so delight to see;
And they have taken all thy smiles,
    And all thy love from me.

"Well, let them seize on all they can; –
    One treasure still is mine, –
A heart that loves to think on thee,
    And feels the worth of thine."

Yes! at least, they could not deprive me of that; I could think of him day and night; and I could feel that he was worthy to be thought of. Nobody knew him as I did; nobody could appreciate him as I did; nobody could love him as I . . . could, if I might; but there was the evil. What business had I to think so much of one that never thought of me? Was it not foolish? . . . Was it not wrong?

Yet, if I found such deep delight in thinking of him, and if I kept those thoughts to myself, and troubled no one else with them, where was the harm of it? I would ask myself.

And such reasoning prevented me from making any sufficient effort to shake off my fetters.

But if those thoughts brought delight, it was a painful, troubled pleasure, too near akin to anguish; and one that did me more injury than I was aware of. It was an indulgence that a person of more wisdom or more experience would doubtless have denied herself.

And yet . . . how dreary to turn my eyes from the contemplation of that bright object, and force them to dwell on the dull, grey, desolate prospect around, the joyless, hopeless, solitary path that lay before me. It was wrong to be so joyless, so desponding; I should have made God my friend, and to do His will the pleasure and the business of my life; but Faith was weak, and Passion was too strong.

In this time of trouble I had two other causes of affliction. The first may seem a trifle, but it cost me many a tear: Snap, my little dumb, rough-visaged, but bright-eyed, warm-hearted companion, the only thing I had to love me, was taken away, and delivered over to the tender mercies of the village rat-catcher, a man notorious for his brutal treatment of his canine slaves.

The other was serious enough: my letters from home gave intimation that my father's health was worse. No boding fears were expressed, but I was grown timid and despondent, and could not help fearing that some dreadful calamity awaited us there. I seemed to see the black clouds gathering round my native hills, and to hear the angry muttering of a storm that was about to burst, and desolate our hearth.

XVIII
MIRTH AND MOURNING

THE FIRST OF JUNE ARRIVED at last; and Rosalie Murray
was transmuted into Lady Ashby. Most splendidly beautiful she
looked in her bridal costume.

Upon her return from church, after the ceremony, she came
flying into the school-room, flushed with excitement, and laughing . . . half in mirth and half in reckless desperation, as it seemed
to me.

'Now, Miss Grey, I'm Lady Ashby!' she exclaimed. 'It's done!
my fate is sealed . . . there's no drawing back now! I'm come to
receive your congratulations, and bid you good-bye; and then
I'm off . . . for Paris . . . Rome . . . Naples . . . Switzerland . . .
London . . . Oh, dear! what a deal I shall see and hear before I
come back again! But don't forget me; I shan't forget you, though
I've been a naughty girl. Come, why don't you congratulate me?'

'I cannot congratulate you,' I replied, 'till I know whether this
change is really for the better; but I sincerely hope it is; and I
wish you true happiness and the best of blessings.'

'Well, good-bye – the carriage is waiting, and they're calling
me.'

She gave me a hasty kiss, and was hurrying away but, suddenly
returning, embraced me with more affection than I thought her
capable of evincing, and departed with tears in her eyes.

Poor girl! I really loved her then; and forgave her from my
heart all the injury she had done me – and others also; she had
not half known it, I was sure; and I prayed God to pardon her
too.

During the remainder of that day of festal sadness, I was left
to my own devices. Being too much unhinged for any steady
occupation, I wandered about with a book in my hand for several

hours – more thinking than reading, for I had many things to think about; and in the evening, I made use of my liberty to go and see my old friend Nancy once again; to apologise for my long absence ... which must have seemed so neglectful and unkind, by telling her how busy I had been, and to talk, or read, or work for her, whichever might be most acceptable; and also, of course, to tell her the news of this important day, and perhaps to obtain a little information from her in return, respecting Mr Weston's expected departure. But of this, she seemed to know nothing, and I hoped, as she did, that it was all a false report.

She was very glad to see me; but, happily, her eyes were now so nearly well that she was almost independent of my services. She was deeply interested in the wedding; but while I amused her with the details of the festive day, the splendours of the bridal party and of the bride herself, she often sighed and shook her head, and wished good might come of it: she seemed, like me, to regard it rather as a theme for sorrow than rejoicing. I set a long time talking to her about that and other things; – but *no one came*.

Shall I confess – that I sometimes looked towards the door with a half-expectant wish to see it open and give entrance to Mr Weston, as had happened once before? and that, returning through the lanes and fields, I often paused to look round me, and walked more slowly than was at all necessary – for, though a fine evening, it was not a hot one – and, finally, felt a sense of emptiness and disappointment at having reached the house without meeting or even catching a distant glimpse of any one, except a few labourers returning from their work?

Sunday however was approaching: I should see him then; for now that Miss Murray was gone, I could have my old corner again – I should see him; and by look, speech, and manner, I might judge whether the circumstance of her marriage had very much afflicted him.

Happily, I could perceive no shadow of a difference: he wore the same aspect as he had worn two months ago – voice, look, manner – all alike unchanged: there was the same keen-sighted, unclouded truthfulness in his discourse, the same forcible clear-

ness in his style, the same earnest simplicity in all he said and
did, that made itself not marked by the eye and ear, but felt
upon the hearts of his audience.

I walked home with Miss Matilda, but *he did not join us*.
Matilda was now sadly at a loss for amusement, and wofully in
want of a companion. Her brothers at school – her sister married
and gone – she too young to be admitted into society, for which,
from Rosalie's example, she was in some degree beginning to
acquire a taste – a taste at least for the company of certain
classes of gentlemen – at this dull time of year – no hunting
going on . . . no shooting even . . . for, though she might not join
in that, it was *something* to see her father or the gamekeeper go
out with the dogs, and to talk to them, on their return, about the
different birds they had bagged. Now also she was denied the
solace which the companionship of the coachman, groom,
horses, greyhounds and pointers might have afforded; for her
mother having, notwithstanding the disadvantages of a country
life, so satisfactorily disposed of her elder daughter, the pride of
her heart, had begun seriously to turn her attention to the
younger, and being truly alarmed at the roughness of her manners, and thinking it high time to work a reform, had been
aroused at length to exert her authority, and prohibited entirely
the yards, stables, kennels, and coach-house. Of course, she was
not implicitly obeyed; but, indulgent as she had hitherto been,
when once her spirit was roused, her temper was not so gentle as
she required that of her governesses to be, and her will was not
to be thwarted with impunity; and after many a scene of contention between mother and daughter, many a violent outbreak
which I was ashamed to witness, in which the father's authority
was often called in to confirm, with oaths and threats, the
mother's slighted prohibitions . . . for even *he* could see that
'Tilly,' though she would have made a fine lad, was not quite
what a young lady ought to be – Matilda at length found that
her easiest plan was to keep clear of the forbidden regions,
unless she could now and then steal a visit without her watchful mother's knowledge.

Amid all this, let it not be imagined that I escaped without many a reprimand, and many an implied reproach, that lost none of its sting from not being openly worded, but rather wounded the more deeply, because from that very reason, it seemed to preclude self-defence. Frequently, I was told to amuse Miss Matilda with other things, and to *remind* her of her mother's precepts and prohibitions. I did so to the best of my power; but she would not be amused against her will, and could not against her taste; and though I went beyond mere reminding, such gentle remonstrances as I could use were utterly ineffectual.

'*Dear* Miss Grey! it is the *strangest* thing – I suppose you can't help it, if it's not in your nature – but I *wonder* you can't win the confidence of that girl, and make your society at *least* as agreeable to her as that of Robert or Joseph!'

'They can talk the best about the things in which she is most interested,' I replied.

'Well! that is a strange confession, *however*, to come from her *governess*! Who is to form a young lady's tastes, I wonder, if the governess doesn't do it! I *have* known governesses who have so completely identified themselves with the reputation of their young ladies for elegance and propriety in mind and manners, that they would *blush* to speak a word against them; and to hear the slightest blame imputed to their pupils was worse than to be censured in their own persons, – and I really think it very natural, for my part.'

'Do you, ma'am?'

'Yes, of course, the young lady's proficiency and elegance is of more consequence to the governess than her own, as well as to the world. If she wishes to prosper in her vocation she must devote all her energies to her business; all her ideas and all her ambition will tend to the accomplishment of that one object. When we wish to decide upon the merits of a governess, we naturally look at the young ladies she professes to have educated and judge accordingly. The *judicious* governess knows this; she knows that, while she lives in obscurity herself, the pupils' virtues and defects will be open to every eye and that, unless she loses sight of herself in their cultivation, she need not hope for success. You see, Miss Grey, it is just the same as any other trade or profession; they that wish to prosper must devote themselves body and soul to their calling, and if they begin to yield to indolence or self-indulgence they are speedily distanced by wiser competitors: there is little to choose between a person that ruins her pupils by neglect, and one that corrupts them by her example. You will excuse my dropping these little hints . . . you know it is all for your own good. Many ladies would speak to you much more strongly; and many would not trouble themselves to speak at all, but quietly look out for a substitute. That, of course, would be the *easiest* plan; but I know the advantages of a place like this to a person in your situation; and I have no desire to part with you, as I am sure you would do very well if you will only think of these things and try to exert yourself a *little* more; and then, I am convinced, you would *soon* acquire that delicate tact which alone is wanting to give you a proper influence over the mind of your pupil.'

I was about to give the lady some idea of the fallacy of her expectations; but she sailed away as soon as she had concluded her speech. Having said what she wished, it was no part of her plan to await my answer: it was my business to hear, and not to speak.

However, as I have said, Matilda at length yielded, in some degree, to her mother's authority (pity it had not been exerted before), and being thus deprived of almost every source of amusement, there was nothing for it but to take long rides with the groom and long walks with the governess, and visit the cottages and farm-houses on her father's estate, to kill time in chatting with the old men and women that inhabited them.

In one of these walks, it was our chance to meet Mr Weston. This was what I had long desired; but now, for a moment, I wished either he or I were away: I felt my heart throb so violently that I dreaded lest some outward signs of emotion should appear; but I think he hardly glanced at me, and I was soon calm enough. After a brief salutation to both, he asked Matilda if she had lately heard from her sister.

'Yes,' replied she. 'She was at Paris when she wrote, and very well, and very happy.'

She spoke the last word emphatically, and with a glance impertinently sly. He did not seem to notice it, but replied, with equal emphasis, and very seriously, –

'I hope she will continue to be so.'

'Do you think it likely?' I ventured to inquire, for Matilda had started off in pursuit of her dog, that was chasing a leveret.

'I cannot tell,' replied he. 'Sir Thomas may be a better man than I suppose, but from all I have heard and seen, it seems a pity that one so young, and gay, and ... and *interesting*, to express many things by one ... whose greatest, if not her only fault, appears to be thoughtlessness ... no trifling fault to be sure, since it renders the possessor liable to almost every other, and exposes him to so many temptations; but it seems a pity that she should be thrown away on such a man. It was her mother's wish, I suppose?'

'Yes; and her own too, I think, for she always laughed at my attempts to dissuade her from the step.'

'You did attempt it? Then, at least, you will have the satisfaction of knowing that it is no fault of yours, if any harm should come of it; as for Mrs Murray, I don't know how she can justify her conduct; if I had sufficient acquaintance with her, I'd ask her.'

'It seems unnatural; but some people think rank and wealth the chief good; and, if they can secure that to their children, they think they have done their duty.'

'True; but is it not strange that persons of experience who have been married themselves should judge so falsely?'

Matilda now came panting back, with the lacerated body of the young hare in her hand.

'Was it your intention to kill that hare, or to save it, Miss Murray?' asked Mr Weston, apparently puzzled at her gleeful countenance.

'I pretended to want to save it,' she answered, honestly enough, 'as it was so glaringly out of season; but I was better pleased to see it killed. However, you can both witness that I couldn't help it; Prince was determined to have her; and he clutched her by the back, and killed her in a minute! Wasn't it a noble chase?'

'Very! for a young lady after a leveret.'

There was a quiet sarcasm in the tone of his reply which was not lost upon her; she shrugged her shoulders, and, turning away with a significant 'Humph!' asked me how I had enjoyed the fun.

I replied that I saw no fun in the matter; but admitted that I had not observed the transaction very narrowly.

'Didn't you see how it doubled – just like an old hare? and didn't you hear it scream?'

'I'm happy to say I did not.'

'It cried out just like a child.'

'Poor little thing! What will you do with it?'

'Come along – I shall leave it in the first house we come to – I don't want to take it home, for fear papa should scold me for letting the dog kill it.'

Mr Weston was now gone, and we too went on our way; but as we returned, after having deposited the hare in a farm-house, and demolished some spice-cake and currant wine in exchange, we met him returning also from the execution of his mission, whatever it might be. He carried in his hand a cluster of beautiful bluebells, which he offered to me, observing, with a smile, that though he had seen so little of me for the last two months, he had not forgotten that bluebells were numbered among my favourite flowers.

It was done as a simple act of good will, without compliment, or remarkable courtesy, or any look that could be construed into 'reverential, tender adoration' (*vide*[1] Rosalie Murray); but still, it was something to find my unimportant saying so well remembered; it was something that he had noticed so accurately the time I had ceased to be visible.

'I was told,' said he, 'that you were a perfect book-worm, Miss Grey, so completely absorbed in your studies that you were lost to every other pleasure.'

'Yes, and it's quite true!' cried Matilda.

'No, Mr Weston; don't believe it; it's a scandalous libel. These young ladies are too fond of making random assertions at the expense of their friends; and you ought to be careful how you listen to them.'

'I hope *this* assertion is groundless, at any rate'

'Why? Do you particularly object to ladies' studying?'

'No; but I object to any one so devoting himself or herself to study, as to lose sight of everything else. Except under peculiar circumstances, I consider very close and constant study as a waste of time, and an injury to the mind as well as the body.'

'Well, I have neither the time nor the inclination for such transgressions.'

We parted again.

Well! what is there remarkable in all this? Why have I recorded it? Because, reader, it was important enough to give me a cheerful evening, a night of pleasing dreams, and a morning of felicitous hopes. Shallow-brained cheerfulness – foolish dreams – unfounded hopes – you would say; and I will not venture to deny it: suspicions to that effect arose too frequently in my own mind; but our wishes are like tinder: the flint and steel of circumstances are continually striking out sparks, which vanish immediately, unless they chance to fall upon the tinder of our wishes; then, they instantly ignite, and the flame of hope is kindled in a moment.

But alas! that very morning, my flickering flame of hope was dismally quenched by a letter from my mother, which spoke so seriously of my father's increasing illness, that I feared there was little or no chance of his recovery; and, close at hand as the holidays were, I almost trembled lest they should come too late for me to meet him in this world. Two days after, a letter from Mary told me his life was despaired of, and his end seemed fast approaching.

Then, immediately, I sought permission to anticipate the vacation, and go without delay.

Mrs Murray stared, and wondered at the unwonted energy and boldness with which I urged the request, and thought there was no occasion to hurry; but finally gave me leave, stating, however, that there was 'no need to be in such agitation about the matter – it might prove a false alarm after all; and if not – why, it was only in the common course of nature; we must all die some time; and I was not to suppose myself the only afflicted person in the world'; and concluding with saying I might have the phaeton to take me to O–.

'And instead of *repining*, Miss Grey, be thankful for the *privileges* you enjoy. There's many a poor clergyman whose family would be plunged into *ruin* by the event of his death; but *you*, you see, have influential friends ready to continue their patronage, and to show you every consideration.'

I thanked her for her 'consideration,' and flew to my room to make some hurried preparations for my departure. My bonnet and shawl being on, and a few things hastily crammed into my largest trunk, I descended. But I might have done the work more leisurely, for no one else was in a hurry; and I had still a considerable time to wait for the phaeton.

At length it came to the door, and I was off; but, oh, what a dreary journey was that! how utterly different from my former passages homewards!

Being too late for the last coach to — , I had to hire a cab for ten miles, and then a car to take me over the rugged hills. It was half-past ten before I reached home. They were not in bed.

My mother and sister both met me in the passage – sad – silent – pale! I was so much shocked and terror-stricken I could not speak to ask the information I so much longed yet dreaded to obtain.

'Agnes,' said my mother, struggling to repress some strong emotion.

'Oh, Agnes!' cried Mary, and burst into tears.

'How is he?' I asked, gasping for an answer.

'Dead!'

That was the reply I had anticipated; but the shock seemed none the less tremendous.

XIX
THE LETTER

M Y FATHER'S MORTAL REMAINS had been consigned to the tomb; and we, with sad faces and sombre garments, sat lingering over the frugal breakfast-table, revolving plans for our future life.

My mother's strong mind had not given way beneath even this affliction: her spirit, though crushed, was not broken. Mary's wish was that I should go back to Horton Lodge, and that our mother should come and live with her and Mr Richardson at the vicarage: she affirmed that he wished it no less than herself, and that such an arrangement could not fail to benefit all parties, for my mother's society and experience would be of inestimable value to them, and they would do all they could to make her happy. But no arguments or entreaties could prevail: my mother was determined not to go; not that she questioned, for a moment, the kind wishes and intentions of her daughter; but she affirmed that so long as God spared her health and strength, she would make use of them to earn her own livelihood, and be chargeable to no one, whether her dependence would be felt as a burden or not. If she could afford to reside as a lodger in — vicarage, she would choose that house before all others as the place of her abode; but not being so circumstanced, she would never come under its roof, except as an occasional visiter, unless sickness or calamity should render her assistance really needful, or until age or infirmity should make her incapable of maintaining herself.

'No, Mary,' said she, 'if Richardson and you have anything to spare, you must lay it aside for your family; and Agnes and I must gather honey for ourselves. Thanks to my having had daughters to educate, I have not forgotten my accomplishments ... God willing, I will check this vain repining,' – she said, while the tears coursed one another down her cheeks in spite of her efforts; but she wiped them away, and resolutely shaking back her head, continued, 'I will exert myself and look out for a small house, commodiously situated in some populous but healthy district, where we will take a few young ladies to board and educate – if we can get them – and as many day-pupils as will come, or as we can manage to instruct. Your father's relations and old friends will be able to send us some pupils or to assist us with their recommendations, no doubt: I shall not apply to my own. What say you to it, Agnes – will you be willing to leave your present situation and try?'

'Quite willing, mamma; and the money I have saved will do to furnish the house. It shall be taken from the bank directly.'

'When it is wanted: we must get the house, and settle all preliminaries first.'

Mary offered to lend the little she possessed; but my mother declined it, saying that we must begin on an economical plan, and she hoped that the whole or part of mine, added to what we could get by the sale of the furniture, and what little our dear papa had contrived to lay aside for her since the debts were paid, would be sufficient to last us till Christmas, when, it was hoped, something would accrue from our united labours.

It was finally settled that this should be our plan; and that inquiries and preparations should immediately be set on foot; and while my mother busied herself with these, I should return to Horton Lodge at the close of my four weeks' vacation, and give notice for my final departure when things were in train for the speedy commencement of our school.[1]

We were discussing these affairs on the morning I have mentioned, about a fortnight after my father's death, when a letter was brought in for my mother, on beholding which the colour mounted to her face – lately pale enough with anxious watchings and excessive sorrow.

'From my father!' murmured she, as she hastily tore off the cover.

It was many years since she had heard from any of her own relations before. Naturally wondering what the letter might contain, I watched her countenance while she read it, and was somewhat surprised to see her bite her lip and knit her brows as if in anger. When she had done, she somewhat irreverently cast it on the table, saying with a scornful smile, –

'Your grandpapa has been so kind as to write to me. He says he has no doubt I have long repented of my "unfortunate marriage", and if I will only acknowledge this, and confess I was wrong in neglecting his advice, and that I have justly suffered for it, he will make a lady of me once again – if that be possible after my long degradation – and remember my girls in his will. Get my desk, Agnes, and send these things away – I will answer the letter directly – but first, as I may be depriving you both of a legacy, it is just that I should tell you what I mean to say.

'I shall say that he is mistaken in supposing that I can regret the birth of my daughters (who have been the pride of my life, and are likely to be the comfort of my old age), or the thirty years I have passed in the company of my best and dearest friend; – that, had our misfortunes been three times as great as they were (unless they had been my bringing on), I should still the more rejoice to have shared them with your father, and administered what consolation I was able; and, had his sufferings in illness been ten times what they were, I could not regret having watched over and laboured to relieve them – that, if he had married a richer wife, misfortunes and trials would no doubt have come upon him still, while – I am an egotist enough to imagine that no other woman could have cheered him through them so well – not that I am superior to the rest, but I was made for him, and he for me; and I can no more repent the hours – days – years of happiness we have spent together, and which neither could have had without the other, than I can the privilege of having been his nurse in sickness, and his comfort in affliction.

'Will this do, children? – or shall I say we are all very sorry for what has happened during the last thirty years; and my daughters wish they had never been born; but since they have had that misfortune, they will be thankful for any trifle their grandpapa will be kind enough to bestow?'

Of course, we both applauded our mother's resolution; Mary cleared away the breakfast things; I brought the desk; the letter was quickly written and despatched; and from that day, we heard no more of our grandfather, till we saw his death announced in the newspaper a considerable time after – all his worldly possessions, of course, being left to our wealthy, unknown cousins.

XX

THE FAREWELL

A HOUSE IN A−, THE FASHIONABLE watering place,[1] was hired for our seminary; and a promise of two or three pupils was obtained to commence with. I returned to Horton Lodge about the middle of July, leaving my mother to conclude the bargain for the house, to obtain more pupils, to sell off the furniture of our old abode, and to fit out the new one.

We often pity the poor, because they have no leisure to mourn their departed relatives, and necessity obliges them to labour through their severest afflictions; but is not active employment the best remedy for overwhelming sorrow . . . the surest antidote for despair? It may be a rough comforter: it may seem hard to be harassed with the cares of life when we have no relish for its enjoyments, to be goaded to labour when the heart is ready to break, and the vexed spirit implores for rest only to weep in silence; but is not labour better than the rest we covet? and are not those petty, tormenting cares less hurtful than a continual brooding over the great affliction that oppresses us? − Besides, we cannot have cares, and anxieties, and toil, without hope − if it be but the hope of fulfilling our joyless task, accomplishing some needful project, or escaping some further annoyance.

At any rate, I was glad my mother had so much employment for every faculty of her action-loving frame. Our kind neighbours lamented that she, once so exalted in wealth and station, should be reduced to such extremity in her time of sorrow; but I am persuaded that she would have suffered thrice as much had she been left in affluence, with liberty to remain in that house, the scene of her early happiness and late affliction, and no stern necessity to prevent her from incessantly brooding over and lamenting her bereavement.

I will not dilate upon the feelings with which I left the old house, the well-known garden, the little village church – then doubly dear to me, because my father, who, for thirty years, had taught and prayed within its walls, lay slumbering now beneath its flags – and the old bare hills, delightful in their very desolation, with the narrow vales between, smiling in green wood and sparkling water – the house where I was born, the scene of all my early associations, the place where, throughout my life, my early affections had been centred; – and left them to return no more! True, I was going back to Horton Lodge where, amid many evils, one source of pleasure yet remained; but it was pleasure mingled with excessive pain, and my stay, alas! was limited to six weeks.

And even of that precious time, day after day slipped by and I did not see him: – except at church, I never saw him for a fortnight after my return. It seemed a long time to me: and, as I was often out with my rambling pupil, of course hopes would keep rising, and disappointments would ensue; and then I would say to my own heart, 'Here is a convincing proof – if you would but have the sense to see it, or the candour to acknowledge it – that he does not care for you. If he only thought *half* as much about you, as you do about him, he would have contrived to meet you many times ere this – you must know that by consulting your own feelings. Therefore have done with this nonsense; you have no ground for hope; dismiss, at once, these hurtful thoughts and foolish wishes from your mind and turn to your own duty and the dull, blank life that lies before you. You might have *known* such happiness was not for you.'

But I saw him at last. He came suddenly upon me as I was crossing a field in returning from a visit to Nancy Brown, which I had taken the opportunity of paying while Matilda Murray was riding her matchless mare.

He must have heard of the heavy loss I had sustained; he expressed no sympathy, offered no condolence, but almost the first words he uttered were, 'How is your mother?' And this was no matter-of-course question, for I never told him that I *had* a mother; he must have learned the fact from others, if he knew it

at all – and besides, there was sincere good will, and even deep,
touching, unobtrusive sympathy in the tone and manner of the in-
quiry.

I thanked him with due civility, and told him she was as well
as could be expected.

'What will she do?' was the next question. Many would have
deemed it an impertinent one, and given an evasive reply; but
such an idea never entered my head, and I gave a brief but plain
statement of mother's plans and prospects.

'Then you will leave this place shortly?' said he.

'Yes, in a month.'

He paused a minute, as if in thought. When he spoke again, I
hoped it would be to express his concern at my departure; but it
was only to say, –

'I should think you will be willing enough to go?'

'Yes – for some things,' I replied.

'For *some* things only – I wonder what should make you
regret it!'

I *was* annoyed at this, in some degree, because it embarrassed
me; I had only one reason for regretting it; and that was a
profound secret, which he had no business to trouble me about.

'Why,' said I – 'why should you suppose that I dislike the place?'

'You told me so yourself,' was the decisive reply. 'You said, at
least, that you could not live contentedly without a friend; and
that you had no friend here, and no possibility of making one –
and besides, I know you *must* dislike it.'

'But, if you remember rightly, I said, or meant to say, I could
not live contentedly without a friend in the *world*: I was not so
unreasonable as to require one always near me. I think I could
be happy in a house full of enemies, if ' – but, no; that sentence
must not be continued – I paused, and hastily added, 'And besides, we cannot well leave a place where we have lived for two
or three years, without some feeling of regret.'

'Will you regret to part with Miss Murray . . . your sole remaining pupil and companion?'

'I dare say I shall in some degree – it was not without sorrow I
parted with her sister.'

'I can imagine that.'

'Well, Miss Matilda is quite as good ... better, in one respect.'

'What is that?'

'She's honest.'

'And the other is not?'

'I shall not call her *dishonest*; but it must be confessed, she's a little artful.'

'*Artful* is she? – I saw she was giddy and vain – and now,' he added, after a pause, 'I can well believe she was artful too, but so excessively so as to assume an aspect of extreme simplicity and unguarded openness. Yes,' continued he, musingly, 'that accounts for some little things that puzzled me a trifle before.'

After that, he turned the conversation to more general subjects. He did not leave me till we had nearly reached the park-gates: he had certainly stepped a little out of his way to accompany me so far, for he now went back and disappeared down Moss-lane, the entrance of which we had passed some time before. Assuredly, I did not regret this circumstance: if sorrow had any place in my heart, it was that he was gone at last ... that he was no longer walking by my side, and that short interval of delightful intercourse was at an end. He had not breathed a word of love, or dropped one hint of tenderness or affection, and yet I had been supremely happy. To be near him, to hear him talk ... as he did talk; and to feel that he thought me worthy to be spoken to ... capable of understanding and duly appreciating such discourse ... was enough.

'Yes, Edward Weston, I could indeed be happy in a house full of enemies, if I had but one friend,[2] who truly, deeply, and faithfully loved me, and if that friend were you – though we might be far apart ... seldom to hear from each other, still more seldom to meet ... though toil, and trouble, and vexation might surround me, still ... it would be too much happiness for me to dream of! Yet who can tell,' said I within myself, as I proceeded up the park, 'who can tell what this one month may bring forth? I have lived nearly three-and-twenty years, and I have suffered much, and tasted little pleasure yet: is it likely my life all through will be so clouded? Is it not possible that God may hear my prayers, disperse these gloomy shadows, and grant me some beams of heaven's sunshine yet? Will He entirely deny to me those blessings which are so freely given to others, who neither ask them nor acknowledge them when received? May I not still hope and trust?'

I did hope and trust – for a while; but alas, alas! the time ebbed away; one week followed another, and, excepting one distant glimpse and two transient meetings – during which scarcely anything was said – while I was walking with Miss Matilda, I saw nothing of him – except, of course, at church.

And now, the last Sunday was come, and the last service. I was often on the point of melting into tears during the sermon – the last I was to hear from him . . . the best I should hear from any one, I was well assured. It was over . . . the congregation were departing; and I must follow . . . I had then seen him and heard his voice, too, probably for the last time.

In the church-yard, Matilda was pounced upon by the two Misses Green. They had many inquiries to make about her sister, and I know not what besides. I only wished they would have done, that we might hasten back to Horton Lodge: I longed to seek the retirement of my own room, or some sequestered nook in the grounds, that I might deliver myself up to my feelings – to weep my last farewell, and lament my false hopes and vain delusions . . . only this once, and then adieu to fruitless dreaming . . . thenceforth, only sober, solid, sad reality should occupy my mind; but while I thus resolved, a low voice close beside me said, –

'I suppose you are going this week, Miss Grey?'

'Yes,' I replied. I was very much startled; and had I been at all hysterically inclined, I certainly should have committed myself in some way then. Thank God I was not.

'Well,' said Mr Weston, 'I want to bid you good-bye . . . it is not likely I shall see you again before you go.'

'Good-bye, Mr Weston,' I said . . . Oh, how I struggled to say it calmly! I gave him my hand. He retained it a few seconds in his.

'It is possible we may meet again,' said he, 'will it be of any consequence to you whether we do or not?'

'Yes, I should be very glad to see you again.'

I could say no less. He kindly pressed my hand, and went. Now I was happy again ... though more inclined to burst into tears than ever. If I had been forced to speak at that moment, a succession of sobs would have inevitably ensued; and as it was, I could not keep the water out of my eyes. I walked along with Miss Murray, turning aside my face and neglecting to notice several successive remarks, till she bawled out I was either deaf or stupid, and then (having recovered my self-possession), as one awakened from a fit of abstraction, I suddenly looked up and asked what she had been saying.

XXI

THE SCHOOL

I LEFT HORTON LODGE, AND went to join my mother in our new abode at A–. I found her well in health, resigned in spirit, and even cheerful, though subdued and sober, in her general demeanour. We had only three boarders and half-a-dozen day-pupils to commence with; and by due care and diligence we hoped ere long to increase the number of both.

I set myself with befitting energy to discharge the duties of this new mode of life – I call it *new*, for there was, indeed, a considerable difference between working with my mother in a school of our own, and working as a hireling among strangers, despised and trampled upon by old and young; and for the first few weeks I was by no means unhappy. 'It is possible we may meet again,' and 'Will it be of any consequence to you whether we do or not?' – Those words still rang in my ear and rested on my heart; they were my secret solace and support.

'I shall see him again. – He will come; or he will write.' No promise, in fact, was too bright or too extravagant for hope to whisper in my ear. I did not believe half of what she told me; I pretended to laugh at it all; but I was far more credulous than I myself supposed: otherwise, why did my heart leap up when a knock was heard at the front door, and the maid, who opened it, came to tell my mother a gentleman wished to see her? and why was I out of humour for the rest of the day, because it proved to be a music-master come to offer his services to our school? and what stopped my breath for a moment, when the postman, having brought a couple of letters, my mother said, 'Here, Agnes, this is for you,' and threw one of them to me? and what made the hot blood rush into my face when I saw it was directed in a gentleman's hand? and why – Oh! why did that cold, sickening sense of disappointment fall upon me, when I had torn open the cover and found it was *only* a letter from Mary, which, for some reason or other, her husband had directed for her?

Was it then come to this – that I should be *disappointed* to receive a letter from my only sister; and because it was not written by a comparative stranger? Dear Mary! and she had written it so kindly – and thinking I should be so pleased to have it! – I was not worthy to read it!

And I believe, in my indignation against myself I should have put it aside till I had schooled myself into a better frame of mind, and was become more deserving of the honour and privilege of its perusal; but there was my mother looking on, and wishful to know what news it contained; so I read it and delivered it to her, and then went into the school-room to attend to the pupils; but amidst the cares of copies and sums – in the intervals of correcting errors here, and reproving derelictions of duty there, I was inwardly taking myself to task with far sterner severity.

'What a fool you must be,' said my head to my heart, or my sterner to my softer self; – 'how could you ever dream that he would write to *you?* What grounds have you for such a hope – or that he will see you, or give himself any trouble about you – or even think of you again?'

'What grounds, –' and then Hope set before me that last, short interview and repeated the words I had so faithfully treasured in my memory.

'Well, and what was there in that? ... Who ever hung his hopes upon so frail a twig? What was there in those words that any common acquaintance might not say to another? Of course, it was possible you might meet again; he might have said so if you had been going to New Zealand; but that did not imply any *intention* of seeing you – and then, as to the question that followed, anyone might ask that; and how did you answer? – Merely with a stupid, commonplace reply, such as you would have given to Master Murray, or anyone else you had been on tolerably civil terms with.'

'But then,' persisted Hope, 'the tone and manner in which he spoke.'

'Oh, that is nonsense! he always speaks impressively; and at that moment, there were the Greens and Miss Matilda Murray just before, and other people passing by, and he was obliged to stand close beside you, and to speak very low, unless he wished everybody to hear what he said, which – though it was nothing at all particular – of course, he would rather not.'

But then, above all, that emphatic, yet gentle pressure of the hand, which seemed to say, '*Trust me*,' and many other things besides – too delightful, almost too flattering, to be repeated, even to one's self.

'Egregious folly – too absurd to require contradiction ... mere inventions of the imagination; which you ought to be ashamed of. If you would but consider your own unattractive exterior, your unamiable reserve, your foolish diffidence, which must make you appear cold, dull, awkward, and perhaps ill-tempered too; – if you had but rightly considered these from the beginning, you would never have harboured such presumptuous thoughts; and now that you have been so foolish, pray repent and amend, and let us have no more of it!'

I cannot say that I implicitly obeyed my own injunctions; but such reasoning as this became more and more effective as time wore on and nothing was seen or heard of Mr Weston; until at last, I gave up hoping, for even my heart acknowledged it was all in vain. But still, I would think of him; I would cherish his image in my mind; and treasure every word, look, and gesture that my memory could retain; and brood over his excellences, and his peculiarities, and, in fact, all I had seen, heard, or imagined respecting him.

'Agnes, this sea air and change of scene do *you* no good, I think; I never saw you look so wretched. It must be that you sit too much, and allow the cares of the school-room to worry you: – you must learn to take things easy, and to be more active and cheerful; you must take exercise whenever you can get it, and leave the most tiresome duties to me: they will only serve to exercise my patience, and, perhaps, try my temper a little.'

So said my mother as we sat at work one morning during the Easter holidays. I assured her that my employments were not at all oppressive, that I was well, or if there was anything amiss, it would be gone as soon as the trying months of spring were over; when summer came I should be as strong and hearty as she could wish to see me; but inwardly her observation startled me. I knew my strength was declining, my appetite had failed, and I was grown listless and desponding; – and if, indeed, he could never care for me, and I could never see him more – if I was forbidden to minister to his happiness, forbidden, for ever, to taste the joys of love, to bless and to be blessed, then, life must be a burden, and if my heavenly Father would call me away, I should be glad to rest; but it would not do to die and leave my mother – Selfish, unworthy daughter, to forget her for a moment! Was not her happiness committed in a great measure to my charge – and the welfare of our young pupils too? Should I shrink from the work that God had set before me, because it was not fitted to my taste? Did not He know best what I should do, and where I ought to labour? and should I long to quit His service before I had finished my task, and expect to enter into His rest without having laboured to earn it? 'No; by His help I will arise and address myself diligently to my appointed duty. If happiness in this world is not for me, I will endeavour to promote the welfare of those around me, and my reward shall be here-after.'

So said I in my heart, and from that hour I only permitted my thoughts to wander to Edward Weston – or at least to dwell upon him now and then . . . as a treat for rare occasions; and whether it was really the approach of summer, or the effect of these good resolutions, or the lapse of time, or all together, tranquillity of mind was soon restored, and bodily health and vigour began likewise, slowly, but surely, to return.

Early in June, I received a letter from Lady Ashby, late Miss Murray. She had written to me twice or thrice before, from the different states of her bridal tour, always in good spirits, and professing to be very happy. I wondered every time that she had not forgotten me, in the midst of so much gaiety and variety of scene. At length, however, there was a pause; and it seemed she had forgotten me, for upwards of seven months passed away, and no letter. Of course, I did not break my heart about *that*, though I often wondered how she was getting on; and when this last epistle so unexpectedly arrived, I was glad enough to receive it.

It was dated from Ashby Park, where she was come to settle down at last, having previously divided her time between the Continent and the Metropolis. She made many apologies for having neglected me so long, assured me she had not forgotten me, and had often intended to write, etc., etc., but had always been prevented by something. She acknowledged that she had been leading a very dissipated life, and I should think her very wicked and very thoughtless, but notwithstanding that, she thought a great deal, and, among other things, that she should vastly like to see me.

'We have been several days here already,' wrote she. 'We have not a single friend with us, and are likely to be very dull. You know I never had a fancy for living with my husband like two turtles in a nest, were he the most delightful creature that ever wore a coat, so do take pity upon me and come. I suppose your Midsummer holidays commence in June, the same as other people's, therefore you cannot plead want of time, and you must and shall come – in fact, I shall die if you don't. I want you to visit me as a *friend*, and stay a long time. There is nobody with me, as I told you before, but Sir Thomas and old Lady Ashby; but you needn't mind them – they'll trouble us but little with their company; and you shall have a room to yourself, whenever you like to retire to it, and plenty of books to read when my company is not sufficiently amusing. I forget whether you like babies; if you do, you may have the pleasure of seeing mine . . . the most charming child in the world, no doubt . . . and all the more so, that I am not troubled with nursing it[1] – I was deter-mined I wouldn't be bothered with that – Unfortunately, it is a girl, and Sir Thomas has never forgiven me; but, however, if you will only come, I promise you shall be its governess as soon as it can speak, and you shall bring it up in the way it should go, and make a better woman of it than its mamma; – and you shall see my poodle too, a splendid little charmer imported from Paris, and two fine Italian paintings of great value ... I forget the artist ... doubtless you will be able to discover prodigious beauties in them, which you must point out to me, as I only admire by hearsay ... and many elegant curiosities besides, which I purchased at Rome and elsewhere ... and, finally, you shall see my new home – the splendid house and grounds I used to covet so greatly. Alas! how far the promise of anticipation exceeds the pleasure of possession! ... There's a fine sentiment! I assure you I am become quite a grave old matron ... pray come, if it be only to witness the wonderful change. Write by return of post, and tell me when your vacation commences, and say that you will come the day after, and stay till the day before it closes ... in mercy to

'Yours affectionately,

'ROSALIE ASHBY.'

I shewed this strange epistle to my mother, and consulted her on what I ought to do. She advised me to go; and I went – willing enough to see Lady Ashby – and her baby too – and to do anything I could to benefit her by consolation or advice, for I imagined she must be unhappy, or she would not have applied to me thus – but feeling, as may readily be conceived, that, in accepting the invitation, I made a great sacrifice for her, and did violence to my feelings in many ways, instead of being delighted with the honourable distinction of being entreated by the baronet's lady to visit her as a friend.

However, I determined my visit should only be for a few days at most; and, I will not deny that I derived some consolation from the idea that as Ashby Park was not very far from Horton, I might possibly see Mr Weston, or, at least, hear something about him.

XXII
THE VISIT

ASHBY PARK WAS CERTAINLY a very delightful residence. The mansion was stately without, commodious and elegant within, the park was spacious and beautiful – chiefly on account of its magnificent old trees, its stately herds of deer, its broad sheet of water, and the ancient woods that stretched beyond it, for there was no broken ground to give variety to the landscape, and but very little of that undulating swell which adds so greatly to the charm of park scenery.

And so – this was the place Rosalie Murray had so longed to call her own, that she must have a share of it, on whatever terms it might be offered, whatever price was to be paid for the title of mistress, and whoever was to be her partner in the honour and bliss of such a possession! Well – I am not disposed to censure her now.

She received me very kindly; and though I was a poor clergyman's daughter, a governess, and a school-mistress, she welcomed me with unaffected pleasure to her home; and – what surprised me rather – took some pains to make my visit agreeable. I could see, it is true, that she expected me to be greatly struck with the magnificence that surrounded her; and, I confess, I was rather annoyed at her evident efforts to reassure me, and prevent me from being overwhelmed by so much grandeur; too much awed at the idea of encountering her husband and mother-in-law, or too much ashamed of my own humble appearance – I was not ashamed of it at all; for, though plain, I had taken good care not to be shabby or mean, and should have been pretty considerably at my ease, if my condescending hostess had not taken such manifest pains to make me so; and as for the magnificence that surrounded her, nothing that met my eyes struck me, or affected me half so much as her own altered appearance.

Whether from the influence of fashionable dissipation, or some other evil – a space of little more than twelve months had had the effect that might be expected from as many years, in reducing the plumpness of her form, the freshness of her complexion, the vivacity of her movements, and the exuberance of her spirits.

I wished to know if she was unhappy; but I felt it was not my province to inquire; I might endeavour to win her confidence; but, if she chose to conceal her matrimonial cares from me, I would trouble her with no obtrusive questions.

I therefore, at first, confined myself to a few general inquiries about her health and welfare, and a few commendations on the beauty of the park, and of the little girl that should have been a boy, a small delicate infant of seven or eight weeks old, whom its mother seemed to regard with no remarkable degree of interest or affection, though full as much as I expected her to show.

Shortly after my arrival, she commissioned her maid to conduct me to my room and see that I had everything I wanted: it was a small, unpretending, but sufficiently comfortable apartment.

When I had descended thence – having divested myself of all my travelling encumbrances, and arranged my toilet with due consideration for the feelings of my lady hostess – she conducted me herself to the room I was to occupy when I chose to be alone, or when she was engaged with visiters, or obliged to be with her mother-in-law, or otherwise prevented, as she said, from enjoying the pleasure of my society. It was a quiet, tidy little sitting-room, and I was not sorry to be provided with such a harbour of refuge.

'And some time,' said she, 'I will show you the library; I have never examined its shelves, but, I dare say, it is full of wise books, and you may go and burrow among them whenever you please; and now you shall have some tea – it will soon be dinner time, but, I thought, as you were accustomed to dine at one, you would perhaps like better to have a cup of tea about this time, and to dine when we lunch; and then, you know, you can have your tea in this room, and that will save you from having to dine with Lady Ashby and Sir Thomas, which would be rather awkward – at least, not awkward, but rather – a – you know what I mean – I thought you mightn't like it so well – especially as we may have other ladies and gentlemen to dine with us occasionally.'

'Certainly,' said I, 'I would much rather have it as you say; and, if you have no objection, I should prefer having all my meals in this room.'

'Why so?'

'Because, I imagine, it would be more agreeable to Lady Ashby and Sir Thomas.'

'Nothing of the kind!'

'At any rate it would be more agreeable to me.'

She made some faint objections, but soon conceded; and I could see that the proposal was a considerable relief to her.

'Now, come into the drawing-room,' said she. 'There's the dressing-bell; but I won't go yet; it's no use dressing when there's no one to see you; and I want to have a little discourse.'

The drawing-room was certainly an imposing apartment, and very elegantly furnished; but I saw its young mistress glance towards me as we entered, as if to notice how I was impressed by the spectacle, and, accordingly, I determined to preserve an aspect of stony indifference, as if I saw nothing at all remarkable – but this was only for a moment: immediately conscience whispered, 'Why should I disappoint her to save my pride? No – rather let me sacrifice my pride to give her a little innocent gratification.' And I honestly looked round, and told her it was a noble room, and very tastefully furnished. She said little, but I saw she was pleased.

She shewed me her fat French poodle that lay curled up on a silk cushion, and the two fine Italian paintings, which, however, she would not give me time to examine, but, saying I must look at them some other day, insisted upon my admiring the little jewelled watch she had brought from Geneva; and then took me round the room to point out sundry other articles of *vertu*[1] she had imported from Italy, an elegant little time-piece, and several busts, small, graceful figures, and vases, all beautifully carved in white marble. She spoke of these with animation, and heard my admiring comments with a smile of pleasure, that soon, however, vanished, and was followed by a melancholy sigh, as if in consideration of the insufficiency of all such baubles to the happiness of the human heart, and their woful inability to supply its insatiate demands.

Then, stretching herself upon a couch, she motioned me to a capacious easy chair that stood opposite – not before the fire, but before a wide open window – for it was summer, be it remembered – a sweet, warm evening in the latter half of June; and I sat for a moment in silence, enjoying the still, pure air and the delightful prospect of the park that lay before me, rich in verdure and foliage and basking in yellow sunshine, relieved by the long shadows of declining day. But I must take advantage of this pause: I had inquiries to make, and, like the substance of a lady's postscript, the most important must come last.

So I began with asking after Mr and Mrs Murray, and Miss Matilda and the young gentlemen.

I was told that papa had the gout, which made him very ferocious, and that he would not give up his choice wines, and his substantial dinners and suppers, and had quarrelled with his physician, because the latter had dared to say that no medicine could cure him while he lived so freely; that mamma and the rest were well: Matilda was still wild and reckless, but she had got a fashionable governess, and was considerably improved in her manners, and soon to be introduced to the world; and John and Charles (now at home for the holidays) were, by all accounts, 'fine, bold, unruly, mischievous boys.'

'And how are the other people getting on?' said I – 'the Greens, for instance?'

'Ah! Mr Green is heart-broken, you know,' replied she, with a languid smile; 'he hasn't got over his disappointment yet, and never will, I suppose. He's doomed to be an old bachelor; and his sisters are doing their best to get married.'

'And the Melthams?'

'Oh, they're jogging on as usual, I suppose; but I know very

little about any of them – except Harry,' said she, blushing
slightly, and smiling again; 'I saw a great deal of him while we
were in London; for, as soon as he heard we were there, he
came up under pretence of visiting his brother, and either followed me, like a shadow, wherever I went, or met me, like a
reflection, at every turn. But you needn't look so shocked, Miss
Grey; I was very discreet, I assure you; but you know, one can't
help being admired. Poor fellow! He was not my only worshipper
but he was certainly the most conspicuous, and, I think, the
most devoted among them all. And that detestable – ahem – and
Sir Thomas chose to take offence at him – or my profuse expenditure, or something – I don't exactly know what – and hurried
me down to the country, at a moment's notice, where I'm to
play the hermit, I suppose, for life.'

And she bit her lip, and frowned vindictively upon the fair
domain she had once so coveted to call her own.

'And Mr Hatfield,' said I, 'what is become of him?'

Again, she brightened up, and answered gaily, –

'Oh! he made up to an elderly spinster, and married her, not
long since, weighing her heavy purse against her faded charms,
and expecting to find that solace in gold which was denied him
in love, ha, ha!'

'Well, and I think that's all – except Mr Weston – what is *he*
doing?'

'I don't know, I'm sure. He's gone from Horton.'

'How long since? and where is he gone to?'

'I know nothing about him,' replied she, yawning – 'except
that he went about a month ago – I never asked where' (I would
have asked whether it was to a living or merely another curacy,
but thought it better not), 'and the people made a great rout
about his leaving,' continued she, 'much to Mr Hatfield's displeasure, for Hatfield didn't like him, because he had too much
influence with the common people, and because he was not
sufficiently tractable and submissive to him – and for some other
unpardonable sins, I don't know what. But now I positively
must go and dress; the second bell will ring directly, and if I
come to dinner in this guise, I shall never hear the end of it from

Lady Ashby. It's a strange thing one can't be mistress in one's own house! Just ring the bell, and I'll send for my maid, and tell them to get you some tea. Only think of that intolerable woman –'

'Who – your maid?'

'No, my mother-in-law – and my unfortunate mistake! Instead of letting her take herself off to some other house, as she offered to do when I married, I was fool enough to ask her to live here still, and direct the affairs of the house for me; because in the first place, I hoped we should spend the greater part of the year in Town, and in the second place, being so young and inexperienced, I was frightened at the idea of having a houseful of servants to manage, and dinners to order, and parties to entertain, and all the rest of it, and I thought she might assist me with her experience; never dreaming she would prove a usurper, a tyrant, an incubus, a spy, and everything else that's detestable. I wish she was dead!'

She then turned to give her orders to the footman, who had been standing bolt upright within the door for the last half-minute, and had heard the latter part of her animadversions, and, of course, made his own reflections upon them, notwithstanding the inflexible, wooden countenance he thought proper to preserve in the drawing-room.

On my remarking afterwards that he must have heard her, she replied, –

'Oh, no matter! I never care about the footmen; they're mere automatons – it's nothing to them what their superiors say or do; they won't dare to repeat it; and as to what they think – if they presume to think at all – of course, nobody cares for that. It would be a pretty thing indeed, if we were to be tongue-tied by our servants!'

So saying, she ran off to make her hasty toilet, leaving me to pilot my way back to my sitting-room, where, in due time, I was served with a cup of tea; and, after that, I sat musing on Lady Ashby's past and present condition; and on what little information I had obtained respecting Mr Weston, and the small chance there was of ever seeing or hearing anything more of him throughout my quiet, drab-colour life, which, henceforth, seemed to offer no alternative between positive rainy days, and days of dull, grey clouds without downfall.

At length, however, I began to weary of my thoughts, and to wish I knew where to find the library my hostess had spoken of, and to wonder whether I was to remain there, doing nothing till bed-time.

As I was not rich enough to possess a watch, I could not tell how time was passing, except by observing the slowly lengthening shadows from the window, which presented a side view, including a corner of the park, a clump of trees, whose topmost branches had been colonized by an innumerable company of noisy rooks, and a high wall with a massive wooden gate, no doubt communicating with the stable-yard, as a broad carriage-road swept up to it from the park. The shadow of this wall soon took possession of the whole of the ground as far as I could see, forcing the golden sunlight to retreat inch by inch, and at last take refuge in the very tops of the trees. At last, even they were left in shadow – the shadow of the distant hills, or of the earth itself; and, in sympathy for the busy citizens of the rookery, I regretted to see their habitation, so lately bathed in glorious light, reduced to the sombre, worky-day hue of the lower world, or of my own world within. For a moment, such birds as soared above the rest might still receive the lustre on their wings, which imparted to their sable plumage the hue and brilliance of deep red gold; at last, that too departed. Twilight came stealing on – the rooks became more quiet – I became more weary, and wished I were going home to-morrow.

At length it grew dark; and I was thinking of ringing for a candle, and betaking myself to bed, when my hostess appeared, with many apologies for having neglected me so long, and laying all blame upon that 'nasty old woman', as she called her mother-in-law.

'If I didn't sit with her in the drawing-room while Sir Thomas is taking his wine,' said she, 'she would never forgive me; and then, if I leave the room the instant he comes – as I have done once or twice – it is an unpardonable offence against her dear

Thomas. *She* never shewed such disrespect to *her* husband – and
as for affection, wives never think of that now-a-days, she sup-
poses; but things were different in *her* time – As if there was any
good to be done by staying in the room, when he does nothing
but grumble and scold when he's in a bad humour, talk disgusting nonsense when he's in a good one, and go to sleep on the
sofa when he's too stupid for either, which is most frequently
the case now, when he has nothing to do but to sot² over his
wine.'

'But could you not try to occupy his mind with something
better; and engage him to give up such habits? I'm sure you have
powers of persuasion, and qualifications for amusing a gentleman, which many ladies would be glad to possess.'

'And so you think I would lay myself out for his amusement!
No; that's not *my* idea of a wife. It's the husband's part to
please the wife, not hers to please him; and if he isn't satisfied
with her as she is – and thankful to possess her too, he isn't
worthy of her – that's all. And as for persuasion, I assure you I
shan't trouble myself with that: I've enough to do to bear with
him as he is, without attempting to work a reform. But I'm sorry
I left you so long alone, Miss Grey. How have you passed the
time?'

'Chiefly in watching the rooks.'

'Mercy, how dull you must have been! I really must show you
the library; and you must ring for everything you want, just as
you would in an inn, and make yourself comfortable. I have
selfish reasons for wishing to make you happy, because I want
you to stay with me, and not fulfil your horrid threat of running
away in a day or two.'

'Well, don't let me keep you out of the drawing-room any
longer to-night, for at present I am tired, and wish to go to bed.'

XXIII

THE PARK

I CAME DOWN A LITTLE BEFORE eight, next morning, as I knew by the striking of a distant clock. There was no appearance of breakfast. I waited above an hour before it came, still vainly longing for access to the library; and after that lonely repast was concluded, I waited again about an hour and a half in great suspense and discomfort, uncertain what to do.

At length, Lady Ashby came to bid me good-morning. She informed me she had only just breakfasted, and now wanted me to take an early walk with her in the park. She asked how long I had been up, and, on receiving my answer, expressed the deepest regret, and again promised to show me the library.

I suggested she had better do so at once, and then there would be no further trouble either with remembering or forgetting. She complied, on condition that I would not think of reading, or bothering with the books now, for she wanted to show me the gardens, and take a walk in the park with me, before it became too hot for enjoyment, which, indeed, was nearly the case already. Of course, I readily assented; and we took our walk accordingly.

As we were strolling in the park, talking of what my companion had seen and heard during her travelling experience, a gentleman on horseback rode up and passed us. As he turned, in passing, and stared me full in the face, I had a good opportunity of seeing what he was like. He was tall, thin and wasted, with a slight stoop in the shoulders, a pale face, but somewhat blotchy, and disagreeably red about the eye-lids, plain features, and a general appearance of languor and flatness, relieved by a sinister expression about the mouth and the dull, soulless eyes.

'I detest that man!' whispered Lady Ashby, with bitter emphasis, as he slowly trotted by.

'Who is it?' I asked, unwilling to suppose that she should so speak of her husband.

'Sir Thomas Ashby,' she replied with dreary composure.

'And do you *detest* him, Miss Murray?' said I, for I was too much shocked to remember her name at that moment.

'Yes, I do, Miss Grey – and despise him too! and if you knew him, you would not blame me.'

'But you knew what he was before you married him.'

'No; I only thought so – I did not half know him really. I know you warned me against it; and I wish I had listened to you – but it's too late to regret that now – and besides, mamma ought to have known better than either of us; and she never said anything against it – quite the contrary – and then I thought he adored me, and would let me have my own way – he did pretend to do so at first; but now he does not care a bit about me. But I should not care for that; he might do as he pleased, if I might only be free to amuse myself and to stay in London, or have a few friends down here . . . but *he will* do as he pleases – and I must be a prisoner and a slave. The moment he saw I could enjoy myself without him, and that others knew my value better than himself, the selfish wretch began to accuse me of coquetry and extravagance, and to abuse Harry Meltham, whose shoes he was not worthy to clean; – and then, he must needs have me down in the country, to lead the life of a nun, lest I should dishonour him or bring him to ruin, as if he had not been ten times worse every way – with his betting-book, and his gaming table, and his opera girls, and his Lady this and Mrs that – yes, and his bottles of wine, and glasses of brandy and water too – filthy beast! Oh, I would give ten thousand worlds to be Miss Murray again! It is *too* bad to feel life, health and beauty wasting away, unfelt and unenjoyed, for such a brute as that!' exclaimed she, fairly bursting into tears in the bitterness of her vexation.

Of course, I pitied her exceedingly, as well for her false idea of happiness and disregard of duty, as for the wretched partner with whom her fate was linked.

I said what I could to comfort her, and offered such counsels as I thought she most required, advising her, first, by gentle reasoning, by kindness, example, and persuasion to try to ameliorate her husband; and then, when she had done all she could, if she still found him incorrigible, to endeavour to abstract herself from him – to wrap herself up in her own integrity, and trouble herself as little about him as possible. I exhorted her to seek consolation in doing her duty to God and man, to put her trust in Heaven, and solace herself with the care and nurture of her little daughter, assuring her she would be amply rewarded by witnessing its progress in strength and wisdom, and receiving its genuine affection.

'But I can't devote myself entirely to a child,' said she, 'it may die[1] – which is not at all improbable.'

'But with care, many a delicate infant has become a strong man or woman.'

'But it may grow so intolerably like its father that I shall hate it.'

'That is not likely; it is a little girl, and strongly resembles its mother.'

'No matter – I should like it better if it were a boy – only that its father will leave it no inheritance that he can possibly squander away. What pleasure can I have in seeing a girl grow up to eclipse me, and enjoy those pleasures that I am for ever debarred from? But supposing I could be so generous as to take delight in this, still it is *only* a child; and I can't centre all my hopes in a child; that is only one degree better than devoting one's self to a dog. And as for all the wisdom and goodness you have been trying to instil into me – that is all very right and proper, I dare say; and if I were some twenty years older, I might fructify by it; but people must enjoy themselves when they're young – and if others won't let them – why, they must hate them for it!'

'The best way to enjoy yourself is to do what is right, and hate nobody. The end of Religion is not to teach us how to die, but how to live; and the earlier you become wise and good, the more of happiness you secure. And now, Lady Ashby, I have one more piece of advice to offer you, which is that you will not make an enemy of your mother-in-law. Don't get into the way of holding her at arm's length and regarding her with jealous distrust. I never saw her, but I have heard good as well as evil respecting her, and I imagine that, though cold and haughty in her general demeanour, and even exacting in her requirements, she has strong affections for those who can reach them; and, though so blindly attached to her son, she is not without good principles, or incapable of hearing reason; and if you would but conciliate her a little, and adopt a friendly, open manner – and even confide your grievances to her ... *real* grievances, such as you have a right to complain of ... it is my firm belief that she would, in time, become your faithful friend, and a comfort and support to you, instead of the incubus you describe her.'

But I fear my advice had little effect upon the unfortunate young lady; and, finding I could render myself so little service-able, my residence at Ashby Park became doubly painful. But still, I must stay out that day and the following one, as I had promised to do so; though, resisting all entreaties and induce-ments to prolong my visit further, I insisted upon departing the next morning, affirming that my mother would be lonely without me, and that she impatiently expected my return.

Nevertheless, it was with a heavy heart that I bid adieu to poor Lady Ashby and left her in her princely home. It was no slight additional proof of her unhappiness, that she should so cling to the consolation of my presence, and earnestly desire the company of one whose general tastes and ideas were so little congenial to her own, whom she had completely forgotten in her hours of prosperity, and whose presence would be rather a nuis-ance than a pleasure, if she could but have half her heart's desire.

XXIV

THE SANDS

OUR SCHOOL WAS NOT SITUATED in the heart of the town: on entering A— from the north-west there is a row of respectable-looking houses, on each side of the broad, white road, with narrow slips of garden-ground before them, Venetian blinds to the windows, and a flight of steps leading to each trim, brass-handled door. In one of the largest of these habitations dwelt my mother and I, with such young ladies as our friends and the public chose to commit to our charge. Consequently, we were a considerable distance from the sea, and divided from it by a labyrinth of streets and houses. But the sea was my delight; and I would often gladly pierce the town to obtain the pleasure of a walk beside it, whether with the pupils, or alone with my mother during the vacations. It was delightful to me at all times and seasons, but especially in the wild commotion of a rough sea-breeze, and in the brilliant freshness of a summer morning.

I awoke early on the third morning after my return from Ashby Park ... the sun was shining through the blind, and I thought how pleasant it would be to pass through the quiet town and take a solitary ramble on the sands while half the world was in bed. I was not long in forming the resolution, nor slow to act upon it. Of course I would not disturb my mother, so I stole noiselessly downstairs, and quietly unfastened the door. I was dressed, down, and out when the church clock struck a quarter to six.

There was a feeling of freshness and vigour in the very streets; and when I got free of the town, when my foot was on the sands and my face towards the broad, bright bay ... no language can describe the effect of the deep, clear azure of the sky and ocean, the bright morning sunshine on the semi-circular barrier of craggy cliffs surmounted by green swelling hills, and on the

smooth, wide sands, and the low rocks out at sea ... looking, with their clothing of weeds and moss, like little grass-
grown islands – and above all, on the brilliant, sparkling waves.
And then, the unspeakable purity and freshness of the air! there
was just enough heat to enhance the value of the breeze, and just
enough wind to keep the whole sea in motion, to make the
waves come bounding to the shore, foaming and sparkling, as if
wild with glee. Nothing else was stirring – no living creature was
visible besides myself. My footsteps were the first to press the
firm, unbroken sands; – nothing before had trampled them since
last night's flowing tide had obliterated the deepest marks of
yesterday, and left it fair and even, except where the subsiding
water had left behind it the traces of dimpled pools, and little
running streams.

  Refreshed, delighted, invigorated, I walked along, forgetting
all my cares, feeling as if I had wings to my feet, and could go at
least forty miles without fatigue, and experiencing a sense of
exhilaration to which I had been an entire stranger since the
days of early youth. About half-past six, however, the grooms
began to come down to air their masters' horses – first one, and
then another, till there were some dozen horses and five or six
riders; but that need not trouble me, for they would not come as
far as the low rocks which I was now approaching. When I had
reached these, and walked over the moist slippery sea-weed (at
the risk of floundering into one of the numerous pools of clear,
salt water that lay between them), to a little mossy promontory
with the sea splashing round it, I looked back again to see who
next was stirring. Still, there were only the early grooms with
their horses, and one gentleman with a little dark speck of a dog
running before him, and one water-cart coming out of the town
to get water for the baths. In another minute or two, the distant
bathing-machines would begin to move: and then the elderly
gentlemen of regular habits, and sober Quaker ladies would be
coming to take their salutary morning walks. But however interesting such a scene might be, I could not wait to witness it, for
the sun and the sea so dazzled my eyes in that direction, that I
could but afford one glance; and then I turned again to delight

myself with the sight and the sound of the sea dashing against my promontory – with no prodigious force, for the swell was broken by the tangled sea-weed and the unseen rocks beneath; otherwise I should soon have been deluged with spray.

But the tide was coming in; the water was rising; the gulfs and lakes were filling; the straits were widening: it was time to seek some safer footing; so I walked, skipped, and stumbled back to the smooth, wide sands, and resolved to proceed to a certain bold projection in the cliffs, and then return.

Presently, I heard a snuffling sound behind me, and then a dog came frisking and wriggling to my feet. It was my own Snap – the little dark, wire-haired terrier![1] When I spoke his name, he leapt up in my face, and yelled for joy.

Almost as much delighted as himself, I caught the little creature in my arms, and kissed him repeatedly. But how came he to be there? He could not have dropped from the sky, or come all that way alone: it must be either his master, the rat-catcher, or somebody else that had brought him; so, repressing my extravagant caresses, and endeavouring to repress likewise, I looked round, and beheld – Mr Weston!

'Your dog remembers you well, Miss Grey,' said he, warmly grasping the hand I offered him, without clearly knowing what I was about.

'You rise early.'

'Not often so early as this,' I replied, with amazing composure, considering all the circumstances of the case.

'How far do you purpose to extend your walk?'

'I was thinking of returning – it must be almost time, I think.'

He consulted his watch – a gold one now – and told me it was only five minutes past seven.

'But, doubtless, you have had a long enough walk,' said he, turning towards the town, to which I now proceeded leisurely to retrace my steps; and he walked beside me.

'In what part of the town do you live?' asked he. 'I never could discover.'

Never could discover? Had he endeavoured to do so, then? I told him the place of our abode.

He asked how we prospered in our affairs; I told him we were doing very well, – that we had had a considerable addition to our pupils after the Christmas vacation, and expected a still further increase at the close of this.

'You must be an accomplished instructor,' he observed.

'No, it is my mother,' I replied, 'she manages things so well, and is so active, and clever, and kind.'

'I should like to know your mother – Will you introduce me to her some time, if I call?'

'Yes, willingly.'

'And will you allow me the privilege of an old friend, of looking in upon you now and then?'

'Yes, if – I suppose so.'

This was a very foolish answer, but the truth was, I considered that I had no right to invite any one to my mother's house without her knowledge; and if I had said, 'Yes, if my mother does not object,' it would appear as if, by his question, I understood more than was expressed, so, *supposing* she would not, I added, 'I suppose so,' but of course I should have said something more sensible and more polite if I had had my wits about me. We continued our walk for a minute in silence, which, however, was shortly relieved (no small relief to me) by Mr Weston commenting upon the brightness of the morning, and the beauty of the bay, and then, upon the advantages A– possessed over many other fashionable places of resort.

'You don't ask what brings me to A–,' said he. 'You can't suppose I'm rich enough to come for my own pleasure.'

'I heard you had left Horton.'

'You didn't hear, then, that I had got the living of F–?'

F– was a village about two miles distant from A–.

'No,' said I; 'we live so completely out of the world, even here, that news seldom reaches me from any quarter – except through the medium of the – *Gazette*. But I hope you like your new parish; and that I may congratulate you on the acquisition?'

'I expect to like my parish better a year or two hence, when I have worked certain reforms I have set my heart upon – or, at least, progressed some steps towards such an achievement; but

you may congratulate me now, for I find it very agreeable to
have a parish all to myself with nobody to interfere with me – to
thwart my plans or cripple my exertions; and besides, I have a
respectable house in a rather pleasant neighbourhood, and three
hundred pounds a year; and, in fact, I have nothing but solitude
to complain of, and nothing but a companion to wish for.'

He looked at me as he concluded; and the flash of his dark
eyes seemed to set my face on fire, greatly to my own disconcer-
tion, for to evince confusion at such a juncture was intolerable.

I made an effort, therefore, to remedy the evil, and disclaim
all personal application of the remark, by a hasty, ill-expressed
reply, to the effect that if he waited till he was well known in the
neighbourhood, he might have numerous opportunities for sup-
plying his want among the residents of F– and its vicinity, or the
visiters of A–, if he required so ample a choice; not considering
the compliment implied by such an assertion, till his answer
made me aware of it.

'I am not so presumptuous as to believe that,' said he, 'though
you tell it me; but if it were so – I am rather particular in my
notions of a companion for life, and perhaps I might not find
one to suit me among the ladies you mention.'

'If you require perfection, you never will.'

'I do not – I have no right to, being so far from perfection myself.'

Here the conversation was interrupted by a water-cart lumber-
ing past us, for we were now come to the busy part of the sands;
and, for the next eight or ten minutes, between carts and horses,
and asses, and men, there was little room for social intercourse,
till we had turned our backs upon the sea, and begun to ascend
the precipitous road leading into the town. Here my companion
offered me his arm, which I accepted, though not with the intention of using it as a support.

'You don't often come on to the sands, I think,' said he, 'for I
have walked there many times, both morning and evening, since
I came, and never seen you till now; and several times, in passing
through the town, too, I have looked about for your school –
but I did not think of the —— road; and once or twice I made
inquiries, but without obtaining the requisite information.'

When we had surmounted the acclivity, I was about to withdraw my arm from his, but by a slight tightening of the elbow was tacitly informed that such was not his will, and accordingly desisted.

Discoursing on different subjects, we entered the town, and passed through several streets; I saw that he was going out of his way to accompany me, notwithstanding the long walk that was yet before him; and, fearing that he might be inconveniencing himself from motives of politeness, I observed, –

'I fear I am taking you out of your way, Mr Weston – I believe the road to F– lies quite in another direction.'

'I'll leave you at the end of the next street,' said he.

'And when will you come to see mamma?'

'To-morrow – God willing.'

The end of the next street was nearly the conclusion of my journey. He stopped there, however, bid me good-morning, and called Snap, who seemed a little doubtful whether to follow his old mistress or his new master, but trotted away upon being summoned by the latter.

'I won't offer to restore him to you, Miss Grey,' said Mr Weston, smiling, 'because I like him.'

'Oh, I don't want him,' replied I; 'now that he has a good master, I'm quite satisfied.'

'You take it for granted that I *am* a good one, then?'

The man and the dog departed, and I returned home, full of gratitude to Heaven for so much bliss, and praying that my hopes might not again be crushed.

XXV

CONCLUSION

'WELL, AGNES, YOU MUST not take such long walks again before breakfast,' said my mother, observing that I drank an extra cup of coffee and ate nothing – pleading the heat of the weather, and the fatigue of my long walk as an excuse.

I certainly did feel feverish, and tired too.

'You always do things by extremes: now, if you had taken a *short* walk every morning, and would continue to do so, it would do you good.'

'Well, mamma, I will.'

'But this is worse than lying in bed, or bending over your books; you have quite put yourself into a fever.'

'I won't do it again,' said I.

I was racking my brains with thinking how to tell about Mr Weston, for she must know he was coming to-morrow. However, I waited till the breakfast things were removed, and I was more calm and cool; and then, having sat down to my drawing, I began, –

'I met an old friend on the sands to-day, mamma.'

'An old friend! Who could it be?'

'Two old friends indeed. One was a dog,' and then I reminded her of Snap, whose history I had recounted before, and related the incident of his sudden appearance and remarkable recognition, 'and the other,' continued I, 'was Mr Weston, the curate of Horton.'

'Mr Weston! I never heard of him before,'

'Yes, you have: I've mentioned him several times I believe, but you don't remember.'

'I've heard you speak of Mr Hatfield.'

'Mr Hatfield was the rector, and Mr Weston the curate; I

used to mention him sometimes in contradistinction to Mr Hatfield, as being a more efficient clergyman. However, he was on the sands this morning with the dog – he had bought it, I suppose, from the rat-catcher; and he knew me as well as it did – probably through its means; and I had a little conversation with him, in the course of which, as he asked about our school, I was led to say something about you and your good management; and he said he should like to know you, and asked if I would introduce him to you, if he should take the liberty of calling to-morrow, so I said I would. Was I right?'

'Of course. What kind of a man is he?'

'A very respectable man, I think; but you will see him to-morrow. He is the new vicar of F–, and as he has only been there a few weeks, I suppose he has made no friends yet, and wants a little society.'

The morrow came. What a fever of anxiety and expectation I was in from breakfast till noon – at which time he made his appearance.

Having introduced him to my mother, I took my work to the window, and sat down to await the result of the interview.

They got on extremely well together, greatly to my satisfaction, for I had felt very anxious about what my mother would think of him. He did not stay long that time; but when he rose to take leave, she said she should be happy to see him, whenever he might find it convenient to call again; and when he was gone, I was gratified by hearing her say, –

'Well! I think he is a very sensible man. But why did you sit back there, Agnes,' she added, 'and talk so little?'

'Because you talked so well, mamma, I thought you required no assistance from me; and, besides, he was your visiter, not mine.'

After that, he often called upon us – several times in the course of a week. He generally addressed most of his conversation to my mother; and no wonder, for she *could* converse. I almost envied the unfettered, vigorous fluency of her discourse, and the strong sense evinced by everything she said – and yet, I did not, for though I occasionally regretted my own deficiencies for his sake, it gave me very great pleasure to sit and hear the two beings I loved and honoured above everyone else in the world, discoursing together so amicably, so wisely, and so well.

I was not always silent, however; nor was I at all neglected. I was quite as much noticed as I would wish to be: there was no lack of kind words and kinder looks, no end of delicate attentions, too fine and subtle to be grasped by words, and, therefore, indescribable – but deeply felt at heart.

Ceremony was quickly dropped between us, Mr Weston came as an expected guest, welcome at all times, and never deranging the economy of our household affairs. He even called me 'Agnes'; the name had been timidly spoken at first, but, finding it gave no offence in any quarter, he seemed greatly to prefer that appellation to 'Miss Grey', and so did I.

How tedious and gloomy were those days in which he did not come! And yet not miserable, for I had still the remembrance of the last visit and the hope of the next to cheer me. But when two or three days passed without my seeing him, I certainly felt very anxious – absurdly, unreasonably so, for, of course, he had his own business and the affairs of his parish to attend to: and I dreaded the close of the holidays, when *my* business also would begin, and I should be sometimes unable to see him, and sometimes . . . when my mother was in the school-room – obliged to be with him alone; a position I did not at all desire . . . in the house, though to meet him out-of-doors, and walk beside him, had proved by no means disagreeable.

One evening, however, in the last week of the vacation, he arrived – unexpectedly, for a heavy and protracted thunder-shower during the afternoon had almost destroyed my hopes of seeing him that day; but now the storm was over, and the sun was shining brightly.

'A beautiful evening, Mrs Grey!' said he, as he entered. 'Agnes, I want you to take a walk with me to —' (he named a certain part of the coast . . . a bold hill on the land side, and towards the sea, a steep precipice,[1] from the summit of which a glorious view is to be had). 'The rain has laid the dust, and cooled and cleared the air, and the prospect will be magnificent. Will you come?'

'Can I go, mamma?'

'Yes, to be sure.'

I went to get ready, and was down again in a few minutes, though, of course, I took a little more pains with my attire than if I had merely been going out on some shopping expedition alone.

The thunder-shower had certainly had a most beneficial effect upon the weather, and the evening was most delightful. Mr Weston would have me to take his arm: he said little during our passage through the crowded streets, but walked very fast, and appeared grave and abstracted.

I wondered what was the matter, and felt an indefinite dread that something unpleasant was on his mind; and vague surmises, concerning what it might be, troubled me not a little, and made me grave and silent enough. But these fantasies vanished upon reaching the quiet outskirts of the town, for as soon as we came in sight of the venerable old church, and the — hill, with the deep blue sea beyond it, I found my companion was cheerful enough.

'I'm afraid I've been walking too fast for you, Agnes,' said he; 'in my impatience to get rid of the town, I forgot to consult your convenience; but now, we'll walk as slowly as you please: I see, by those light clouds in the west, there will be a brilliant sunset, and we shall be in time to witness its effect upon the sea, at the most moderate rate of progression.'

When we had got about half-way up the hill, we fell into silence again, which, as usual, he was the first to break.

'My house is desolate yet, Miss Grey,' he smilingly observed, 'and I am acquainted now with all the ladies in my parish, and several in this town too; and many others I know by sight and by report; but not one of them will suit me for a companion . . . in fact, there is only one person in the world that will; and that is yourself; and I want to know your decision?'

'Are you in earnest, Mr Weston?'

'In earnest! How could you think I should jest on such a subject?'

He laid his hand on mine that rested on his arm: he must have felt it tremble . . . but it was no great matter now.

'I hope I have not been too precipitate,' he said, in a serious tone. 'You must have known that it was not my way to flatter and talk soft nonsense, or even to speak the admiration that I felt; and that a single word or glance of mine meant more than the honeyed[2] phrases and fervent protestations of most other men.'

I said something about not liking to leave my mother, and doing nothing without her consent.

'I settled everything with Mrs Grey while you were putting on your bonnet,' replied he. 'She said I might have her consent, if I could obtain yours; and I asked her, in case I should be so happy, to come and live with us – for I was sure you would like it better. But she refused, saying she could now afford to employ an assistant, and would continue the school till she could purchase an annuity sufficient to maintain her in comfortable lodgings; and meantime she would spend her vacations alternately with us and your sister, and should be quite contented if you were happy. And so now I have overruled your objections on her account. Have you any other?'

'No – none.'

'You love me then?' said he, fervently pressing my hand.

'Yes.'

Here I pause. My diary, from which I have compiled these pages, goes but little further. I could go on for years; but I will content myself with adding, that I shall never forget that glorious summer evening, and always remember with delight that steep, rugged hill, and the edge of the precipice where we stood together watching the splendid sun-set mirrored on the restless world of waters at our feet – with hearts filled with gratitude to Heaven, and happiness, and love – almost too full for speech.

A few weeks after that, when my mother had supplied herself with an assistant, I became the wife of Edward Weston, and never found cause to repent it, and am certain that I never shall. We have had trials, and we know that we must have them again; but we bear them well together, and endeavour to fortify ourselves and each other against the final separation – that greatest of all afflictions to the survivor; but, if we keep in mind the glorious heaven beyond, where both may meet again, and sin and sorrow are unknown, surely that too may be borne; and meantime, we endeavour to live to the glory of Him who has scattered so many blessings in our path.

Edward, by his strenuous exertions, has worked surprising reforms in his parish, and is esteemed and loved by its inhabitants – as he deserves—for whatever his faults may be as a man (and no one is entirely without), I defy anybody to blame him as a pastor, a husband, or a father.

Our children, Edward, Agnes, and little Mary, promise well; their education, for the time being, is chiefly committed to me; and they shall want no good thing that a mother's care can give.

Our modest income is amply sufficient for our requirements; and by practising the economy we learnt in harder times, and never attempting to imitate our richer neighbours, we manage not only to enjoy comfort and contentment ourselves, but to have every year something to lay by for our children, and something to give to those who need it.

And now I think I have said sufficient.

ABBREVIATIONS

Allott   Miriam Allott, ed., *The Brontës: The Critical Heritage*, London, 1974.

Biographical   'Biographical Notice of Ellis and Acton Bell', in
Notice   *Wuthering Heights and Agnes Grey* by Ellis and Acton Bell. A new edition with a Biographical Notice of the authors, a selection from their literary remains, and a Preface by Currer Bell, London, 1850.

BL   British Library

BPM   Brontë Parsonage Museum, Haworth

Chitham   Edward Chitham, ed., *The Poems of Anne Brontë*, London, 1979.

Gaskell   Elizabeth Gaskell, *The Life of Charlotte Brontë*, London, 1857. I quote from the Penguin edition, 1975.

LL   T. J. Wise, and J. A. Symington, *The Brontës: Their Lives, Friendships and Correspondence*, 4 vols., Oxford, 1932.

OED   Oxford English Dictionary

TWH   Anne Brontë, *The Tenant of Wildfell Hall*, London, 1848. I quote from the Penguin edition, 1979.

NOTES

INTRODUCTION

1. Gaskell, pp. 307–8.
2. Biographical Notice.
3. See Allott, pp. 67–113.
4. LL, II, p. 154.
5. Ibid., p. 165.
6. Allott, p. 233; 243; 228.
7. Ibid., p. 219.
8. Ibid., p. 227.
9. LL, II, p. 187.
10. Allott, p. 263.
11. Ibid., p. 251, 259, 262.
12. TWH, pp. 29–31.
13. LL, III, p. 156.
14. Biographical Notice.
15. 'History of the Year 1829', BPM.
16. Gaskell, p. 94.
17. LL, I, p. 112.
18. Original MS at the BPM.
19. LL, I, p. 130.
20. Ibid., p. 157.
21. Ibid., p. 129.
22. Biographical Notice.
23. Gaskell, p. 160.
24. Roe Head Journal, BPM.
25. Ibid.
26. Chitham, p. 60.
27. Ibid., p. 63–4.
28. Original MS. at BPM.
29. Chitham, pp. 53–4.
30. LL, I, p. 164.
31. Ibid., p. 175.
32. Ibid., p. 229.
33. Ibid., p. 234.
34. Ibid., p. 238.
35. Ibid., p. 239.
36. Ibid., p. 247.
37. Ibid., p. 244.
38. Ibid., p. 243.
39. Ibid., p. 250.
40. Chitham, p. 87.
41. LL, II, p. 12.
42. Ibid., p. 57.
43. Ibid., p. 52.
44. Ibid., pp. 49–50.
45. Ibid., p. 52.
46. Ibid., pp. 49–50.
47. Biographical Notice.
48. LL, II, p. 256.
49. Letter from Charlotte Brontë to M. Heger, 24 July 1844. Original in BL.
50. Biographical Notice.
51. LL, II, p. 77.
52. Chitham, p. 128.
53. 'Editor's Preface to the New Edition of Wuthering Heights,' in the 1850 edition of *Wuthering Heights and Agnes Grey*.

54. Ibid.
55. LL, II, p. 241.
56. Ibid., pp. 288, 289.
57. Ibid., p. 287.
58. Allott, p. 247–8.
59. LL, II, p. 241.
60. Ibid., p. 321.
61. Ibid., p. 327.
62. Ibid., p. 339.
63. Ibid., p. 321.
64. Biographical Notice.
65. LL, I, p. 175.
66. Harriet Martineau, *Deerbrook*, London, 1892, p. 448.
67. LL, I, p. 229–30.
68. Elizabeth Missing Sewell, *Principles of Education*, II, pp. 238, 279.
69. *The English Woman's Journal*, IV, 21, pp. 145–6.
70. LL, II, p. 308.
71. *Fraser's Magazine*, 30 (1844), p. 572.
72. Ibid.
73. Ibid.
74. Ibid., p. 573.
75. *Fraser's Magazine*, 37 (1848), p. 411.
76. Allott, p. 109.
77. Patricia Thompson, *The Victorian Heroine*, p. 53.

BIOGRAPHICAL NOTICE
OF ELLIS AND ACTON BELL

1. *One writer*: See the *Palladium* September, 1850.
2. *interpretation*: Daniel 5:7–8.
3. *Upharsin*: Daniel 5:25.

I. THE PARSONAGE

1. *passed*: The Newby edition has 'past'.
2. *had been wrecked*: In November 1812, just before Anne Brontë's mother married her father, she wrote of a similar misfortune: 'I suppose you never expected to be much the richer for me, but I am sorry to inform you that I am still poorer than I thought myself. I mentioned having sent for my books, clothes, etc. On Saturday evening, about the time when you were writing the description of your imaginary shipwreck, I was reading and feeling the effects of a real one, having then received a letter from my sister giving me an account of the vessel in which she had sent my box being stranded on the coast of Devonshire, in consequence of which the box was dashed to pieces with the violence of the sea, and all my little property, with the exception of a very few articles, being swallowed up in the mighty deep.' (LL, I, 21, Nov. 8 1812.)

3. *mamma*: The Newby edition uses both 'mama' and 'mamma'. I have altered the spelling throughout to conform with the latter.

4. *you draw pretty well*: All four Brontë children had drawing lessons from the Leeds artist William Robinson. Anne worked hard at this skill and achieved a fairly high level of competence. Many of her sketches are still extant. The suggestion that Agnes Grey execute water-colours to sell is further developed in *The Tenant of Wildfell Hall*, where Helen Huntingdon makes her living by selling paintings. The Brontës hoped that Branwell could make a career as portrait painter, but this expectation was crushed by his failure to present himself at the National Academy when sent to London for that purpose.

5. *Delightful ... shoot*: These lines are from James Thomson's poem 'The Seasons' (1726–30). George Eliot also referred to them in a chapter title of *The Mill on the Floss*. Thomson's poem was a favourite among readers of the early nineteenth century.

6. *my heart sank*: The Newby edition has 'sunk' here.

II. FIRST LESSONS IN THE ART OF INSTRUCTION

1. *from the nurses*: Mrs Bloomfield is referring principally to accent. One of the purposes of engaging a governess was to ensure that children acquired the 'genteel' accent only a 'gentlewoman' could instil.

2. *partake a frugal supper*: The Newby edition omits 'of' here, a usage now obsolete.

III. A FEW MORE LESSONS

1. *I found it doubly disagreeable*: The Newby edition omits 'it'.

2. *charges*: The Newby edition has 'charge'.

3. *boxes on the ear*: The Newby edition has 'in'.

4. *meed*: Recompense or reward. The OED cites Sir Walter Scott's *Lord of the Isles* (1814): 'A lordly meed to him that will avenge the dead.'

5. *tire-woman*: A woman who assisted at a lady's toilet.

6. *They may crush ... not of them*: Anne Brontë is quoting Byron's 'Stanzas to Augusta'. Emily Brontë in particular admired Byron, but his work was also an important influence on the juvenilia of Charlotte, Branwell and Anne.

IV. THE GRANDMAMMA

1. *work bag*: 'Work' meant needlework for nineteenth-century women.
2. *Gorgon ferocity*: In Greek mythology, the Gorgons were three sisters, with snakes for hair, whose look changed the beholder to stone.
3. *as heart could wish*: Anne Brontë also uses this expression in Chapters 13 and 32 of *The Tenant of Wildfell Hall*.
4. *drugget*: A coarse woollen stuff used for floor-coverings, table-cloths, etc.
5. *painfully*: The Newby edition has 'painsfully'.
6. *much*: The Newby edition has 'many'.
7. *Douglas-larder*: An expression that has its source in a famous battle that took place during the reign of Edward II. Sir James Douglas (1286?–1330), a Scottish patriot known as 'The Black Douglas', invaded England several times and plundered many villages of the north. During one of his absences, the English had taken Douglas castle, stationed a garrison there and stored it with provisions. On Palm Sunday, 1306–7, Sir James Douglas surprised the English garrison, broke up the barrels of provisions, killed all prisoners and, piling up their bodies, set fire to his own castle. Sir Walter Scott based several of his stories on this and other black deeds of Sir James Douglas. In the *History of Scotland*, Scott wrote: 'It was said that the name of this indefatigable and successful chief had become so formidable that women used in the northern counties to still their froward children by threatening them with the Black Douglas.' (Ch. XI) The Brontë children were all avid readers of Sir Walter Scott.
8. *a good whipping*: As Lawrence Stone points out in *The Family, Sex and Marriage in England 1500–1800*, the practice of disciplining children with physical punishment had fallen into disrepute in the latter part of the eighteenth century. By the beginning of the nineteenth century, many contemporaries were complaining of the spoiled, undisciplined behaviour of English children. Anne Brontë clearly means to attack the excessive permissiveness that she believed characterized the attitude of fashionably 'modern' parents. Her account of the beastly Bloomfield children is supported by a remark Charlotte Brontë made in a letter to Ellen Nussey, warning her friend that she could 'never live in an unruly, violent family of modern children, such, for instance, as those at Blake Hall' (LL, I p. 196).

V. THE UNCLE

1. *fettle 'em off*: In Yorkshire dialect, to 'fettle' a person was to beat him, but the word could also mean 'to clean up' or 'tidy up' when applied to a house, as it is later on in the novel.
2. *obtain mercy*: Matthew 5: 7.

VI. THE PARSONAGE AGAIN

1. *dependent*: The Newby edition has 'dependant'.
2. *canty old dame*: Cheerfully brisk, lively, active. A colloquialism common to dialects of the north of England. Emily Brontë uses the expression in *Wuthering Heights*: 'My mother lived till eighty, a canty dame to the last' (Ch. XXII, p. 264).
3. *away*: The Newby edition has 'sway'.
4. mauvaise honte: False shame, modesty. Charlotte also uses this expression in a letter describing her first experience as governess in a private family: 'at home you know Ellen I talk with ease and am never shy – never weighed down and oppressed by that *mauvaise honte* which torments and constrains me elsewhere' (LL, I, p. 184).

VII. HORTON LODGE

1. *German wools*: Fine, dyed wools used for knitting, tapestry and the like. Also referred to as 'Berlin wools' later on in the novel (p. 182).
2. *hoyden*: A boisterous, noisy girl; a romp. The Newby edition has 'hoiden'.
3. *a slight grimace*: The Newby edition has 'sligh'. Charlotte Brontë, in preparing her posthumous edition of the novel, evidently regarded it as a misprint and added the 't'. Since 'sligh' is a variant, now obsolete, spelling of 'sly' the printer's 'error' may in fact reflect the author's intention. I have chosen to follow Charlotte's reading, however, as it seemed to fit the context more logically.
4. *Dogberry*: A garrulous constable in Shakespeare's *Much Ado About Nothing*. Anne Brontë also refers to the play in Chapter 26 of *The Tenant of Wildfell Hall*.
5. *roystering*: Uproarious, wild, given to revelling.
6. *or discomfort to themselves*: The Newby edition reads: 'without present trouble to discomfort to themselves'.
7. *Valpy's Delectus*: Ann Brontë purchased a copy of Valpy's *Delectus* in November 1843, while she was governess to the Robinson

children at Thorp Green. She apparently used this text in their instruction. Her pencilled notes indicate a knowledge of the language much beyond that of most governesses of the time. Among the other books she acquired then (now preserved in the Brontë Parsonage Museum) was a German dictionary, Hannah More's *Sketches and Opinions*, *Deutches Leserbuch* and sets of piano music.

8. *meek and quiet spirit*: The quote is from the First Epistle of Peter – Mrs Murray is mistaken in attributing it to St Matthew. Her misquotation is a kind of private joke at the expense of the *real* Mrs Murray – the worldly Mrs Robinson, Branwell's seductress – who was in fact a canon's daughter.

9. *Miss Murray*: 'Miss', with only the surname following, was commonly used to indicate the eldest daughter of the house.

10. *fancy-work*: Ornamental needlework. Anne Brontë's description of Miss Murray's 'showy accomplishments' is more or less typical of the education thought proper for an upper-class girl.

11. *venture*: The Newby edition has 'ventured'.

12. *suffereth long . . . all things*: I Corinthians 13:4–7.

VIII. THE 'COMING OUT'

1. *debut*: Coming out.

IX. THE BALL

1. *a mare*: The sphere of language permitted to ladies in the nineteenth century was severely restricted. Expletives, colloquialisms and any sort of explicit language were considered vulgar. A lady's speech, like her demeanour, had to be refined. The Brontës' unconventional use of language aroused a great deal of hostility on the part of critics. All of their novels were at one time or another charged with 'coarseness'.

X. THE CHURCH

1. Nota bene: Note well.

2. *prostration*: The Newby edition has 'prostraction'.

3. *Church discipline*: Mr Hatfield's attitude toward Dissent as well as his general behaviour is almost a parody of High Church Toryism.

His views of salvation, however, are strangely incongruous – they seem much closer to the Calvinism a Dissenter would espouse. The term 'Dissenter' described any one of a number of Protestant sects that rejected the Church of England in the seventeenth century. Mrs Gaskell noted that the part of Yorkshire that the Brontës lived in was known as a haven for Dissent: 'The descendants of many who served under Cromwell at Dunbar, live on the same lands as their ancestors occupied then; and perhaps there is no part of England where the traditional and fond recollections of the Commonwealth have lingered so long as in ... the West Riding [of Yorkshire]' (Gaskell, p. 63.). Anne Brontë's attitude toward Dissenters was unusually sympathetic for the daughter of an Anglican minister. When she underwent her religious crisis as an adolescent at Roe Head, she turned to the Moravian minister, the Rev. James La Trobe for comfort and reassurance. In *The Tenant of Wildfell Hall* the Rev. Michael Millward is disparaged because he is 'intolerant of dissent in any shape, acting under a firm conviction that his opinions were always right, and whoever differed from them, must be, either most deplorably ignorant, or wilfully blind' (p. 42).

4. *thought*: The Newby edition has 'thoughts'.

5. *bind heavy . . . fingers*: Matthew 23:4.

6. *Make the word . . . of men*: Anne Brontë is paraphrasing Matthew 14:6: 'Thus have ye made the commandment of God of none effect by your tradition,' and Matthew 15:9: 'But in vain they do worship me, teaching for doctrines the commandments of men.'

XI. THE COTTAGERS

1. *cottagers on their father's estate*: It was fashionable for young ladies of the upper classes to visit the poor. The heroine of Jane Austen's *Emma* regularly occupies her leisure hours in this way.

2. *religious melancholy*: Charlotte Brontë applied this phrase to Anne herself in the 'Biographical Notice of Ellis and Acton Bell': 'the tinge of religious melancholy communicated a sad shade to her brief, blameless life'.

3. *the seventh verse*: 'Beloved, let us love one another: for love is God; and every one that loveth is born of God, and knoweth God.'

4. *as much as aught*: Troubled me as much as anything. The Newby edition has 'ought', but Anne Brontë altered it 'aught' in her own copy.

5. *He that . . . not God*: I John 4:8.

6. *Methodists*: Methodism was a movement of reaction against the apathy of the Church of England that prevailed in the early part of the eighteenth century. Anne Brontë's Aunt Branwell was a staunch Methodist and the *Methodist Magazine* was a staple of the Brontë household while the author was growing up.

7. *strait gate*: Luke 13:24.

8. *kicked my cat*: Cruelty to animals was the sure mark of a villain for Anne Brontë. Ellen Nussey, recounting the story of her first visit to Haworth in the summer of 1833, remembered: 'The Brontës' love of dumb creatures made them very sensitive of the treatment bestowed upon them. For any one to offend in this respect with them was an infallible bad sign, and a blot on the disposition' (LL, I, p.115). Mr Weston's rescue of Nancy Brown's cat is contrasted with Hatfield's callousness.

9. *sounding brass . . . cymbal*: I Corinthians 13:1.

10. *canting* : 'Canting' was speech characteristic of Dissenters.

11. *siding*: In Yorkshire dialect, to 'side' was to put in order, clear away, or tidy up. Mrs Gaskell uses the expression in her novel *Ruth* (1853): 'Whenever things are mislaid, I know it has been Miss Hilton's evening for siding away!' (Ch. II).

12. *with his lips*: Psalms 106:33.

13. *anent him*: Facing him or opposite him. Obsolete northern dialect.

14. *manifest in the flesh*: I John 4:8. These lines are also quoted in *The Tenant of Wildfell Hall*.

15. *whosoever loves Him . . . begotten also*: I John 4:9–11. The Newby edition has 'loved'.

16. *dwell in love*: I John 4:13.

17. *a soft answer . . . anger*: Proverbs 15:1.

18. *Come unto me . . . rest*: Matthew 11:28.

19. *that follows*: Matthew 11:29: 'Take my yoke upon you, and learn of me; for I am meek and lowly in heart: and ye shall find rest unto your souls,' and Matthew 11:30: 'For my yoke *is* easy, and my burden is light.'

20. *threaping*: To argue, dispute. A colloquialism peculiar to the north of England. Charlotte Brontë uses the word in *Jane Eyre*, surrounding it with quotation marks: 'They were so agreeable with each other – never fell out or "threaped"' (Ch. 29).

21. *another guess sort of man*: Another kind of man. *Fraser's Maga-*

zine, which Aunt Branwell subscribed to, uses the expression thus: 'Every one ... knows what guess-sort of wiseacre France gave birth to in the person of that algebraical gentleman' (1834, Vol. X, p. 668).

XII. THE SHOWER

1. *paid*: The Newby edition has 'payed'.
2. *stop till dusk*: The Newby edition has 'while'.
3. *the fire*: In Charlotte Brontë's *Shirley*, Caroline Helstone exhibits similar behaviour in front of the man she loves. She refuses to take part in the conversation and won't take a chair in front of the fire.

XIII. THE PRIMROSES

1. *blue bells*: While at Thorp Green, Anne Brontë wrote a poem entitled 'The Bluebell'. The flower's significance to her is made clear in these lines:

> But when I looked upon the bank
> My wandering glances fell
> Upon a little trembling flower,
> A single sweet bluebell.
>
> Whence came that rising in my throat,
> That dimness in my eye?
> Why did those burning drops distil –
> Those bitter feelings rise?
>
> O, that lone flower recalled to me
> My happy childhood's hours
> When bluebells seemed like fairy gifts
> A prize among the flowers,
>
> Those sunny days of merriment
> When heart and soul were free,
> And when I dwelt with kindred hearts
> That loved and cared for me.

2. *possible with thee*: Mark 14:36.
3. *Thou wilt not despise!*: Psalms 51:17.

XIV. THE RECTOR

1. *vengibly*: The Newby edition has 'vengeably'. This word also appears in Chapter 13 of *The Tenant of Wildfell Hall*. 'Vengibly' (or 'vengeably') seems to have been largely out of use by the nineteenth century. The only example cited by the OED after 1607 is from *Agnes Grey*.
2. *Moss-lane*: The Newby edition has 'Moss-lane' here. Later in the text the word is hyphenated.
3. *poser*: A puzzle.
4. tête-à-tête: A private conversation between two persons.
5. *un-methodical*: The Newby edition has 'im-methodical'.
6. *ready to perish*: Job 29:13.
7. *budget to her*: To speak one's mind. The expression was probably obsolete when Anne Brontë wrote *Agnes Grey*; the last use of the word cited by the OED is from 1681.
8. *unprecedentedly*: The Newby edition has 'unprecedently'.
9. *stone upon another*: Anne Brontë is paraphrasing Mark 13:2: '. . . there shall not be left one stone upon another, that shall not be thrown down.' These lines are also quoted from in *The Tenant of Wildfell Hall* (Ch. 9, p. 100).
10. *annihilate them*: The Newby edition omits 'them'.

XV. THE WALK

1. *one lamb*: Agnes Grey is recalling II Samuel, 12:2–3.

XVI. THE SUBSTITUTION

2. *Whatsoever . . . things*: Philippians 4:8.

XVII. CONFESSIONS

1. *marked features*: Ironically, Anne was the only Brontë sister who was generally considered to be attractive. Much has been made of Charlotte Brontë's innovation in making the heroine of *Jane Eyre* plain. In Harriet Martineau's obituary of Charlotte Brontë, she recalled that '[the author] once told her sisters that they were wrong – even morally wrong – in making their heroines beautiful as a matter of course. They replied that it was impossible to make a

heroine interesting on any other terms. Her answer was, "I will prove to you that you are wrong; I will show you a heroine as plain and as small as myself, who shall be as interesting as any of yours." Hence 'Jane Eyre', said she in telling the anecdote: 'but she is not myself, any further than that"' (Gaskell, p. 308).

2. *eclat*: Public display; conspicuous success.
3. *billets-doux*: Love letters.

XVIII. MIRTH AND MOURNING

1. *vide*: See.

XIX. THE LETTER

1. *our school*: When Anne Brontë began writing *Agnes Grey*, the three Brontë sisters were looking forward to starting a school of their own, as Agnes and her mother do. By the time the novel was finished, however, the school project had failed.

XX. THE FAREWELL

1. *A–, the fashionable watering place*: Scarborough, where Anne Brontë went with the Robinson family.
2. *friend*: The Newby edition has 'frend', an error that Anne Brontë failed to correct in her own copy.

XXI. THE SCHOOL

1. *nursing it*: Though as late as the mid-eighteenth century, it was still common among the upper classes to put a baby out to nurse, by the time this was written, the practice was frowned upon. Most mothers, even very wealthy ones, breast-fed their own children.

XXII. THE VISIT

1. vertu; Curios, *objets d'art*.
2. *sot*: To soak; to drink to excess.

XXIII. THE PARK

1. *it may die*: Infant mortality was in fact on the decline in the early
nineteenth century.

XXIV. THE SANDS

1. *terrier*: Pilot, Mr Rochester's dog, also plays a part in the scene at
the end of *Jane Eyre* in which the heroine is reunited with her
'master'.

XXV. CONCLUSION

1. *a steep precipice*: Anne Brontë describes the same spot in *The
Tenant of Wildfell Hall*: '. . . on gaining the summit of a steep
acclivity, and looking downward, an opening lay before us – and
the blue sea burst upon our sight! – deep violet blue – not deadly
calm, but covered with glinting breakers . . .[Helen] felt its exhilarating influence . . .' (p. 86).
2. *honeyed*: The Newby edition has 'honied'.

READ MORE IN PENGUIN

In every corner of the world, on every subject under the sun, Penguin represents quality and variety – the very best in publishing today.

For complete information about books available from Penguin – including Puffins, Penguin Classics and Arkana – and how to order them, write to us at the appropriate address below. Please note that for copyright reasons the selection of books varies from country to country.

In the United Kingdom: Please write to *Dept. EP, Penguin Books Ltd, Bath Road, Harmondsworth, West Drayton, Middlesex UB7 0DA*

In the United States: Please write to *Consumer Sales, Penguin USA, P.O. Box 999, Dept. 17109, Bergenfield, New Jersey 07621-0120*. VISA and MasterCard holders call 1-800-253-6476 to order Penguin titles

In Canada: Please write to *Penguin Books Canada Ltd, 10 Alcorn Avenue, Suite 300, Toronto, Ontario M4V 3B2*

In Australia: Please write to *Penguin Books Australia Ltd, P.O. Box 257, Ringwood, Victoria 3134*

In New Zealand: Please write to *Penguin Books (NZ) Ltd, Private Bag 102902, North Shore Mail Centre, Auckland 10*

In India: Please write to *Penguin Books India Pvt Ltd, 706 Eros Apartments, 56 Nehru Place, New Delhi 110 019*

In the Netherlands: Please write to *Penguin Books Netherlands bv, Postbus 3507, NL-1001 AH Amsterdam*

In Germany: Please write to *Penguin Books Deutschland GmbH, Metzlerstrasse 26, 60594 Frankfurt am Main*

In Spain: Please write to *Penguin Books S. A., Bravo Murillo 19, 1° B, 28015 Madrid*

In Italy: Please write to *Penguin Italia s.r.l., Via Felice Casati 20, I–20124 Milano*

In France: Please write to *Penguin France S. A., 17 rue Lejeune, F–31000 Toulouse*

In Japan: Please write to *Penguin Books Japan, Ishikiribashi Building, 2–5–4, Suido, Bunkyo-ku, Tokyo 112*

In South Africa: Please write to *Longman Penguin Southern Africa (Pty) Ltd, Private Bag X08, Bertsham 2013*

READ MORE IN PENGUIN

A CHOICE OF CLASSICS

Matthew Arnold	**Selected Prose**
Jane Austen	**Emma**
	Lady Susan/The Watsons/Sanditon
	Mansfield Park
	Northanger Abbey
	Persuasion
	Pride and Prejudice
	Sense and Sensibility
William Barnes	**Selected Poems**
Anne Brontë	**Agnes Grey**
	The Tenant of Wildfell Hall
Charlotte Brontë	**Jane Eyre**
	Shirley
	Villette
Emily Brontë	**Wuthering Heights**
Samuel Butler	**Erewhon**
	The Way of All Flesh
Lord Byron	**Selected Poems**
Thomas Carlyle	**Selected Writings**
Arthur Hugh Clough	**Selected Poems**
Wilkie Collins	**Armadale**
	The Moonstone
	No Name
	The Woman in White
Charles Darwin	**The Origin of Species**
	Voyage of the *Beagle*
Benjamin Disraeli	**Sybil**
George Eliot	**Adam Bede**
	Daniel Deronda
	Felix Holt
	Middlemarch
	The Mill on the Floss
	Romola
	Scenes of Clerical Life
	Silas Marner

READ MORE IN PENGUIN

A CHOICE OF CLASSICS

Charles Dickens	**American Notes for General Circulation**
	Barnaby Rudge
	Bleak House
	The Christmas Books (in two volumes)
	David Copperfield
	Dombey and Son
	Great Expectations
	Hard Times
	Little Dorrit
	Martin Chuzzlewit
	The Mystery of Edwin Drood
	Nicholas Nickleby
	The Old Curiosity Shop
	Oliver Twist
	Our Mutual Friend
	The Pickwick Papers
	Selected Short Fiction
	A Tale of Two Cities
Elizabeth Gaskell	**Cranford/Cousin Phillis**
	The Life of Charlotte Brontë
	Mary Barton
	North and South
	Ruth
	Sylvia's Lovers
	Wives and Daughters
Edward Gibbon	**The Decline and Fall of the Roman Empire** (in three volumes)
George Gissing	**New Grub Street**
	The Odd Women
William Godwin	**Caleb Williams**

READ MORE IN PENGUIN

A CHOICE OF CLASSICS

Thomas Hardy	**Desperate Remedies**
	The Distracted Preacher and Other Tales
	Far from the Madding Crowd
	Jude the Obscure
	The Hand of Ethelberta
	A Laodicean
	The Mayor of Casterbridge
	A Pair of Blue Eyes
	The Return of the Native
	Selected Poems
	Tess of the d'Urbervilles
	The Trumpet-Major
	Two on a Tower
	Under the Greenwood Tree
	The Well-Beloved
	The Woodlanders
Lord Macaulay	**The History of England**
Henry Mayhew	**London Labour and the London Poor**
John Stuart Mill	**The Autobiography**
	On Liberty
William Morris	**News from Nowhere** and **Other Writings**
John Henry Newman	**Apologia Pro Vita Sua**
Robert Owen	**A New View of Society and Other Writings**
Walter Pater	**Marius the Epicurean**
John Ruskin	**Unto This Last and Other Writings**
Walter Scott	**Ivanhoe**
	Heart of Mid-Lothian
	Old Mortality
	Rob Roy
	Waverley

READ MORE IN PENGUIN

The Tenant of Wildfell Hall   Anne Brontë

An imprudent and unhappy marriage causes the wife's departure and her determined bid for freedom. The story of Helen Huntingdon is notable for its psychological truth – and for its startling modernity.

Jane Eyre   Charlotte Brontë

In *Jane Eyre*, Charlotte Brontë portrayed the refusal of a spirited and intelligent woman to accept her appointed place in society with unusual frankness and with a passionate sense of the dignity and needs of her sex.

Villette   Charlotte Brontë

Published in 1853, *Villette* was Charlotte Brontë's last novel and is often regarded as her most satisfying work, whose central character expresses the anguish of unrequited love.

also by Charlotte Brontë in Penguin Classics:

Shirley
The Professor

Wuthering Heights   Emily Brontë

Emily Brontë's dark, brooding vision finds expression in this, her only novel and her masterpiece. The love between Catherine and Heathcliff is recorded with such intensity that it acquires the depth and simplicity of ancient tragedy.

Agnes Grey, The Tenant of Wildfell Hall, Wuthering Heights, Jane Eyre, Shirley, The Professor and Villette *are also available as Penguin Audiobooks, read by Juliet Stevenson.*